PRAISE FOR

# THE VALE OF SEVEN DRAGONS

"*The Vale of Seven Dragons* is a wild and wonderful fantasy adventure. Compelling characters, plenty of action, romance, and snark!"

—Jonathan Maberry, *New York Times* bestselling author of *Red Empire* and *Ghosts of the Void*

"Five stars. Jendia Gammon's done it again! With breathtaking plotting, complex world-building, and the voracious readability of an instant classic, *The Vale of Seven Dragons* truly has it all. This tale of magic and mayhem, friendship and family, will appeal to fans of fantasy and coming-of-age stories alike. Highly recommended!"

—Danika (D.K.) Stone, best-selling, multi-genre author of *Switchback, All the Feels, Internet Famous, Inescapable* and the Waterton trilogy.

"An enchanting adventure."

—Caitlin Rozakis, *New York Times* bestselling author of *Dreadful*

"Gammon's wildly entertaining stable of characters and epic fantasy settings coupled with her uncanny knack for adventure will have you flipping through the pages of *The Vale of Seven Dragons* into the wee hours of the morning."

—Michael Boulerice, author of *Inhalation* and *Feeding the Wheel*

"*The Vale of Seven Dragons* puts the epic in epic fantasy. With a vivid world that continues to grow with each chapter and a fantastic cast of characters, this propulsive coming of age story blends genres and familiar tropes with ease. From fae groves to cosmic horror and a mind-blowing climax, I'm raring to read more in this expansive universe Jendia Gammon has created!"

—Harvey Hamer, Diamond Dimensions Universe author and Star Wars Insider contributor

# The Vale of Seven Dragons

ALSO BY

# JENDIA GAMMON

**As Jendia Gammon:**

*Godfestation*
*Dungeon Crawl at the Haunted Mall:*
  *A Choose Your Own Adventure Book*
*To Wonder and Starshine*
*Atacama*
*Doomflower*

*Coming soon:*
  *Coursers of Wings and Flame (2027)*
  *The Vale of Fire Wrought (2028)*

**As J. Dianne Dotson:**

*The Inn at the Amethyst Lantern (Nebula and BSFA Award Finalist)*
*The Secret of the Sapphire Sentinel*
*The Shadow Galaxy: A Collection of Short Stories and Poetry*
*The Questrison Saga:*
  *Heliopause: The Questrison Saga: Book One*
  *Ephemeris: The Questrison Saga: Book Two*
  *Accretion: The Questrison Saga: Book Three*
  *Luminiferous: The Questrison Saga: Book Four*

*Coming soon:*
  *The Dawn of Dusk and Twilight (2026)*

# The Vale of Seven Dragons

### Jendia Gammon

Copyright © 2026 by Jendia Gammon

All rights reserved.

No part of this publication may be reproduced, distributed, or transmitted in any form or by any means, including photocopying, recording, or other electronic or mechanical methods, without the prior written permission of the publisher, except as permitted by U.S. copyright law. For permission requests, contact Sley House Publishing.

The story, all names, characters, and incidents portrayed in this production are fictitious. No identification with actual persons (living or deceased), places, buildings, and products is intended or should be inferred.

ISBN: 978-1-957941-27-1

Cover artist: Chris Panatier

Cover design: Ranxvrus

Interior design: Dreadful Designs

Editor: Scarlett Algee

First Edition

2026

*For my family, and for the dragons (and the parrots).*

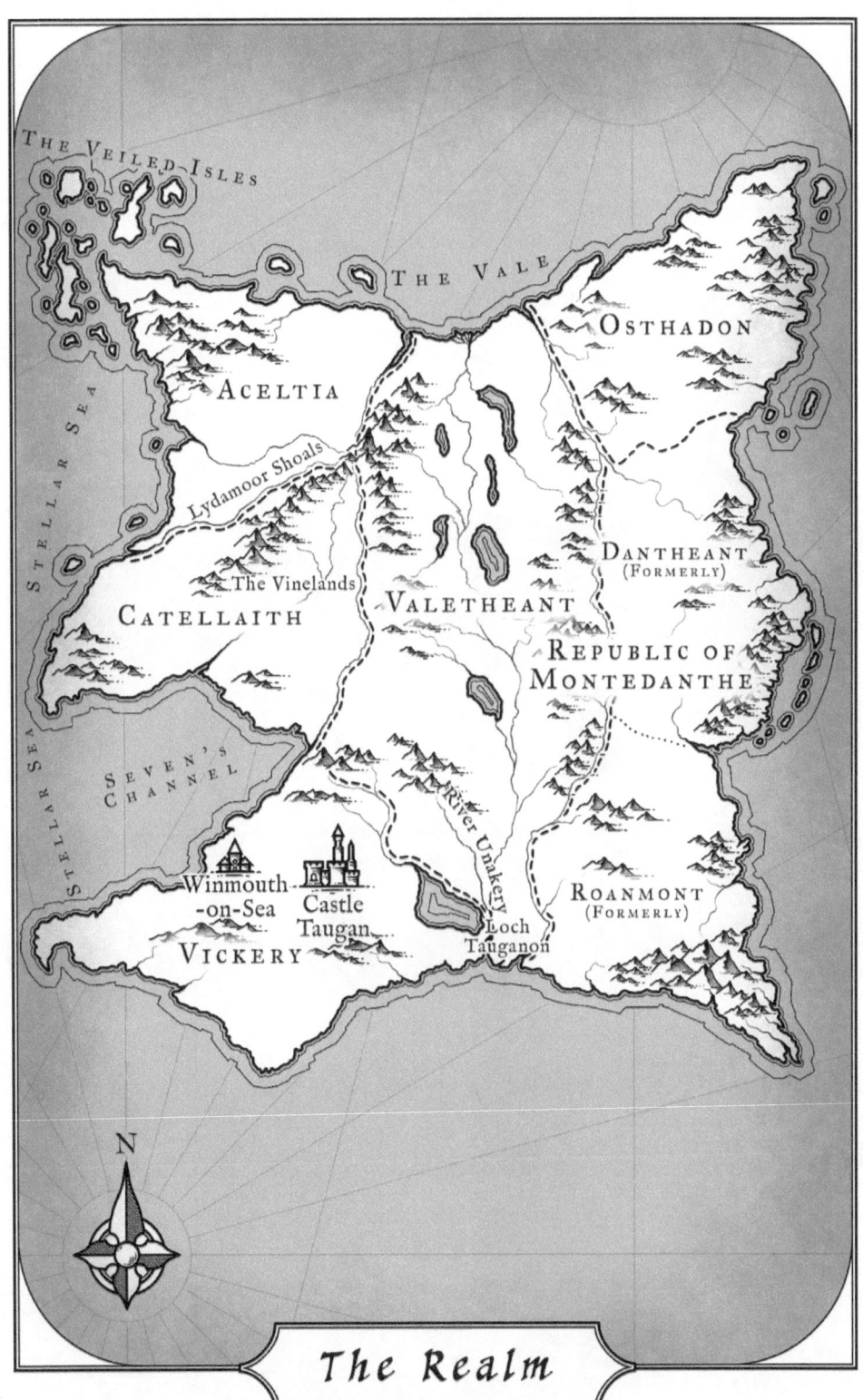

# CHAPTER 1

## A MOST WILLFUL PRINCESS

Thilly slipped outside the library with impish intention in her wry smile. Down the spiral stone stairs, out the window that faced the hilltop apple orchards to the south, she slid out and down on her bottom, staining her skirt, which she promptly removed to reveal the trousers hidden beneath. She rolled up the skirt, tucked it out of sight next to the stairs, and twisted her curly dark auburn hair into a bun so that it would fit under her hooded cloak. It would take perhaps one minute before Chamberlain noticed she had gone; he would wheel slowly about to stare at her over his aquiline nose, under knotted white eyebrows stretched overly long across his wrinkled pate and find only an empty seat pushed aside in haste. Indeed, she heard a wheezing, indignant cry echoing from the parapet: "Githilien!" She grinned as she sprinted out of sight of the tower and into the edge of the woods, where the ringing of axes upon felled trunks echoed through the castle grounds.

"Gods' knickers, what are they doing that for?" she asked aloud, and no sooner had she asked when a woodsman bowed low. She tried very hard not to roll her eyes.

"Your Royal Highness," said the woodsman. She could see he must have been in his late thirties, his hands rough, his outfit smeared in sap and soot, and he took off his cap to reveal salt-and-pepper dark brown hair. He had a scar on his shaved chin, old by the look of it, and crinkled blue eyes.

"Thank you," Thilly said crisply, "that won't be necessary. But can you tell me why you are chopping down all those trees?"

The man seemed surprised by the question, but quickly supplicated, and she sighed in frustration.

"That will do," she said, her cheeks burning. "Speak plainly, good woodsman. But first, what is your name?"

"Nicol Farthington, Your Highness," the man replied, avoiding her gaze.

"Mr. Farthington," Thilly said, "do please tell me, ah! *Without* the formality, I beg you!" For the man had begun to bow again. He straightened and fumbled his hat. "Do please tell me the purpose for chopping all the trees there? I don't recall Father saying anything about it. I rather liked those trees."

"Your High—" he began, but she fixed him with her hazel glare, and he altered course and said, "Princess Githilien," and she stopped him again.

"Thilly. Please. It's all right! I don't want to seem otherworldly," she said, more warmly this time.

Nicol Farthington opened and closed his mouth a few times, not sure how to act, but he stumbled forth the words, "His Majesty the King has requested the trees be removed ahead of the arrival of the King and Queen of Catellaith."

Thilly gasped. "Oh, gods! They're coming *here*?"

The poor woodsman was completely out of his element by now, and looked as though he could wither on the spot. So Thilly reached out and touched his arm with her ungloved hand, and said softly, "Thank you, good sir. I shall speak to Father about this. You've been tasked, and I've kept you away. Carry on, then."

He bowed, and she cringed inwardly and sprinted off before anyone *else* should see her and bow and supplicate and all the deeply uncomfortable activities that she endured from people she saw as equals to herself. Of course, that attitude was highly frowned upon by the Court, and she knew it. Hence her disguise, which she had hoped would allow her some freedom from her station.

But now she was curious in a manner most unpleasant. She had not known the Royals Catellaith would be visiting, and with them, no doubt, Prince Beaumain and Princess Tantienne. She rather liked both the prince and princess, except she found Beaumain rigid at times, and she suspected he disapproved of her somehow. He was eighteen, and of the age to be taking on more royal duties, as he would one day succeed his father, King Ardenour, to the throne. His sister Tantienne was eleven now, and it had been over a year since Thilly had seen her, but the last time she had, the two had got along like a house on fire. Thilly felt the girl had some promise in bucking the trends of her mother, Queen Maulielle, and that filled Thilly with secret glee.

Queen Maulielle was unlike Thilly's own mother in every respect. The Queen of Catellaith steeped herself in tradition, outrageous raiment, and unbounded gossip. She was the leader of society through the entire Realm, and closely governed ladies who came of age to be out in society. Thilly loathed this. She was about to turn sixteen and…

"Oh, gods!" she gasped as she halted her climb up Sunset Hill. She felt sick. Now she had some inkling for why the Royals Catellaith

# THE VALE OF SEVEN DRAGONS

might visit. Her birthday was coming up, and at sixteen, she would be of age to debut in society, and Queen Maulielle would want a look at her.

She rubbed her eyes and looked out from the crest of the hill to the castle. Its rampart flickered like a tongue of flame, for the flag of Vickery bore a great fire-colored dragon: one of the ancient, mythical Seven Dragons of the Vale, and the sigil for her father King Gathlade's house as well. Thilly felt mutinous.

"Why do I have to follow this track?" she asked the air itself. "Why can't I be like Mother? Or be a knight? Or anything *but* a lady of the Court?"

Her own mother, Woadlynn, had rejected all titles and absconded to the far north, to the mist-shrouded islands of Aceltia, where she practiced secret arts unknown to men. Woadlynn rarely visited, and each time she had, she seemed stranger to Thilly. Their parting was never easy for the girl, for she always wanted to go back with her mother. It had been seven years since Woadlynn's last visit. But Thilly was the only heir of Gathlade and Woadlynn, and so she must eventually be Queen, and be married off as well to the king of another land.

Thilly felt nauseous. Of course the closest other land was their long-former adversary and now ally, Catellaith.

"This isn't about my being out in society," she hissed. She startled a crow, who jumped a full two feet in the air and squawked at her.

"Well?" she asked the irritated crow. "I'm right, aren't I? They want to pair me up with that stick in the mud, Beaumain. Do you know, crow, I won't have it. I reject it and him utterly."

The crow tilted its head and considered her with its onyx eye.

"Are you judging me?" she demanded. "We used to be enemies. Even our dragons were enemies! Or so the stories tell us. Vickery and Catellaith, warring from time immemorial, our dragons Antares and

Nistraan forever at each other's throats…and lands burnt to cinders. I suppose that's why they're so lush now," she reflected. "Plenty of fertilizer from the ashes of the dead, back then."

She put her face in her hands for a moment and felt cold spikes going up and down her neck.

"I won't," she told the crow. "I won't become a queen. And besides, maybe Father will live far longer than I. And then I won't have to worry about it! Right?"

The crow preened and clicked its beak.

"Some help you are, sleek friend," she muttered, putting her hands on her hips. She sighed. "I'd planned to visit the village and sneak a cider. Now I feel quite as if someone has poured cider all over my head."

She retrieved from her pants pocket a sausage roll, broke the tip of it off, and tossed it at the bird, who dipped its head gratefully. She began to descend just as a host of other birds took notice of the treat and jousted with each other for any remaining crumbs. The crow bounced down each step behind her.

"Gods! I may run away yet. But," and she sighed so loudly that it became a groan, "I won't let Father down this time. I'll plan my escape, though. Mark me, crow!" The crow did not answer, as it flew off like a black dart with its prize, chased by a small vortex of other birds.

As Thilly stepped down the narrow path, with the view of the castle grounds tinged by autumn afternoon sunlight in pale amber shafts between clouds, she spied a horse and rider kicking up dust upon the road to the castle at a brisk gallop. Such a sight was uncommon. She wondered what news the rider might bring, and she hastened her steps to find out.

# CHAPTER 2

## A DISTANT TEMPEST

Stealthily darting back to the castle steps she'd slinked down earlier, Thilly unfurled her hidden dress and stepped into it. She kept her trousers on so that she could change later in her quarters. Somehow it comforted her to wear them, like a secret. She then smoothed the ochre dress, which while simple for a princess was far too fussy for her tastes. She made her way to the back gardens to avoid the hawk-eyed Chamberlain.

Castle Taugan was ancient, its pale grey stone walls etched by many rains and encrusted with lichen and the scars of time…and supposedly of dragons. The last visitation by the house dragon, Antares, had been over a thousand years ago, and now seemed more mythological than historic. A mound in the flower gardens, rimmed by round-canopied trees, was said to house a dragon skull beneath its sod. Thilly doubted this, just as she doubted the existence of dragons. That was heretical, which made her double down. But she had mostly

# THE VALE OF SEVEN DRAGONS

learned when to say such things and when not, and her father was one of the few people she felt comfortable admitting that to.

Not to say that King Gathlade felt at ease listening to his daughter's heretical doubt of the dragons of the Vale. In fact, whenever she spoke of these beliefs to him, he squirmed a bit and cleared his throat, and his bushy black and grey eyebrows went to war with each other to try to contain his emotions.

Thilly bypassed the supposed dragon skull mound and found the kitchen gardens next, and there she chose to make her entry, dodging cooks carrying great quantities of food from the garden gate to the north, where deliveries arrived by coach. The sight of so much food made her skin crawl.

"That's got to be for the Royals Catellaith," she muttered as the various cooks halted their busy steps to curtsy or bow to her in kind. She greeted each warmly with a smile, but inwardly, she trembled.

She winnowed her way through the kitchens, which were all a clamor and a fuss, with pots clanging, coal fires burning, and the heady smell of cakes baking and soups simmering. Pepper and potato and goose fat and onions filled the air alongside gossip, which fell into silence at the sight of her.

"Carry on," she said to them. They did, but more quietly, and with watchful eyes.

The downstairs staff, she knew, had its own set of rules. Presently, she met the king's head butler and valet, Birkswood, an extraordinarily tall and impressive older gentleman with a mostly bald head ringed by thin white hair, and a white goatee. He bowed and nodded to her, taking the only casual gesture of the entire downstairs staff, who all scurried around her like river water around a boulder.

"Your Highness," said Birkswood pleasantly. He wore the black waistcoat, jacket, and trousers of the highest echelon of Vickery's royal court, embroidered with B and the dragon Antares sigil in red and orange on his cuffs, as he waited upon King Gathlade himself.

"Good evening, Birkswood," answered Thilly. "What news of the Royals Catellaith? This is for them, is it not?" she asked, gesturing at the politely annoyed kitchen staff, whom Birkswood glared at from his deep-set brown eyes.

To her surprise, Birkswood regarded her with a look of…mischief? She could not tell. She caught a smile sneaking in at the corner of his mouth.

"Yes and no," he answered. "Did you think we'd forgotten your coming of age? This would not be happening otherwise, dear Princess Githilien."

"Thilly," she hissed, barely tapping his elbow and leaning in conspiratorially. "I've not been given much warning, quite honestly," she said to him quietly.

"It's all the part of the great machine of the Crown, Your Highness," said Birkswood, lowering his head a moment before barking orders at a slim young man in a tall white hat quavering under the weight of a tiered cake covered in marzipan autumn leaves. "Not *there*! The icing will melt!"

As he watched the young pastry chef swerve around the whirlwind of activity, he said to Thilly in a lower voice, "You're to have your new lady's maid as of this evening, in fact. I've arranged everything with Mrs. Florence."

"Oh, gods!" muttered Thilly. "Who'd she pick, the stodgiest, oldest—I'm sorry," she quickly said, watching Birkswood's eyelids lower a tick, "*you're* not old. You're timeless."

"How diplomatic of you!" he exclaimed. "And in answer to your question, I understand she found a northern maiden for your lady-in-waiting."

# THE VALE OF SEVEN DRAGONS

"A northerner!" said Thilly, truly surprised and—she hated to admit it—intrigued. "What, from Catellaith?"

"No, ye gods!" murmured Birkswood, plucking lint from the shoulder of a passing steward. "That would not do. Not until you are wed, anyway."

Thilly frowned at that.

He went on, "Farther north, near Valetheant. A good, sturdy girl, perhaps a little willful." He glanced sidewise at Thilly. "Not unlike someone else I know."

Thilly snorted.

"And Mrs. Florence did not choose her," added Birkswood. He looked sly but kept his face otherwise inscrutable. "I did."

Thilly covered her mouth and giggled. "I'll bet she hated that!"

Birkswood began to weave among the staff and work like a symphony conductor, carefully adjusting foods and collars, inspecting goblets, and so on. Thilly knew he must return to his duties, though she wished she could speak more to him. As she turned to leave, however, he held up his white-gloved hand.

"She did," he replied at last, and Thilly laughed and skipped out of the kitchens and up to the court.

Sweaty, out of breath, and growing hungry and irritable, Thilly found the side stairs that members of the royal court could use in clandestine situations. She had heard rumors for such things, but never encountered any herself. Then it dawned on her.

"I *am* the clandestine situation," she said, huffing as she kilted her skirts and charged up the steps. This brought her out onto a balcony overlooking the great staircase below. She could hear music now, a soft guitar strumming, and she knew her father waited in his public office and inner quarters on this floor. Some commotion at the front of the castle led to the rise and fall of voices, and the clanging of metal on stone as someone's footsteps approached. Leaning just out of view, Thilly beheld someone bent over, gasping to catch their breath, and soon she spied Birkswood and a host of pages seeing to the man. Birkswood himself then ascended the stairs. Thilly drew back into an alcove and watched as he entered the King's office. Then she tiptoed over to it after Birkswood closed the door behind him. She leaned her face against the door and listened.

"Yes, he said he'd been riding two days. Said a host of pirates might follow suit," she heard Birkswood say in a low voice.

"No other word, then?" her father's voice asked.

"None, Your Majesty."

"Do you believe him?"

Birkswood cleared his throat. "Your Majesty, I respect your appreciation for my judgment of character. As you know, I keep a clear eye upon all the comings and goings of Castle Taugan and the Court. I know from my service as a young man what it means to look with the eyes of terror. And his eyes shine with it like a beacon of portent."

"Very good, Birkswood. Send him in."

Thilly fled to the other side of the balcony and pretended to emerge from the library. Birkswood exited the king's office and turned toward the walkway to the grand staircase. Then he paused and looked over his shoulder to see Thilly walking with her chin high. He smirked and put his finger to his lips. She tilted her head at him, feeling a thrill of being in on something for a change.

"You should attend to His Majesty," Birkswood said softly. "You're of age tomorrow. Time to participate in these matters."

"Really?" she cried, a little too loudly.

Birkswood barely lowered his head, and then turned away from her. He approached the head of the stairs and, facing them, clapped his hands together once. The footmen dashed down to retrieve the exhausted stranger. Thilly then quickly stepped across the deep scarlet and orange rugs, embroidered with miniature likeness of the great Antares, and tapped on the door to her father's office.

"That you, Birkswood?" he called.

"No, Father," she answered.

"Come, child, but quickly," he said, and she opened the tall door with its wrought iron handle and then shut it behind her. Her father had stood from his craft table, which was laden with small carvings of insects of all kinds, and little paint pots and brushes. A telescoping bronze lens of exquisite make from the East stood curled over the scene, illuminated by many dripping taper candles. He hastened to his desk and straightened a sheaf of parchment papers that lay strewn about. Then he gestured to the sitting room. He pulled the cord for tea service and arranged himself on his great wingback chair, its edges mahogany and carved with red dragons. Above him hung a fine tapestry, quite aged, depicting Antares and Nistraan in battle, and then later, Nistraan in surrender, symbolizing peace in the Vale, the Realm, and all the islands and territories.

Thilly said, "I've not done this before," and she twisted her fingers together. "Also, I'm a bit...disheveled."

The king glanced at his daughter and waved his hand. "It does not matter. There is a man in distress; he will not be focused upon comportment. Your place is here standing beside me, for one day you will need to sit in this chair and decide the fates of those who call for aid. Let us see what this man has to say."

King Gathlade arranged his hands in his lap, fidgeting; noticing dried paint on his leg, he quickly flicked that off, just as they could hear footfalls outside his office door. Gathlade was in his early fifties, with black hair shot with silver, which presently he kept tied back. His remarkable eyebrows looked stern by turns and quizzical by others. He kept his mouth in a straight line for business, hidden in his greying beard; but Thilly had brought forth true laughter from him since her childhood, so she knew that he was kind and good. He simply did not seem like other kings of song and story. He preferred painting his miniatures, playing his guitar, and reading about far-off lands rather than managing any himself. But he was her father, and that was all she cared about.

With some pomp, Birkswood announced, "To the Office of His Majesty the King Gathlade, I grant Mr. Belter Riggs of Winmouth-on-Sea."

And the valet opened the door and strode in, taking up a fair amount of real estate with his stature, and stepped aside with his hands behind his back. He did not make eye contact with either the king or Thilly. The footmen entered, aiding an exhausted-looking man, his battered and tarnished suit of armor caked in grey mud and sand.

*Is he a knight?* Thilly wondered.

The man Riggs knelt before the king, who waved his hand and said, "Do stand, good Mr. Riggs."

Riggs stammered, "Thank you, Your Majesty, and Your Highness," and he bowed to Thilly. He must have been thirty at the oldest, and his hair was greasy and dark ash blond. She could not tell his eye color. He bore a shaven face lined with anxiety and fatigue. She inclined her head and watched him intently.

King Gathlade then said, "Tell us your troubles, Mr. Riggs, that we may assist."

"Thank you," the man stammered again. "I'm most grateful. I have come…I have come at great speed, on account of my own witness to a horror."

The king raised one of his wild eyebrows. "Continue," he said.

Riggs nodded and swallowed, and then suddenly he shook all over and tears sprang into his eyes. Birkswood kept his own face level, but his eyelids lowered, Thilly noticed.

# THE VALE OF SEVEN DRAGONS

"Your—Your Majesty," he sputtered and sniffed, "I come from the port of Winmouth. Something has happened. I—I am not even sure what. I cannot think of it without nearing madness, but felt you must know. Death! So much death!"

Then he stood very still and stared at the tapestry behind Thilly and her father the king, and he pointed. "Monsters," he breathed.

The king shifted in his seat and said, "Speak plainly, Mr. Riggs. What are these monsters you speak of?"

"Like those…dragons, yes? But not…not like," and Mr. Riggs stood quivering.

Birkswood stepped forward, but the king raised his hand.

"Continue," he said, and Birkswood retreated to his station by the wall on the left.

"From the sea," the man choked out. "Monsters. Long strings of—of something. Ropes? I cannot say! My eyes, they burned at the sight, and then they took—they took the entire seafront. All its people. They swallowed everyone in sight. Even some of the pirates, and there was cannon fire and madness, and fire and death! O gods!"

And he broke down then and sagged to his knees. Birkswood and the pages swooped forward.

"'Tis a tempest," whispered the man. "A tempest. A tempest. Tempest. Tempest. Tempest. Temp—"

"That will do, Riggs," said Birkswood sharply, and with a nod, the pages lifted the man back to his feet.

"Mr. Riggs," said the king suddenly. "You saw monsters killing people, and pirates fighting them, am I to understand this aright?"

The man swiveled his head back and forth and wept, and said gurgling, "Tempest! Tempest! Tempest!"

So Birkswood and his men hauled the terrified Mr. Riggs outside, just in time for the tea service and Mrs. Florence to arrive outside the door.

"One moment," Birkswood told Mrs. Florence, and a silent look passed between them, which Thilly barely caught. He shut the door so that she could not continue watching, and she turned to her father, who sat still as stone, ruminating.

"What was that?" Thilly whispered.

"I don't know," her father admitted. "I don't like it. I've never seen anyone so frightened in all my life."

"Monsters!" she hissed.

"Thilly, beloved," murmured her father urgently. "Not a word of this to anyone, I beg you. The Royals Catellaith already march in a host to us. They should arrive in the morning. We do not know what is happening at the Stellar Sea, but I daresay we will learn more soon. Best to keep quiet. And darling, it is your birthday. Let us focus on that tomorrow."

Thilly sighed, frustrated. She wanted to learn more.

"Must I?" she whispered.

Her father smiled fondly up at her. "Well, first tea. Then to bed. We will sort it all out after. I see Mrs. Florence has brought your new lady-in-waiting. Let us greet them."

Thilly said, "Hmmph," but she kissed the top of her father's head and sat in the seat next to him.

As the door opened for the tea service, however, she wanted nothing more than to race out of it and seek out some of the knights…including one particular knight with a roguish grin, and see what they might know about these so-called monsters.

*Only after tea, though.*

# CHAPTER 3

## THE KNIGHT AT NIGHT

Mrs. Florence, flanked by two prim maids and followed by a third just in the shadow of the doorway, brought forth the tea service. King Gathlade did not always adhere to the greatest luxuries, for he was a man of simple tastes who enjoyed peace and quiet. Thilly knew that he did, however, always appreciate evening tea. Born into the role of future king and heir, he had frustrated his parents with his obstinate love for nature and books and music...and solitude, except for a remarkable woman named Woadlynn, whom he had met on a tour of the Vale as a young man. She had awakened him to other possibilities, and had made the path to his coronation easier, because she stood by him. Until she chose not to.

Thilly's parents were still married, but Queen Woadlynn had abdicated her duties to join the Covenant of the Veiled Isles in the far north...islands so shrouded in fog, the stories told that they were ever cloaked by dragons' breath. When the queen had left, she chose to give her daughter the life of a royal, for she bore no other children to Gathlade, nor indeed to anyone else. She recognized the need for the king's only heir to remain, for other relatives in succession left much to be desired, from her point of view (to say nothing of others'). But Woadlynn had established certain assurances for Thilly before she had left, and Mrs. Florence was one of them.

So Thilly had known Mrs. Florence all her life, and the matronly woman ran the household alongside Birkswood, lock and step most of the time. Mrs. Florence found her charge to be most obstinate, not unlike both her parents, but she was fond of Thilly in her own right and clucked privately about the young lady's fate. There was a fevered air about her now, though, what with the approaching visit of the Royals Catellaith. Thilly had never seen Mrs. Florence so flustered. And then the third maid entered.

Thilly knew at once this must be the young woman who would be her personal assistant henceforth, and at first the girl did not look up at the princess. That was a bad sign, as far as Thilly was concerned. But she waited.

"Your Majesty, Your Royal Highness," announced Mrs. Florence. "May I present to you Miss Hana Buellton. I have chosen her with the aid of Mr. Birkswood, and she comes from a good and loyal family in the north."

The girl, who looked about Thilly's age, blushed scarlet, and curtsied even more deeply. She was a little taller than Thilly, and solid, with broad shoulders. Her quite rosy face was framed by brown curls secured under a flame-colored cap, the same as all the housemaids. But now it bore an embroidered scarlet dragon sigil to distinguish Hana. Mrs. Florence watched her the way a snake watches a mouse, ready to spring.

"Hana," she said, belying her watchful glare with a honeyed voice, "you're to attend to Princess Githilien starting this evening. You will lead the household within presence of Her Royal Highness in all matters. And you will prepare her for her coming of age tomorrow, as well as the arrival of the Royals Catellaith."

Hana's pale gold eyes met Thilly's then, and Thilly grinned.

She stepped forward and could almost feel Mrs. Florence's disapproval, but she knew there was nothing Mrs. Florence would do about her forward—or as Birkswood had put it, willful—attitude. That battle had been lost long ago, even before the Queen had absconded to the Veiled Isles.

"Welcome, Hana," Thilly said warmly, and the maid curtsied again. "I'll definitely need your help in all sorts of ways."

She thought, *Starting tonight, I'll see how good you are at keeping secrets.*

"Very good," Mrs. Florence said, lifting her chin with pride and appraising the two with her button nose and softly lined cheeks. Her own scarlet cap covered up steel grey hair and set off her green eyes. She turned ever so slightly to Birkswood, who slowly blinked in reply.

She said to Hana, "Hana, dear, don't judge our obstinate princess too harshly. She is without her mother, and so we must guide her accordingly, and respect her office at all times."

"Yes, Mrs. Florence," said Hana, and she curtsied again to Thilly.

"Hana," Thilly addressed the girl, "would you be so kind to set out my things for the celebrations tomorrow?"

Hana, blushing again, said, "Yes, Your Highness. 'Tis already done." Then the blush went nearly magenta. "Begging your pardon," she stammered. "'Tis my—it is my—northern accent. I shall control it."

Thilly laughed, startling everyone in the room.

"Please don't!" she said, and she reached her hands out to Hana, who took them, baffled. "I should like to hear your speech anytime you wish."

# THE VALE OF SEVEN DRAGONS

Mrs. Florence drew herself up like a full sail and huffed out her own gale to exclaim, "That is all well and good, Your Highness. Shall we prepare for your evening?"

Thilly smirked at Hana, who looked very much as if she would like to smirk back.

*I like her*, Thilly thought.

"Not yet, good Mrs. Florence," Thilly replied, smoothing her ochre skirt. "I want to speak more to my father. I'll return to my quarters on my own."

And so their company left.

Birkswood lingered, and the king said, "Thank you, Birkswood. A moment alone with my daughter, please, and then do return so we can discuss tomorrow."

"Yes, Your Grace," Birkswood answered, stiff, yet inclining his chin from its lofty height. He left the room and closed the door.

Gathlade turned to his daughter, and his eyes danced with humor.

"What do you think?" he asked her.

She grinned up at him. "She'll do. To be honest, I was worried. I thought I might get another version of Mrs. Florence."

Gathlade tilted his head. "Florence is a fine ladies' maid, Githilien."

"Ah, so formal, Daddy!" cried Thilly, and she flung an arm around him. He kissed the top of her curly head. "What were you playing earlier?"

The king glanced over at his guitar. "The song I played for your mother the night I proposed to her."

Thilly smiled and sighed. She knew the song, of course, and she knew the story, yet she never tired of his retelling it.

"Tell me again," she begged. "I know Mother won't be here for my birthday."

Her father smiled sadly. "She is here in other ways, just the same. And while we are on that subject, upon your coming out, I would like for you to tour the Realm. Including Aceltia. It is time you visited the Veiled Isles."

Thilly gasped. "Really? Go see Mother?"

"Yes, of course," said her father. "I always had it in mind."

Thilly felt an electric thrill course through her. "I never thought the day would come."

"It has!" said the king warmly. "Or it shall, tomorrow. Thilly."

She was already daydreaming, wondering what those misty isles looked like. Wondering what her mother looked like, for Thilly could not remember her face well, and the paintings of her never seemed to capture the essence that she *could* remember. She knew her father thought the same, but he seemed to have coped well.

"Thilly," he said again.

"Hmm, yes, Father?" she answered.

She was surprised to see him clasp his hands and look at her with a slight crinkle of the brow.

"How do you feel about tomorrow? Really?" he asked her. "If it won't work, we will find another way."

"What do you mean?" she asked, but she already knew, and it made her stomach twist. Her hands grew sweaty.

"You know the prince is a good lad," began Gathlade.

"Must we talk about this now?" said Thilly, bristling.

"We must, dearheart," said her father, his voice calming. "Would that you could stay this wild and free person, and I am so very proud of who you've become. The weight of the crown grows heavy, and it is easier shared."

"Won't it be *his* crown?" she replied, gritting her teeth. "I don't want to marry."

# THE VALE OF SEVEN DRAGONS

The king sighed. "I know you say that now, but you are the rightful heir, and you must have a King by your side."

"Why not keep him a Prince?" grumbled Thilly. Her mind went back to the Veiled Isles. "Mother wouldn't have wanted this for me."

Gathlade took a deep breath and exhaled slowly. "Your mother abdicated this life of ours, and expressly wished for you to carry it on."

"What about what *I* want?" demanded Thilly. "I've come of age, or will after midnight. What of this makes any sense? You'll be king a good long time, anyway."

"Well, of course I hope so," replied her father, but Thilly caught something in his voice.

"Do you miss her?" she asked suddenly.

His eyes darted to the guitar. "Every moment of every day, with every draw of breath, with every beat of my heart, I miss your mother."

Thilly seized him in a hug.

"Why not join her, then?" she pondered into his sleeve. "Let me take on the kingdom and you go be with Mother."

The king laughed softly.

"Ah, daughter. That is not the way of things."

"Why isn't it? Why shouldn't it be?" she wanted to know. "I'm serious. None of this makes sense."

"From time imm—"

"Oh, Daddy," interrupted Thilly. "I know enough of the history, though I find it all rather tedious, to understand. I just—I wish you could be with the person you loved."

"I am with our daughter," said the king, cupping her cheek in his hand. "There is much of your mother in you, Thilly. And thank the gods for that. You are what the Realm needs."

Thilly snorted. "I'm not sure the Realm is what I need," she said, tossing her frizzled hair. "And I'm not sure Prince Beaumain is *who* I need."

"I understand that," said Gathlade, nodding. "But you could do far worse."

"I've not seen him in over a year, and the last time he barely looked at me," complained Thilly.

"He'll be here in the morning," he reminded her. "Two dragons, meeting as adults."

"Am I an adult now?" teased Thilly.

"Never in my eyes, child," her father said, and Thilly felt her eyes well up. "You will forever be my baby, my one and most precious darling. Your mother would be so proud of you. But before any of that business with the prince, go and see her."

Thilly nodded and sighed.

"Very well, Father," she said, her voice shaking. "I shall make you proud."

"You always have," he told her.

She darted out of his office, holding back tears, and Birkswood watched her go. He also, before entering to attend the king, noticed Thilly did not take the proper corridor back to her quarters.

"Hmm," Birkswood murmured to himself.

And indeed, Thilly did not return to her quarters. She slid among the shadows and candlelight and the soft closing of the castle for the evening to head outdoors, and again tossed her gown aside and placed her cloak upon herself and stole into the night.

Startling a tabby cat and a dusky-feathered night parrot, she made her way to the keep. There she could hear the murmurings and laughter of the knights. She stood with her back against the south-facing stone wall near their quarters and listened, stealing glances when she dared.

# THE VALE OF SEVEN DRAGONS

The knights sang and joked and laughed. Thilly could hear them playing games and slamming down mugs or steins, and shouting thickly for more beer.

"—different after tomorrow, you'll find," said one grizzled older knight.

Thilly perked up, for she heard a younger man say, "Ah, that is a lucky prince indeed."

His mates roared with laughter.

"Not you taking an interest in Her Royal Highness? Put the drink down, man! You've had enough!" Gales of laughter rang through their quarters.

"The mead is fair, but not as fair as she," the voice answered to more laughter.

Thilly's cheeks burned.

"Well, she'll never be yours, lad, so put that dream to rest," said the first knight.

"Aye, but that's what songs are for," answered the younger man.

"Oho!" another cried. "He's a bard, now, eh, Vyrent?"

And Sir Vyrent answered, "Not yet," to more laughter.

Thilly's heart hammered.

*O gods! Did I really hear that? About* me?

She heard the door swing open, and she scrambled to get out of sight.

The door shut, and she heard a voice say, "Who goes there?"

She quaked, hidden behind one of the still-standing trees, praying to the dragons themselves that she would not be found out here at night, before her coming of age, spying on knights.

Footsteps shuffled through leaves, and she scarcely breathed.

"Hello?" called a voice softly. And not hearing a response, he said in a harder voice, "I would advise you, whoever you are, to step forth and reveal yourself. My blade is sharper than my wits."

Thilly said nothing, but the footsteps advanced, and she bit her lips.

"Show yourself!" the voice hissed, and she heard the air sing with a blade, and she gasped.

He heard.

"Who's that?" he demanded, and he reached into the thicket of trees and caught her cloak and yanked.

"Oh!" she cried, and she tumbled forward, colliding with his chin, and nearly impaling herself on his blade.

"Gods be good!" he cried. "Your Highness!" And he bowed low.

"Hush," she hissed. They both glanced with wide eyes back to the door, which remained closed.

"Milady," cried the knight, bowing. "Er, Your Highness! I could have killed you!"

"Good thing you didn't," snapped Thilly. "Nearly scared the shit out of me, though, Sir Vyrent."

His eyes grew wider then, and she yanked her hood down, and her hair flew in all directions, untamed and frizzing in the damp evening air. They stared at each other.

Even in the dark, he was ruggedly handsome, with a wisdom in his eyes and station that was beyond his years. His hair, looking darker at night, fell into his eyes, and he swept them out again.

"What—Your Highness—what are you doing here?" he asked her.

"I—I—" began Thilly. Her entire body vibrated just then, in embarrassment, thrill, and attraction. "I heard there was trouble at the seafront," she stammered. "I wanted to see if I could find out anything."

He screwed his face up. "What trouble?"

Then she gasped. "Oh, gods. Nothing, forget I said anything."

"Wait, no, Your Highness," he asked, daring to step forward and raise his hands. "What trouble?"

"I shouldn't have spoken, and I should not be here," she answered, furious at herself and her foolishness.

"No indeed, you should not; no lady should, especially not the Princess Githilien on the eve of her coming of age. Nor should she be at any other time," said Sir Vyrent. "I shall escort you back to the castle."

"No, you shall not," she hissed. Then he looked at her trousers.

"Ah," he said. "You don't want to be seen. But gods! Get away from here, at least. Come, let's head through the woods; it'll be a shortcut, and then at least I can see on the other side that you've made it back safely. I'll keep watch."

So they climbed quickly through the woods behind the knights' quarters, and on the other side of the dense firs, the land sloped back down toward Castle Taugan. Seeing it in view, and trembling from her head to her feet, she looked up at Sir Vyrent, who caught her gaze and held it.

"So you think he's lucky, then?" she asked him.

His eyebrows lifted, and he looked even more handsome.

"Who, Your Highness?" he asked innocently.

She bit her lip.

"Well, that was you, wasn't it? You think the prince is lucky? Because I'm...supposed to marry him, or some such ghastly fate?"

Sir Vyrent coughed and ran his hands through his hair. That act flustered her even further.

"Whatever do you mean?" he asked, not looking at her. "Anyway, we're here. I'll keep a lookout for you."

"Don't you follow orders from me, technically?" she asked impishly. She felt hot all over.

The knight shifted from one foot to the other.

"Your Highness, I am ever at your service," he declared.

"Are you, indeed?" she replied. She leaned close to him, and he stood stock still, head held high. "I'll hold you to that."

She dashed off then, her heart feeling as though it would launch from her chest to join the stars above, and she knew he watched her go, and she grinned the whole way back to her quarters, cheeks aflame and hair wild. There she met Hana and sighed as she sank back to her reality. But a smile twitched upon her lips, and she fell asleep the moment her head hit her pillow.

# CHAPTER 4

## THE PRINCE AND THE BIRTHDAY

*Singing. Who is that singing?*

She stirred, and the echoes of an ethereal voice rang in her mind. She found she had drooled on her pillow, and she blinked in the dim light. A hiss of curtains and a blast of light in her face, and she cried out.

"Ack! Gods! Who's there?" she mumbled, reaching for the kerchief on her bedside table. It lay like a fairy's coverlet in front of a crystalline frame with a painting made of crushed opals. It was a painting of a woman with loose, fair wavy hair, and a fine long neck, a wry smile, and large, knowing eyes: her mother, Woadlynn, a witch and a priestess, who was not there for her daughter's sixteenth birthday.

Thilly wiped her mouth with her kerchief and groaned.

"Good morning, Your Highness!" called a melodic voice with a bit of a brogue.

Thilly sat up on her elbows. "Oh! Hana. Good morning!"

# THE VALE OF SEVEN DRAGONS

The girl tilted her head and beamed from her rosy face. Over her arms she held a simple but well-crafted dressing gown, an exquisite deep violet in hue.

"I've rung for tea," the young woman told Thilly. "Many happy returns!"

Thilly grinned.

"You're a bit more casual than Mrs. Florence's usual," she said, to which Hana blushed deeply.

"I'm so sorry, Your Highness, I didn't—"

Thilly laughed softly. "No, dear Hana, do not apologize! I find all the frippery ridiculous."

Hana looked scandalized, and Thilly realized her error.

"I'm sorry, milady," Hana stammered, and Thilly felt bad.

She swung her legs over the bed and stood, approached Hana, and said, "No, I apologize. I've made light of your station. I may not enjoy this life, but I live it in privilege, and I disrespected you. *I* am sorry."

For a moment the two girls looked at each other, and Hana's shoulders dropped, and she curtsied. Thilly dipped her head and felt relieved. She let Hana drape the dressing gown over her. Then Hana pulled the elaborate cord next to the window, which was embroidered with red, orange, and gold dragons interspersed with autumn leaves and bramble fruits.

Hana said, "I've pressed your gowns for the day's events, and Mrs. Florence is preparing for the arrival."

Thilly grimaced. "I hoped I'd dreamed all that."

Hana glanced at her, her eyebrows raised. She asked shyly, "What's he like?"

And it was Thilly's turn to blush, for she thought back to the previous evening, and how she wished she could have lingered with Sir Vyrent a bit longer.

"Who...who do you mean?" she asked, and then thought, *Well, now I've done it.*

"The Crown Prince Beaumain, Your Highness," answered Hana, her eyes round.

Thilly snorted, which shocked Hana.

"Oh, *him*," she said in a gravelly voice. "I'm sure he's adequate. Considering our ancestors fought each other with literal warring dragons."

"You'll be the queen of two lands, one day," Hana mused.

"I admire your imagination, Hana!" exclaimed Thilly. "I might decide to take my mother's course of action, though, after all," and she smirked wickedly, watching Hana's face flicker from one form of surprise to the next. Thilly looked over at her bedside table to the picture of her mother, gleaming softly from a shaft of filtered sunlight, slanting from the tall window.

She blinked. *Singing.* The finest melody had traversed her dreams, from an enchanting voice. But what *had* the voice been singing? Words? Nonsense? Simple notes, rendered nearly holy? She wished she could go back to the dream and listen. It seemed...important, somehow.

The tea service arrived, as did Mrs. Florence. The older woman shut the door after the maids stepped out, and her brow looked stern.

"Gods almighty!" she hissed, and Thilly held her teacup in the air, mid-sip.

"What is it?" she asked.

"They've arrived," Mrs. Florence replied in a tone of doom.

Thill nearly sloshed her tea by standing abruptly. She set the cup down with a clatter from trembling hands.

"What?" she asked. "I thought they'd get here later...at least late morning!"

Mrs. Florence looked as if she had eaten three lemons soaked in chiles.

"So we did think! Thank the gods for some of the wood parrots and ravens, who saw their host coming and got in a wicked fight in the air, competing to bring the news...else we'd be scrambling. More than we already are, at any rate. Hana, get her morning dress, there's a good girl. Your Highness, it's time you met your future husband."

Thilly's face went hot. *Who's to say I didn't last night?*

She sighed. "Why must everything seem so inevitable? Mother didn't settle."

Mrs. Florence shot Thilly a look that sent a chill down her spine. "You say naught of your mother's choices, young lady. You may be a princess by birth, but your mother"—and she stopped abruptly.

"My mother," said Thilly in a downcast voice, "is not here on my birthday, on my coming out, and on my day of a possible marriage proposal."

Mrs. Florence twisted her face in all manner of ways, and Thilly could not fathom what the woman was going through, but she decided it must have been a struggle.

"She is not," agreed the older woman. "But she left me and Birkswood to fill the vacuum. And I intend to do that today, Princess Githilien of Vickery, for all our sakes."

Mrs. Florence's severe tone stilled Thilly then. She gave herself over to Hana's fussing, and two additional ladies' maids were brought in to help prepare Thilly. Mrs. Florence huffed and grumbled under her breath and then excused herself. Thilly felt on edge.

*I hate this*, she thought, scowling into her mirror as the young women dressed her. Her morning gown was yellow, with an empire waist and short, capped sleeves with their edges embroidered in carnelian flame patterns that also extended to the scooped neck of her gown. The maids hung a long strand of pale-yellow river pearls around Thilly's neck. They pulled her difficult hair back, leaving some of it down, and fastened it with a cluster of the same pearls. She protested at the application of light coral-hued lip balm.

"Every bite I take will wipe that right off," she said.

Hana shook her head. "No, Your Highness, this is a new one, part of a set Mrs. Florence ordered weeks ago, she said. It won't budge. Not even for a kiss!"

And Hana and the other maids broke into giggles, then covered their mouths. They were in great cheer and excitement. Thilly felt leaden with dread.

When it was time to go down, Thilly felt a bit light-headed, as if this were all an out-of-body experience. She heard the trumpets heralding the entrance of the Royals Catellaith and her stomach turned. She was glad for her pale-yellow gloves, which covered the sweat that her palms now pulsed forth. The great stairs looked a bit too steep to her, and she cast about. Two footmen came to stand beside her, and then they all descended together. Hana and the maids watched furtively from the balcony and whispered behind their hands as the princess stepped carefully toward a group gathered at the bottom of the stairs.

Her father stood among them in state dress, with red metallic dragon epaulets and garnet cufflinks, and a simple gold circlet on his brow. He looked at her and smiled, and Thilly for a moment forgot that all other eyes were upon her...especially those of the queen, but she did not forget for long.

The two royal families faced each other, and Thilly blinked, feeling something in her right eye.

*Ah, shit*, she thought, for she desperately wanted to rub her eye, but instead kept blinking.

Before her stood King Ardenour, his skin rich brown and his eyes blue-green, his hair mixed russet and white and finely curled, cropped close. He wore a deep grey morning suit with blue and silver epaulets, and a silver circlet on his head. He looked as aloof as she remembered, but something in his gaze seemed unusual. Like he was distracted.

*Maybe he's got something in his eye.*

Still, he bowed to Thilly, and she curtsied deeply.

And then there was the queen.

Queen Maulielle turned heads wherever she went, and Castle Taugan proved to be no exception. She stood in a deep periwinkle silk gown with an empire waist, draped with strands of silver and pale blue beads. Her alabaster skin, famed throughout the realm as being without flaw, was exposed only at her neck and face. And her face was most arresting: pale, framed by thick, jet-black hair coiffed into a high beehive, and eyebrows that lifted archly above deep-set dark violet eyes with thick black lashes. Those deep eyes narrowed as they examined Thilly, and the young woman felt as though the queen could see down to her bones and into her marrow. There was something predatory in the gaze that chilled Thilly and confused her. She took a deep breath and slowly exhaled, and moved her gaze to the queen's right, where Prince Beaumain stood.

The prince was tall and had his father's sea-colored eyes and ginger hair, and his skin was light brown. He had grown in stature and in build, since Thilly had seen him last. He had his mother's closely tucked ears and her high cheekbones, and his father's strong jaw and determined mouth. His face was expressionless, but he bowed. He wore a morning suit of grey, with a cravat embroidered with a silver and blue dragon: Nistraan of old, the house dragon of Catellaith.

"It is an honor, Your Highness," Thilly said in a perfunctory tone.

"The honor is mine," Beaumain said to her in a stiff, even voice.

*Gods, what a bore,* she thought, and she dipped her head only from politeness.

Next to the prince, Princess Tantienne stood with her hands clasped tightly in front of her, with long, dark wavy hair, tan skin, and large, open dark blue eyes. Her ears looked like her father's, and she was so slender and delicate that Thilly fancied she must be descended from fairy folk. Certainly she did not have the severe look of her mother or the stern look of her father. Thilly smiled at her and outstretched her hands, which the younger princess took, while Prince Beaumain watched.

"Your Highness, it is so good to see you again!" said Thilly warmly, and the young girl's face lit up. She curtsied and became more animated. She glanced up at her brother, and his face finally broke into a soft smile at her. Thilly lifted one eyebrow.

*He thaws!* she thought.

They walked into the dining hall, brightly lit for breakfast with many hanging candles and some oil lamps, and above the long ancient oak table, fastened with ancient swords twisted about its legs, two immense banners hung: one for Vickery with the dragon Antares, and one for Catellaith with the dragon Nistraan.

"Two dragons, under the same roof at last," announced King Gathlade, sitting at the head of the table with King Ardenour next to him, to his left; beyond Ardenour, Prince Beaumain sat, and Queen Maulielle presided between her son and daughter. The queen turned her dark eyes to Thilly, who blinked. Her eye grew irritated again, and she smiled politely back.

*She disturbs me*, Thilly thought. There was something strange about the queen's eyes. Not merely their ethereal color, but something in them. Thilly dared not study too closely, though she didn't understand why she felt that way. Those eyes made her feel as though they held something maybe she shouldn't have seen. She fought a shudder.

A small tone rang out, and King Ardenour called out in a rich, resonant voice, "A glorious day, the day of Princess Githilien and Prince Beaumain, reunited: a symbol of the joining of our kingdoms made flesh."

Thilly felt the urge to gag.

*Wait, isn't this* my *birthday? Can I at least get* some *recognition for that before I'm to be paraded before the prince?*

She caught the look of Queen Maulielle again, who smiled with too-white teeth in a strangely unlined face…waxen, Thilly thought.

"To the union of our families," the queen said then, in a deep, velvety voice, and all raised a glass to that. "But of course, I must have a look at the princess this evening, for her coming out ceremony. On this, her sixteenth birthday! For which we must rejoice. To Princess Githilien!"

A tinkling of goblets shivered through the dining hall, and the servants brought forth the courses for the breakfast tea. Thilly's was brought first: a tiny, tiered cake, which smoldered and fizzed, and when she cut into it, minuscule sparkling lights in the shape of red dragons sprang out of it and danced about above her head before disintegrating. Applause rang forth.

"Many happy returns, Thi—Your Highness," said Beaumain then.

Thilly smirked. "Thank you, good Prince."

"Your mother would be proud, I'm sure," Beaumain remarked, sipping his tea.

"Would she?" countered Thilly. "But not proud enough to be here, right?"

Beaumain shifted uncomfortably. Thilly caught her father's eye and he frowned ever so slightly, and the queen lowered her eyelids nearly to slits.

"Ah, but you see," said the queen, her smile glittering, her jewel-like gaze piercing Thilly, "your days of not having a mother about shall come to an end with the marriage."

Thilly choked on her bite of cake. She quickly sipped from her water goblet.

"You're mistaken," she said nervously. "My mother took the vows of the Covenant of the Veiled Isles. She cannot leave to come here right now; it is a lifelong vow with little respite."

"Oh darling," said Queen Maulielle in a simpering voice, "we are all too aware of your father's great sacrifice."

"My *father's* sacrifice!" cried Thilly, growing hot.

The queen extended her long fingers dramatically before her. "The King could easily have taken a second wife, but he chose to indulge in your mother's abdication without ending the marriage."

Thilly glared at her. "Are you really telling me my father should have moved on from the love of his life, my mother?"

The queen shrugged her bejeweled shoulders. "It would have been an acceptable choice, as she abandoned him, and you."

Thilly took a breath and then quite suddenly her father said, "It was a mutual choice, something the entire realm does indeed recall," and Thilly heard in that voice something rare indeed: steel. "We do communicate still, as our marriage requires."

Thilly jerked her head to stare at him.

"What?" she asked. "You've never told me this. I thought she couldn't!"

"Perhaps," said Beaumain suddenly, his voice shaking slightly, "we could discuss my upcoming tour."

"Yes," said King Gathlade, glancing sideways at King Ardenour. "I think that might be a better avenue for discussion. Githilien, darling, we shall speak in the morning."

"I think I'll excuse myself," said Thilly hotly.

# THE VALE OF SEVEN DRAGONS

The queen raised her eyebrows and shook her head. "I must say, Your Majesty," and she looked with great disdain from Thilly to her father, "there is some of the mother in this one after all. More than we had thought."

"Indeed," said Gathlade, his brow creased, "for which I am very proud. Thilly, you may be excused; but only after listening to our guest, the prince, discuss his plans."

Beaumain adjusted himself and swallowed; she watched the pulse in his neck, just above his stiff collar. His pupils had gone tiny in the brightly lit space.

"It is—it is just that my own age is marked by duty, much as yours is," he said, glancing uneasily at his mother, who looked down her nose and clucked something to her daughter, who looked as though she wished she could be anywhere else; she appeared almost shrunken in her seat, and her large eyes stared at Thilly.

"I'm to tour Catellaith," Beaumain went on, and he nodded to the murmurs of intrigue around the table. "This will be part of my duty to the Crown and to the Realm, and to visit our subjects. It should also be an opportunity for you to join me, Princess."

Thilly snapped her head up at that.

"I beg your pardon?" she said, overly loudly. The hall went silent.

"The prince," King Ardenour then said in his operatic voice, "would like to ask for a host from Vickery to join him, given that our lands should unite eventually under a new King and Queen."

"I've not agreed to any of this!" cried Thilly, standing, which made Princess Tantienne gasp. "And I was to visit my mother! Father, you said—"

"Githilien," said her father in a warning tone.

"I—I must be excused," said Thilly, feeling dizzy, in shock at both her father's revelation about her mother, and his seeming dismissal of her trip to visit her. "I have taken a turn. I shall—I shall see you this evening at the ball," she said to Beaumain, but she avoided his sea-colored eyes.

She walked quickly from the hall, feeling all eyes upon her, hearing the undulation of disapproving murmurs.

As soon as she was out of the door, she turned to sprint, and then halted quite suddenly. Birkswood and Mrs. Florence stood in her way.

"Your Highness," said Birkswood in his deep voice, towering over her. "Are you feeling quite well?"

Thilly's heart raced, and she actually did feel unwell at the moment, so great had her anxiety grown. Mrs. Florence caught her arm and looked sternly at Birkswood.

"Birkswood, will you help me with the princess?" she asked, her tone level. "Let us take her to her quarters to rest. She seems to have need of a nap."

"A nap!" gasped Thilly, coming around to her senses enough to feel outraged. "I don't need a nap! I'm quite fully awake and alert, and…and…"

Mrs. Florence shot Birkswood a half-lidded look and said in a low voice, "Be that as it may, we need to get you away from the prying eyes and ears of the host of Catellaith. We can discuss this more in your quarters." Louder, she said, "Birkswood?"

The man nodded a touch and said, "Would you like for me to ring the physic?"

"Let us see how our princess does first, shall we?" said Mrs. Florence. Thilly detected a hint of anger in the woman's voice, which made her curious. Were they arguing?

On either side of her, they helped Thilly up the stairs and to her quarters. Hana stood before the door, face full of shocked concern, and she opened it.

"Hana," said Mrs. Florence, "draw the princess a hot bath and add some petals of arcswithy, will you? There's a dear."

Then she turned to Thilly, glancing first at Birkswood as she did so. "Child, you absolutely will visit your mother. We will go with you."

Thilly stared. "What?" she gasped.

Birkswood cleared his throat, and Mrs. Florence bit her lip.

She whispered, "Let us keep our voices down along with our tempers, princess. You will travel to see your mother as planned. We've got it all arranged. But you'll have to play along with the prince as well. Come to some compromise, the two of you. We can do many things, but not that. Speak to him tonight about it."

Birkswood said very quietly, "Do not let the queen hear a word you say, either."

Thilly stared at them both, amazed. "What are you getting at, the two of you?"

Birkswood answered, "When we are on the open road as a group, we will tell you; but not within these walls, not right now…not with her here."

*Her* meaning the queen. Thilly was stunned. This was already the strangest birthday she had ever had.

# CHAPTER 5

## *DEBUTANTE*

In her quarters, Thilly found a table set up with small gifts.

"The larger ones are in the library," Hana told her, drawing back Thilly's bedcovers. "Mrs. Florence says you're to have a nap," she said, in answer to Thilly's crinkled eyebrows.

Thilly shook her head. "No. No, I can't nap. I...don't feel settled enough to."

Hana approached her and looked into her hazel eyes with concern.

"What happened, milady?" she asked warmly.

Thilly sat on the edge of her bed. Hana knelt to remove her shoes, which Thilly allowed.

"Please sit next to me, Hana," she said. She rubbed her temples. "Something isn't right. A lot of somethings."

Hana shrugged, gave a little laugh, and said, "Them's just wedding jitters, Your Highness," and she gave Thilly's shoulder a quick squeeze.

Thilly looked sidewise at her and smirked.

"I wish that were all. It's...well. The queen..."

"Oh!" cried Hana, face rosy with excitement. "What's she like? We—that is, the girls and I—got a peek at her. Isn't she beautiful!"

"Quite," agreed Thilly, sighing. "Beautiful, but strange. Cold. There's...she makes *me* feel cold."

Hana shrugged again. She rose and walked over to adjust the tea table by the window. "Maybe she's nervous too, you know. Getting a new daughter-in-law, her only son, and all that. Got to be a bit stressful, yes?"

Thilly pressed her lips together. "Well, it's true I never thought of it that way. Maybe you're right, Hana. I hope that's all it is. Thank you. Now, what are these, do you think?"

She gestured to the small gifts laid carefully out. Some were in silk-covered boxes, some in bundled velvet. One was about the size of her hand, yet exquisitely made from pearled gnarlwood, which bore a softly iridescent sheen. She vaguely remembered that small forests of those rare trees grew upon the windy bluffs of the northeastern coast of Catellaith. A little silver cord tied around it bore a blue tag.

"For Thilly," she read aloud. "Who do you suppose sent this?"

"Not sure, milady," said Hana, pulling the cord for tea and adjusting the curtains. The light in Thilly's quarters flickered back and forth between clouds and sunshine.

Thilly pulled the silver cord from the wooden box and found that its lid lifted easily off. The inside of the box was lined with periwinkle velvet and held a gauzy silver bag. She lifted the bag and found it surprisingly heavy in her hand. She looked up and found that Hana stood by her again, with a little smile.

"Look, there's a card underneath!" she pointed out. Thilly had missed it, for it was the same periwinkle hue as the velvet.

"Keen eyes, dear Hana," said Thilly appreciatively. She held out the gauze bag to the maid, who took it with awe.

"Oh, it's heavy!" Hana marveled.

"Isn't it?"

"Well, open it, then!" urged the girl, forgetting herself. She clapped her hand over her mouth then. "Oh, I'm sorry, I've overstepped, Your Highness!"

Thilly laughed, "Oh, Hana, I am so very glad you're my chief lady in waiting."

"But I'm no lady!" protested Hana, and then her mouth formed a horrified "o" shape. "I mean, I'm just a country girl, I honestly don't know why—"

Thilly stood and took her hands, and said, "I couldn't have asked for better, Hana. In my quarters, or away from others, you may be casual with me. I prefer that you are. Knowing full well the requirements of your post, do so as you feel comfortable. But please, never worry. I would rather you were real and true to yourself, at all times."

Hana blushed and curtsied. Then she glanced down at the card in Thilly's hand.

"Oh," said Thilly, and she turned it over. "Ah. Well, then."

Hana's eyes darted from the card to Thilly's face and back again.

"It says," she told the maid, "'To our friendship, and our future. May it be better than the past, and may our dragons meet again. Yours, Beaumain.'"

"Ahhh!" cried Hana, and she twirled on her feet. "That's so romantic!"

Thilly swallowed. "Well, I don't know about that, but…it's something."

Hana then handed her bag back to her. "Oh, sorry!"

Thilly laughed again. "I forgot, for a moment, there was even a gift."

# THE VALE OF SEVEN DRAGONS

Hana looked distraught, but Thilly shook her head. "It's all right, Hana. We've had an exciting day."

Thilly held the bag, weighed it in her hand, and finally, with a short sigh, opened it. She poured its contents into her hand: a finely wrought chain, made of silver and gold, its links shaped like flames, and at its end, an amulet of two intertwined dragons, one of silver and blue, one of red and gold: Nistraan of Catellaith and Antares of Vickery.

"Oh!" said Hana, her face now round with smiles and awe. "Your two kingdoms together. It's just beautiful!"

Thilly tilted the amulet back and forth. "It's really heavy," she noted. "But yes, it is lovely."

Hana's fingers twitched. "You'll wear it to the ball, of course?"

Thilly's stomach lurched.

"I suppose it'll be expected," she said in a flat voice.

The tea service arrived, and so did Mrs. Florence. Her eyes shot from Hana to Thilly, and to the necklace. She lifted her chin, set her shoulders back, and looked like an aloof raven.

"Good, you got it before the others," she said simply.

Thilly lifted her right eyebrow and said, "Well, it was unusual, anyway."

"His idea, so I was told," sniffed Mrs. Florence.

"Whose, Beaumain's?" asked Thilly, wondering at the woman's attitude.

"Always the nature lover, that one," said Mrs. Florence. "Went out of his way personally, I heard, to find driftwood—driftwood! Along the shore, so nobody would disturb the grove of trees it originally came from."

"Really?" asked Thilly. Her face tingled. "That's…thoughtful."

Mrs. Florence helped Hana set out the plates for tea and said, irritably, "That boy's always been climbing around in trees, his whole life. Risks his neck and the Crown of Catellaith wandering the stormy shores to find a piece of wood for you. Anyway, Princess, you'd better thank him for his ridiculous gesture."

Thilly blinked.

"There's more to Beaumain than I thought," she declared.

Mrs. Florence tutted. "One of you lives in a library or skulking about watching knights, play-fighting with sticks for a sword"—Thilly's face went full scarlet—"and the other slinks about the woods and hedges and stormy shores. What the two of you would be together, gods know."

Hana twirled again, and exclaimed, "It's so lovely!"

Mrs. Florence turned her full fury upon the girl and barked, "Do remember yourself, Hana!"

To which Hana's eyebrows shot up and remained that way while Thilly busied herself with a scone and cream and tried not to think much about that one gift's revelation.

Soon after, a knock on the door revealed a set of ladies' maids, bearing a great and bulky item between them.

"Well, finally," snapped Mrs. Florence. Thilly recognized that voice: the woman was stressed out, but also Thilly wondered if she might be masking something else. It was unusual to see her so worked up. "Your gown for the evening," said Mrs. Florence, "underneath this great balloon, apparently."

Thilly's throat tickled from a desire to laugh, but she knew the woman well enough not to press her luck with that at the moment. So she watched as the maids untied the "great balloon," and the filtered sunlight from the curtains illuminated its contents as if they were made from embers. For there Thilly beheld her ballgown, her coming-out extravagance, and even she had to admit it was remarkable.

# THE VALE OF SEVEN DRAGONS

The gown was a drop-shoulder affair with long, fitted sleeves, its bodice drawn snugly to the waist, and the skirt was full. Made from raw silk in a vivid orange-red hue, it was stitched with the patterns of flames at the edge of its sleeves and along the collar, and the great dragon crest of Antares himself was woven into a wearable tapestry on the bodice. The skirt fell from the waist in many folds, so that it would flare when Thilly danced. Over the vibrant silk, copper-colored tulle encrusted with garnet rhinestones set the dress ablaze. Gazing at it, Thilly felt a deep pang of longing that took her by surprise.

"I wish Mother could see this," she murmured. Then Mrs. Florence thawed, and she put her arm around the girl.

"As do I," said the older woman. "But she will see *you* in the near future, and that is better than any gown, even one as remarkable as this."

Thilly's throat hurt, and she swallowed. She nodded and dabbed her eyes with the tips of her fingers.

"Oh, ain't it just grand?" breathed Hana.

Mrs. Florence shot her a ferocious look, and she cowered.

Thilly sat back down and shoved a small sandwich into her mouth in one bite and stared absently at the blazing dress.

"If I never wear another dress again," she mused, "at least I've gone out with a bang."

Mrs. Florence snorted at that, and said, "Well, you've got to come out first, and let's start getting you ready for dinner before that."

"Another meal at the table with *her*?" said Thilly under her breath, and Mrs. Florence pinched up her mouth and said nothing.

Thilly shivered, for she already dreaded seeing the queen again.

"She's a bit put out, methinks," said Mrs. Florence, "down her favorite maids and all."

"Doesn't she have several dozen to choose from?" countered Thilly. "She likes that sort of thing, or so I've heard. I'd rather have one great maid than so many dozens."

Mrs. Florence fluffed out the bottom of the fiery gown and stood with her hands on her hips, admiring it. "Well, they had a trip to the seacoast, and apparently some of them caught the cold air or something like that. Fell ill, but fortunately not the queen herself."

"Too bad," said Thilly so quietly that she thought nobody heard, but of course Mrs. Florence did.

"You watch yourself, Princess," she admonished. "The Realm's eyes are upon you, and I daresay their ears are too."

"She just...something seems...I mean, I never really bonded with her when I was younger, not that we saw much of each other," noted Thilly. "But I...I felt quite uncomfortable today. Did anyone else?"

"You're nervous," said Mrs. Florence flatly. "And you were out late, were you not?"

Thilly blushed, thinking of Sir Vyrent's heated gaze and the words she'd overheard him say to the other knights.

"Anyway," the older woman went on, "you're seeing things that aren't there because she's going to be your mother-in-law, and that would make anyone nervous. For it to be Queen Maulielle? Child, how could you not be? But you're a spirited lass, and you're *our* princess; one day you'll be our queen, not her."

Thill shook her head and sighed. She imagined Sir Vyrent lifting her upon his horse, and riding off with him into the Vale, never to return. Rather than indulging that fancy, she endured having her wildly unruly hair brushed to prepare for the ball and winced at the many tangles that required extra pulls and tugs from Mrs. Florence herself. *I hate being a Princess*, she thought, not for the first time.

# THE VALE OF SEVEN DRAGONS

❦

It took hours, during which Thilly nearly went mad, but the maids transformed her for the ball. Her coming out would be the grandest event Castle Taugan had witnessed since the coronation of Gathlade. No fanfare would be spared, and yet Vickery never had been a kingdom of gaudy show, unlike Catellaith under Queen Maulielle's luxuriant eye.

Yet the women of the castle came together to prepare their Princess for the most public and important moment of her entire life. To her hair, they added white starflowers and pins of gold and garnet. Next, they applied rouge, powdered her face, tinted her lips red, and sprinkled the powder of glittering crushed garnets on top of her elaborately coiled hair that still wanted to frizz despite all their combined efforts and much lavender-scented pomade. To Thilly's neck, one girl applied touches of subtly musky perfume, but Thilly held her hand up.

"Not too much, please, else I'll sneeze all night!" she said.

Once they had finished and Thilly stepped into her glittering carnelian-hued shoes, the women all cooed at her, even Mrs. Florence, who clasped her hands to her chin. Her eyes glinted suspiciously.

"No, you're not crying!" Thilly cried.

Mrs. Florence covered a small hiccup-sob with her fist and shook her head.

"You're the picture of both your parents, and still somehow better. Oh, my dear girl!"

Thilly lowered her head and looked down at her full skirt, her gloved hands, and then raised her head to look at all the maids in her quarters, their eyes shining and their smiles broad.

"I know it's not something I'd ever choose for myself," she said, "but this is marvelous, and I thank each of you. I'll probably tear out of it like a banshee at midnight and run screaming into the night"—some gasps and some titters answered her—"but for now, I'll take it."

Hana then ran over and held out the amulet Prince Beaumain had given Thilly.

"Don't forget this, Your Highness! I think it goes just right," said the young maid, beaming.

She fastened the entwined silver and gold flame chain around Thilly's neck, and the coupled dragons rested just above her bosom. Thilly put her hand there for a moment, feeling its cool touch against her bare skin. The maids clasped each other's hands in delight at the sight.

*Well*, she thought, *at least the necklace fits.*

"Shall we go down, then?" asked Mrs. Florence.

"I suppose we should," said Thilly, "although we could use Antares himself, wherever he's at, bless him, to pluck me from the top of the stairs and drop me at the bottom!"

Mrs. Florence grinned at that and opened the doors to Thilly's room. Birkswood and two footmen stood there. And so Thilly set foot upon the stairs down to guide her to this next phase of her life, one which she did not want but felt no way to escape.

*What a beautiful trap I'm in*, she thought, watching all the admiring gazes, hearing the gasps of delight at the sight of her. Waiting for her at the bottom of the stairs, King Gathlade watched his daughter proudly, and his own eyes looked red, and his mustache and beard twitched. Thilly felt a burst of love for her father, and he took her arm and patted her hand.

"My beautiful daughter!" he said softly. "How can you be sixteen? When just yesterday, I held you in my arms, newly born from your wonderful mother."

# THE VALE OF SEVEN DRAGONS

"Thank you, Father," Thilly answered back quietly. "I still want to see her, by the way."

"All in good time," he murmured.

"I hope that time is soon."

The king guided Thilly into the grand ballroom, which she had never seen so polished or bedazzled in her life. She shivered from it, for she knew it was all for her…and for Prince Beaumain. The music swelled and Birkswood himself made a great clap of his hands to call attention.

"His Majesty King Gathlade of the Court of Castle Taugan, of the Land of Vickery borne of the dragon Antares, presents his daughter, Princess Githilien."

# CHAPTER 6

## *MOVING AHEAD*

Thilly's eyes and ears swam from the sensory overload of dragon tapestries, candles flickering, music, ladies fanning themselves in their exquisite gowns and tall hair, and the general din of the most remarkable celebration she had ever attended. It all blurred together for her: choruses in her name and honor, twirling dancers with flame-hued ribbons signifying the fiery breath of Antares himself, and all manner of greetings from royals and lords and ladies from throughout the Realm. She looked for any anchor in the fray, and she found two: Prince Beaumain and, to her great shock, Sir Vyrent!

This jolted her back awake, and she became hypervigilant. Every sense shunted to the fore and her heart pounded. Thilly did not realize it, but she began to smile. But then her eyes fell upon Queen Maulielle, and that smile died. Thilly glimpsed something flickering on the wall before Queen Maulielle stepped fully into view. She was not sure what she saw; it reminded her of the way water danced in the sun, but it seemed inverted somehow…not light dancing, but shadow, maybe. Then the Queen advanced, and gasps of awe undulated through the crowd. But not from Thilly. The Queen turned and smiled with too-white teeth, porcelain skin, and bright lips. Her hair was midnight-hued and bound in great coils and spirals on her head. The queen wore an indigo gown shot with silver filigree, its skirt drawn into a bustle, and she leaned upon a silver cane with a dragon for its head, the long wings and tail winding around the cane itself. The air seemed to draw into a vacuum for a moment. Thilly felt cold. The queen's eyes then turned to her from across the hall, and Thilly's throat caught as if the wind had been knocked out of her.

Everything muffled in Thilly's ears, and she watched the wall behind the queen, the shadows behind the woman twisting and dancing into strange shapes. The queen lowered her deep violet eyes subtly, locking their gaze with Thilly's, and the girl squirmed.

*Shadows*, thought Thilly. *Shadows in her eyes.*

"Princess," a voice spoke next to her, and she jumped, and placed her hand on her breast, covering the amulet. She looked up to see Prince Beaumain, who bowed.

"I see you received my gift," Beaumain said.

Thilly blinked and decided not to look back at his mother. She quickly took in the prince in his deep navy suit, glittering with all the official epaulets and medals of his rank as Crown Prince of Catellaith, and how his aqua eyes gleamed through his ginger eyelashes. She was close enough to him to notice, for the first time, a series of freckles across his nose and cheekbones.

She swallowed and answered, "Yes, obviously. Thank you," she added, and she realized she had sounded brusque. "Pearled gnarlwood box, yes?"

"That's right," answered the prince, with a smile. "I'm impressed you know of it."

"Of course I didn't," she snapped, feeling on edge, with the queen's eyes upon them. "Mrs. Florence told me you got it yourself. That was a tad foolish, wasn't it?"

The prince tilted his head and furrowed his brow.

"Foolish?" he repeated. "That's a fair way to describe it if you've never been to the coast. Which it sounds like you haven't."

Thilly shivered. "Can we—I—let's find something to drink."

"Very well," said Beaumain stiffly. She hurried ahead of him, and the crowd parted for her. She wanted to run out of there, away from the cold and strange eyes of Queen Maulielle, but she settled for sitting out of direct view of the woman, under a set of potted cycads from the southeastern land of what was once the kingdom of Roanmont. Now it was part of the eastern republic of Montadanthe, combined with the former kingdom of Dantheant to the northeast. Some of that republic's dignitaries were in attendance, with their blended dragon raiment, all rather staid in comparison to the royals of Catellaith and Vickery. Each dignitary wore the embroidered crest upon their coats. These shields bore two dragons, the red and black Sunder of Dantheant, and the orange and violet Meteor of Roanmont, who stood on their hind legs, back-to-back, wings joined like hands to their sides, as if facing the world together.

*A republic sounds quite excellent to me right now,* Thilly thought with a frown. *I'll bet they don't arrange marriages!*

Heaving a great sigh, Thilly settled into a fine deep gold velvet chair, and footmen arrived offering trays of drinks and food to her and the prince, who sat next to her on a divan.

"You could sit next to me," he suggested.

She turned her head slowly and looked at him as if to say, "Really?" but she refrained for the moment.

"I promise I don't have peeling pox," said the prince.

"Oh well, that's a huge relief then," snorted Thilly. She caught sight of Sir Vyrent and admired him from afar without his knowledge.

"I did wonder if my explorations might send me to the physic, though." He tried catching her eyes.

She rolled her eyes and said, "And why is that?"

"Got myself into some mushrooms," he added slowly. His eyes lowered halfway.

Her cheek twitched. "Had some visions, did you?" she asked, aware that so very many people watched them that they could have nothing resembling a normal conversation. Yet the prince was trying.

"Well, I had to verify whether or not they were safe, you know," said Beaumain, a grin forming on his lips. "I didn't want to turn into a mushroom or anything."

"Were you at risk?" she asked, lowering her head and looking up at him with her eyes incredulous, and she took a sip of green wine from her glass.

"I might just be a fungi," he said.

Gilly choked on her wine and coughed, and a footman raced forward to take the glass. She recovered and darted her eyes back to Beaumain and shook her head.

"You're funnier than I remember," Thilly said to him.

"And you're meaner," he answered.

She tilted her head and squinted at him, and he looked clearly and openly back at her, until something caught his attention. She turned to see what it was, and in doing so, one of the starflowers fell from her deep russet curls. Beaumain reached out to catch it. He tucked it away out of sight before she noticed.

She had followed his original gaze to the other end of the hall, where the tall and slender blonde Lady Patranne stood fanning herself, surrounded by gentlemen of the Court. The Lady was nearly twenty, Thilly knew, and without a husband…a minor scandal, but not enough to warrant any blacklisting. The reason for that was her inherent fabulosity and great beauty, which shone like a lamp no matter where she stood and cast shadows upon everyone else around her. Thilly's mouth turned down in a scowl.

Thilly had no use for women like Lady Patranne, who incidentally never gave her so much as a second glance, and if she did, it was down her perfect, long nose, under her cobalt eyes, and filled with distaste.

Beaumain said to Thilly, "Excuse me," and she felt chilled by his tone. He set his jaw and walked away from where she sat, toward the Lady Patranne.

Thilly felt a fiery sensation tingle all over her, something she had never felt before.

*What's he doing? Going to court the Lady?* she wondered, and she shifted irritably in her seat.

Still scowling, and clenching the arm of her chair, she stewed in her confused and disturbed state until a shadow passed over her. She looked up to see Sir Vyrent, and then she looked behind her…but no, the knight was looking down at *her*, and extending his hand.

Sir Vyrent stood like a god, edged in the light of the candles of the great hall, his dark gold hair falling forward a bit, tracing the edge of his chiseled jaw. His grey eyes considered Thilly with a deep glint of something in them…humor? But she was not sure. She felt her mouth open a bit, and then she closed it and swallowed.

"Your Highness," said Sir Vyrent, and his voice was deep and husky. Thilly felt a new sensation, looking up at him, and she rather enjoyed it.

"Hi, hello," she stammered, and she found herself staring at that hand, wondering what it might do, without even thinking about what the knight was doing.

# THE VALE OF SEVEN DRAGONS

He grinned at her, and his grin was slightly lopsided, and she enjoyed that.

"Your Highness," he repeated, "may I have this dance?"

Thilly found herself thrusting her hand into his, and taking it with some strength, to which he laughed. He pulled her up and she felt slightly giddy, so he steadied her and put his hand on her waist, while she draped her hands on his shoulders.

The very air seemed to go silent then, as if the world paused, and Thilly found it had indeed gone quiet, for now there were two pairs upon the floor: Thilly and Sir Vyrent, and Beaumain and Lady Patranne. Delighted gasps arose from the onlookers, and then in pairs, many of them joined in dancing. The music swelled with horns and harps and cymbals. But Thilly did not hear them. She only heard Sir Vyrent, speaking softly, only to her.

"Many happy returns," he said first. She blushed.

"Thank you," she answered.

"You've made quite an impression on the Royals Catellaith, I see," he remarked, and his wry smile charmed her.

*He's too good-looking. There has to be* something *wrong with him*, she thought.

"I don't think it was a good one," said Thilly, and Sir Vyrent laughed.

"Better that than to bore them," he told her. "And you are anything but boring."

She bit her lip.

"But how would you know that, Sir Vyrent? I have been but a girl of this court my whole life. And you are a knight."

He grinned at her. "And you *want* to be a knight."

She began to halt her dance, but he held her gently.

"Let's keep dancing," he said quietly.

"How do you know?" Thilly demanded quietly.

"Did you think me stupid, Princess?" he asked her, his eyes half-lowered. She blushed, and her heart raced as he held her closer.

"To be quite honest with you, Sir," she answered, returning his gaze until he flinched, "I think you're quite bold, after last night."

"Is that so?" he countered. "One thing I never quite understood, though. Why do you spy on me sometimes?"

The surge of blood to Thilly's face must have been seen by the entire court, she thought, so deeply had she blushed.

"How would you know if I spied?" she hissed.

He twirled her around and whispered, "Send your onlookers a smile so they don't pay close attention to what we're saying."

He spun her again, and she smiled into the crowd, to delighted sighs.

"In answer to your question," said Sir Vyrent, "I've seen you. Ah! Don't flinch. All eyes are on you. Every single one. Look how the prince himself cannot take his eyes off you...poor Lady Patranne!"

Thilly twisted her eyebrows at the knight and glanced, and caught Beaumain's eyes, and he glanced away from her, his cheeks going red.

"You didn't answer my question," said Sir Vyrent, and he spoke it into her ear, close enough so that her curls went hot from his breath, and she wished that he would linger there.

"I wanted to see how you do things," she admitted.

"What...things?" he asked her, grinning impishly, and she blushed again.

"Not your whoring, if that's what you're getting at," she snapped quietly.

His eyes went wide. Then he burst out laughing.

An awkward silence settled over the court, but Thilly made a fake laugh, and then everyone carried on.

"Your practice," she went on. "I wanted to see how you did things. So that I could."

"Ah, an admission," he whispered. "Good. In that case, may I offer you some lessons? In the guise of self-protection, perhaps?"

Thilly grinned. "Hells yes," she murmured.

At that moment, the knight halted, for the prince stood before them, and despite the tall knight's stature, the office of the prince shone from Beaumain. Thilly realized then that he had indeed matured and could bring forth the power of the Crown now for all to see. She was not sure she liked this new side of him. She liked better what Mrs. Florence had told her: the image of Beaumain clambering about on a rocky coast hunting for driftwood was far more interesting than his playing the role of future king.

"May I have the next dance, Your Highness?" Beaumain asked her stiffly.

Thilly glanced at Sir Vyrent, who bowed and gave her a very slow wink from his right eye, so that Beaumain could not see it. Thilly smirked and turned her eyes to Beaumain.

"I would be honored, Your Highness," she said, and curtsied.

Beaumain took her in his arms, and she looked at his chin.

"It would appear you know more about courtly behavior than you let on when you go gallivanting in the woods," said Beaumain quietly.

She looked into his blue-green eyes then and furrowed her brow.

"And what would you know about that, Your Highness?" she murmured.

"I know *you*," he answered simply.

"I don't think you do, Beaumain," said Thilly archly.

"I do," he insisted, and he guided her quite skillfully across the floor. "I know you hate this," he told her, glancing about at the hall. "And yet you fit in perfectly."

"I fucking do *not*," she whispered angrily.

A slow smile crept across Beaumain's mouth.

"And anyway," Thilly hissed, "it would seem you've paired nicely with Lady Patranne of Yon Willowy and Most Available Form."

"You seem a little defensive, Thilly," said Beaumain. His jaw muscle twitched. Seeing that irritated her more.

"Are you serious?" she gasped. "You're making a fool out of us out here, flirting with that lady, when..."

"When *what*?" said Beaumain, looking down at her then.

Thilly wanted to lash out at him, but she bit the words back. She glared at him, and he lifted his ginger head.

At that moment, the music came to an abrupt halt, and someone stirred at the entrance to the great hall. The great banners fluttered, the dragons of each of them set in motion as the wind from outside had been allowed to burst forth, and candles flickered. The Court's voices rose and undulated as whispers traveled.

"Happy birthday, Githilien," said Beaumain then. He released Thilly, stood taut and tall, bowed, and walked back to his parents, who had been watching the pair with interest. The Queen wore an expression of disapproval. Which was fine, thought Thilly; her son had learned it well.

Sir Vyrent was summoned, and he looked back at Thilly, again winking, and Thilly grinned back at him, feeling relieved that at least *someone* had made her smile this evening. It would be the last smile of that night for her, and indeed for anyone there.

A great roar and a stream of profanity echoed through the ballroom, and in bounded an extraordinary figure: a great ginger-bearded man, tall and broad and blocky. His copper-colored hair sprang wildly in all directions, and both that hair and his beard were woven with rubies and golden-dipped giant shark's teeth. He wore a black leather jacket with gold fastenings, leather pants, and thick black boots, their soles caked in grey mud. His eyes were wild and golden, and in his tattooed hands he held a sack that dripped black liquid onto the fine stone floor of the ballroom. Guards and knights sprang for him, and he threw them off like ants. Then he plunged his hand inside the sack and drew forth something black and oozing, and he threw it into the center of the ballroom.

Screams echoed throughout the room, and the soft thuds of fainting women—and some men—could be heard in otherwise dead silence. On the floor lay a cauterized head of what might have been a man, with black and green tentacles and branches forking out of it, its jaw ruptured, its eyes missing, its tongue lolling out and dripping.

Thilly ran forward, to many gasps, and leaned in to look at the thing.

"Disgusting!" she breathed, and she looked up. "And you are?"

"The name's Aldebaran Copperbox. That's Cap'n Copperbox to you, Your Grace." He bowed before her. "I'm no lord, I'm but a pirate, and I'm not invited. But I'm here to give you a warning. Summin's crawling out of the Stellar Sea and killin' everyone it touches. This was my first mate, and it might be the rest of you soon."

# CHAPTER 7

## *THE FULCRUM*

The shrieks and roars and rush of guards and knights toward Thilly charged the air around her, and sent her skirts and hair billowing casting the white starflowers out of her hair in the maelstrom. She had locked eyes with the brazen Captain Copperbox, and he stared at her continually, even as the guards shackled him.

"Aye, *you* know," he said to her in a thick brogue as guards attempted to drag his great form away. "Better than these dull twits. Every one of them a coward with sandbags for brains, but not you. Steppin' in to see that head. Might be a chance for your kingdom yet, lass."

"You are under arrest by order of the King!" barked the captain of the guards, the crest on his shiny helmet flickering with the jerks of his head. He nearly spat in the pirate's face. "You will disrespect Princess Githilien and this kingdom no longer!"

Copperbox laughed wildly, his eyebrows bouncing, his feral, huge, golden eyes bulging. "Aye, lock me up!" he brayed. "Delay the inevitable! I'll just get out in the mornin'. I'm right with the fae, y'know, and while not every pirate can pick a lock, the fairy folk can, and we're pals and that. Get each other out of scrapes. But maybe not this time—"

"Shut your mouth, heathen!" hissed the captain of the guard.

King Gathlade, meanwhile, looking rather as if he would prefer to be anywhere but there at the moment, walked steadily forth and stood before the melee. He glanced at his daughter, and Thilly quickly looked at him, and then back to Copperbox.

Gathlade said, "Unhand the man, will you, Broderick?" and the captain obeyed. Gathlade then stepped right up to the pirate and stared up at him. Thilly realized that Copperbox might be even taller than Birkswood, and Birkswood was taller than anyone she'd ever seen. With his blazing hair and beard and blocky form, the pirate Copperbox more than lived up to this name. He nodded to the king and looked shrewdly back to Thilly.

"Yours?" he asked Gathlade.

The king frowned and turned to Thilly. He gestured to her, and she stepped up next to him.

Thilly heard a disapproving hiss from the direction of the queen, so she jutted her chin up defiantly.

"My daughter, the Princess Githilien," said Gathlade.

"Thilly," she said, standing straight and proud.

"At least one of you's got gumption," grumbled Copperbox.

"She does that," agreed the king. "Tell us plainly, good sir, what is the meaning of this display? To disrupt my daughter's season and engagement thus?"

Copperbox pulled on his great fiery beard. "I apologize, Princess Thilly," he said gruffly. "I didn't know 'twas your birthday and that. I knew there was a great fuss a-goin' on and all. But if you wed that prince over there, you'll have your hands full, for them monsters are eatin' up the shores of his land, and soon they'll turn to yours, if they've not already."

Thilly bit her lip and peeked at Beaumain, who slowly walked toward them. King Ardenour joined him.

"What is this mockery?" demanded Ardenour. His brow bent in even more of a taciturn set of wrinkles than usual, Thilly noted. "Why do you release this man, Gathlade? And allow him to disrupt the union of our families thus?"

King Gathlade turned slowly to Ardenour, and asked, "Did you know of any attacks on the shore?"

Ardenour shrugged his silver epaulets impressively. "I hear a good many tales from the shore and take few to heart. Besides, my good Queen recently returned from there, and bore no ill experience, as you can see."

Thilly, however, *did* see. Something. The queen looked more menacing now than she ever had before; her teeth sparkled in a faux smile during the talk, but it was an awful smile, full of ghastly intention. Thilly had never felt more certain of anything than that before in her life. The queen more than disliked Thilly; she *hated* her.

*Why would she feel like that toward me?* she wondered, but she had no answer.

Her father cleared his throat. "Ardenour, good friend," and Thilly held back from saying, *But is he really?* Gathlade said, "We had a rider here, also from the shore, and in a shock, before your arrival, saying something about the sea. That makes two people bearing ill news from the Stellar Sea. Yet you've heard and seen nothing?"

King Ardenour shook his head, and Queen Maulielle joined him by his side.

"Really," she said, grandly placing her gloved hand at her porcelain bosom, flicking her dark eyelashes quickly, "are we allowing our children to be sullied in the presence of this…this *person*?" And she glanced with slitted eyes at Copperbox. By the queen's tone, Thilly knew that the woman nearly said something else, far more derogatory.

Thilly felt cold in the presence of Maulielle until Beaumain stepped between them. He looked down at Thilly. His expression was even and unreadable, but she met his aqua eyes, and he looked as if he wanted to say something to her but withheld in the presence of so many.

Copperbox drew himself up. "Throw me under the castle if you must, Your Majesty," he said to Gathlade. "But it won't matter for long. That head you see on the floor? 'Twas a man's once. A man I knew. And now look at it."

Gathlade could not help but do so, and he flinched and focused again on the pirate.

"There's summin' twistin' and warpin' our men," said Copperbox in a low voice, but it was resonant, and it rang through the hushed throngs. "And not just the men. Things crawlin' from the water. You know the tales of the kraken?"

"I have heard them, yes," admitted Gathlade.

"Children's stories," snorted Copperbox. "There are no krakens. We like to embellish things out on the seas. But in all my life I've never seen the like of this. I watched grown men overtaken by shapes, shadows maybe; I couldn't see"—Thilly felt the urge to look at the queen just then, but stood shivering and staring at the pirate instead—"but whatever they were, they made friends of mine into monsters. And we…I…we had to put them down, Your Majesty." The pirate made an S-shaped sign across his chest, which clearly meant something to him, but Thilly did not know the reference. He went on, "They overtook one ship and attempted to overtake another. We lit some pitch barrels and set them to flame. One of the beasts got up close to my party. I knew the man. You see those branches stickin' out of his head? They were sproutin' all over his body and shootin' out at us. So we tarred him and set him alight and cut off his head."

At this, the pirate's deep voice trembled a moment before he recovered. "Only fire seemed to kill the things. And not simple torch fire; we tried that too. It took summin' stronger."

Thilly cleared her throat. "If you please, Captain," she said.

"Aye, lass—Your Highness," said Copperbox, and the corners of his mouth twitched, but he did not fully smile.

Thilly asked, "So you can't kill these creatures with regular fire, only pitch fire?" She tapped her finger on her chin and looked down at the cauterized head while shivers traversed her spine.

"Aye," Copperbox answered. "Might be we could try some other methods, but it seemed that only a penetratin' fire worked. Granted, we didn't have all the time in the world to experiment, lass."

"It would seem to me," Thilly said, "that you could kill the things with flaming tar as soon as they come out of the ocean. That would be the end of them."

Copperbox sighed. "If we knew that would stop them, it might be worth it. But if there are many more, how many men will we need? How many buckets of flamin' tar? Your Majesty, you'd best be fortifyin' your own walls. We'll figure out how to survive at sea or we'll die tryin'. I'm only here to pass on the warnin' before it's too late."

"I understand that," said the king, "but where might these...creatures be coming from?"

Copperbox shrugged. "Unknown. Never seen nor heard anythin' like them. The water's been unusual warm-like for some time, and I've seen some fishes that ought to be more southerly in origin. Could be these things are up from the equator or summin'. I'd like to avoid seein' them again! But we're down one ship. And gods know, there might be fewer when I get back."

Gathlade stood straight and regal, his chin high, and he said clearly to everyone, "I will send a regiment at dawn to the shores to face this threat and decide what is to be done upon their return. For now, let us return to the festivities once more, in honor of our Princess Githilien and of Prince Beaumain of Catellaith."

The musicians took their cue and burst forth music to encourage the onlookers to return to dancing, and many did. Two footmen came to retrieve the mutated head with thick gloves and a large bucket between them. One of the men gagged while placing the head in the bucket. The other one coughed and covered the ghastly thing with a cloth. A third footman dashed in to clean the mess, and his face looked sallow as he mopped up the black-green ooze. This happened within the space of a few minutes, and the collected royals began to step back, but King Gathlade, Thilly, and Beaumain remained by the pirate Copperbox.

"You are welcome to stay," Gathlade told the immense man. Everyone heard the click of Queen Maulielle's tongue, and she withdrew with a muttering King Ardenour into the shadows toward Princess Tantienne.

Thilly stole looks at the back of the queen and felt great sympathy toward the young Tantienne, whose large eyes stared out at the crowd plaintively. Thilly then turned back to the pirate, and her eyes went wide as Sir Vyrent appeared by the man's side.

"Good Sir Vyrent," said Gathlade, and the knight bowed, while lifting his eyes just enough to meet Thilly's gaze as a rose flush crept across her cheeks. "Take this man for food and water, and ready him for tomorrow's journey. You'll be part of the regiment."

Thilly took in a sharp breath. She swallowed and tried to meet Vyrent's gaze, but he had bowed and turned, holding an arm out to guide Captain Copperbox away.

The pirate nodded to the king and said, "I reckon we're tippin' on the edge of summin'. Like a fulcrum. Could go either way. Many mercies to ye, Your Majesty. And to you, Your Highness," he addressed Thilly, "now's the time to take up the sword, and not the skirt."

Beaumain gasped, but Thilly lifted her head triumphantly.

"I quite agree," she said. She nodded back at him, and Sir Vyrent led the man away. She would have liked for the knight to lead her away as well, preferably to someplace more private. With a little quiet sigh, she turned back to her father and the prince.

"We'll be going in the morning, then," Beaumain said to them both. "My parents seem to have made a judgment this evening, if my guess is correct. I'm sorry."

King Gathlade raised his eyebrows. "Then is the engagement off? Tell us clearly, lad."

Beaumain clenched his jaw. "It would seem so. I'll begin my tour of the lands and leave my parents to return home."

"Do you think it wise, given what that man had to say?" the king asked.

Beaumain shook his head and looked to Thilly and her father. "I do not know. My mother insists she found nothing of concern on her trip to the coast. I will certainly remain wary, and I'll send word if I see anything. And Thilly, I wish you well on your trip to your mother. I know you want that more than anything."

Thilly felt a sudden, strange pang that confused her, as if she had made a mistake, for she found him kind and very attractive in his maturity. "I'm sorry, Beaumain. Really. I—I just think perhaps this isn't the right time, or—"

He held up his hand, and his aqua eyes looked at her unblinking. "It is understandable. You need to see your mother. And you need time for decisions; you've just now come of age. I think it is for the best as well."

Gathlade shook his head. "I had hoped for a different outcome," he told the two teens. "Our countries united by marriage: an ending to the old rivalry for good."

"There is no rivalry anymore," Beaumain said, holding his hands out. "Know that. I will ensure my kingdom is your ally, always. But," and he turned to Thilly, "I can offer something, meanwhile."

"Yes?" Thilly asked him, her eyebrows questioning.

"The shortest passage to Aceltia," said Beaumain, glancing between her and Gathlade, "is through Catellaith. And while it is not as flat as going straight through the Vale itself, it is manageable. I would like to guide your host through my land to the border of the north. From there I'll return home. Then we accomplish two things: I see that eastern border of Catellaith, and I see you safely abroad."

Thilly felt warm inside, for Beaumain looked at her kindly.

"Would that be an acceptable compromise?" he asked the king.

King Gathlade nodded. "Indeed, and I am most grateful. I shall sleep better knowing that you're helping Githilien in this way, and it spreads more goodwill between our two countries. But did your parents approve this?"

The prince put his hands behind his back and straightened himself. "I am old enough to make my own decisions about how I'm to tour my country and the Realm," he said stoically. "Regardless of their opinions, I am prepared to do this. Will you be ready in the morning?" he asked Thilly.

She felt an electric thrill bounce through her. "I will," she said.

"Then it's settled," said the prince, and he bowed to her and the king, and retreated to join his family.

Gathlade turned back to Thilly. "Darling, I confess I'm relieved. I knew you did not want to wed; and after all it is still your decision, no matter the pressures of politics and crowns. Your happiness and safety mean more to me than any of that!"

Thilly embraced her father quickly, and said, "Good! Now I'm off for one final dance, and then I suppose I had better gear up for a long journey. But still, I want to know…how did you communicate with Mother?"

The King held her hands in his and said warmly, "Some things must remain private because they are sacred, dearheart. This is one of them. But! You will see your mother soon, and that makes my heart glad. Dance well and rest well, daughter."

Thilly nodded, knowing she could not press her father further. She caught sight of Birkswood and Mrs. Florence overseeing the staff, and she beamed at them on her way back to the dance floor. She accepted one final dance from one of the Republic's administration, and found the man dreary but at least a competent dancer. Then she made her farewells and joined Mrs. Florence to return to her quarters. After Hana helped her out of her finery and left, Thilly stayed awake. She had no intention of sleeping just yet.

# CHAPTER 8

## *PROMISES*

The hour was late, and Thilly lay alert in her bed. She waited for the clock to chime softly and then she sat up, fully clothed in tunic and pants. She donned her riding dress and her boots over the peasant attire and padded quietly to her door. She glanced back at her quarters and saw her mother's picture gleaming a bit in the dim light. Next to it lay the amulet with the two dragons that Beaumain had given her. She shoved down all thoughts of him just then, however. She could hear her own pulse and she took deep, slow breaths to calm herself; she put her ear against the door, and it felt cool against her skin. It was quiet, dark, and the hallways were lit with sconces; she could see their light glowing softly under the door. She opened it and stepped out.

Looking left and right, she dashed over to the staff stairwell and, checking over her shoulder, she entered it and began her descent. Down she tiptoed from her third floor, past the guttering sconces that hung above the landings, until she heard a voice...no, two voices, murmuring at the second floor.

"No, it will be fine," said one deep baritone voice: Birkswood's.

Thilly froze and waited in the darkness of the landing.

"Let's hope so," a gruff woman's voice murmured. That was Mrs. Florence. "You look nervous. Go to bed! His Grace will survive a couple of weeks. You've more than earned the break."

"It will take longer than a couple of weeks," grumbled Birkswood. "And I am reluctant to call such a journey a *break*."

"Aye, but her own staff will meet us," said Mrs. Florence. "Then you can turn 'round and head back."

"I don't like the sound of things," Birkswood muttered. "It seems like a bad time to leave."

"What, the business with that great ginger brute?" scoffed Mrs. Florence. "*If* he's right, the regiment will take care of it. I'm not too worried."

"I am," said Birkswood. "Many of those lads aren't battle-tested."

"Well!" Mrs. Florence replied crisply, "Maybe it's time they were, then."

"I don't like it," growled Birkswood.

"You don't like a great many things," noted Mrs. Florence.

"Yes, and that's why I'm old," retorted Birkswood, and his voice grew fainter.

Thilly knew they were moving away from the landing. She didn't like the sound of their talk, but she did not waste time. She continued down the stairs and finally made it out and found her hidden bundle. She tugged at her dress quickly and replaced it with her cloak. She found a wedge of darkest shadow, away from the torches of the castle wall, and she followed it toward the hill above the keep. She could hear much more activity on this night than she had before: a hushed readying, metal and stone scraping as riders prepared for the morning, with horses snorting and restless hounds yipping. She slipped a bit on pine needles as she wove through the smooth trunks, and then she looked down upon the keep, where instead of revelry the knights were quite restive, packing and joking by turns. A few shouts of laughter met her ears. She squinted at the torchlit scene from her perch and sighed.

*There's no way to see him tonight, then,* she thought.

She felt dreary then, and tired, and realizing she had not quite processed the day's events thoroughly, she blinked and leaned against a tree for a moment.

*I had better get back.*

Then she heard a *shiff-shiff-shiff*, and she turned to see a shape in the woods. She edged slowly deeper into the trees to watch.

"Thilly," a quiet voice said.

She stepped forward, every part of her suddenly awake, and there she found him: Sir Vyrent, dressed in a great coat over his own simple pants and shirt. He approached her and grinned down at her, illuminated just a bit in the soft firelight from the keep below and by gentle moonlight from above.

"Hi," she said in a low voice, grinning sheepishly at him.

"Hello," he said. "I hoped you'd come."

"How'd you guess?" she said, her voice shaking a bit, but maybe that was from the chilly night.

"It was a feeling," Vyrent answered, his hair falling into his eyes. "Since we're all leaving in the morning, I thought…hoped there might be another chance to see you again, before we go our separate ways."

He reached out to touch her hair. He pulled his hand away and showed her one of the starflowers in his palm.

"I guess I didn't remove them all," she whispered.

# THE VALE OF SEVEN DRAGONS

Vyrent placed the flower carefully into the pocket of his coat. She felt a surge of emotion, watching him. He cupped her face in his hands and looked into her eyes.

"I wish we had more time," he said to her.

"Well, we've got now," Thilly said, her heart pounding.

"If this is all we have, then I'm happy," said Vyrent, and he bent his head and kissed her. He drew back then, suddenly shy. She stared at him in surprise. "Forgive me," he said, "I've imposed."

Thilly stepped forward. "The hell you have," she said, and she swept his hair back with her small hands and kissed him in return, and he put his arms around her waist. They sank to their knees onto the soft pine needles.

"You are a princess," he whispered, trembling.

"Not with you," she answered, and she kissed him again. "I'm going away, you're going away…I won't be back for a long time. So give me something to look forward to when I come back."

Vyrent touched her lips with his fingers and kissed her forehead. She repositioned herself where he knelt and wrapped her legs around him. He held her, tasting her lips and the sweat on her neck, and when he did this, she felt her entire body tingle, and she threw her head back and gasped, startling an owl above them. They laughed into each other's ears.

The knight brushed his lips in the same place on her neck, and she shook all over. "What was that?" she wondered.

"The promise of a very good future for us, when I return," said Vyrent with a roguish smile. "You should go. It is late, and if your ladies show up, they'll wonder where you are."

"Must you go west?" she asked him, between kisses.

"I must, so that I can protect *you*," said Vyrent.

"I can protect myself," said Thilly. And she kissed him again.

"I know that you can, Githilien, oh, I very much know that." He sighed, and they rubbed noses. She did not want to leave. She did not want her title. She wanted only him, and all the time in the world. "Go, and when you return, I'll be here waiting."

"Don't be gone too long yourself," Thilly said to him.

"Will you wait for me?" Vyrent asked. He did so shyly, and she held his face in her hands, and they kissed deeply.

She wondered what he meant by waiting, if there were something deeper to his meaning. She decided she didn't care; she would wait for him no matter what he had in mind.

"I shall," said Thilly.

After a few more caresses and a long embrace, she stood up and brushed off her clothes. Vyrent held her hands for a moment, and they turned away from each other. She glanced back at him as he watched her go but could only see his silhouette. She hastened back to the castle, slipping among the shadows toward the staff entrance. She considered her stashed bundle, and with a resigned sigh she removed her cloak and pulled her dress over her pants and shirt. Then she gathered the bundle in her arms. *I won't be here for a while, so there's no sense in leaving this out in the weather.* Her heart hammered as she thought of the sizzling effect Vyrent had made her feel simply by kissing her neck. She wished they had had more time and more privacy, for she wanted to know what it would feel like if he kissed the rest of her...

Something caught her eye among the wisps of fast-moving clouds to the southeast. She blinked.

*It's late, and I am tired, but that looked...like a great bat, or something.*

She searched the sky again. If she looked straight ahead, she could not see anything other than a smudge. Yet out of the corner of her eyes, she could see a black shape, something twisting and warped, and moving at great speed through the sky. And a few moments later, another form followed it, and another. She shuddered.

*Not dragons?* She wondered. But some instinct, ancient and protective, set her on edge. Those were no dragons now, she knew; and she could not explain *how* she knew. What she beheld in the sky was something *other*. Something that did not belong there…or perhaps anywhere.

Shivering, she slinked inside and hurried up the stairs as quietly as she could. She stopped at the second landing and listened; she heard footsteps out in the great hall. Peeking around the edge of the staff entrance, she then recoiled. The queen stood there, illuminated by the reflection of sconces in a large mirror that stood in the court. Beyond her, her shadow resembled dark wings that danced and morphed into whipping shapes like tentacles. Yet the queen stood alone in her finery, sapphires sparkling in her hair, her face paler than candles, and she turned her head slowly toward the staff stairwell.

Thilly jerked out of sight and ran up the stairs, not caring if anyone saw or heard her now. She scurried back to her room, shut the door, and locked it.

"You're tired, you're tired, that's all," she wheezed to herself. "You're just really *fucking tired*." She shed her clothes and crawled into her bed and tried to focus only on the kisses Sir Vyrent had given her…rather than the icy Queen who for some reason was up late in a place that was not her home, the night before her return home.

It was all too much for Thilly, and it was now well past midnight. She would have liked to learn more, but her own fatigue defeated her at last, and she sank into fitful sleep.

# CHAPTER 9

## SET UPON A PATH UNKNOWN

She woke thrashing her sheets, and she realized she was fighting someone: Hana, who looked frantic.

"Milady!" cried the maid, her round face pinched in concern. "It's just me, Hana! It's all right!"

Thilly wailed, and then she sank back onto her sheets, which were soaked with her sweat.

"Gods!" she gasped. "Hana, I'm so sorry. I was—I was dreaming—"

She felt exhausted and depressed, and she clutched her throat. "I was—suffocating, paralyzed, I couldn't move, I tried to shout—" and she let out a choked sob.

"There, there," said Hana, "it was just a nightmare. I've rung for tea, and that'll set you right. Got to be all the pressure you've been under, and now with your leaving and all, and the engagement off."

Thilly groaned. "Gods…what a mess. Were you quite scandalized?"

Hana helped Thilly up and averted her eyes from the pile of tunic and pants and boots by the bedside even as she managed to cover them all with the top sheet from Thilly's bed. Thilly noticed the tactic and smiled ruefully.

"Well," said Hana, flushed to her hairline, "I won't say scandalized is the right word, Your Highness, but maybe…maybe a bit sad, innit?"

Thilly shrugged and shook her head. "There's no need to feel sad, Hana," she told the girl. "It's clear that the Queen—that is, the King and Queen—didn't approve of the match, and so it was called off quite tidily. I'm relieved."

For the most part, she was telling the truth, but there was one little flicker of shame deep down, like a cut that gets aggravated by touch, and so she avoided that tiny wound.

*There's too much else to think about, and I don't need to dwell on something that never existed*, she reasoned with herself.

The ladies' maids arrived with the tea, as well as a parade of boxes and bags.

"What in Antares' name is all this?" cried Thilly.

With a rustle of brown crepe skirts, Mrs. Florence entered, looking quite severe and prim, her iron-grey hair pulled in the tightest low bun Thilly had ever seen. She wore the scarlet cap with Antares on top of her head, and her mouth looked like a perfectly drawn line. Her eyes glowed ferociously.

"We're to pack and load your things, Your Highness," she said briskly. "You're to leave at midday."

"But—surely I don't need anything other than riding clothes!" said Thilly.

"You are a woman of society, and a princess of Vickery," said Mrs. Florence fiercely. "You will travel with the appropriate host and the appropriate attire."

Thilly went hot all over.

"No," she said, facing Mrs. Florence with her own dark auburn hair wild, frizzled, and curling down her back. She clenched her jaw. "I do not need all of this frippery, and I do not want it."

"Your Highness, need I remind you—" began Mrs. Florence.

"Mrs. Florence!" Thilly said loudly, drawing herself up despite her dressing gown.

The maids, including Hana, all paused what they were doing to stare with huge eyes and mouths agape.

"Mrs. Florence," Thilly repeated, lowering her voice, "as Princess and heir to the throne of Vickery, I forbid this excessive display. It is gauche."

Mrs. Florence looked as though all the blood had drained from her face. She opened her mouth and shut it again, and her jaws worked.

Thilly's hazel eyes stared at the woman, and her cheeks burned. She felt powerful, but then felt bad about that as well.

"I'm sorry. But I can't allow this. We are traveling to the far north to visit my mother, among priestess-witches. They'll have ample clothing. So I'll only need traveling clothes. Do we have an understanding?"

Mrs. Florence drew herself up and said, "If this is to be your order, then I must follow it," she said flatly. "But," she dared, and one of the maids gasped, "I will ensure that one or two articles of your esteemed office *do* make the trip, Your Highness. That is part of *my* office, to make sure that you do yours correctly."

Thilly's little tongue of shame in her soul burst into a small bonfire, but she swallowed and blinked rapidly and said, "Very well. I—" but Mrs. Florence turned away from her.

# THE VALE OF SEVEN DRAGONS

"Hana," Mrs. Florence called, and the girl trotted over to her. "Help me choose more practical attire befitting the north. As you're from there, I assume you can contribute in this way?"

"Yes, Mrs. Florence," said Hana, flustered, wringing her hands.

"Then get to it," snapped Mrs. Florence. She avoided Thilly's gaze while the princess had her tea.

Then the older woman said to Hana, "Dress the princess to say farewell to the Royals Catellaith, as they leave within the hour."

"But Beau—Prince Beaumain said he'd be accompanying us," Thilly protested.

Mrs. Florence turned her vivid green eyes to Thilly.

*Gods!* thought Thilly. *If looks could kill, I'd be dragon's cinders right now.*

Mrs. Florence said, in as perfunctory a tone as Thilly had ever heard, which terrified her, "The good Prince Beaumain indeed shall guide your host through his lands, but not before he bids his own parents farewell. As I understand it, they're taking the royal ferry back across the Seven's Channel rather than taking the road. And, Your Highness, I realize you are quite fatigued after your late evening"—Thilly gulped—"but you must be present to wish King Ardenour, Queen Maulielle, and especially Princess Tantienne, who thinks highly of you, a safe and happy journey home. Goodness knows we've enough strange tales and stranger fellows about. A good wish or two from a princess makes sense. Now, get to it!"

Thilly did not have to be told twice.

After enduring the application of dress, the torturous detangling of hair, and dithering over jewelry, Thilly began her descent to meet her father to help see off the king and queen of Catellaith. Thilly felt nauseous with dread, thinking back to the night before, when she beheld the queen standing alone…and the earlier ball, when she had those strange shadows in her eyes. She took her father's arm and noticed his eyes were slightly red, and she bit her lip to hold back a cry of sudden sadness, for then she fully realized she was leaving soon also. He patted her hand and looked straight ahead. She placed her other hand against her neck and touched the amulet Beaumain had given her.

*For goodwill*, she told herself.

He noticed.

The prince bowed to her and Gathlade, as his parents stood off with what attendants they had, before their royal coaches and horses. King Gathlade approached the couple, and Princess Tantienne ran forward to hug her older brother.

"You won't be long, will you?" the young girl asked, her large blue eyes beseeching. She looked so frail to Thilly.

"Of course not!" said Beaumain. "I'm only seeing Thi—Princess Githilien to the border of Aceltia. I'll bring you something back, how's that?" He rumpled her hair just a bit, and she squealed and laughed. She dashed back and stood next to King Ardenour.

Beaumain turned to Thilly. "Shall we, then?"

Thilly grimaced. "If we must."

Beaumain looked sidewise at her. "Don't worry. She's been on about this or that young lady all through the countryside already. She's moved on, and I say, let her."

Thilly shrugged in irritation. "Seems rather sudden," she said.

"No more sudden than your actions," noted Beaumain.

Thilly huffed and walked more quickly to get away from him.

*I'm going into the pit. Save me,* she thought. She walked straight up to King Ardenour and Queen Maulielle and worked up the nerve to look both of them in the eyes.

She curtsied and said, "I wish you the speed of dragons' wings, and the warmth of the sun and the shine of the moon upon your journey."

The king was all comportment, and nodded to her, but said nothing. Thilly looked at the queen, and realized she'd been holding her *breath*, so she exhaled carefully. The queen merely looked at her in cold politeness. Her eyes were simply dark violet, but her face was so expressionless that somehow that disturbed Thilly even more. She looked away from the princess and sniffed.

*Well, that went fabulously,* thought Thilly sourly. Still, she was relieved. *It could have been far worse.*

She began to wonder if she'd imagined everything the day before: the shadows in the queen's eyes, the darkness behind her, the strangeness of her behavior. She shook it off and stepped back, and with her father and Beaumain, waved the royals away. As soon as their coach rounded the bend out of sight, Thilly's shoulders relaxed, and she exhaled…rather too loudly. Her father and Beaumain turned to look at her; Gathlade's wild eyebrows jumped up and down, but he said nothing to her.

He said to the prince, "It is good of you to escort the princess to the border of the north. I know her mother appreciates this also."

Thilly walked forward to stand beside her father.

Beaumain inclined his head to the king and glanced at Thilly.

"It is an honor, Your Majesty."

"I confess I'm relieved," said Gathlade, and for a wild second Thilly thought he might be referring to the exit of the king and queen, "as this strange business at the coast unsettles me."

The prince held his palms up. "Who's to say if it's true? You had a raving man, and a rather boorish pirate."

"Yes," agreed Gathlade, "but I'll feel better when our men bring back reports of absolutely *nothing*. Here they are now, in fact."

Thilly's mouth went very dry then. The regiment marched up from the keep, helmets and armor gleaming, horse tails flicking, and orders echoing among the knights. Thilly searched among them and found a figure whose shape she knew…better than she had the previous morning. She stepped forward to greet the regiment.

"Githilien," said her father in a tone that she knew meant he was concerned, but not about to make a fuss.

She continued, and all the horses lowered before her. She stood in awe and looked among the sea of bent faces. One remained unbent, and he looked up at her: Sir Vyrent.

"May your search be fruitful," she called out, but she looked only at him. "May your worries be unfounded. But if"—she swallowed—"if you should meet an enemy, may their resistance be brief as they break under your swords." A series of shouts roared into the air from the knights, and they clanked their sabers upon their armored thighs. Thilly was blushing but excited. "Come back to us with happy news, with the speed of the wings of Antares and the wind at your backs, and we will sing your praises evermore."

Deafening roars of excitement and pride rang forth as the horses all rose, and Sir Vyrent smiled openly at Thilly. The horses began marching, and she stood and watched, her feet and hands twitching. Just as the knight was about to pass by her, she dashed forward, loosed her hair, and ran up to Sir Vyrent, and tied her ribbon around his arm. She gasped then, for she saw he bore the flower from her hair, embedded into a little charm set in the armor above his heart. Then she turned and ran back to her father, cheeks aflame, and ignored the stare of Prince Beaumain. She watched the horses continue and prayed silently to all the gods of the heavens and the earth, and to the dragons too, wherever they might be, for Sir Vyrent to return safely.

Prince Beaumain turned on his heel and walked toward the entrance to the castle, while Gathlade lingered with Thilly. She could see, then, that Mrs. Florence and Birkswood had been watching the whole time. They exchanged an important look but said nothing.

# THE VALE OF SEVEN DRAGONS

Thilly linked arms with her father as they made their way back to the castle, and a group of footmen and other servants brought forth boxes as more coaches rode up. She sighed. It was nearly time to be off.

"I've got to change for the ride, Father," she said casually. Gathlade looked lost in his thoughts, his brow furrowed, his mustache completely covering his pursed mouth.

"Thilly," he said quietly.

"Yes, Father?" she asked, glad the prince had gone ahead.

"That was a marvelous farewell. Just what those fine young soldiers needed to hear. Well done!" Thilly beamed. "Now, is there something you would like to tell me about a certain knight?" Gathlade asked.

Thilly halted her steps for a brief moment and then kept walking. Her heart raced, and she knew her cheeks betrayed her. She thought quickly.

"I was shown tremendous respect by Sir Vyrent," she said carefully, and she cleared her throat, "at my coming-of-age last night."

The king nodded. "There was talk of your dancing. Ah, do not worry: it was very fine to see you enjoying your birthday. But the queen disapproved, audibly, and wondered. I think she discouraged Beaumain from continuing with any plans for marriage."

Thilly stopped walking and stared up at her father. His eyes were kind, but they were sad.

"Are you…are you very disappointed, Father?" she asked.

"Dearheart," said Gathlade softly, "I am never disappointed in you. But you must know a knight is not a suitable partner for helping you rule."

Thilly attempted a small laugh, but it rang feebly, and she said, "Well, we've just danced, we're not—" and she stopped.

Her father lowered his head and met her eyes.

"Githilien," said he, "it is no small gesture to send a man off to battle, particularly by giving hm the favor of your ribbon. Did he propose to you?"

Thilly panicked. "N-no, of course not," she stammered. "He's really just—we're friends, that's all. We—we respect each other. I wanted to see him off because—because I'm leaving and—"

"That will do, daughter," said the king, and she thought she caught a look of bemusement in his eyes. "He is fortunate to have a friend like you."

Thilly licked her dry lips. "I'm fortunate to have a friend like him."

"Yes," agreed Gathlade. "But you have a great friend in Beaumain, and I hope you will not forget that."

"I won't," said Thilly. "I promise."

She wanted to believe it, for her father's sake.

"Now, off you go, be ready. I'll see you both off," and Gathlade gave her shoulder a squeeze.

She ran up the stairs, cheeks burnished, and wondered what kind of state she must look. And she never cared about the way she looked.

Seeing her father standing alone, without even Birkswood by his side but with other attendants, Thilly felt a raw ache in her throat and eyes. The coach bearing her and the prince rolled away from Castle Taugan, its fiery dragon rampant aloft in a strong breeze as rain began pelting the land and pounding on the coach. She and her father stayed in eye contact as long as they could, and when he was finally out of sight, her lips trembled.

Beaumain, reading through some scrolls he'd brought along, set aside his work and looked up at her.

"He'll be fine, Thilly," he said quietly.

## THE VALE OF SEVEN DRAGONS

"Will he?" she asked him, narrowing her eyes. Then she looked out at the rain, as if the sky itself wept from her parting with her father for the first time.

*Will I?*

# CHAPTER 10

## *UNSETTLED*

Thilly stared out the window at the lead-hued sky, the rain, and the wind, now lashing the coach, the countryside, and the poor horses pulling them along. She felt so fatigued from the events of the past few days that the rocking back and forth of the coach made her fall into a stupor. She watched the waves of bending grasses and the swaying of gold-tinged trees at the edges of farmland in service to Castle Taugan, and she began to blink slowly.

She heard the buckling of a bag and then heard it fall in a thud at her feet. She kept blinking at the rainy scene outside.

Beaumain broke the quiet by saying, "That was quite a rousing battle cry you gave back there."

She sniffed.

"Had you been practicing it?" he pressed her.

"Gods, no. How dreary!" she exclaimed.

"Well, then I'm even more impressed."

Thilly rolled her eyes. "It must not take much."

"Only you, when you're not being difficult." He shifted in his seat. She straightened up and looked at him.

"Are you saying I'm impressive?" she asked him.

"I'm saying you can be."

"But not enough to defy your mother's wishes over."

"That's interesting," noted Beaumain, cocking his head while looking at her. "I thought you favored a knight. You gave him your ribbon, after all."

"It shouldn't matter to you whom I favor, since we aren't engaged," snapped Thilly.

"Too true," agreed the prince. "We dodged a travesty there, I think."

"So will it be Queen Patranne?" She glared at him.

"Why should you care?" Beaumain asked, shrugging.

"I don't."

"Clearly. Your cares are in the hands of a knight marching to the coast to look for pirate tales."

"Do you think yourself bold, then?" Thilly said furiously. "I saw that man's head close up."

"Maybe the pirate was having a laugh," suggested the prince, blinking slowly.

"No," said Thilly, leaning forward, her hands clasped under her chin. "It was horrific. The man must've been in tremendous pain before—before they set him on fire."

"Tough way to go."

"Don't you care?" demanded Thilly.

"I care more about a great many things than you want to give me credit for."

"You don't know what I want."

"You want that knight."

"How fucking *dare* you?" she hissed.

"I dare, Princess Githilien, because I came here with a host from my country to join our lands together in marriage *to you*," said the prince, jaw tight, aqua eyes serious.

"You never actually proposed, remember," she muttered, smoothing out her riding coat.

"Maybe sharing this coach was not the best idea," said Beaumain suddenly, sitting ramrod straight.

"Definitely not," Thilly retorted.

"We'll arrange to switch out at the next stop," said Beaumain in his stiff, official tone.

"Good."

"Excellent."

And Thilly turned away from him to stare at the outdoors again, while Beaumain yanked up the case that had fallen and loudly rustled through his papers. She did not want to deal with him. She'd had enough. She leaned her head against the wall of the coach and felt the rocking lull her further and further, and then she dozed off.

She dreamed…first of the stolen kisses with Sir Vyrent, which made her shift pleasantly in her seat, but then she found herself in the great hall of Castle Taugan, in the darkness. And she was not alone. She gazed into the immense mirror in the hall, with its fine copper and gold frame of flames and dragons, and it reflected her wild hair, loose and frazzled, and her hazel eyes, flecked with both amber and green. The light that shone from the mirror onto her came from that frame, and it pulsed as if made from living fire. Behind her there stretched darkness, the shadows of the great hall. She breathed into the mirror and left a foggy spot to fade away. But as she looked at herself, she saw something behind her…something stretching from the ceiling, dark, bottomless, coiling and writhing, dripping, slinking down, and then standing, huge, shapeless, and breathing on her with a sickly air. She wheeled around and found Queen Maulielle standing there, wraith-pale, violet eyes lustrous, but her hair was down her back, and it spilled upon the floor, and then became black, whipping tentacles that sprang out at Thilly. And then the Queen's jaw unhinged, crackling, breaking its own bones, and something black and spiked shot from her mouth, right at Thilly's face. Thilly screamed.

Someone shook her, and she screamed again, and she thrashed with arms and legs. Then she opened her eyes and found Beaumain beside her, restraining her.

"It's all right!" he hissed. "You're fine! It was a dream!"

Thilly fought him for a moment, eyes wide in terror, and then she went limp and let tears spill from her eyes. But she did not sob. She pulled her arms from his grip, which loosened, and she put her face in her hands.

The coach had halted, and a Catellaith footman in a navy and silver hat stood outside in a rain slicker.

"Is everything all right?" he asked, and the prince opened the little window.

"Night terrors," said Beaumain. "Let's stop here for a few moments and refresh ourselves, yes?"

The footman nodded, and he then strode behind the coach and waved for the caravan to halt. He and a second footman extended rain shields from the top of the coach on either side. Then the first footman walked back to the coach door by the prince and opened it, and pulled down a platform in the door to make a makeshift table. He and his fellow footman set to work with small stoves filled with shalefire stones for a steady flame in the damp weather, and set kettles upon them. They brought forth a hamper full of snacks and set everything where the prince could reach it.

But Beaumain's eyes were only on Thilly, who refused to look at him.

"They're making tea," he said softly. "That will help. Are you cold?" He unspooled a thick blanket and held it out to her.

Then she drew her hands away from her face. She looked at him, studying him, looking for any sign of his mother. She shuddered. Beaumain bore some of Maulielle's features, but favored his father for the most part, and she was glad. His steady gaze from his blue-green eyes reassured her. She slowly lowered her tense shoulders. He placed the blanket on her lap.

"I'm fine," she said simply.

Beaumain shook his head. "You were terrified. Would you like to talk about it?"

Thilly shook her head and clenched her teeth. "It's none of your concern," she said.

"You're under my care," he replied, and he took a cup of tea from the footman and handed it to her. "So yes, it is my concern."

"Hopefully not for much longer," she retorted.

Beaumain sighed. "All right. I won't push. But you were...Thilly, you *fought* in your sleep. Was someone...attacking you?"

Thilly shivered and finally accepted the blanket, pressing it closer around herself, and then the tea.

"I don't want to talk about it," she muttered, cradling the hot metal cup in her hands gingerly, letting the peat-like scent and steam of the tea rise into her nose. Then, "Why does she hate me?"

Beaumain had been blowing on his mug of tea when she asked, and he raised his eyebrows.

"Who?"

"Your mother," answered Thilly, watching him, her brow stern; she looked more like her father just then.

Beaumain tilted his head at her.

"Hate you? Mother? She doesn't hate you, Thilly," said he, shaking his head. "What a ridiculous thing to say. No one could hate you!"

"She does," insisted Thilly. She was beginning to warm under the blanket, and from drinking the tea. Beaumain handed her a small hand pie, golden and flaky, with dark purple-blue berry juice staining its edges. "I felt it, I saw it. She despises me."

"Nonsense," scoffed Beaumain. "Disapproves, sure. She disapproves of everyone, though. That's her societal role. But hate you? Never! Especially since we were going to be betrothed."

He glanced at Thilly, noticed the stern little crease between her eyes, and said, "Look, it was awkward, of course. But better to have that rather than a greater tension between our lands, don't you think?"

"I worry," Thilly murmured. "What will happen after they're back home? Now that we aren't uniting our countries. What will that do to relations? Have I doomed Vickery?"

Beaumain laughed at that. "Why in the heavens and the hells combined would that doom Vickery?"

Thilly squirmed. "I don't know. I just feel like…like something is very wrong."

"What sort of thing?" Beaumain asked.

"You're still sitting next to me, for one thing," snapped Thilly, pulling her blanket up over herself. She felt a strange electricity in the air, this close to Beaumain, in such tight quarters. It befuddled her, and she already felt off enough from the nightmare.

Arching one eyebrow, Beaumain shrugged and moved across from her again to the opposite seat. "I was only trying to put you at ease."

"I'm calm now," Thilly said angrily.

"No, you're not," said Beaumain. "I want to know more. Why do you feel like something is wrong?"

Thilly stared at him. "Don't *you* feel it?"

He blinked at her. "I'm not sure what I'm supposed to be feeling," he answered.

Thilly shook her thick curls. "Just tell me plainly, Beaumain. Has anything about your mother felt different lately?"

She watched him blink a few times, sip his tea, and shift in his seat. He still looked rather formal, but he had unbuttoned his collar, and she could just barely see dark red hair on his chest. That distracted her momentarily.

"I—I'm not sure how to answer that," Beaumain admitted. "We were preparing to come and visit you and your father. Mother had been at the coast. She seemed…preoccupied."

"After the coast trip or before?" pressed Thilly. She felt she was on the verge of something. It was so very close.

"I don't know," said Beaumain with a sigh. "I can't keep up with her social outings. I knew some of her ladies' maids had taken ill, but I didn't know more than that. Or what kind of illness they had. I never fussed with that group, to be honest with you. They seemed far too skittish around the queen, and far too savage away from her."

Thilly grimaced. She could not imagine being in service to that queen under the best of circumstances. She had no interest whatsoever in the frippery and societal rules that Catellaith's sapphire queen held so dear. Yet she had heard the queen was intelligent. Thilly couldn't understand such a person, or how one could be both smart and judgmental.

She took a bite of her hand pie and caught some of the berry syrup within it before it spilled onto the blanket covering her lap. Realizing she was hungrier than she thought, she relished the little tart and her tea, and began to feel cozy and comfortable…and safe, she had to admit, within that small space with the prince. She did not want to fall back asleep again, though. Not for a long while. After the footmen packed the food away and the caravan started up again, the rain stopped, and the fields rolled by covered in steam while the treetops captured wisps of mist. It was getting on late in the day, and finally Beaumain opened his window and stuck his head out, and he grinned.

"We're crossing the border soon," he said. "Another rise, and we'll be there. Say goodbye to Vickery, Thilly."

Thilly turned in her seat and looked back, and the sky was lowering and dark, laden with moisture, but interspersed with small pockets of brightness from the afternoon sun. She considered the gentler lands of Vickery one last time and sent love to her father in the wind. She turned back to face Beaumain, and he sat with a tiny smile at the corner of his lips.

"You're glad to be back," she observed.

"I am!" he agreed. "No offense. But it's wilder here. There's a rawness to Catellaith. Not like the far north, mind you. You'll see *that* contrast soon enough."

"I never came this way into Catellaith before," said Thilly, thinking back over the few visits to the Royals Catellaith in her life. Still, she dwelt upon the queen, and the coldness and strangeness in her, and especially the loathing. That had definitely never been present when Thilly was younger. Why would it be there now? She puzzled over it.

The coach halted, and Beaumain nodded. "We're at the border crossing. We'll soon be through."

Thilly heard the horses snorting and pawing. Their fastenings jangled, and they twitched. A tap on her window made her jump.

It was one of the footmen. She unhinged the window, and the man said, "The patrol isn't here."

Beaumain frowned. "What?"

He opened the door and stepped onto the muddy, gravelly road, and then turned to look back south toward Vickery.

He glanced at Thilly. "No one is here at all, for either side," he said.

Thilly felt tiny cold pinpricks climb up and down her spine. She leaned out of the coach, looked back at the caravan, and saw Birkswood advancing toward them. He caught her eye and gave her a light nod.

To Beaumain, Birkswood said, "I take it this is something new, Your Highness?"

Beaumain chewed on his lower lip. "I...don't know."

"You didn't come this way before, on your way to Castle Taugan?" Birkswood asked him.

"No, we came along the southern path heading east, then curved around the river mouth," muttered Beaumain.

"I'm going to take a look at the patrol station," Birkswood said, and he gestured to the footmen. "Get back inside, Your Highness." Thilly noticed that he laid his hand on something at his waist, and she sat up straight.

Looking reluctant, Beaumain sat in the coach again.

"What is it?" she whispered to Beaumain. He blinked a few times and watched the men proceed to the station building, which was small and sheltered; it used to be part of an ancient fort, and now only held the one toll booth and sentry tower. The remainder of the fort had crumbled into the earth years before, leaving only the foundation stonework hiding beneath the long grasses. The wind set those grasses rippling just now, and thunder boomed in the distance.

Thilly jumped over to Beaumain's side of the coach and craned her neck to watch with him. She was close enough to smell him: tea on his lips, some hidden spicy-woodsy scent elsewhere, and she took a furtive but deep breath of that smell. She rather liked that smell, and it stirred something warm in her that took her by surprise.

Then the coach began to shake. At first it was so subtle, she thought it was the horses. But they whinnied and stomped, and then the coach shook again, harder. Everything shook.

Beaumain seized Thilly. "Earthquake!" he hissed.

"Are you holding onto me so you don't fall out of the coach?" Thilly shouted at him, and his hands shot away from her waist and his face turned red.

He looked as though he might say something, but the horses bucked, and the two of them were jolted in their seats. The footsteps of running men met their ears.

The other footman climbed up to manage the horses alongside his mate, and the shaking began again.

Birkswood appeared by the window.

"Well?" asked the prince.

Birkswood gave Thilly an inscrutable look and said to Beaumain, "There is no one there at all. No sign anyone's been there in a few days, in fact. Molding bread, half-eaten. Tracks washed away. I'd say we're the only people who have been on this road since then as well. Very strange."

"And now earthquakes," said Thilly, feeling nauseous. Something about all this unnerved her. But she threw off her blanket and opened the door to get out.

"Githilien!" said Beaumain with an edge to his voice. "You'll be safer in here."

"In the care of your arms, no doubt?" she shot back over her shoulder, and swung herself out onto the muddy road to stand next to Birkswood. She felt the cool wind in her face, with much colder gusts, and she shivered. But the chill was not what bothered her the most. She watched the sky and looked at the open road and the vastness of the land. She could see no animals of any kind.

*There should at least be birds. Did the earthquake scare them all?*

"I don't like it," Birkswood said with a scowl. "We'd better get to proper shelter before nightfall." He looked at the prince. "What towns are close by?"

Beaumain considered. "Well, there's Valewhistle a bit northeast, on the edge of the Vale, and then there's a little village on a hill—Nistraan's Wold. Just to the west, probably five miles or so."

"Let's head there," said Birkswood, "if you don't mind my suggestion. We should be off this open road, and soon. When was the last time Catellaith had an earthquake that you can remember?"

Beaumain shook his head. "Never," he said. "I knew it was possible, but it's not geologically active like the northeast; in fact, it's been dormant for centuries, at least."

Thilly could see in Birkswood's face that he didn't like that little fact either.

"To Nistraan's Wold, then," he said to the prince.

Beaumain nodded, and Birkswood alerted the footmen.

"Your Highness," Birkswood said to Thilly, his eyes keen, "if you would prefer other accommodation, we can arrange it." The twitch of his goatee made her squint. She looked back at Beaumain, who was watching them, and he turned away.

She put her hands on her hips. "Well, it's only another five miles to the town. I don't want to waste time getting there, so I'll stay put for now. After that, however...we shall see." Birkswood nodded, and his goatee twisted just a bit again.

*Is he smiling?* Thilly wondered, slightly irritated.

Birkswood began his walk back to his own coach, and Thilly climbed back in opposite the prince.

"There are no birds, did you notice?" she said to him.

Beaumain gazed out the window. "'Tis a strange air," he mused.

"In a strange land," Thilly remarked, tucking her blanket back around her, but unable to shake the chill from her mood.

# THE VALE OF SEVEN DRAGONS

The horses were nervous, and so needed no urging to go, and the coach bounced and shimmied over the roads into Catellaith and then veered northwest at a turnpike. Thilly gripped her seat and felt on edge, and Beaumain's jaw muscles worked.

He turned to her, and she realized, with a blush, that she had been staring at him.

"I'll get you across my lands, I promise," he told her. "This is just a detour for your safety."

"Is it?" she asked. He stared back at her, and then they both fell to brooding. She bit her lip, and he rubbed his head.

*This was not how things were supposed to go*, thought Thilly, and she could tell by his expression that Beaumain felt the same.

# CHAPTER 11

## *THE DRAGON'S HEAD*

The road to the town at first seemed as empty and quiet as had the main road north, but by and by, Thilly could see signs of activity, to her relief. There were farms with long hedgerows, and birds darting above and into them as pale blades of sunlight pierced the clouds. The telltale small puffs of white on the hills revealed sheep farms, and Thilly at one point heard a cow moo. For the time being, the earthquakes had stopped. She rubbed her neck, having tensed up over everything. She still could see no people about, but the sights of animals comforted her. She even heard the distant chatter of a flock of wood parrots, and that cheered her more than anything.

Down a narrow slot of road, they wound around ponds and then climbed up again to a plateau, which looked out upon the hills and valleys, and ultimately the great Vale itself beyond those. There stood the town of Nistraan's Wold, and it looked old and weathered, but pleasant and lived-in as well. The flag of Catellaith, with the slender silver and blue dragon Nistraan, spread high and flat in the stiff breeze. Here and there, little rows of blue and silver bunting dotted cottage window boxes and gates. At last, Thilly saw people; a few in the town's circle, but more hanging about what was clearly a pub, with a swinging sign and a carved sigil of Nistraan. Its name was etched in two languages: Vickering, the common tongue dominant through much of the Vale, and the older, more melodic language Catelle, of the country Catellaith. The name itself was The Dragon's Head.

At the sight of the caravan, more people emerged from houses to watch, and soon the news spread, so that a good number of villagers and children spilled forth from homes to look at the Royal Contingent. The coaches came to a halt, and Birkswood and Mrs. Florence emerged and approached the royal coach bearing Prince Beaumain and Princess Githilien.

Thilly, for her part, was eager to get out of the coach and into the open air. Mrs. Florence helped her out, while Birkswood joined the prince and the head footmen on the other side of the coach. Thilly then stood alongside Beaumain, and everyone within view bowed to them both. They looked at each other. Beaumain smirked.

The mayor of Nistraan's Wold emerged, a short man flushed and resplendent in a dark blue suit, wearing a cravat with a pattern of blue and silver dragons, and he bowed low to the two young royals. Seeing the sigil of Antares on both Thilly's gown and her staff's outfits, the man practically bounced in excitement, glancing back and forth between her and Beaumain.

Birkswood said in a deep, carrying voice, "We present Prince Beaumain of Catellaith and Princess Githilien of Vickery. We would like to take shelter for the night before returning on our northern route."

"Greetings, Your Royal Highness Beaumain, and welcome, Your Royal Highness Githilien!" said the mayor, nearly sputtering with enthusiasm. "I am Jackdaw Quelle, Mayor of Nistraan's Wold and the Vinelands. I welcome this unexpected delight."

*Do you, now?* Thilly wondered. He swabbed the sweat from his brow with his handkerchief, and his skin was so flushed that she thought he resembled a stewed turnip. Then she felt bad about the comparison…but unfortunately, she couldn't shake it from her thoughts.

"Thank you, Mayor Quelle," Thilly spoke up, pushing the barbed vision down and curtsying.

The man bowed low, sweeping his left hand out at a right angle as he did so, and Thilly feared he might tip over. Then she caught the unmistakable whiff of sloe gin and stifled a smile. She caught Beaumain's eye, and his lips pressed together. He had to look away from her, and so she knew that he was about to laugh as well.

Then it was a swarm of activity: Birkswood and Mrs. Florence and the footmen and ladies in waiting swept into the pub and mingled with the staff there, who looked either intrigued or put out by the circumstance, by turns. Hana approached Thilly and made a little curtsy and held up a case.

"For Your Highness, to freshen up," said Hana, and her face turned quite red near the roaring fireplace of the pub. She guided Thilly to the privy so the princess could clean herself up a bit and tidy her humidity-wrecked hair.

It was a weeknight, but the pub clearly centered the Wold and the surrounding communities, and it was bustling. ("Heaving," muttered Birkswood to Mrs. Florence, who nodded and pursed her lips.) So Thilly felt a pang of guilt that they'd intruded upon the town this night. But there was much chatter rising and falling as long tables were cleared and two of the best of the quite aged oaken chairs were

## THE VALE OF SEVEN DRAGONS

set at its head. Birkswood snipped and bossed the Catellaith staff and the pub staff, until nearly all the workers looked on edge and flustered.

The mayor, however, swept forward grandly with two young assistants trotting behind who could not have been more than twelve, each with bobbed, curly russet hair and wearing the typical handwoven garb of the Catellaith countryfolks. Thilly suspected they were twins. Each held rather elaborate glass pitchers full of a deep burgundy liquid that looked wholly out of place in a pub, for they bore silver carvings on them of Nistraan, with bright turquoise eyes. Thilly wondered if these might be the most valuable items in the entire region. In each of Quelle's hands, he held goblets that matched, with the base of each being the dragon's tail, its head curving up toward the lip, its wings wrapped around each glass.

The mayor gestured to the two chairs at the head of the great, weathered old table, and so Thilly and Beaumain sat next to each other. She glanced at him, and he smirked for the fraction of a second. The mayor set the two glasses upon the table, and the crowds hushed to murmurs. He took one of the pitchers from his child helpers, and the other child set the remaining pitcher on the table. They then scurried off back to the kitchens, where a woman who surely was their mother beckoned them inside. She, however, held back to watch. Mayor Quelle poured the deep garnet, flowery-fruity-fragrant liquid into each goblet. Then he bowed again, extravagantly, and set the first goblet before Thilly, and the second before Beaumain.

At that moment, the pub door creaked open, and a tall man in a weathered dark coat and hood entered. Heads turned to see him, and then turned back. Thilly watched him for a moment. She could only see his chin, and it was covered in a scrappy light brown beard. He retreated off to a corner, and a barmaid met him with a stein.

*A regular,* Thilly surmised.

She looked up at the mayor then, and he said, "To the health of our Crown Prince Beaumain and his future bride, the Princess Githilien of Vickery!"

Thilly tensed all over and looked at Beaumain, pained.

"Fuck's sake," she whispered so that only he could hear.

"I'm sorry," he hissed back, keeping his lips stiff as he did so, so that no one could see him speak.

The mayor continued, "May Nistraan's wings carry them far, and may their vines be laden, and their children be many."

Thilly shut her eyes at that final statement.

A collective roar rose from the onlookers, and mugs, glasses, and steins rose and fell, with the quaffing of much cider and beer and liquor. Thilly, meanwhile, took her goblet and sniffed it again. It smelled like gossamer summer, as if the last burst of heat and light and fruit had been bottled at the start of autumn, but it also momentarily heightened her senses and made her feel excited. This was before she took her first sip.

Beaumain held his glass to hers, and they clinked together, and then Thilly took a drink.

The contents burned through her mouth, down her throat, and into her stomach. She felt a powerful, searing sensation in her sinuses, as one might from eating horseradish. She stifled a cough. She saw Beaumain shiver after his sip.

"This is a most fortified port!" he exclaimed diplomatically, and Mayor Quelle laughed, as did most of the pub. Sly winks and snickers rippled around, and Thilly raised her eyebrows.

"What are we drinking?" she said under her breath.

"Ah, Your Highness," the mayor said, mopping humored tears from his cheeks, and rubbing his bald head, "that is no port! That is vinapsys, the pride of the Vineland, and the rarest drink in the Realm.

# THE VALE OF SEVEN DRAGONS

The stories of old sing that the seven dragons themselves sought it out to slake their thirst, and also the priestesses of the Veiled Isles!"

Thilly's eyes went wide. "And why would they have done so?" she asked.

The mayor lifted his chin and grinned like an impish child.

"Wait a few more minutes, Your Highness. You will see. And you will, indeed, *see*."

A few laughs rippled among the crowd, but by now a bard had set up in a corner, well stocked with Vineland cider, and he sang while a banjo began twanging out old tunes in the ancient tongue, intermixed with the modern, and with the laughter of their rapt audience. It did not take long for Thilly to understand what Mayor Quelle had meant. Just as her vision blurred, the earth shook again…not as violently as it had upon the road, but enough to excite everyone there, and to align her eyes with someone across the room, his hood now back, and his bearded, weathered face quite like someone's she had kissed.

"Vyrent?" she mouthed, but the man shook his head.

And then Thilly's reality imploded.

Every sound muffled to near silence, yet she could hear singing.

*Such beautiful singing. Where have I heard this singing?*

She looked down and screamed, for she was in the air, and the air was the color of flame, and she rose and fell upon giant, fiery-hued scales. She whipped her head from side to side and beheld great wings stretching beneath her, beating slowly and powerfully up and down, and then she jerked forward to look straight ahead. An immense reptilian head at the end of the scarlet-scaled neck turned enough for her to see its golden eyes, and then she felt beneath her the creature's body expand…and with a great rush, a current of spectacular flame erupted from the beast.

*ANTARES!*

"Thilly!" a voice called, and she turned to her left, and there she beheld Beaumain…but he looked weathered, his outfit coarse and torn, and he rode a sleek silver and blue creature with vibrant blue-white wings and crystal blue eyes.

*NISTRAAN!*

Thilly looked behind her and could see the shapes of several winged creatures in a strange black sky. Then she turned and looked ahead, and another spout of flame burst from the mouth of the dragon she rode, toward something huge, something incomprehensibly immense and black, twisting, and foul. It opened a gaping maw to swallow them all…

And then she was falling, falling…down through fire and mist. She was caught by someone or something. And she was cradled, with long silver and gold hair draping over her head, and kind hazel eyes staring into hers. A woman, singing in an inhuman, ethereal voice, surrounded by fog, but holding Thilly in strong arms.

"Daughter," she whispered.

Thilly jerked her head up. She was in the pub again, and she turned quickly to Beaumain, who met her gaze with huge eyes.

"Did you see?" she whispered.

"I saw," he answered.

Mrs. Florence and Hana were at her side, eyes full of concern.

"Are you quite all right, Your Highness?" asked Mrs. Florence in a hard voice. Birkswood, Thilly noticed, had approached Beaumain.

Thilly looked down at her glass, and it seemed that within its garnet depths a coil of fire spiraled deep, deep, down into impossibility, into something smaller than small, and yet what she had seen before had been so enormous. She felt something nudge her side, and she found Beaumain's right hand reaching out to her, out of sight of everyone else, and she reached back and squeezed his with her left hand. They then released each other as the drink was taken away, and in its place, water and sloe gin and wine were laid, as were plates of pears, late mulberries, and cheese and cured meats, with baskets of bread and butter.

Another small aftershock rumbled through the pub, and someone shouted, "Lay off the beans, Raddam!" to guffaws from onlookers.

Thilly blinked and looked for the stranger again, and he was gone. She shook her head. Mayor Quelle walked up next to her, and she looked up at him with her vision slowly shifting back into focus. He smiled down at her.

"Your Highness," he said, and she could swear for a moment that little iridescent sparkles surrounded the man in a sort of aura, and that he bore deep blue and silver robes rather than a suit, "your necklace suits you well. The two of you give the Realm much hope."

Thilly looked down, and the amulet of two dragons that Beaumain had given her swayed above her breast.

*I thought I had removed this.*

She closed her eyes and tried to listen for the singing: the singing of her mother's voice. It was gone, she knew, and the sights she had beheld began to fade like dreams upon waking. She ached in sadness and longing, and tears formed in her eyes.

"You did indeed see," said the mayor in a warm voice. He was simply the mayor again, in his suit, patting the sweat from his brow and smiling jovially. He sat to her right and began to fill his own plate, while servants came to fill Thilly's.

"I did, indeed, see," repeated Thilly. And she felt it too.

Everything had changed quite suddenly, down to her blood, her bones, the very fibers of her being, and within the depths of her soul.

# CHAPTER 12

## *IDLE TALK*

After enduring the evening entertainment, Thilly reached the point at which she could not concentrate on anything anymore. She found it especially difficult to think of the present when she wanted to think of the trance she'd been in earlier. Was it the future? A shared hallucination? Of course, she suspected the latter, given Beaumain's reaction to the vinapsys and their moment of recognition.

"To your health!" one hale-looking, middle-aged man with copper skin and long, straight black hair suddenly called out, and a chorus of "Hear, hear!" erupted from the townspeople. They all raised their mugs high and drank deeply, laughed, and joined in the bard's songs.

Hana watched Thilly closely, and when the princess began to blink and smile and nod at a perfunctory rate, the maid edged toward her. But Mrs. Florence stopped her.

Thilly heard the older woman say, "Don't be bothering Her Grace at this dinner, Hana. We've got to get her set up for the evening."

Thilly wanted to cry out, "Wait for me!" but instead sat stiffly next to the prince and heard yet another set of yodeling songs from the bard. She craned her neck to look for the strange, hooded man from earlier, but he had apparently left for good. That bothered her, for something about him was very like Sir Vyrent. Then again, she had heard talk among her ladies-in-waiting at the castle, without her knowing, and one of them had said once, "You look for the person you love in everyone."

*Do I love Vyrent?* She closed her eyes for a second, remembering that kiss on her neck. The tingling all through her body. How could that have been only the night before?

Thilly shook her curls and made eye contact with Hana and tried her best to implore the girl with her eyes to rescue her, but ultimately Hana was too stressed to pick up on the silent call for aid. Mrs. Florence pulled her aside to prepare the simple upstairs guest rooms for the two royals, and Hana's face remained flushed when she returned later to the dining hall of the pub. Thilly could see the girl was under Mrs. Florence's iron grip and looking stressed out, so she decided to speak up.

"Hana, dear," she called out, and the girl looked flustered but eager at the same time, her hair under her fiery cap curling madly in the heat of the pub. Thilly was also sweating, for the crowd had not died down yet. Another few light earthquakes set off more rounds of laughter and pulls of cider and ale.

*Is it so humorous to be shaken?* She wondered, for even though the aftershocks were mild, she despised them. They set her on edge.

Hana quickly wove through the morass of increasingly tipsy villagers and country folk who had streamed in to see the princess and prince, and by the time she'd reached Thilly, she looked tortured.

"Yes, milady, I mean, Your Highness?" she asked, gripping her hands together in front of her.

*Hmm...she needs a break*, thought Thilly. She abruptly stood, and the entire pub stilled.

"Carry on!" she said with a small laugh. "I just want to feel the night air on my face."

She turned to Hana and whispered, "Come with me outside, please." Then she glanced back at the prince, who watched her, and then she sighed with annoyance when he stood as well. The room stilled again.

"Thank you for your hospitality," he told the mayor and the crowd before him. "We must leave early in the morning, for I am to escort Her Royal Highness of Vickery to our northern border. I shall continue my tour of the lands afterward and treasure our time here."

A piercing whistle and shouts of good cheer and "Long live the prince!" thundered through the pub, and some of the revelers began to leave. Beaumain looked as though he wanted to join Thilly, and she paused for a moment before heading out the back door away from the crowd and watched him. He looked as regal as his office commanded, but he also looked reluctant, somehow, to leave the merry throng.

"You're not leaving the princess alone in Aceltia, are you?" Mayor Quelle asked, swiveling his head from the prince to Thilly. Beaumain gave him a questioning look.

"That was our agreement," he said simply.

The mayor's expression puzzled Thilly. Was it worry, or disappointment?

# THE VALE OF SEVEN DRAGONS

"Ah, that is too bad," said Quelle, twitching. "Perhaps reconsider?"

"Our Royal Highness must proceed on to see her mother in the Veiled Isles," Beaumain told him, and Thilly felt a surge of gratitude for the prince's diplomacy.

He tried catching Thilly's eye again, but she shrugged and shook her head and left.

The night air was dank and the dark sky partly cloudy, much as it had been the night before at Castle Taugan. The back door of the pub had led Thilly and Hana to a partially covered deck overlooking a kitchen garden, and the scent of herbs wavered up, pungent and astringent, tickling Thilly's nose. Thilly glanced up at the broken clouds above and the waning moon's light edging those clouds, and she leaned against the rail of a wooden staircase that led to the garden.

"I had to get out of there," she said to Hana. She rubbed her eyes and pushed her hair away from her face, letting the night air cool her.

Hana, for her part, let her shoulders sag, and her face relaxed. "Your quarters are ready, milady," she said, and she caught herself almost yawning, and slapped her hand over her mouth.

*Mrs. Florence is working this girl half to death!* though Thilly. Then she heard a woman's voice, and Hana snapped to attention. Thilly rolled her eyes. There would be no break for Hana, as it was Mrs. Florence's voice they heard. But the woman did not appear, so Thilly wondered where she was. She stepped quietly down the stairs, whereas Hana remained stiff and watchful on the deck. Thilly listened.

"Well, we'd heard of some odd things too, but nothing like that pirate…Copperbox? Extravagant creature, to be sure," Mrs. Florence was saying.

Another woman answered in a thick, western accent, "Eh, but we seent it, or somethin' like it."

"You never!" hissed Mrs. Florence.

"Now, Sigrid," said the woman, "maybe not a decapitated head, but somethin' flyin' in the sky. Fast...like big bats they were!"

Mrs. Florence actually *snorted*. "Ever think they *were* bats, Nat?"

"Bats the size of dragons, eh?" said the woman, Nat. "I know what I saw. T'weren't no *bats*. Fast movin'. What if they *was* the dragons?"

"I should think you'd have seen fire and that, don't you?" scoffed Mrs. Florence.

"Too true. And likely t'weren't bats. I like bats, you know."

"Well, I learn something every day. Time to get back in, we're leaving in the morning."

"But they really aren't gettin' married, then?"

Thilly felt angry at herself for blushing, even though no one could see in the dark that she did.

Mrs. Florence let out a soft sigh. "I never met two more bull-headed people in all my life."

"I have," laughed Nat, "and you're one of 'em!"

Soft laughter rang out, and Hana twitched where she stood. Thilly looked back at her and felt wracked with sympathy.

"I've kept you up as well," she said ruefully. "Let's go in. You go ahead, I want to look at the moon once more."

Hana obliged, darting back in, and Thilly scanned the sky. She shuddered. Whatever she had seen the night before, down above Vickery, was not isolated; she knew that now. She heard someone clear their throat, then, down and to the left, as if from the garden. She froze.

She called, "Who's there?" but she could see no one. Footsteps to her right on light gravel met her ears, and Mrs. Florence emerged, and then raised her hands, seeing Thilly. Thilly breathed a sigh of relief at the sight of her.

# THE VALE OF SEVEN DRAGONS

"Heavens above!" exclaimed the woman. "Your Highness, you mustn't be out here alone at night! Let's get you inside. Where's that Hana? I'll have a word—"

"No, please don't," begged Thilly. "I've sent her in. She's exhausted. Can we let her go to bed?"

Mrs. Florence herded her inside, but Thilly still felt perturbed by the sound of whoever was outside. She shivered, and welcomed the warmth and light of the pub as tables were being cleared and the final guests were politely—or more vehemently—urged out for the night.

"Let us send a few folks with you," the mayor was urging Beaumain. The look on his face puzzled Thilly, as it was one of an almost pained concern. Was there something about Aceltia that frightened him? "It would be our honor."

*For that matter, should I be frightened?*

Beaumain nodded. "I will consider it. Either way, we ride in the morning."

"We'll make sure you all have good tea and a proper breakfast," assured Mayor Quelle, bowing deeply. "Now, mind, the effects of the vinapsys might give you odd dreams, and occasional sight over the coming days: these are considered great blessings and good omens."

"Is that what they are?" Thilly asked dryly. "You might give a person fair warning next time."

The mayor blushed. "It does affect individuals quite differently. Some more than others," and he glanced from Thilly to Beaumain. His brow furrowed, but then he said, "Not to worry. But once you do reach your mother, you might want to tell her what you saw."

Thilly blinked in surprise. "Do you know her?"

"Princess Githilien, the Lady Woadlynn is well known to all the north," said the mayor, looking surprised himself.

"Oh," said Thilly, not sure what else to say.

"That will do, Mayor Quelle," Mrs. Florence said sharply. "It is time we let our ladyship and lordship rest after their long journey today."

"Of course, of course," said the mayor, and he bowed to both Thilly and Beaumain, and then retrieved a fancy peacock-blue hat edged in bright green from a coatrack and bade them goodnight as he left the pub.

Birkswood appeared by Beaumain's side then, along with one of the Catellaith footmen.

"We've prepared your room, Your Highness," said Birkswood.

"Very good, Birkswood, thank you," said the prince. He turned to Thilly.

"Good night, Princess," Beaumain said to her, and his eyes looked as though he wished he could talk to her alone. She crinkled her brow at him and then smirked.

"Good night, Prince," she replied, lowering her eyelids at him. "Perhaps we will see each other again, flying."

"I hope so," said Beaumain, raising one eyebrow.

"Hmm," said Thilly. She turned away from him, ascended the creaking, popping, narrow stairwell of the pub, and followed Hana and Mrs. Florence, each holding lanterns, to her room at the end of the hallway on the right.

It was a simple room, but immaculately clean, and Thilly did not want to know how much work had been put into making it more "royal," for it made her uneasy. She wished they had just let her have the room as it was meant to be, rather than this sterilized version. The simple wrought iron bed bore a white quilt, and a thick woolen grey blanket was folded up at the end of it. An oil lamp shone on a side table, and a wash basin sat in one corner. Above the basin, a mirror with a faded blue and white border of simple flowers stood just a tiny bit off-center. The room smelled of rosemary and lavender, like the garden, and Thilly found a sprig of both tied together with rough kitchen twine upon the sill of the lone small window.

"I'll bid you good night, Your Highness," said Mrs. Florence. "Hana can see to your care; she'll be right next door."

"Just give a knock on the wall if you need me, milady," assured Hana.

"Thank you both," said Thilly.

After they left, she locked the door. She listened as Beaumain was led to his room opposite hers, and for a wild second, she wondered what it would be like to chat with him all through the night. For she felt detached from her home in every respect, and he was somehow now an anchor to that home, even though he was from this strange land. What would the morning bring to her, and how would it be when they separated at the border? She thought about what the mayor had said. She considered what Nat, the pub's servant, had shared with Mrs. Florence. She finally lay upon her simple bed under her covers, enjoying the weight of the wool blanket at the end of the bed, and she hugged herself, for it seemed like everything she had known was beginning to recede. She closed her eyes, and she felt herself rise and fall, heard the wind howling in her ears, and she looked out on at the reddish-orange tops of clouds, and felt he rough and brilliant scales of a great beast beneath her…and she slept.

# CHAPTER 13

## AN UNINVITED PASSENGER

The cooks at the pub had outdone themselves, scurrying about before dawn to prepare the final feast for Thilly and Beaumain and their mayor, as well as the accompanying staff of the royals. Thilly felt every sense sharply that morning; she could hear the kitchen staff clanging pots, she could smell sausages and toast and fresh flowers, and even though the sky threatened rain again, she could see from her window the edge of every cloud.

"The vinapsys, I suppose," she muttered. She was about to dress herself, but a knock on her door made her halt, and she sighed irritably. "One day I'm doing this myself. Only me," she whispered. She walked to her door and unlocked it.

"Your Highness," said Hana through the door, "I'm here to dress you."

Closing her eyes for a moment, Thilly put her hand on her forehead, and then she let it fall, straightened herself, and managed to lift her cheeks into, if not a full smile, at least a more cheerful appearance. Then she opened her door.

Hana looked puffy-eyed, as though she had been crying or slept poorly. *Or both*, considered Thilly, watching the young woman walk in and begin to smooth out Thilly's outfit.

"Hana, are you quite all right?" she asked gingerly.

Hana ducked her head, "Yes, milady, thank you," but she avoided eye contact with Thilly.

Thilly felt a hot spike of anger toward Mrs. Florence. She just knew that Hana *had* been crying and was obviously overworked. As Hana gestured for Thilly to raise her arms so she could slide a dress over her head, Thilly said, "You know, you could ride in the coach with me and the prince, going forward."

Hana looked scandalized. "Oh, no, Your Highness, that wouldn't be proper! That's the royal coach!"

"Yes," agreed Thilly, raising her eyebrows, "and you're part of my royal company."

Hana shook her head vigorously, her dark curls bobbing on either side of her round, blushing face. "It wouldn't be proper," she repeated. "And besides, it's not much farther to the border, and won't the prince be taking leave of us and going on his way for that tour of his?"

Thilly kept trying to avoid thinking about this inevitability, but she knew the moment was indeed coming when Beaumain would say farewell. She grew angry with herself for feeling ambivalent about this. Of course, she wanted to have her own coach, with Hana in it and no one else (certainly not Mrs. Florence, but she began to realize this might also be inevitable). But the thought of all those miles with just her ladies' maid…and Thilly quite liked Hana already, but she was no Beaumain.

*Why do I give a shit about that? I should be glad we're parting. I am* glad *we're parting.*

So she told herself.

"Very well," Thilly said aloud, "but we will travel together soon, Hana."

Hana stood back and put her hands on her hips to admire Thilly, dressed in periwinkle blue as a nod to Catellaith, and the girl looked pleased for the first time in a while, Thilly thought.

"If you ask me, he's a right fool," said Hana, and then she covered her mouth. "I'm so sorry! Why did I say that?"

Thilly grinned at Hana and held out her hand.

"We aren't meant to be together," she said. "That's all, and there's no regret, no ill will. Only friendship, as it should be."

Hana nodded, but she did not say anything else about what she really thought just then, and instead opened the door so that Thilly could descend. So she did, stepping carefully down the worn, protesting stairs, running her hands on the much-smoothed handrail as she held onto it. At the bottom, Mrs. Florence stood, a discontented raven of a woman with an expression that left no doubt what she thought about the pub and everyone in it who was not part of the royal party. Save the pub server Nat, Thilly realized.

Mrs. Florence guided Thilly and Hana to the dining room, and there the long table had been spread with a fresh white tablecloth, and the flowers Thilly had smelled were in vases and crocks among the plates and cutlery. Everyone stood at the sight of Thilly, and she felt her cheeks tingle. Beaumain's eyes opened more upon seeing her.

"I'm so sorry I'm late," she said, both to him and the company.

Mayor Quelle was there again, this time wearing a deep teal suit. She blinked at him. There was something about him, a light or something…he stood out from everyone else, yet was wholly unremarkable in nearly every respect. It was as if light scattered around the edges of the man. He made eye contact with her, and her stare was so intense that he began to sweat.

*What is it with this man?*

She broke eye contact and sat next to Beaumain. Once everyone was seated and the tea was served, Mayor Quelle said, "We send you forth on your journeys with many blessings, and we thank you for traveling this way."

A zealous cheer arose from the assembled guests, some of whom Thilly had seen the night before, and others, some of the more well-to-do farmers and vintners, had come for this morning alone.

The breakfast left nothing to spare: heaps of scones and pots of clotted cream, jars of local jam, carafes of fresh juices and ciders, piles of sausages and black puddings, tatties and fat beignets, and clusters of late muscadine grapes and green-gold pears graced the table. It was good, simple, well-prepared food, abundant and unpretentious, and Thilly felt more nourished after eating it than she had ever felt after any other meal in her life. Her sense of taste seemed heightened, and she felt almost feisty, so good was the feast.

"Blue suits you," Beaumain said to her idly, watching her sneak another black pudding when offered.

Thilly looked down at her dress.

"Hana chose it. I don't normally wear this," she said simply.

Beaumain tilted his head toward her and said, "I meant what I said. It suits you: the color of Catellaith, one of them anyway. The land suits you too. Or it would, under any normal circumstance. You look quite alive today."

Thilly snickered. "I should hope so."

The prince himself looked alert, his eyes bright turquoise and green mixed, and she could see little darker flecks in those eyes, set in his golden-brown face with his fiery, curly hair. Glancing at him, Thilly felt a strange tug deep within her that she found both painful and somehow pleasurable at the same time. She had never felt such a thing before. She looked away from him and drank her tea to cover her face. She busied herself with chatting to the other good folks at the table, who were all keenly interested in her visit to her mother.

"What an exciting time for you, Your Highness!" exclaimed a middle-aged woman named Pegrinnon, who was an independent farmer, one of the few women farmers in the county, so she said. She was bronze-skinned and black-haired, like many northern Catellaith families. She wore her hair at chin length, which was also common for many of the women there; the men either wore theirs long or very short, but never in between, Thilly noticed. "I've heard tales of the Veiled Isles, and that is all that they are. But to think your own mother, Lady Woadlynn herself, resides there! What an honor!"

"Thank you," said Thilly, relieved that Pegrinnon was not passing judgment on Woadlynn. She would have liked to talk more with the woman, but Birkswood stepped into the room and gave her a tiny nod. She looked sideways at Beaumain, who dipped his head in acknowledgement.

"Mayor Quelle," Beaumain said then, loud enough over the chatter of the breakfast that everyone else hushed instantly. "Thank you for your hospitality here. Princess Githilien and I are forever in your debt."

The mayor truly looked forlorn at their leaving.

"It was our honor," he said. He avoided looking at Thilly, and she shook her head, deciding not to think about it.

As everyone stood, Mrs. Florence joined Birkswood, and Thilly noticed they both looked more taciturn than usual…and she had thought that was a high bar to top. The mayor approached them and said in a low voice, which Thilly could just hear, "There is a decent road heading to the crossing at Lydamoor Shoals, just to the west of the weir. It'll keep you headed the right direction while staying off the main route."

*So we're still worried about the road,* Thilly thought.

The mayor opened the door of the pub with a grand sweep of his arms, and the morning sun burst forth briefly, making him look nearly iridescent to Thilly.

"Can you see that?" she said in a low voice to Beaumain.

"See what?" he asked her, following her line of vision and then twisting his brows at her.

Thilly blinked, but she could see quite plainly that Quelle stood wreathed in some sort of aura. "Mm, nothing, I suppose," she answered, gawking.

*How is it I can see that and no one else can? And just what sort of person is this mayor?*

Distracted by the light around Mayor Quelle, she blinked several times as she thanked him and wished him farewell. He swept his hat in one of his vigorous arcs and watched as she waved to him from the coach. She craned her neck to look back, and found that instead of a man standing there, she could only see an iridescent light. She straightened and sat very still and then she shivered.

"Everything all right?" asked Beaumain as the coach bounced along the country road.

"I—I think so," said Thilly, but really, she was befuddled. *Must be a lingering effect of that damned drink!*

"I'm sorry for this," he said then.

"For what?" Thilly asked.

"This...detour. The weirdness on the main road. The awkwardness...I didn't want you to have to apologize for anything," Beaumain said, his hands outstretched.

She realized he was not wanting her to take hold of his hands; he simply made a peace offering.

"Well," she said with a shake of her frizzy hair, "you don't have to worry about that. I'm not apologizing for anything about this."

She folded her arms across her chest, and he snickered. He pulled forth one of his scrolls and began to read, and Thilly watched the undulation of land outside her window, with the vineyards rolling in draperies of gold and russet leaves, the grapes either long since picked or dried upon the vine. Apple and pear trees and late plums hung with some fruit still bending their branches among colorful leaves, but by and large the season was late, with little harvest for fruits remaining, and acres of winter wheat and kale stretching in combed rows of both pale and dark green among all the surrounding gold. She enjoyed the sight of a few brown and white spotted cattle grazing by ponds, reflecting the steel-grey sky that forever pressed down and occasionally released some of its rain. Then she saw something she did not quite understand. It was a little green and brown something, rising and falling and pumping ahead, and finally she could see it bore hard-working wings. And it was headed right for the coach.

"Oh!" cried Thilly, afraid that the bird, for bird it was, would crash into her window, and without thinking she threw the window open, and the bird burst in and rolled right at her feet. Then it straightened, listed a bit, and shook itself. Its curved beak quickly groomed its ruffled feathers.

"A wood parrot!" said Beaumain. "What are you doing in here?" and he darted his eyes accusingly to Thilly.

"What was I supposed to do, Beaumain?" she demanded. "Let it perish against our window?"

"Well," said he, reaching his slim but tough hands down toward the still-woozy and preening bird, who blinked up at Thilly, "you'll have to be off, little friend."

The parrot whipped its head around and snapped Beaumain's fingers.

# THE VALE OF SEVEN DRAGONS

"Damnit!" he gasped, and then cried out, "Let go, damn you!" for the bird had latched fully onto his hand and would not let go, its beak fully embedded in Beaumain's finger, its eyes wild and golden, its green-brown wings flapping. It squawked despite its mouthful of royal finger.

Thilly feared Beaumain might fling the bird down hard, as his eyes had grown wide from pain and shock, so she reached out and seized the bird from behind and held its wings down. It released the prince, who panted for a moment and nursed the deeply dented finger. Remarkably, it had not broken the skin. But it had bitten a nerve.

The parrot, in Thilly's hands, acquiesced, and clucked innocently.

"Princess," said the bird.

Thilly turned the stocky psittacine around to face it, and it hopped out of her hands and onto her knee, looking up at her, tilting its head to one side.

"Yes!" said Thilly, stunned.

"Here," said the parrot, and it held out its left foot. Something shiny dangled from it, the size of a small coin, and for a moment, that was what Thilly thought it was. The object was tied with something, and Thilly placed her hand on her mouth. It was a strip of the scarf she had given Sir Vyrent when he had left.

Hands shaking, she untied the scrap fabric, and the little object fell into her hands. It was a round piece of metal, into which had been untidily pressed the flower Vyrent had taken from her hair the night of her birthday. She turned it over, and it said, "With love, V."

"I—I don't understand," she stammered, trembling. She was aware that Beaumain watched her closely. Feeling a little silly, but desperate to know more, she asked the parrot, "Is this from Sir Vyrent?"

"Yes," said the parrot simply. It hopped over to her little water bottle and gnawed at the lid.

"Oh, sorry," said Thilly. "You must be thirsty." She uncapped the bottle and poured water into the cap, and the parrot dipped its dark gold beak in, tipped its head back, and repeated the gulping until it was satisfied.

It fluffed its feathers and said, "Thanks!"

Shaking her head in confusion, Thilly asked, "Are—are you his bird?"

The bird held out its right foot, and Thilly could just see a little copper band on it. She squinted, and read, "Blinky," and the bird blinked at her with its radiant eyes.

"Your Blinky," said the bird, hopping back onto Thilly's lap. "Your Blinky now."

And it snuggled up to her, burrowing its head into her armpit until she cradled it. Tears spilled down her cheeks.

"Is he gone, then?" she whispered, feeling cold spikes of horror down her back.

"Your Blinky now," repeated the parrot, and it began to groom Thilly's hair.

"Oh, Thilly," said Beaumain, as she sat cradling the bird, her teardrops slowly dropping onto its back.

# CHAPTER 14

## *NEVER A KNIGHT*

Thilly could not accept that Sir Vyrent was gone. She forcibly had to accept, however, that his parrot, Blinky, was now a passenger in the coach. She did not know how to take care of a parrot, so she set her handkerchief down on the seat beside her and then reached for the bird. It evaded her, however, and hopped on the ledge of the window and tapped.

"Do…do you want out, now?" she asked the bird, and she opened the window. Blinky turned around to face her, extending its tail outside, squatted down, and sprayed out its poop.

"Ah, gods!" cried Thilly, scowling.

Beaumain burst out laughing to the point that he doubled over and gasped.

"At least!" he cried between spasms, "at least that didn't happen in *here*!"

Thilly frowned at him, and after Blinky shook itself off, it hopped back inside and settled agreeably upon her handkerchief.

Beaumain cleared his throat, but his lips twitched.

Thilly sighed and looked away from him, back outside.

"Hey," he said to her. "I'm sorry. I guess I...I needed that laugh. I'm truly sorry if—"

"We don't know anything," said Thilly flatly. "He's probably still out there, fighting..."

*Fighting* what, *though?* She swallowed. Her mouth felt parched.

Blinky nudged her with its beak and bent its head down, so she scratched its neck, and its pupils dilated.

"He's a tough bird," said Beaumain, observing Blinky. "That is a very long way to travel. He must have flown at night to catch up."

"How do you know Blinky is a boy?" demanded Thilly. "Wood parrots all look alike."

"I just assumed because he's so stocky and solid," said Beaumain with a shrug.

"How original of you," snapped Thilly.

So they traveled for some time, and Blinky tucked its head under its feathers and snoozed. Thilly would have liked to have joined the bird, for she felt somewhat hungover from the vinapsys. But by and by, she could see a little flash of something as they rolled along, and she shifted to try to get a better look.

"Are we almost to the border, do you think?" she asked Beaumain. He turned to look.

"Ah, very nearly, yes. We're almost to the river crossing."

"What is that in the sky?" she asked suddenly, pointing.

He joined her in looking at the horizon. A little ribbon of water shone in the noon sun, which had finally broken out, but what lay beyond it was most unusual. It looked like a wall of fog, stretching across the northern horizon...but it shimmered along its upper edge.

"I...don't...know," said Beaumain. "A...a storm?"

"That doesn't look like any storm I've ever seen," Thilly said doubtfully.

"Nor I," admitted Beaumain. "It's…it's right at the border. And it looks like maybe it drops down into the Vale to the east, but I can't tell from here."

A loud squawk frightened them both as Blinky flapped its wings and jumped onto Thilly's shoulder, then burrowed under her masses of hair. Its little claws dug into Thilly's neck, and she cringed and tried to extract the bird, but it would not come out.

"What—what is it, Blinky?" she grunted.

Beaumain had moved to the other side of the coach and looked out to the west.

"Um, Thilly," he said. "There's something happening at the river crossing."

He looked back at the bird and its head poked out, saw with its bright golden eyes what Beaumain had, and it shrieked again and dove for cover.

"What *is* it?" cried Thilly, and she managed to scoot across the seat up next to Beaumain and looked out.

"Gods," he whispered, "I do not know."

Thilly shook, for she could see amorphous dark shapes flickering above the river, and thrashing in it to the west of the weir, just at the shoals. Below the weir, riverboats had been driven and sat bobbing in disarray. She could hear screams, and she saw one of the great shapes pluck a person from their boat and soar off into the sky, back west.

"Oh hells," she breathed.

The coach halted abruptly then, and they heard running.

Birkswood appeared by the window. He looked ferocious, his eyes wild, his pulse pounding in his neck just above his stiff collar.

"Your Highness," he said urgently, looking between them. His gaze briefly halted on Blinky, and his mouth opened and shut, but he continued, "Do not leave this coach. Do you understand? Keep the windows shut."

"Birkswood," said Thilly, tense, "is everyone else all right?"

"So far," said the man, "but if whatever those…things are notice us, we might not be all right for long."

"What are they?" Beaumain asked.

Birkswood studied the prince, his face grim, and he pulled at his white goatee. "I think it is safe to say that Captain Copperbox was correct, and what visited your coast has made its way upstream."

"Are they birds?" asked Beaumain, squinting at the immense shapes.

Blinky let out a protesting squawk, and Birkswood grimaced at the bird.

"No," said Birkswood, his voice an octave higher than usual, "I don't know what they are. But they mean to do harm."

"What do we do?" asked Thilly.

The sound of hooves clattered up next to Birkswood, and he looked up. Thilly did as well, and she gasped.

"Vyrent?" she asked, for the man on the reddish-brown horse looked so like her favorite knight. But then she felt chilled. He was older, his hair lank, his clothing worn and filthy, but the sword at his side gleamed silver at the hilt. This was the man she had seen in the Dragon's Head.

"No," said the man to her, his eyes half lidded so that she did not see their color.

Blinky fluttered toward the window. The man swung off the horse, and the bird flew out and landed on his shoulder. He retrieved something from a pouch on his belt, and the bird munched contentedly.

"And you are?" demanded Birkswood, taking in the scene while also glancing toward the attack at the weir.

"Evgrent," said the man. He nodded to his mare. "This is Umbra. I'll lead you to the border."

"But who are you?" asked Beaumain, his aqua eyes fixated on the stranger.

The man bowed briefly while glancing with a smirk at Thilly, who returned his look with a stern glare.

"Your Highness," he said to her, "I am the brother of your good Sir Vyrent."

He looked very like the knight, yes, and was just as handsome, but much more rugged, and there was an air of disdain about him.

"I see you received his gift," said Evgrent, and he held his gloved finger out to Blinky, who stepped up on it. Evgrent then passed Blinky through the coach window back to Thilly, who took the bird in her hands. Blinky promptly returned to the back of her neck and drew her hair through its beak.

"Have you been following us?" said Thilly loudly.

Birkswood raised his eyebrows at her. "We might want to keep our voices down, Your Highness," he warned, glancing over his shoulder. More echoes of distant screams met their ears. He turned to Evgrent. "Well? What did you have in mind?"

Evgrent opened a flap on one of the packs upon his horse. He held out what looked like a flagon. It held a peacock feather.

"Some assistance from Mayor Quelle," said Evgrent simply.

"And what sort of assistance might that be, fortified wine?" asked Birkswood acidly.

Evgrent grinned and closed his eyes. "Nothing that exciting. It's glamour."

Birkswood drew himself up. "Do you know how to use it, then?"

Evgrent shrugged, and his attitude irritated Thilly. "Let's hope so. It's the only way we're getting across unseen."

"Well, get on with it, then," snapped Birkswood. He said to the drivers of the coach, "Wait until Sir—"

"Not 'sir,'" corrected Evgrent bluntly. "Never was a knight, never will be."

Birkswood grumbled and said, "Wait until...*Evgrent* makes whatever trick he's got and then proceed. Understood?" The footmen agreed.

Thilly, watching the river attack, sat bolt upright.

"Fucking hells," she breathed, and she ignored Birkswood whipping his head to rebuke her speech, and she pointed. He turned back and she could see his muscles tense, and he stood in what looked to her like a fighting stance.

"Well, mister Never-a-Knight," growled Birkswood, "now's the time for that trick."

A looping, winged, flat black shape turned toward them and let out a call that made the horses leap into the air and scream, and sent shudders up and down Thilly's spine while Blinky shrieked.

The way it flew disturbed her. She remembered from seeing the other strange creatures in the night sky before leaving Vickery that they had reminded her of bats, but this was now, she could see, not correct either. It was something about their irregular flight, not their shape, and certainly not their appearance. This thing flew differently than a bird might as well. It was as if it used the air in another manner, as if it structured itself not just to propel through that fluid but to occupy space in a way no animal could.

She knew instinctively, then, that it was no animal. It was something undefinable and other, filled with nothingness save one thing: malice.

Then she recalled the feeling she had experienced from Queen Maulielle: hatred. Beyond disapproval and dislike, it was a power that radiated a craving for not merely destroying something, but making it suffer before doing so. Yet there was no madness to it. There was great purpose, and that purpose wore a winglike frame, a shifting visage with no eyes but with a jagged hook, long arms, and other unnamable appendages that could seize and rip and crush. The winged instrument of malice flew at her...at *her*, she was convinced...as if it knew her and marked her. It wanted only her suffering and her destruction. She could feel it.

Evgrent stood in front of them all and opened the flagon. Out of it streamed an iridescent smoke that billowed impossibly forth, clouding everything in sight, and then Thilly could no longer see him or Birkswood. But she heard the echoes of their voices, as if they were all closed together in some sort of bubble.

"Go!" shouted Birkswood to the footmen, and the coach bounded forward.

Beaumain jumped over to Thilly's side and put his arm around her shoulder.

"Get away from the windows," he urged, but Thilly could not see anything outside of them except swirling, rainbowy iridescence. They squeezed in tight against each other, with Blinky scrambling under Thilly's hair.

The unearthly scream of the flying creature bounced off them, echoing, and the coach flew ahead as the horses charged in complete terror. The going was rough and swerving, and at one point Thilly thought the coach might fall over.

*How are Hana and Mrs. Florence?* she thought desperately, but she could do nothing but press herself against Beaumain and smell his sweat mixed with his cologne, and they held each other that way for so long that it began to hurt. Then Thilly gasped, for it felt like they

## THE VALE OF SEVEN DRAGONS

were falling, and the horses screamed, and so did she. They fell and fell, and she feared they would be dashed to bits whenever they landed. But what happened was far stranger: they began to slow in their fall, and then began to move so slowly it seemed impossible, and then the iridescent clouds disappeared, and they were on solid ground…inside of a fog that smelled most peculiar.

They had crossed the border into Aceltia.

# CHAPTER 15

## ACELTIA

The horses settled, but only a little, and they shivered and jolted the coach. Beaumain loosened his hold on Thilly, and they both sighed and looked away from each other. She disentangled Blinky from her hair and set the bird down, but its feathers were drawn close to its body and it trembled. She stroked its head, and it fluffed up and looked a bit restored. She dug into her own bag and found a small, wrapped oatcake and, holding it with her left hand, she broke a piece off her right with the other and offered it to Blinky. But Blinky made a little flying jump and snatched the larger oatcake and held it in one claw while nibbling it with the other.

"Well, at least someone is feeling better," grumbled Thilly. She turned the handle of the coach door to step out.

"Thilly, wait!" cautioned Beaumain. "We don't know what could be on this side of the border, either!"

Thilly huffed out a sigh and rolled her eyes. "Only one way to find out. I'm tired of being trapped in here. You and Blinky can entertain each other, but I'm getting out."

She swung open the door and nearly struck Birkswood, who had walked up next to her. He offered his hand, and she took it, giving her a look of both disapproval and admiration at her courage. She stepped onto the ground and looked all around her. The fog still swirled about and was so thick that she could see nothing beyond the horses. She heard the canter of another horse and looked up to watch a form emerge from the fog. It was Evgrent, his face partially covered with a cowl. He still, for a moment, reminded her greatly of Vyrent. She slid her hand into her pocket, and she closed her fingers around the little round starflower, now immortalized in metal. She shook her head.

*I will not believe he is dead. I have not seen his body, so I will not believe it until I do.*

"What is this place?" she asked aloud. Beaumain exited the coach and stood behind her, and Blinky sprang out of the open door, flew in a couple of circles around the coach, and then settled onto Thilly's shoulder, to her annoyance.

"Must you?" she whispered to the bird, frowning, and Blinky bopped her cheek with its beak.

"Your Blinky," it said in a singsong voice.

"Well, my Blinky," she said, irritably, "kindly don't shit all over me."

Evgrent swung off his horse and unhooked one of his saddlebags. He brought forth a rectangle of felt and approached Thilly. He lowered his cowl.

He was lined in the forehead and about the mouth, and his coloring was different, but he so resembled Vyrent that she felt an uncanny feeling, as if she were viewing a future version of her favorite knight. But there was some aura about this man that made her feel ill at ease, and she could not decide what it was. He was, for lack of a better word in her mind, *rough*. Yet she found him attractive, and she rather despised herself for it.

Evgrent looked down at her, as she stood with her hands on her hips, her hair feral in the fog, with Blinky on her shoulder, and the lined corners of his mouth deepened almost into a grin, but there was something insolent about the expression. So Thilly glared at him. He then held out the fabric piece and inclined his head with a hint of deference, but only just.

*You're a bit of an ass*, she thought.

"If you don't want Blinky shitting all over you, you'll want to wear this," he said simply.

Beaumain fumed, "You are to address the Princess Githilien as 'Your Royal Highness,' you abject churl."

Thilly snorted. "Such a way with words, dear prince," she said. "Fine, Evgrent, Not-a-Knight, I will take your lovely shit-shield. No need to feign fealty to me."

Evgrent held his finger out to Blinky, who stepped agreeably onto it, and then carefully lifted Thilly's hair and placed the felt onto her shoulder. Blinky wasted no time in jumping back to perch there, and promptly began chewing on the felt.

"I had no intention of doing so," replied Evgrent with a shrug. "Royal titles mean nothing in Aceltia, anyway."

"And what would you know of that?" demanded Birkswood. He stood looking down over the proceedings, being the tallest person there, and in the fog becoming a sort of landmark by height alone.

Evgrent turned and looked up at him, with another of his little nods. "I get around," he answered simply.

"I'll bet you do!" exclaimed Mrs. Florence, appearing with Hana.

# THE VALE OF SEVEN DRAGONS

"Your Highness!" cried Hana, and she lunged forward to embrace Thilly, while Blinky launched up and landed on Beaumain's head and began grooming the prince's tight ginger curls.

Thilly laughed loudly at the prince, who looked up while Blinky bent forward and hung upside down to make eye contact with him and nibbled on the end of his nose.

"Ah, Blinky, that will do!" said the prince, and he reached up and tried to grab the bird, but Evgrent stepped in and offered his hand, and the wood parrot promptly stepped on board.

Prince Beaumain huffed and adjusted his hair and his outfit, and his scowl greatly amused Thilly. She was glad for any humor just then, because none of the trip had gone as she might have imagined it. It was certainly not what he had planned, either.

"I'm sorry," she said to him, feeling a pang of guilt. "I know you meant to leave us at the border. And now...well."

"Yes," he mumbled. "Now. Well, I'm here, and our party is safe. I can't stay here, though. You know I'm needed back home. How can we know what's happening there from here? And where is 'here,' anyway? Has all Aceltia been consumed in fog? I still can't work out how we got here."

"Your Highness," called Birkswood, "we owe much to the clever thinking of Mayor Quelle, providing a glamour that Mr....Evgrent used. As to how he obtained it, I find that little piece of data quite lacking. Meanwhile, we should try to seek our way out of the fog and—"

The fog quite suddenly lifted...at least in front of them. The strange smell, a mix of sweet-smoky with a hint of sulfur, dissipated somewhat, and it was clearer to breathe.

"Well, that's convenient," Thilly said. "Now we can proceed through the countryside."

Evgrent cleared his throat. "Not without horses to pull your coaches," he said.

"What do you mean?" Thilly asked.

"By the gods!" cried Birkswood. "The horses are gone! How?"

Evgrent, sitting upon his mare, tilted his head to one side and said, "Listen."

They did, and they could hear hooves and whickering echoing from somewhere in the distance.

Prince Beaumain's eyes went wide at first, but then he drew a knife at his belt and wheeled around to face Evgrent.

"Did you do this?" he demanded.

Evgrent raised his eyebrows, looking at the knife with what Thilly could only interpret as bemusement, and held out his hands. "Do I look like I could have? I've been here the whole time. Someone took advantage of this fog and stole the horses right from under you. Don't you have footmen? Where are they?"

At that moment, the men showed up out of the fog behind them, looking all about, completely bewildered. Birkswood's face went nearly purple.

"Where were you?" he bellowed, startling the young men.

"Do not chide your men," a deep, rich voice spoke.

Everyone turned then, and they found an array of four people standing a little apart from each other. Thilly gasped: for a moment, each of them bore the same strange, scintillating aura that Mayor Quelle had...which only Thilly had apparently been able to see. Then the effect vanished. Each person wore scarves over their mouths, deep jewel-toned outfits with fine weaving and embroidery, and they looked tall and athletic in build. The speaker had dark skin, golden eyes, and cables of black, gold, and teal hair. It appeared to be a man, but Thilly was not sure the person was quite human. She then began to doubt Mayor Quelle had been, either. The speaker wore garments

# THE VALE OF SEVEN DRAGONS

that looked like a blend of teal velvet and dark green gossamer fabric, with a long-sleeved tunic, close-fitting dark pants, and an opalescent amulet resting on the chest.

Thilly stepped forward, and Beaumain called, "Thilly, no!" while Birkswood barked, "Your Highness, stand back!" Blinky, riding on her shoulder, clucked, but did not make a show of fear. Meanwhile, Evgrent snorted, watching her.

Thilly ignored them all and looked up at the speaker, who she realized was every bit as tall as Birkswood.

"I am Githilien, daughter of King Gathlade of the kingdom of Vickery," she said to the person.

The tall being knelt then, and the other three companions did as well.

"Welcome to Aceltia," said the speaker, "Githilien, daughter of High Priestess Woadlynn of the Covenant of Veiled Isles. We have been expecting you."

# CHAPTER 16

## *THE GLOAMING GROVE*

Thilly felt reverent and overcome by the greeting, but she was surprised that the quartet of strangers did not address Beaumain the same way. They did not kneel for him at all, but they politely bowed. Their focus remained chiefly upon Thilly, although they did give palms-out greetings to Birkswood and Evgrent, she noticed, as well.

*They know Evgrent, then,* she thought. It was another mystery about the man. She began to suspect they knew of Birkswood, at the very least, for they gave a deferential approach to him. But their greeting of Mrs. Florence was the most interesting to Thilly.

"Long have the stars turned and the mists sighed since your last visit," said the speaker to Mrs. Florence. She looked embarrassed, but she smiled.

"That will do, Ki'roth," she said, patting the tall being's hands with her small hands. In her prim, dull long dress, juxtaposed against Ki'roth's exquisite, colorful appearance, she seemed rather grandmotherly just then. Only her distinctive cap, with scarlet and gold dragon embroidery, made her stand out.

Thilly gawked at Mrs. Florence in surprise. "You know each other?" she asked.

"We do, Your Highness," said the fae. "I am Ki'roth. And these are Val'dreth, Mal'treth, and Ul'trok."

Thilly could not help it, and said in a rush, "There's…an aura around you. What is it? Why do you have it?"

Ki'roth grinned and looked at their fellow associates, who grinned and nodded. "That is most observant of you, Princess Githilien."

"Please," Thilly said, clasping her hands under her chin, "call me Thilly. No titles. You know Mrs. Florence, and I am in my mother's land. Sorry. Go on!"

Ki'roth tilted their head to the side and said softly, "You are independent, quite like your mother. We will respect your wishes, Thilly."

"Thank you," she said, and the tension melted from her shoulders. She felt a current of nervous excitement about any comparison to her mother. But now that she was in Aceltia, the nervous part welled up more than anything else, as did another tickling mix of emotions swirling in her. After all, it had been a decade since she had seen Woadlynn. She couldn't decide how to feel about this yet.

"In answer to your question," said Ki'roth, and Beaumain looked attentive, while Birkswood bore the slightest frown. "We are fae, and not everyone *can* see the aura. But you can, Thilly, and that is most interesting to us."

"Fae," said Thilly. "I thought those—you—were just stories. Fairies."

Ki'roth shook the long cables of their mane and said, "Fae and fairies…we do know each other. But those are the wee folk, and little tricksters they are sometimes. I will say, though, if you make friends with fairies, you have them for life!"

Thilly thought back to what the pirate Copperbox had said about fairies. She tried to picture the great ginger pirate conversing with small fairies, and she suppressed a giggle. Ki'roth looked at her with a rather canny expression then, and she blinked, and then wondered. Could these fae hear her thoughts?

"You have been through an ordeal," said Ki'roth then to all their party. "We will guide you to a place to camp, so that you can rest."

"Thank you," said Thilly.

Beaumain said, "We're forever in your debt, and to all the fae."

Ki'roth drew up their mouth and said, "Do not stretch yourself over a cliff's edge, young Prince Beaumain."

Beaumain and Thilly stared at each other, and she covered her mouth and snickered.

Birkswood and Mrs. Florence led the footmen and maids behind the royals, while Thilly and Beaumain followed the four fae as they stepped quietly and carefully over soft, moss-covered paths. The moss was resilient and cushiony, not penetrated by the heels of Thilly's travel boots. Old, twisted trees arched over the mossy trails, including oak, cedar, and other species Thilly did not recognize. Another form of moss hung in shaggy, green-gold curtains from the branches of several of the trees. Thilly saw no birds save Blinky, who had been dozing under her hair after the previous drama. Now that they were walking, the bird grew agitated and nibbled on Thilly's earlobe.

"No, Blinky," she murmured quietly, and she fished through her pocket for oatcake bits, and the parrot quickly downed those and then launched up into the sky suddenly. "Oh," said Thilly, watching the stocky parrot venture ahead, undulating and wheeling.

Beaumain twitched and sighed next to her, and she frowned, growing annoyed at his agitation.

"What's with you?" she hissed. "We survived, didn't we? Aren't you glad?"

He looked sidewise at her and rolled his eyes.

"This wasn't supposed to happen," he said. "I should have seen you off at the border and then ventured downriver along the northern border. And now my horses are gone and we're following fae folk to gods know where. I'm a bit concerned, Thilly. Aren't you?"

She was, but that worry rested like a dormant geyser in her soul, and she knew that at any point it would erupt and could only bring her a flood of tears. "Only as worried as I feel we need to be right now," she answered. "But...well, that could change."

"Mother and Father," murmured Beaumain, and Thilly tried to prevent herself from shuddering.

*We are away from that queen...that strange monster-queen who hates me,* thought Thilly. *So from that point of view, we're better off.*

Aloud, she said, "Fine, yes, I'm worried about Father. And— and"— she traced the little flower token of Sir Vyrent's in her pocket with her right hand. "Others," she finished, not knowing what else to say. She shook off the queasy sensation that someone watched her. When she turned to look over her left shoulder, she saw Evgrent riding his horse along the perimeter of their party. He caught her glance and smirked with that insolent manner of his. She narrowed her eyes and fumed.

The fae quartet led them on, and eventually they could hear a great chattering and flapping of wings. They came upon a small valley whose bracken had turned russet for the autumn, and along its edge great old oak trees bent their boughs with acorns. Among their branches and golden-brown leaves, the green-brown coats of wood parrots were barely distinguishable from the last green streaks of autumn leaves. But their noise was tremendous. The sky above had cleared enough to reveal some spots of blue, and sunlight caught the tops of the parrot-laden oak trees. Thilly smiled.

"Blinky must be among them," she reasoned.

"Perhaps that's where he's from," suggested Beaumain.

"Will you stop assuming Blinky's male?" said Thilly. "Anyway, maybe you're right."

"You can rest easy, knowing he—it's back with its own kind, and you can go on your journey without that inconvenience," said Beaumain.

Thilly halted her steps and wheeled on the prince, balling her fists.

"How dare you!" she cried. "That bird flew all the way from its owner's side to find me. Do you think I'd abandon it?"

Beaumain shook his head and held his hands up.

"Forget I said anything," he said. "I'm going on ahead to ask the fae about what manner of transport I can get to return to Catellaith." And he marched off, continuing to shake his head.

Thilly huffed.

Hana caught up with her then, and asked, "Milady, do you need anything?"

Thilly snapped, "I need the prince to stay away from me for a bit. Or perhaps forever!"

Hana stared at her, and Thilly kicked some errant pinecones in her path.

"You don't mean that!" Hana exclaimed.

"I do," said Thilly bitterly. "Anyway...no, I don't need anything. But," and she looked at Hana's concerned face with affection, "I would love your company."

The girl flushed with delight and smiled, and whenever Hana smiled, Thilly felt rather like the sun was out, and that she did not need to worry about anything. She was a useful person to have around, thought Thilly.

"Then I'm honored to keep you company, Your Highness!" said the girl.

"You can call me Thilly, you know," said Thilly, smirking and nudging her with her elbow.

Hana's face grew serious, and with a large-eyed expression, she said, "No, milady. I cannot. I'm beneath your status."

Thilly made a raspberry sound and said, "You're beneath nothing. And here, titles like that *mean* nothing. It's rather relieving, I think."

Hana looked deeply uncomfortable, so Thilly suppressed a sigh and said, "I'm hoping Blinky comes back, but what if that doesn't happen?"

"Nay, Your Highness," said Hana confidently. "You've got a companion for life, I'd bet."

"Do you like parrots?" Thilly asked her.

Hana shifted and shuffled as she walked and darted her eyes from Thilly to the roadside.

"Well," she said, cringing, "not so much, milady. I hope…I hope you'll understand. I'm sure it's a fine bird, but I would prefer—I mean to say, I don't think—" and she clamped her mouth shut.

Thilly nodded. "Don't worry, Hana," she said to the girl. "Blinky is my bird, and I don't want anyone else to feel obligated to care for it."

Hana instantly relaxed and smiled, and even began to hum. Thilly turned away from her and grinned to herself. Again she could see Evgrent off to the side. They all began to head toward a bank of tall trees, much taller than the oaks and quite dark. The party slowed as Ki'roth halted.

"We're entering the Gloaming Grove shortly," Ki'roth announced. "Nothing within it will hurt you. But it might seem...perhaps unusual to many of you. You might hear and see things that never venture far from the protection of the grove's canopy, and so are used to its ever-present twilight. There is a stream within it, with clear water, and we will make camp by that for the night."

Birkswood gestured for the footmen to join the group of fae, and Beaumain moved back and to Thilly's lefthand side.

"I admit," said Beaumain, looking at his shoes, "that I hope our camp isn't much farther."

Thilly did not dare look back at Evgrent, but she could not help but think that he certainly would be prepared to walk quite far, with or without his horse.

"That man," said Beaumain suddenly, "should have offered his horse to *you*."

"Why?" Thilly asked, keeping her expression neutral. "He cares nothing for our conventions, after all."

Beaumain brightened at that. "You're quite right," he said. "Don't forget that he never will, either."

"Oh," drawled Thilly, lowering her eyelids, "I won't."

They entered the forest, and the immediate shutting out of light disoriented Thilly. She could see, however that some of the hanging moss from the oak groves survived within this new ecosystem as well. As the light faded, Birkswood and the footmen, laden with what stores and provisions they were able to bring from the coaches, lit lanterns for everyone. The fae folk did not need lanterns, however, as they bore lights on their clothing. Thilly marveled at this.

"Look at that!" she breathed to Hana and Beaumain. "They're glowing!"

One of them, Mal'treth, lit the end of their staff with a green jewel. As they did, the hanging moss burst into a golden glow, all through the dark woods, and softly lit a tunnel-like path before them. Thilly drew in her breath at the sight. So it was that they did not walk in total darkness. But she began to worry about some of the odd hoots and booms and clicks and rasping sounds from deep within the dark shadows. Blinky had not joined them yet, and Thilly kept looking behind her for any sight of the bird. She chewed her lower lip.

Eventually she heard the distinctive, high rushing sound of a swift stream dashing down rocks, and the humidity level of the forest deepened. She could smell firs and hemlocks and the tannins they produced, acrid and sharp in her nose, and the dried evergreen needles beneath her feet were slightly slippery, even with boots. She was growing hungry, having run out of her oatcakes, and longed for a night's rest. Finally the fae folk slowed, and she could see an almost cathedral-like arch of the tallest trees above them, lit by the golden-glowing mosses.

Birkswood and his cadre of footmen worked with the royal tents, with the help of the fae folk. He offered for them to stay in one of them, but each refused.

"Why would you not want to stay in a tent?" Thilly asked.

"That is not our way," explained Ki'roth to her. "We have no need. The forest shelters and protects us; our clothing serves any other functions for the task." Ki'roth then unwrapped a garment tied about the waist and demonstrated that it could expand to create a blanket large enough to envelope the whole body. Thilly loved this, and when she looked at the rigid, stiff, musty-smelling royal tents with their silly little dragon ramparts, she felt a surge of distaste.

*The way of the fae is much more natural,* she thought.

Everyone helped share food and sat around small fires housed in little stone rings that had clearly been used for many years, as the rocks were black, and the ground permanently singed in little pits.

Thilly wondered what sorts of folk had traveled and camped there over time, and who might come after her own party one day. Mrs. Florence rounded up the maids, including Hana, to share a tent with her. Thilly was to have a tent adjacent in case she needed anything.

"I'm sorry, Your Highness," she said to Thilly, "that we can't provide you with the most comfortable bed, without the coach."

"It's fine, Mrs. Florence," Thilly told her. "And I'm not quite ready for bed either, so I think I will listen to the fae singing until I am so tired even the hard ground would be comfortable!"

"Our stubborn princess," Mrs. Florence replied, and she clucked her tongue. "As ever." But she smiled, and Thilly could feel her fondness.

Beaumain sat cross-legged before the fae and listened to various stories about the forest. Thilly wanted to hear them as well, but as she cast her gaze about, she did not see Evgrent, and she wondered where he might be. She had given up on Blinky returning to her at night, so she merely hoped the bird was tucked away with its other parrot friends until morning. She decided to look for Evgrent.

Slipping away from the warm light of the fires and the rigid forms of the tents, she kilted her skirts and stepped along the dank streamside, following the water as it bent deeper into the forest, and she found another small clearing. There stood Evgrent, with his own little fire, and he combed his horse and hummed softly to her a tune that Thilly could not quite make out. She tried to walk quietly, but he heard her and turned swiftly. In the light of the fire, she could see him frown.

"What are you doing here?" Evgrent asked in an irritable tone, turning back around.

"Your horse didn't run off," Thilly said.

"How observant of you," retorted Evgrent, not looking up. "What do you want?"

# THE VALE OF SEVEN DRAGONS

Thilly felt a flare of outrage surge in her, but she held her tongue.

"I just want to thank you, Sir—I mean, thank you, Evgrent," said Thilly. "You know, for getting us out of Catellaith alive. I know Vyrent would—"

Evgrent put down the brush and held his left forefinger up.

"If you think I did this as a favor to my brother, you're mistaken."

Thilly stared at him with a furrowed brow. *Why are you like this?*

"What do you mean?" she pressed him. "Why else would you follow me and help me...us?"

He turned back to the mare, stroking her face in a calming manner, and said, "Coin, pure and simple."

"Bullshit," said Thilly, hands on her hips. He glanced at her. "Whose coin?"

Looking at her with his eyes narrowed and glinting, he muttered, "I never share my patrons." He curved his mouth into a menacing half-smile.

"Bastard," snapped Thilly, tempted to spit on him.

"Probably," he said with a grin, "but our parents are dead, so who can say?"

"Do you want me to feel sorry for you?" she countered.

"I don't want anything from you, least of all your pity." He put the brush away and spoke something soft to his horse. She tossed her mane.

Thilly closed her eyes for a second, opened them, shook her head and said, "That's good, because you won't get it from me."

"Then we understand each other," he said, unstrapping his bedroll from his baggage.

"I wouldn't say that," Thilly replied, gritting her teeth. "I don't understand mercenaries."

"Your one flaw," he said, almost so quietly that Thilly thought for a second that she had imagined it. She blushed.

"And why is that?" she wanted to know, maybe a bit too much.

Evgrent unrolled his bed for the night, sighed, and walked over to her. Looking down at her, his face outlined in firelight, he said, "Because this realm will not survive an all-out assault, if that's what's happening at the coast. Not in any way you recognize now. Your crown will be meaningless, if you even keep your head long enough to wear it."

Thilly lifted her chin proudly. "So I should abdicate like my mother and join the Covenant?"

Evgrent sneered. "What good is a covenant against monsters?"

Thilly shrugged, trying to ignore the heady scents of woodsmoke and fir and something else foreign to her nose that enveloped Evgrent, for he stood very near her.

"I'll guess we'll find out, won't we?" she countered. "Why, what did you have in mind?"

She looked at him with her eyes questioning, her mouth drawn in a bit.

He leaned toward her, locking eyes with her, and hissed, "I don't give a flying *fuck*, Githilien of Vickery. But I've made it this far as a mercenary. And you wanted to wield a sword."

He marched away from her, unfastened one of his bags, and withdrew something just over two feet in length, in leather wrappings. He walked up to her, scowling, and held out the package to her. She stared at it.

"What is this?"

Evgrent snorted. "How can you want a sword and not know what it is? Ignorant snippet."

"Fuck you!" hissed Thilly, leaning forward, fists clenched, hair flying.

"No, *girl*," said Evgrent with a nasty smirk. "But take the sword so nobody *else* fucks with you. Consider it a gift from my dearly departed brother."

Thilly breathed heavily in rage. "You don't know he's dead!"

Evgrent shook his head. "He's as good as, and there's not a godsdamned thing I can do about it now anyway."

Thilly tried to still her quick breathing. "I still don't believe you," she said to him. "So now what?"

Evgrent pressed the package into her arms, and it was the only thing that separated them.

"Go to your mother," he said, voice even, jaw working. "At least you have one. Then it's none of my concern what you do. Fight or die like the rest of us without titles and kingdoms. See what that feels like."

He released the package, and she caught it and found it heavy. He snatched his bedroll, strode to his fire, kicked dirt upon it, and extinguished it. Then he walked back to his horse and led her off, away from Thilly into the darker forest, and did not look back.

She looked down at the package, in the sudden dark lit only by glowing moss from above, and she hefted it.

*I have a sword.*

# CHAPTER 17

## *THE BLADE AND THE SONG*

Thilly murmured, "Thank you," but either Evgrent didn't hear or didn't care, for he was out of sight of her. The wind rustled her wild, tangled hair and her boots were scuffed, her skirts soaked with night dew, and her arms strained, holding the unexpected sword bundle.

"I did want a sword," she murmured to the trees and the chirping night insects, "but how did he know that? And what do I do with it now?"

The only voice to answer her was that of the night and of the eerie circus of sounds, pops and buzzes and a long, repeating *whoosh* that she was not quite sure she heard underneath it all. This forest was alive in a manner wholly unlike the gentle groves of her native Vickery. It had a beat to it, and a glimmer on the periphery of Thilly's vision. She reasoned that might have been from the glowing mosses above her, but occasionally she could see something flicker, little winking lights. Yet even with the moss and those odd lights, this forest was *dark*. Dark in a manner which she had never experienced in her sheltered life in Castle Taugan and its relatively genteel grounds…which were still considered rustic compared to those of the Royals Catellaith in their palace. Dark and pulsating and wheezing, perhaps. Yet not dark in the manner of those monsters she had seen, for that was different. Those were things where light went to die, she thought, whereas the Gloaming Grove was a place where twilight lived. But she was still a stranger here, and somehow, she felt that the forest did not want her to forget that.

She held the sword in its wrappings.

"If I wait until I'm at the camp to open it, then everyone will know about it and ask questions. I think I want to see it now." So she began to unwrap it.

It was in a scabbard, a simple leather one, but finely wrought, and stitched with little patterns that she could not quite discern in the darkness, but she ran her fingers across the little bumpy threads and realized that these were probably flowers she felt. She felt another shape stitched above the blade, and she tried squinting under the dim light of the glowing moss.

"A dragon," she murmured.

She pulled the sword free from its scabbard, which fell into the low bushes around her feet. She held the sword up, and it reflected that faint glow of hanging moss, but as far as she could tell, it was made of polished steel with no peculiar strengths other than its sharp edge. Its hilt was small and felt correct in her hands, and where it met the silvery blade, a dragon of a deep rosy metal wound, with a flame from its mouth stretching up the center of the blade, where it eventually vanished in an infinitesimally small line into the steel.

"Exquisite," she breathed. "Where did he get this?"

She wanted to ask Evgrent, but feared his answer…for she was certain no mercenary would find a lovely sword like this just lying around. He was not there, so she could not question him, but she made that a priority. For now, she held the sword and with both hands swung it left and right, and then wheeled with it...and nearly struck Beaumain in the neck.

"Fuck!" he cried, and Thilly gasped. Then she burst into giggles.

"Finally I get a proper swear from you," she gasped, doubled over snickering, pressing the sword into the ground as she did as if it were a cane.

"Well, yeah, because you nearly killed me!" he hissed. "Thilly, what are you doing? And where'd you get this—oh."

Beaumain looked down at the remnants of Evgrent's fire.

"Him," he said.

Thilly shrugged. "Yes. I wasn't knighted or anything."

He laughed at that. "You won't be, either," he said.

"Must you always ruin my fun?" Thilly said with a sigh.

Beaumain retrieved the fallen scabbard and handed it to her, along with the wrappings she had also dropped. She looked up at him, and his aqua eyes glinted. He seemed unusually calm to her, and relaxed.

"Come back, please," he told her, "before Birkswood completely loses his mind worrying about you."

"He sent you, then?" she asked, taking the scabbard and sheathing the sword rather reluctantly.

"I volunteered," Beaumain told her.

So they stepped carefully over perilous roots that nearly tripped them both, under the odd hovering little twinkles in the trees and the faint glimmer of hanging moss.

"Tomorrow, we travel northwest," he said softly. "I've been talking to Ki'roth and the other fae. What an interesting people they are! I never knew!"

Thilly considered. "I hadn't either, and I find that strange. Was Aceltia always like this? I don't remember learning that in my courses from Chamberlain."

"Aceltia is…" and Beaumain looked up at the dark tree canopy. "It's unique. There was a throughfare that bordered along Valetheant's western border, and that extended up to the sea and ran over to Osthadon. But few people bother to venture into Aceltia from the south; more come from the Vale. And for that matter, more of my people deal with Valetheant instead. Aceltia was always a place to…wander off to, seek knowledge or maybe deliberately get lost, or so Father used to describe it."

"Deliberately get lost," repeated Thilly, and she kicked up pine needles as she walked. "Like my mother."

Beaumain glanced at her and said, "I didn't mean…I, well. Not like that. I'm sorry."

Thilly said nothing then, but held her sheathed sword across her body, almost like a shield. She was trying to block something from hurting her; her mind tilted on the edge of it.

"What will you do?" she asked him suddenly, pulling away from that unnamed sensation she fought. "How will you get back home?"

"I don't know yet," admitted Beaumain. "But Ki'roth has advised against leaving until after we've visited the Veiled Isles. I hoped I could return before that. It's not exactly convenient to go up there and then return home. But he—they—seemed to think that your mother and the other priestesses might know of a safer way to return home. I wonder if anywhere is safe at all, though. How safe are we here? The fae seem to think we're quite protected, but how?"

Thilly shivered. "I don't know, but something about this forest feels alive to me, and I wonder how much of these lands are protecting themselves."

"The fog, though," said Beaumain. "I wonder how far it extends. All the way around every part of Aceltia? Even to the sea?"

"Well, they are the *Veiled Isles*," said Thilly, the corner of her mouth curving a bit.

"That's a different kind of fog," insisted Beaumain, gesturing with his hands. "That's just coastal fog. Coastal fog doesn't extend inland this far."

Thilly threw her head back and sighed as they approached the ember-strewn fire pits of their camp.

"Beaumain," she said, feeling suddenly quite fatigued, "let's add that to the list of questions for my mother, shall we? It's a long list growing longer all the time."

She walked toward her tent, but then halted. She looked over her shoulder at the prince, who stood with his hands behind his back, watching her holding her covered sword, with her mussed hair and disheveled skirts.

"There's nothing to be done for it, then," said Beaumain to her. "I'll go with you to the Isles, and we'll ask your mother every question we can think of. Together."

Thilly turned her head away, not wanting to smile but finding it hard not to.

"In that case, I'm coming back with you to fight monsters afterward," she said.

"No, you're—" Beaumain began.

"I've got family in the south too, remember?" said Thilly. "And now I've got a sword. Try and stop me."

Beaumain swung his head left and right and said, "I think I have more fight in me for monsters than trying to talk you out of something."

Thilly beamed. "Finally!" she exclaimed. "I think you're starting to get me."

# THE VALE OF SEVEN DRAGONS

Beaumain continued shaking his head as he walked back to his own tent. "Good night, Githilien, Sword Maiden."

"Good night, Beaumain," she called back, lifting the flap of her musty tent, "Friend of the Fae."

Inside the tent, she found a bedroll and blankets, everything made, and though a great part of her wanted no fuss, she recognized the benefit of even a simple camping bed made as comfortable as possible for a princess in a rustic place. She pressed her hands upon her heart and gave a blessing to the stars and to her maids, who had clearly worked hard in this strange land. She took off her traveling gown and stood in pantaloons, swaying, exhausted, and then she sank to her knees, fell flat on her face, and rolled herself up in the covers. And she dreamed.

*Singing.* In her dreams she was conscious enough to decide that she had heard the singing before. *Such glorious singing.* A feminine voice, high and yet deep at the same time, singing notes and words she did not know, and yet somehow her mind translated for her:

*Sleep and sleep*
*Upon the mantle born*
*Quiet and deep*
*Until the fateful morn*

*And so we sing*
*So clear, so fair*
*'Til dragon's wing*
*Takes to the air*

Then the words became incomprehensible, garbled, or it was simply the woman's voice looping in strange ways, unlike any other music Thilly had ever heard before. She felt herself rising and falling, or perhaps that was because she had been in the coach so long, and then walking, and so she felt she still moved, slowly up, slowly down, over and over, as if upon a bellows.

*"Come closer, Githilien,"* a voice said clearly to her, and she jerked awake.

She was soaked with sweat and yet cold, heart thumping madly in her chest, and her right foot was asleep. She tried tensing and releasing it again and again and rubbing it. And she listened. She could not hear the singing, only the pops in the sagging logs of a dying fire close by, and the constant rush of the stream. She sat upon her elbows, rotating her right foot, and faced the door of the tent, half expecting something to draw back the opening. But nothing ever did. She felt herself drooping, and then she fell asleep again.

*Githilien.*
*Githilien.*
*Githilien.*

# CHAPTER 18

## A DUTIFUL PATH

With sleep-creased skin and the spirals of dreams still spinning in her mind, Thilly awoke to something pulling at her hair. She cried, "Ack!" and was met with a reproachful squawk.

"Blinky!" she cried. The parrot shook its feathers and clucked its tongue.

"Good morning!" said Blinky. "Who's a good bird?"

"Not you, you little scamp!" chided Thilly, but she smiled and took the parrot into her arms and kissed its beak. The feisty bird let out a long whistle, and Thilly laughed. "You had me worried."

Blinky made a tick-tick-tick sound. "Time to get up!" it said in its funny, raspy voice. Blinky tilted its head at Thilly and nibbled at the ends of her compressed, frizzed wreck of hair. The wood parrot was right, as the dawn had just begun to seep through the canopy of trees. The Gloaming Grove never quite dawned, but it was a gradation above the darkness of night and slowly brightening. She listened. The sounds of pots and the smell of woodsmoke and fried bread met her nose.

She called out, "Hana?" and the maid appeared so quickly, Thilly realized she must have been waiting for her to awaken. Hana held folded clothes out to her and looked at Blinky disdainfully, which greatly amused Thilly.

"Blinky," said Thilly gently, "why don't you go find something to eat while I dress?"

Blinky tilted its head to one side, looked up at Hana, and said, "Biscuit?" and her mouth pursed into a thin line. She held the tent flap open just wide enough for Blinky to waddle out, and then they heard the parrot fly over toward a small group of people preparing food over the campfire. A small exclamation of shock rang out, and Thilly cringed, wondering what the bird had done.

She dressed in clean clothes, and then she began to wonder about how much longer it would be before they all ran out of clean clothes…and when she might be able to bathe. She took it in stride but wondered how the rest of the camp might be faring. They could have stayed in Catellaith a little longer, were it not for the invasion of the hellish creatures. She shivered, remembering the focus the one had given her as it flew toward her coach.

"Thank you, Hana," she told the girl, and exited the tent. No sooner had she done so than a footman swooped in to break it down. She spied Mrs. Florence, who met her halfway under the brightening canopy of trees, and the older woman appraised her.

"Your Highness, you look as though you were out a bit late!" Mrs. Florence remarked, and she leaned in to examine Thilly's face. "Dark circles under your eyes. You must get more rest! We've still a long way to go."

"How many days?" Thilly asked, not entirely sure she wanted to know, but also thinking she had better have *something* in mind.

Mrs. Florence looked thoughtful. "We've likely got a couple more nights ahead of us at least, assuming all goes well. And so far, so goo—"

Blinky let out a piercing shriek and darted through the air to Thilly's shoulder, startling the entire camp and embarrassing her, so she stroked the bird, but it trembled violently.

"What in the heavens?" gasped Mrs. Florence.

A shadow passed over them all, and everyone looked up. Thilly felt a sickening chill sweep her, for high above, a great dark shape swung back and forth, but it was indefinable.

"It's another monster," she said, feeling numb for a moment. "But I can't see it well."

Ki'roth walked toward her calmly, and yet their face looked troubled. "That is because the Covenant's shield is blocking our view of it," said the fae. "And by doing so, they help block us *from* it."

Beaumain joined the group and held out a cup of tea to Thilly, who took it gratefully with shaking hands.

"How good is this...shield?" he asked Ki'roth.

The fae looked upward, and they all shuddered as the shadow darkened the already dim morning forest even further. Thilly clutched Blinky to her breast. She could see another shape, and another...they were like sharks that way, swirling, schooling perhaps, and yet not. At least sharks made sense, she thought. Sharks were something natural and of her world. But the things high above seemed out of place in more ways than she could describe.

"A tempest," she murmured, and Birkswood heard her and looked at her with startled eyes. "I wonder if that's what the rider who came to Castle Taugan saw."

Beaumain glanced at her along with Birkswood, and she met the prince's gaze with troubled eyes. His jaw tensed.

# THE VALE OF SEVEN DRAGONS

Ki'roth, watching the skies above, said, "The Covenant must surely be using considerable power to keep this shield running, and I am not sure how long or how well it will hold. I think we can make it to the Veiled Isles. But I feel much more wary about walking in the open now. We will stick to forests. And this is but one; we have others to go through, and those of the Isles are stranger than this one."

The sound of hooves rang through the woods. It was Evgrent, his face taciturn, straddling his mare, Umbra. She came to a halt by the little circle where Thilly and the others conversed, and Evgrent slid off her back.

"I've gone ahead a bit," he announced, avoiding Thilly's gaze. "There is another path that seems more sheltered. Do you know of it, Ki'roth, and where it goes?"

"I do know of it," said the fae. "That follows a darker, denser undergrowth, and the stream veers away from it, but there are springs deep in those woods. Camping by one of those would give fresh water." Ki'roth then turned to Thilly. "We will get you safely to Priestess Woadlynn, Your Highness."

Thilly nodded and looked all around at everyone; they were all focused on her, and she felt her cheeks tingle from the spotlight.

"Then let's take the forest trail," she said to them all. "Stay out of sight of...whatever those creatures are, and stick together. Ki'roth, if you and the fae would lead, I would be most grateful."

"So shall we commence," Ki'roth said, "linked as we are with the forests and by the good, strong magic your mother and the Covenant provide. But surely," the Fae then said, turning to Evgrent, "you can lead us on that horse, if the knight would be so willing to allow it. That way, should the shield not hold, you could race ahead with the princess to the Veiled Isles at speed."

Evgrent's mouth turned downward, and his eyes narrowed. "I do not think Umbra would allow another rider," he said, his voice more neutral than when he had been with Thilly alone.

Ki'roth raised their eyebrows, shrugged, tossed back their hair, and suggested, "Perhaps Princess Githilien could ask Umbra what she thinks."

Thilly let out a small laugh, and said, "I'm afraid I'm not much of an animal person," but Ki'roth and the three other fae turned their gaze to Blinky, who was drawing its vibrant, hidden emerald lower wing feathers through its beak, evidently quite pleased with itself on its perch of Thilly's covered shoulder.

Evgrent leaned down and whispered into his horse's ear, and Umbra perked up both ears and snorted. Sitting back, Evgrent turned the mare toward Thilly. Blinky then flew from Thilly's shoulder to rest on Umbra's saddle pommel, and the mare did not flinch at all. Evgrent rubbed Blinky's head, and the bird gave him an appreciative, gentle nip on his forefinger.

"Well," said Thilly, "I suppose that settles it."

She walked up to Umbra and let the horse sniff her hands, and she stroked the horse, feeling the hot breath upon her cheeks. Evgrent then slid off and offered his cupped hands for Thilly to step up.

"I could probably manage on my own," she said, not looking at him.

"No, you can't," he said simply. "That much is clear."

Thilly heard someone laugh in the collected throng, and she gritted her teeth.

"Don't worry," said Evgrent acidly, "Umbra is more forgiving than I."

Thilly wanted to hurl a string of epithets at the man, but she bit them back, stepped into his hands, and he hoisted her up lightly. She

# THE VALE OF SEVEN DRAGONS

sat side-saddle and then he easily climbed up after her. Blinky crawled up her front, its claws prickling her skin so much that she winced and took its place on her shoulder again. Thilly hung onto the pommel, scooted as far up against it as she could with Evgrent behind her, but she was close enough to him that she could smell him, and she felt his arms just touch hers with the reins. Beaumain watched her constantly, and she tried to avoid looking at him in turn, but she wondered about the expression in his ginger-lashed, blue-green eyes.

"I'm finally taller than you," she said to him lightly.

"So you are," he replied, gazing up at her, and lowering his eyes halfway when he looked at Evgrent, who gave a simple nod that Thilly could not see.

"It's sorted," she declared, and she enjoyed being that high up, despite the company seated behind her.

Evgrent did not wait for any commands; he squeezed his legs around Umbra, and she proceeded slowly at first, and then at a brisker pace. The trees whispered as they rode past, or so it sounded to Thilly. She loved the feel of the wind in her hair, and wished she could fly into it, away from everything. Blinky did fly a bit, ahead and up, and then back again.

"Your Highness!" called Birkswood, and Thilly bit her lip. She felt a tinge of guilt.

"We'll lose them if you go this fast," Thilly said, looking over her shoulder.

"Keep yourself facing forward," replied Evgrent tonelessly.

"That's a bit boring, isn't it? I'd like to look back from time to time," Thilly said, feeling irritable already.

"Boring!" squeaked Blinky, turning its head up from its pommel perch to blink at Thilly.

"What, facing the unknown is boring to you now?" asked Evgrent in a low voice. "All that bullshit about wanting to be a knight was just that? Bullshit?"

"No, but I—" began Thilly. Then she shook her head, and the ribbon Hana had tied in it fell away, so that her hair flung out wild and long. "It would be improper of me to be out of the sight of my party," she ended up saying irritably, with a sigh at the end.

Evgrent nudged Umbra lightly with his left knee, and she slowed, and then curved around and cantered back to the party. The looks on Birkswood and Beaumain's faces told Thilly all she needed to know: that they disapproved of what Evgrent had done. Thilly shivered for a moment, but she realized just how much she had enjoyed being away from them all.

*What if I just took off and never looked back? What if I lived in the wilderness?*

Beaumain looked up at her, taking in her feral hair, and said, "You have a duty, Princess Githilien, and a course ahead. The two must coincide."

She bristled, feeling he had cut too close to the mark, and replied with her chin held high, "We merely scouted ahead. The woods are changing. The air is much more humid, too."

Ki'roth nodded and said, "We're coming upon the Titeltian soon. That river flows from the springs on Moon's Spine into the forest streams ahead, and eventually those form cascades that tumble down a deep forge where it travels toward the lowlands of the coast. There it spills into the sea close to the Veiled Isles, wreathed in fog."

One of the other fae spoke then, and added, "We cannot travel the forge with this party; it is too rough. So we will need to take the dell passage through Absinweald."

"Can we all travel through this…Absinweald?" Thilly asked. "We've one horse. It sounds like rough going." She glanced down at

Hana and Mrs. Florence. Then she swung off the horse and landed on the ground. Blinky flew to her shoulder, and when she looked back at Evgrent, his face remained as inscrutable as ever.

Thilly said to the assemblage, looking Beaumain in the eye as she did so, "If we will only ever have one horse, I do not want to ride it. We take turns. With Mrs. Florence going first," she added, looking at the older woman pointedly.

"Well, I never…Your Highness!" exclaimed Mrs. Florence. "No, that would be most inappropriate."

Thilly shook her mane of wild hair and grinned at Hana, who stared at her with round eyes. She had a feeling Hana was itching to secure her hair.

"I'm not asking, Mrs. Florence," Thilly declared, and she drew herself up as tall as she could, but she hoped her massive hair gave her at least a little more presence in its unrestrained state.

Mrs. Florence's mouth fell open, but she shut it quickly and looked shrewdly toward Evgrent. He had drawn himself up a little more formally and nodded to her.

"Milady," he said in a low voice, and Thilly watched fascinated as Mrs. Florence fought her own mix of emotions.

"Well" she exclaimed. "In that case, I suppose I can try it. But we are taking turns, Princess, and I'll stick to your word on that."

Thilly grinned, looking back and forth at Mrs. Florence and Evgrent respectively. "Perfect," she said. Whatever Evgrent's unreadable expression meant, Thilly felt triumphant.

"Whatever your arrangements, Your Highness," said Ki'roth, "we had better get some distance covered today. Maybe we will find the horses again, but certainly we cannot wait for them. No doubt if those creatures are menacing the whole of the land, no horse would want to venture forth."

"I hadn't thought of that," Thilly mused.

"It doesn't bode well for your father's regiment," agreed Beaumain.

Thilly cast her eyes quickly to Evgrent. He looked away from her, and she squeezed the floral coin in her pocket. *Not until I see Vyrent will I believe anything's really happened to him.*

As if in response to her thoughts, Blinky nipped her earlobe.

"Ow, Blinky," she hissed. The bird preened and blinked at her. She walked up to Birkswood and looked up at his lofty, white-goateed chin, and he looked down his long nose at her, his brow stern.

"You and Ki'roth know the way to the Veiled Isles," Thilly said to him.

"We do, Your Highness," answered Birkswood in his deep baritone.

"Then let Mrs. Florence have a ride for a while, and then she can trade with another maid if she likes," and Thilly nodded to Mrs. Florence, who shook her head and shrugged.

"I will try it for a bit," conceded Mrs. Florence.

"Good!" said Thilly. "Then Prince Beaumain, Birkswood, and I will follow. We should have the footmen bring up the rear of our party, and any of the fae who might like to assist can ride alongside or to the rear as they prefer. Just in case these forests get strange."

Ki'roth laughed. "It is not a debate as to whether the forests of Aceltia get strange; they simply *are*. It is only a matter of degrees, and what your human eyes and ears might tolerate."

The fae looked up at the sheltered sky, with tall fir and pine boughs crisscrossing in their canopy. Muted dark shapes swam to and fro high above, but they had thinned...or traveled elsewhere.

Another fae called, "The Covenant needs our assistance sooner rather than later, so whatever the dark woods bring, we must face.

# THE VALE OF SEVEN DRAGONS

And I daresay whatever we do come across will be preferable to what is outside this protective dome."

"Then we're going now," Thilly declared, and they set off into the darker path, into the rushes of streams and the whisperings of secret forest creatures and the yawning of spirits Thilly had no name for.

*Better a forest spirit than a sky demon,* she thought, and she shivered as they delved further onto the path toward her mother and so many unanswered questions in her heart.

# CHAPTER 19

## ABSINWEALD

The moment arrived in which Thilly shivered head to toe, and not from cold, but from the distinct feeling she had entered a place alien to prior experience at the edge of the dark, living cathedral that was the Absinweald. She mistrusted her vision, for out of the corners of her eyes she thought she beheld glowing orbs of phosphorescent green and palest yellow rising and falling; yet when she turned her head swiftly to try to study them, they vanished. The Gloaming Grove had hinted at but a taste of what lay ahead, and that thicket of woods to the southeast seemed now quaint like a walled garden, compared to this immense living organism that humans called a forest, and yet the fae knew better its true nature and its extent.

The lights were the least unusual things in that forest, as Thilly soon learned.

Ki'roth, walking alongside her and Beaumain, spied her swift peeks into the depths of darkest green, indigo, grey, and rich brown of the Absinweald.

"You will not see anything," said the fae, "except for what the Absinweald *allows* you to see. And," Ki'roth clasped an amulet around their neck, "you will hear and feel and...*experience* things that may not make sense to you, Princess Githilien. Or at least...not make sense *yet*."

Blinky made a gurgling sound, and Thilly said dryly, "Well, if it's anything stranger than this wood parrot, that will be quite something."

Blinky turned a bright eye to her and to the fae, who smirked.

"Count on it," said Ki'roth, eyes shining.

Evgrent and Mrs. Florence did not charge ahead very far, as the man had done with Thilly, and it gave her no end of amusement imagining what the two might discuss, if indeed they said anything at all.

"Do you suppose they'll out-silence each other?" Thilly asked Birkswood.

The man said, "Hmmph," and Thilly thought that might be the end of it. Then he said, "Do you know, Mrs. Florence was once a magician?"

Thilly stopped abruptly and stared at Birkswood, mouth agape.

"You're joking, good man!" cried Beaumain, looking askance at Thilly with a twinkle in his eyes.

Birkswood shrugged. "It's true. But she'll have my hat and coattails if you tell her I told you. Oh, it wasn't *real* magic. Simple tricks before an audience, sleight-of-hand; that sort of thing."

Thilly put her hands over her mouth for a second, then flung them out and exclaimed, "Oh, she'll be furious you told!" She then brought her hands back to her lips to stifle herself from shouting with laughter, and she doubled over, until Blinky fluttered up and away from her in irritation.

Beaumain snickered as well and pinched his nose to keep from laughing louder.

"I'm finding it quite hard to imagine that your dear, but let's be truthful, rather severe Mrs. Florence *ever* pulled a hare out of a hat or anything," he gasped.

"Well, I've gone and done it now, haven't I?" grumbled Birkswood, and the corner of his mouth twitched.

Thilly looked at him slyly.

"Do you mean it, Birkswood? Or were you just trying to distract us from…everything?" she asked him.

He drew himself up and looked most impressive, a tall raven among sparrows, and said serenely, "Two things may be true at once, Your Highness."

Beaumain nodded. "Then it is most appreciated," he told Birkswood, "no matter the intent."

He sighed, and Thilly considered the prince as he walked. He looked tired, his broad shoulders slumped a bit, and dark circles had formed under his eyes.

"It's getting to you, isn't it?" she asked him softly. "Not knowing."

Beaumain at first did not answer, but he did move closer to her, and looking down at her, he nodded.

"It is," he answered quietly. "I don't want to tell my people how worried I am. Can I trust you?"

"Of course!" said Thilly, and she reached out to touch his sleeve briefly, then withdrew her fingers quickly, as if they were butterflies fluttering away.

Beaumain said then, "Then I must tell someone. I am frightened of what is up there, beyond whatever this…protective spell is. What is menacing my lands, my parents, *my sister*, far to the south, right now as we march into this dank wilderness? It's whispering...do you hear it? The forest. *Whispering.*"

Thilly closed her eyes, and when she did, she could hear more and more the reverberations, murmurs, and indeed whispers of a multitude of voices rippling through the trees. She shuddered. She felt like an intruder, not only by being there, but by even attempting to listen.

"Don't close your eyes while you walk," Beaumain said, bending close to her ear. "You'll be disoriented quickly. I tried it and nearly fell."

He was right, and she began to sway and almost stumbled. She opened her eyes.

"Whose voices do you think those are?" she asked him in a murmur. "Can you tell what they are saying?"

Beaumain visibly shook. "I sometimes catch a word or two. I—I think I heard my own name, Thilly. And I heard the name Tantienne. Thilly, I do not think I can stay in this land much longer."

"You must," she hissed, and then she took hold of his hand and pulled him aside from the procession.

"No one is letting us out of here, I feel pretty sure of that. Not without aid," Thilly told Beaumain, looking up at his studious, serious face. "You are my friend...no matter what other expectations there were. And even though we...don't always get along."

"A bit of an understatement," agreed Beaumain.

"Still, I'd rather bicker with you than face what's up there," Thilly muttered, glancing up and feeling nauseous. She could no longer see the sky now, but she felt the presence of whatever those ill creatures were, as if the air pressure itself were being changed by them somehow. "Whatever my mother's people are doing...the Covenant, or whatever...it's working for now. And if you were to go outside this protection, I feel sure those things would head straight for you.

Although maybe…maybe not. Maybe with you, they would not interfere…"

And for a moment Thilly almost told him about his mother and her suspicions. But something stalled her, and while she very nearly continued anyway, a loud stream of whispers funneled into her ears from the Absinweald, and she turned her head to search where they had come from. She could only see darkness and the odd glowing things in her peripheral vision. Then she turned back to Beaumain, and he was gone.

Everyone was gone.

Thilly was alone.

*Githilien.*

*Githilien.*

*Githilien.*

She had heard this voice before. Then…singing. The exquisite voice, presumably of a woman, resonating through the air or the earth, she was not sure. It entered her mind and wound its way through her thoughts, past the surface, deeper into the layers of which she was both aware and unaware. She began to feel small, and younger, and scared, and sad.

*"Where is Mummy going, Father?"* little Thilly asked, deep in her memory. *"Why can't I go with Mummy?"*

No answer had been enough for Thilly, despite her asking many times…until one day she simply stopped. Her mother remained an old dream, a vision in a frame by her bed. And yet, the voice.

Thilly realized she had sunk to the forest floor and lay curled up on her side. She leaned up on an elbow and she could see a slow rising and falling of objects deep in the trees: the green and yellow orbs from earlier. Up and down, up and down, and they grew closer. She could not comprehend what they were. She was unsure how to feel about them. Should she be terrified? But part of her brain did not seem to operate properly. As if she had taken a potion for fever. Or as if she *had* a fever. Here they came, those glowing orbs. One green, one yellow, very bright, followed by others, and then she could discern figures within the lights. Some of them had two legs. Some had four. Some had hundreds.

She blinked, rubbed her eyes, and tried to stand to face them. She felt her scabbard against her thigh. She put her hand on her sword's hilt but did not draw it.

"That will have no power here," a whisper said to her from one of the approaching glowing beings.

The visage congealed into something resembling a person. Whether fae or human or another being, Thilly could not decide at first. And then that person grew clearer, still glowing, almost unbearable to look upon, so bright did they glow. It was a woman.

"Mother?" Thilly breathed, staring up.

The woman was brilliant, with light spinning and bursting all around her, her thin face and tall, slender form swaying, her long hair rippling beneath a hood covered in starbursts of green and gold and turquoise. The woman smiled.

"You are dreaming, daughter," said the lady. "You are dreaming in the elixir of the Absinweald."

"So…you're not my mother?" Thilly asked, feeling again very young and very small.

"I am Woadlynn," said the woman softly.

Thilly's eyes began to sting, and her throat ached. She hiccupped, trying to stifle a sob.

"Mother," she said.

The woman stood just beyond Thilly's reach, though the girl tried to approach her several times.

"I was your mother, yes," said the lady. "But you are your own person now, and do not need a parent."

Thilly shook the tears from her eyes.

"No," she said emphatically. "No! I do need you. And Father. Why did you leave me?"

The woman stood, her face placid, but Thilly could see what she interpreted as kindness in her eyes. And maybe…sadness? Or something else.

"I am not the person I was when I bore you, Githilien," said Woadlynn's image.

For now, Thilly realized she could never touch the lady, because all she beheld was an image, and not a woman in the flesh.

"An enchantment, a vision," said Thilly, reaching out to the phantom Woadlynn.

"A projection, darling," said the woman. Then, "I fear your party does not fare so well as you do, here in the deep. You are stronger than they. Except for Birkswood. You must help guide your people to the Veiled Isles. I will answer your questions there. Now, sleep a while longer, dear daughter. And awaken to your path ahead."

Thilly fought the urge to sleep, but she felt heavy and warm, as if covered by a soft blanket, and the light of her mother's image began to diminish until the orbs retreated into the darkness of the forest. The Absinweald's whispers dulled, and Thilly slept.

# CHAPTER 20

## *INTO THE QUIET DEEP*

Thilly jolted. She felt warm hands upon her forehead, and through blurred vision, she beheld a round, rosy face. It resolved into an expression of concern ringed by brown curls and topped with a scarlet hat.

"Your Highness!" gasped Hana, and then the maid hissed, "Not now, Blinky!"

For Blinky pulled at Thilly's hair and said shrilly, "Up! Up! Up!"

Thilly sat up and regretted the act instantly, for everything wavered for her. She felt deeply unpleasant and then leaned over and vomited on the ground. That made her feel somewhat better, but her head throbbed. She let Hana cluck and daub her mouth with a kerchief. Then she looked around her.

Some of the footmen were chatting nervously, their weapons drawn.

"Did you see it? The legs! The legs!" cried one.

"I'll bloody kill it if I see it again," hissed another.

Someone else wailed up ahead, and Thilly tried to stand to look, but the ground took hold of her again, for she felt heavy and dull.

"Who is that?" cried Thilly, holding her aching head. "What's happened?"

Hana winced, as though unsure what to say and fearing reprisal.

"Milady," she began, and then she bit her lip and pulled at her hat.

"Go on, dear Hana, it's all right," said Thilly thickly, feeling anything *but* all right. "Tell me."

"Well—well," stammered Hana, "that's just it, Your Highness. We don't know what happened. There were lights in the forest and then…people screamed, fainted, and went mad! Gloria and Whemhail ran off into the trees and haven't come back."

The girl trembled and Thilly, despite feeling wretched, pressed her hand on Hana's arm and locked eyes with her.

"It's all right," Thilly said. "We will find everyone."

"I don't like it here," Hana whispered, as if ashamed to admit it openly. "It's not natural."

A chorus of whispers funneled out of the woods, and Thilly felt a cold burst of air waft down her neck. She shivered, and clasped Hana's hand.

"I think it's natural," she said to her maid, "but it's not nature like we're used to in Vickery. It's…stranger. But it's very real."

"There is real," a booming baritone rang out in the air, and she looked up to see Birkswood's hawkish nose leading to his hooded eyes, "and there is imaginary. Absinweald seems to blend the two, but that is its whole trick. Nothing we see here is imaginary. It is simply not the 'real' that is more familiar to you, Your Highness, and good Hana."

Ki'roth approached them and nodded, sending the long cables of hair swaying, and added, "You choose what you wear, to an extent," and they nodded to Hana, staring at the girl's Vickery cap, "and so Absinweald chooses what it wears. Its denizens cloak themselves how they see fit, in the way they choose based upon many things. Some of these things even we fae do not comprehend, nor do we try, for what would be the point? Passage through is all that we seek, and if wisdom can be gained by what besets or allows us to proceed, then we benefit no matter how difficult the trial."

Hana shook her head. "I don't know anythin' about any of this," she remarked. "All's I know is the whispers give me a frighten, and that the cold air makes me think there's surely a ghost about!"

Beaumain turned to Ki'roth and asked, his eyebrows wriggling, "You're not admitting there *are* ghosts here, are you? Among the…denizens?"

Ki'roth tilted their head and smirked. "Again, Absinweald's creatures choose their appearance. Who is to say what form that is, and that it should fit your princely education?"

"I'm a man of research and facts," Beaumain declared, standing straight and tall, "not stories and myth."

Thilly felt torn. She was book-smart, but the thought of a realm of upended logic appealed to her. She was not certain why, for she did actually love learning about the laws of nature. It just seemed to her that they did not apply in Absinweald.

"It is a wide world, among many worlds," Ki'roth murmured, looking up, "and we do not know how they all work, nor do we know fully how this one does. Respecting the spirits of the forest requires some suspension of what your conventions and your gods might approve of."

*Now that I do like, very much*, thought Thilly.

"Enough arguing," she said to them.

"We aren't arguing," Beaumain said crisply.

"Now you are," Thilly pointed out, and she grinned at him and walked past him.

"We should keep going," she called, marching straight for Evgrent and his mare.

Birkswood wasted no time and loped on his long legs to catch up with her, not only because she was technically the outranking royal among them, but also because he was not certain of her path to Evgrent, in any sense of the word. Thilly did not see the intention in Birkswood, but she stubbornly followed Evgrent, as if he were some sort of anchor in this strange forest.

In many ways, he was. She had been visited by a projection of her mother, and it differed more from her ancient memory of the woman than Thilly had cared to admit. She did not want to engage Beaumain, for the moment, because she both dreaded his eventually finding out *something* about Queen Maulielle, and because she began to question her own experiences with the queen.

*That's crazy*, she thought. *I saw what I saw.*

To go from Beaumain's unexpectedly hateful and monstrous mother to the strangeness of her own mother in the span of not very many days set Thilly on edge. With each step toward Evgrent, she grew angrier, for somehow anger made her feel safe and strong when she was out of her depth now, with her footsteps set upon a path of unknowns.

Mrs. Florence ceded her ride at the sight of Thilly, tapping on Evgrent's shoulder and saying a crisp "Thank you" to the man before attempting to climb down off Umbra. Evgrent hopped down to help her, and Thilly stared up at the woman with her hands on her hips.

"Mrs. Florence!" cried Thilly. "You should stay on Umbra!"

"No, Your Highness," said Mrs. Florence, her jaw set, "I should not. Let someone else take the seat for a bit. Mrs. Dockmire, perhaps." And she waved back toward the contingent of still-befuddled footmen and maids. Thilly's eyes settled on Mrs. Dockmire, a rail-thin, severe woman with a long neck, dour expression, and tightly pulled steel-grey bun secured under a scarlet Vickery hat. Thilly shuddered and glanced at Evgrent.

He looked away from her, tactfully checking Umbra's bridle and offering the mare something from his pocket.

"Mrs. Dockmire, then," agreed Thilly, her lips twitching. "Will you please ask her, Mrs. Florence?"

"Of course, Your Highness," said Mrs. Florence, glancing between Thilly and Evgrent, her lips turning down just a bit into a frown.

So it was settled, but Thilly had little time to think about Mrs. Dockmire's opinion of things, and despite the woman's bone-tingling glare upon being asked by Mrs. Florence, the maid had no further reaction, and marched with a proud stance toward Thilly and Evgrent.

"I will ride alongsi—" Thilly began.

The earth shook. A small tremor, but noticeable. Umbra's ears lay back, and with a burst of feathers, Blinky descended upon Thilly's shoulder. She held the bird against her chest, its head just under her chin, and stroked its back.

"Shaky-shaky," croaked the parrot.

Then a quite large earthquake set the trees themselves trembling and swaying. Umbra neighed and Blinky squawked and twitched, and then ultimately crawled under Thilly's still-loose mane of tremendously frizzy hair. The missing maid and footman, Gloria and Whemhail, tumbled out of the forest, wild-eyed and disheveled, their pupils dilated as if they were drugged. Thilly breathed a little sigh of relief at their return.

*Like shaking apples from a tree*, she thought.

"That was a bad one," Beaumain said, looking nauseous.

# THE VALE OF SEVEN DRAGONS

Ki'roth then stepped up to them and said, "That…isn't so typical here. Not like in the northeast."

"I thought we'd got away from strange earthquakes," Thilly remarked.

"We may have more yet," said Birkswood grimly.

"Why here, though?" Beaumain asked him. "This region isn't known for seismic activity."

"So," said Thilly, "Ki'roth seems in agreement, which tells me that perhaps there's something else going on."

"Do we not have the capacity to agree on this?" Beaumain asked her pointedly.

"You don't seem to agree with anyone, generally," said Thilly, "but rather you insist on being the authority in all things."

Beaumain twitched and narrowed his eyes. "I should be the authority," he declared, "as I'm a future king."

"Bully for you, then," muttered Thilly, her anger from earlier foaming within her to help quell her anxiety.

Birkswood cut through the awkward moment by saying to the prince, "You are right in one regard, Your Highness, in terms of some aspects of seismic activity. But not all."

"I don't understand," said Beaumain. "This simply isn't the kind of area that should have such large earthquakes. Nothing would be built for that. I worry for the people of this land."

"The people of this land," said Ki'roth suddenly, with an undercurrent of something Thilly could not decide on. *Bitterness?* she wondered. "Begging your pardon, Your Highness, but I am one of the people of this land. We fae are as important here as anyone in your family in the bounds of Catellaith."

The prince looked stunned. "I didn't mean to imply otherwise," he said quickly.

One of the other fae, Val'dreth, stepped up beside Beaumain, towering over him, and the bronze and gold striped spikes of hair on their chiseled head extended down toward the prince like knives.

"To your kind, we will always be *other*," they hissed. "You do not represent us."

Thilly said nervously, "Please, let's not get into this here, in these…" and she flung her arms wide, unsure how to express the scale, "whispering lands, lands of my mother's chosen people. Which includes everyone, fae or human or fairy. We must get to the Veiled Isles, and bickering won't help us."

"In that case," said Beaumain, his face twitching and his brow furrowed, "why must you bicker all the time?"

"Oh, well," said Thilly, flushing, "I'm not capable of resisting a good argument with you or Evgrent, but you both deserve it, so…"

And Val'dreth and Ki'roth roared with laughter at that. Val'dreth bowed to Thilly.

"Your mother's spirit flickers in you, Princess Githilien," said Val'dreth.

Thilly blushed again. "Well then. Let's see what she's like in person, shall we? Evgrent! Onward we go, quakes or otherwise."

The quakes ebbed into aftershocks, and the way grew steeper and darker, and the ceiling of great black boughs seemed entwined over them like the joined hands of a great creature. Yet from time to time, Thilly could hear distant booms, and the hair on her neck rose. Blinky quavered and clucked and squawked at first, but eventually settled, as did the entire party. For the feeling was ominous. As the forest grew darker, Thilly thought it might rain, but all that fell was a fine mist, as if it were passed through a filter, and the cap of both the protective shield of the Covenant and the forest canopy prevented any hard rain.

*A filter my mother made.*

No one spoke for some time. Thilly felt her temper ebb, ultimately, and without her coping mechanism and any banter with either the prince or Evgrent, she felt her anxiety twist in her like a parasitic creature in her gut. She walked steadily alongside Hana for some time, and then lanterns were lit, and Hana carried one to help light Thilly's way. Thilly looked at her in surprise, for the maid's cheeks shone from more than the fine mist.

"Hana," she said softly. "Are you all right?"

Hana jumped, and then daubed her eyes with her sleeve.

"I'm—I'm fine, milady. Your Highness. Just the rain, that's all," said the girl, avoiding eye contact.

Thilly moved closer to her.

"You feel it, don't you," she murmured, glancing up at the darkness. "Those things up there. Trying to get in."

Hana trembled, her eyes pooling with tears.

"This isn't what you signed up to do," Thilly said sadly, touching Hana's arm. "I'm sorry. I would never have asked you, had I known."

At that, Hana drew herself up and took a deep breath.

"No, milady," she declared, "I would have signed up regardless. I don't know what's up there and I don't understand it, and it may have us all yet. But my duty is to you. I only wish I weren't such a coward."

Thilly stopped, mouth agape, and said, "Hana, you are no coward. You are brave and strong, and you've never once shirked your duty. Here you are in the middle of this—this strange, dreamlike place, and you've not turned back once. You're helping me just by being here! But if ever you don't want to stay, you are welcome to leave for safer grounds."

Hana half-smiled and said, "Well, Your Highness, may I ask where those might be?"

Thilly bit her lip. "I only wish I knew. But for now, we are still protected from what's above."

"Maybe," said Hana, sounding quite as though she didn't believe Thilly, "but are we protected from what's in the forest? Everyone acted like they'd tasted Deep Vale mushrooms before...look at the lads back there, still drooling like teething puppies."

Thilly laughed out loud, startling the sleeping Blinky. She settled the bird with some pats and walked on. She felt self-conscious then, as if the forest resented her laughs, for the whispers began again. She looked for any sign of her mother's strange appearance or the beings who had accompanied her. She did not see them. She was glad, especially, not to see the creatures with myriad legs. But she felt as though her contingent had entered a place quite opposed to all light and sound, the heart of Absinweald, and through it the artery of strange water rushed, sending up its own mist through the dense trees. She felt at every second that eyes gazed down upon her from those trees, or up at her from stones, and she drew closer to Hana and began to shiver more herself.

By and by the party stopped and broke their fast, and Thilly fed Blinky some crumbs. Evgrent and Umbra stood away from the group, and Thilly approached them. The man scowled as she walked toward him.

"What did I do to deserve that look, Sir Evgrent?" she asked.

"Do not ever call me 'sir,'" he hissed.

"You're in a foul mood," Thilly noted with a frown of her own.

Turning away from her, Evgrent ran his hands across Umbra's face.

"This place does not want us here," he said quietly.

"So you feel it too," she whispered. "Do you...do you feel what's above us?"

"How could I not? Umbra and I both do. Mrs. Dockmire is lucky Umbra didn't bolt a thousand times."

"What do you think the booms were? Thunder?" she asked.

"No," Evgrent said. "Not…not thunder from a storm." He then paused, and in the swaying light of the lantern he held, he looked thoughtful. "Do you remember…well, maybe you never heard them. There were tales we were told as children, about the dragons. I told them to my brother when he was small." Thilly took a long, slow breath and exhaled, feeling her throat tighten. "Antares and Nistraan, cracking the sky in their flight, that sort of thing."

"I hadn't heard those, no," said Thilly, and despite her sadness of thinking of Vyrent, she grew immensely curious. "What did they say?"

Evgrent's eyes glazed a bit as he said quietly, "The winds rose in the heart of the Vale, in great coils that tore up the earth, and the two dragons met in the sky and chased each other, faster and faster, splitting the sky. The sound of it traveled across the Vale through all the realm, and the force of it ripped the clouds apart. Antares and Nistraan flew to the moon and then back down again, so the stories told, and met the other five dragons then, fighting for the champion. Antares won, of course."

Birkswood strolled up and said, "Antares won, indeed. But the price was a devastated Vale."

By now their group had crowded around Evgrent and Thilly, their lanterns bobbing like a mass of flame that set the forest shimmering, but that did not stop the storytelling. Now the fae joined in.

Val'dreth told them, "The great flood of Valetheant that formed the long-gone inland sea was said to have been caused by the dragons' pummeling back to earth."

"I've heard that tale," Evgrent remarked, "but I wonder about it."

Prince Beaumain chimed in. "I don't think the dragons caused that great valley's formation. I think it was a meteor."

"Well," said Birkswood in his rich, deep voice, "certainly there was a meteor; that is, of course, the rambunctious dragon's name of the land of Roanmont of old."

"Meteor never dwelt in Valetheant, though," said Thilly. "That was Jadesilver's home."

They fell to talking of dragon lore, and pondering the strange, beautiful, yet sinister dragon Antimon of the far northeast in Osthadon. Sunder, the vicious red and black dragon of former land of Dantheant, garnered the most interest among the footmen.

"She'd win in any fight," one enthused. "Temper and what."

"Ah," said Birkswood, "yet the old Maelwyrm fought valiantly, and he was never one to muster up a temper."

Thilly and Hana grinned at each other, and Thilly was glad to see the maid smile.

They decided to stay there for the night, for the fae warned the going would be much steeper the next day, before the descent to the sea. Thilly lay with Blinky nuzzled up against her, listening to many tall tales of the seven dragons, and felt herself grow heavy. She then settled into uneasy sleep. For after the dragon stories ebbed and the fires popped and crackled down to embers, the whispers returned, swirling all around Thilly, settling in with her, and ricocheting in her mind like echoes, from what or when she did not know. But her dreams turned to Maelwyrm, a dragon slow and old and not prone to anger, and in her dreams, she was lying upon his back between weathered and scarred spines, staring up at a cloudless sky, and rising and falling as the great beast breathed.

# CHAPTER 21

## *THE COLUMN*

Dawn in Absinweald did not make its presence known by the advent of daylight, but rather more by the softening of darkness. The forest shifted into daytime in the form of song: mournful coos from what Thilly surmised were doves, crescendo trills of some peculiar thrush, and the sudden cacophony of cicadas, hardy in the moist microclimates among the trees. Still the forest roof felt stifling, and the air bore the peculiar scent Thilly had noticed in their first entry to the land of Aceltia. It became more noticeable now. She felt glad, at least, that the whispers had stilled, or perhaps the untold millions of cicadas drowned them out. Whatever the case, the constant background noise of myriad insects calmed her, and for the first time in many days, she felt energized and determined, and ready to see her mother.

The ground trembled from time to time, but not as striking as the one great quake from the day prior. The members of the company who had succumbed to the strange visions of the forest beings

# THE VALE OF SEVEN DRAGONS

looked dreary and sagging from fatigue, and Thilly felt sorry for them. She hung back a bit and walked alongside Hana once more as Umbra bore Evgrent and a footman with a sprained ankle. Thilly recognized him as Whemhail, the young man who had disappeared during everyone's hallucinogenic forest visitations. He looked a tad sheepish as his mates goaded him on with various saucy epithets. She suspected Evgrent loathed this arrangement.

Blinky left Thilly's shoulder to explore the upper reaches of the forest, and she spied the parrot munching on pine nuts, flicking from tree to tree, then sailing over Umbra and ultimately landing on her pommel again. Thilly could see that Blinky drew some of Umbra's mane through its beak and she grinned. Then she sighed, for her anxiety would not abate.

"Mrs. Florence," she called, watching the dirt-stained dark skirt hemline of the older woman sway ahead of her as she strode beside the towering Birkswood. Mrs. Florence turned and waited for Thilly and Hana, and she dipped her head at the princess. Thilly twisted her hair with her hands and Mrs. Florence raised her eyebrows at her. "It's just…I've been thinking. Should I be…a certain way when I meet Woadlynn—I mean, my mother—because it's been so long, and I don't want to mess this up."

"You were visited by her, were you not?" asked Mrs. Florence, her green eyes burrowing into Thilly's hazel ones.

"Yes, of course," said Thilly, and her mouth went dry. "It's just that…that's all it was, was a vision. I don't know, or don't remember anyway, what she was *really* like, and I don't want…I just," and she sighed, unable to say what she meant, for such a swirl of emotion roiled in her that she felt dizzy.

Mrs. Florence nodded. "You're worried you won't know her, won't bond with her, that sort of thing," said the lady astutely.

Thilly nodded and her shoulders relaxed. "Basically, yes."

Mrs. Florence smiled and shook her head. "There's no need for that, Your Ladyship! Priestess Woadlynn is your mother. That bond will never break."

"But she left," Thilly blurted out, and then she went cold, ashamed.

Hana glanced at Mrs. Florence, so said to the maid, "Go on, Hana, we'll catch up." The girl nodded and tactfully walked out of hearing range.

Mrs. Florence placed her hand on Thilly's shoulder and said, "Dear child, your mother has always loved you. The reasons she abdicated had nothing to do with you beyond wanting you to be safe and making sure the Realm was secure for as long as she could. I daresay she must be just as worried about what you might think of her, and maybe more. Don't you think? You'll find common ground, I know that. She was a willful young woman, just like you in so many ways."

"So many people say I've got my mother in me," mused Thilly thoughtfully.

Mrs. Florence smirked. "Aye, you do, Princess. And there's that bull-headed nature of your father, some of his bookishness, but at the end of it, Githilien, you are your own person. Totally unique. I know your mother will be so happy to have you back in her arms."

Thilly's eyes stung. She could not speak, but she hugged Mrs. Florence so fiercely that the woman gave a little yelp, and then brushed herself off and returned to her place by Birkswood, who, if he had heard any of their conversation, feigned indifference.

Beaumain had watched Thilly and decided to walk beside her now, and she did not see the look in his eyes, but she could feel his gaze on her. She felt her cheeks go hot.

"Thilly," he said softly. She still did not look at him. "No matter what happens, I just want you to know, I'm glad to be here."

She looked at him then and nodded and said, "Likewise."

"But could you," Beaumain began, and he sighed and rubbed his head. "Could you tell me what's bothering you about my mother?"

Thilly bristled and tried to cover the fact she had, but he saw. "I—I don't think I sh—"

A great gust of wind funneled suddenly from above them, and a hideous scraping sound rang out from the tree canopy. Thilly heard Umbra scream, and she reared on her legs, and Evgrent set her running off just as a great black shape like a finger stretched down to the ground among the party. It touched the earth and connected and made sickening sucking noises, and as Thilly looked up, she beheld a bizarre sight; the finger pulsating through what looked like a hole in the sky.

"Gods," she whispered. "They've broken the shield."

Beaumain looked at her and said, "Run!"

Thilly wasted no second, tugging at Hana and urging her to flee, and so they ran full bore, with everyone scattering into the woods—but some of them did not make it far. The black, quivering column sent out whipping tendrils and snatched at the party, and Thilly looked over her shoulder to see one of the footmen ensnared by the thing, and then she screamed: he gurgled and moaned and was burst into pieces, blood spraying everywhere, and she could hear a sort of tapping, laughing sound among the sucking. The column kicked up dirt, for it attempted to burrow into the earth while seizing anyone close by. Thilly did not see Mrs. Florence, Birkswood, or Evgrent and Umbra.

She ran into the depths of the forest and then something flew into her face and she shrieked, and heard the familiar shrill voice of Blinky, who screamed, "Run! Run! Run!" and the bird flew off away from the melee. Beaumain and Hana sprinted alongside her, Hana gasping and crying but managing, Beaumain determined, keeping a watchful eye ahead, behind, and on Thilly.

"Where the fuck are we going?" Thilly hissed at him.

"As far from that thing as we can!" gasped Beaumain.

"We can't run forever," she wheezed, seeing Hana doubling over and stopping, her face scarlet, sweat streaming down her cheeks.

Hana then sank to her knees and vomited and wept. Thilly turned sharply behind her, and she could not see the black shape extending from the sky, but she could hear it churning and squelching and she heard more screams. She knelt to help Hana, and Beaumain approached them both, his eyes huge, the veins in his neck pumping.

"F-fire," Thilly gasped, looking up at him. "We need fire."

He shook his head. "But not a regular fire. Pitch. How do we get pitch?"

"You don't," a booming voice said, and Thilly cried out. It was Birkswood.

"Birkswood," she choked, "gods..." and she found he was hunched over and breathing heavily, for he had carried Mrs. Florence on his back and run. She slid off and yanked her skirts down, her hair flying out, hat gone, and her cheeks burnished from embarrassment.

"Stay here," Birkswood told Mrs. Florence. "I'm going back to see who else I can carry."

"Not alone, you aren't!" cried Beaumain.

"No, Your Highness," said Birkswood sharply. "The heirs to Catellaith and Vickery need to survive. Let me do my task of serving you both."

"No," said Thilly. "Not without help."

The snapping of boughs startled them, and Blinky called out from a high branch, "Ki'roth!"

Thilly felt her mouth go slack as she looked up and beheld Ki'roth hovering in the air above them, slowly descending, their eyes gone pale green-yellow. Behind them, the other three fae also lowered from the air.

"How—how are you doing this?" Thilly cried.

"Never mind, Your Highness," said Ki'roth. "We have milked the pines for pitch. Stay here and we will fight." Ki'roth held up a bow with an arrow wrapped in gauze and soaked in black, sticky liquid, and without touching the ground, the four fae soared off.

"Stay here," Thilly said to Hana, and she began to run.

"Thilly!" Beaumain yelled. "Godsdammit!" and he ran after her, with Birkswood swearing and telling Mrs. Florence and Hana to stay put.

Thilly felt she had lost control of herself, with one exception. She held her sword at her side and ran full bore, clinging to it, her eyes upon the sky, seeing the great rending of clouds and trees, as the horrible column extended like a thin tornado of slithering, shimmering blackness, a rope of palpable evil stretching who knew how high into the atmosphere above Aceltia and perhaps the earth itself. Her mother's Covenant had failed. *Would the rest of the sky fall as well?* she wondered. She needed to know, and she could not explain why she did, but she had to see: what was this thing, what was it doing to her people, and what was it doing *here*? She ran hard and then she struck something with such force that she dropped instantly in shock, fell on her back, and lay still, unable to move and barely able to breathe.

# CHAPTER 22

## *WHISPERS*

"Thilly! Thilleeeeee!" Beaumain's voice rang urgently through the air, but she could only hear muffled sounds as she stared up at the sky, swirling, rippling above the dark pines and firs of Absinweald. She could see the rent in the sky, the vortex or umbilicus or whatever the foul dark thing was that had ruptured the dome her mother's Covenant had built. She stared at it stupidly, imagining it like a drain, only emptying somewhere in the sky, and then her thoughts confused her. But she felt her body fight and she breathed again. She tried to get up.

*"NO,"* said a voice, familiar but hard. *"You are not ready, Githilien."*

"Ma-ma-ma—" Thilly tried to say, the words dying on her lips.

She could see a shape moving, but nothing solid stood there. The air around her looked like the surface of water trembling in a soft breeze, and she could see through the effect to the forest, and she could also see the shapes of the four fae move through that surface effortlessly.

She strained and finally managed to sit up on one elbow. She watched, exhausted yet mesmerized, as Ki'roth lit the end of his pitch-wrapped arrow and sent it flaming skyward toward the great doom-finger. In response, one if its stalks shot out from the amorphous column, but the arrow rang true and burst into flame upon that stalk, and it recoiled with a shrill scream back to its source. Ki'roth glided back to the earth and Thilly could see their face was coated with sweat.

"We can only go so high," Ki'roth gasped. "And we don't have the energy to stay up for long. I don't think we can reach the tear in the dome. But we can distract that thing. Give your people a chance to flee until the Covenant can repair the fissure."

As one fae rose and fired arrows, another descended to rest. Thilly watched with a pang and fear for her people and for the fae, and she could see an arc of body parts spinning off the heinous, undulating abomination penetrating the land.

"Mother!" she cried. "Can't you do something to help?" She stood, reeling, and almost swooned, and the black coil made her sick to look upon. As she looked, she could almost see eyes in it, eyes in the sky, dark violet eyes: the eyes of Queen Maulielle. She looked behind her and found Beaumain staring up, transfixed, his face blank, his lips partly open.

"Beaumain!" she shouted. She moved with aching slowness toward him, and he seemed not to hear or see her. "Oh, gods!" she wailed. "Don't look at it, Beaumain!"

He walked forward as if pulled, away from her, and she tried to stand in his way, but he pushed ahead unseeing. She felt a chill sweep through her.

*It's his mother. She's going to lure him to that thing and tear him apart!*

"No! No!" she shouted, pulling at Beaumain, but he was beyond her reach, and she hit the wall again, an invisible barrier that blocked her proceeding toward that dark presence. "Mother!" she screamed. "Let me pass! Let me stop him!"

She beat at the air in front of her, and it held as if made of warped glass. A flash of anger and horror surged through her, and she felt helpless, for the prince had picked up his pace. The thing in the sky had not thrown a stalk out to him; it was busy lashing at the fae and reacting to their flaming arrows. But it did not need to, for Beaumain walked hellbent toward it.

Hana reached her at last, and begged, "Please, milady, please! Get back from here. There's nothin' you can do!"

"Hana," croaked Thilly, "please get back to safety. I won't lose you too! That's an order!"

Hana shook her head. "I'm going nowhere away from you, Princess."

Thilly watched the prince continue his strange, stilted walk toward the column of malice, and she wept openly.

"Mother, do something," she sobbed.

Almost as if in response, a spiraling tendril shot forth, and one of the fae missed it with their arrow, and it coursed its way toward Thilly. Hana shrieked. Thilly turned to see it.

But strong arms seized her and pulled her away. A flash of metal swung in the air and the stalk fell to the ground, writhing. It was Evgrent with his sword.

"Get the fuck out of here!" he shouted at Thilly, his eyes cold and his teeth bared. He whirled around and Thilly watched in horror as the piece of the creature—if it could be called thus—coiled up like a snake and leapt at Evgrent. He whipped his sword and cut it again.

To his right, Ki'roth descended and lit the end of one of his arrows and stabbed at the thing. It hissed and recoiled and withered. They spent several minutes cutting and burning the pieces of the stalk, while the other three fae kept aiming arrows. A tremendous *clap* rang in the air, and Thilly looked up to see the sky sealed, and the column cut, and falling...falling toward them all.

Evgrent seized both Thilly and Hana around their waists and ran.

"Beaumain!" screamed Thilly, but Evgrent held her fast.

She could no longer see the prince.

"Let me go!" she shouted at Evgrent. "Damn you! We're going to lose him!"

Evgrent gritted his teeth and rushed the two young women back into the depths of the forest, and he let Hana go, and she bent over and gasped for breath. He did not release Thilly.

"No, Thilly," said Evgrent firmly. He held her tightly as she fought and shrieked.

"Will you stop!" he hissed. "We need to stay hidden."

"But Beaumain," she wailed.

"Forget about him for now. We'll hope the fae can fight off that thing. I need you to stay here, *please*."

Thilly did not want to listen to him, but she knew he was right. His hair swung forward in his grey eyes, and he held her face in his hands and looked into her hazel eyes.

"I am sworn to protect you, Githilien of Vickery," Evgrent told her. "I need to know I can trust you. We can't help the prince if you risk your own life. Will you stay here? In memory of my brother, if for no other reason? I beg you."

Thilly slowed her breath and released her clenched fists. Her tears flowed freely.

"Please help him," she whispered, gazing up at him.

"I will do what I can," said the man to her, and he looked down at her side. "Where's your sword?"

Thilly gasped and looked down. "I must have dropped it when I hit that—barrier or whatever it was."

"Godsdammit," muttered Evgrent, and he let Thilly go and rubbed his face. "I'll find it and see what's going on. And you," he turned to Hana, "must make sure the princess does not leave this spot until I'm back. Swear to me, girl."

Hana, bedraggled and rosy-cheeked and hat long gone, nodded. "I will not leave her," she said. "I swear it."

Evgrent nodded and turned back to Thilly.

"Wait for me," he said.

She breathed in deeply and exhaled. "I will," she promised.

And he was off into the forest, off toward the faint light ahead in the clearing where the hellish creature wreaked whatever havoc it would. Thilly watched him until he was out of sight, and she turned to Hana, who looked shellshocked.

Thilly approached her and put her arm around the girl. They sank then to the forest floor by an immense tree, their backs against it, and stared up into the interlocking boughs of green-black fir and pine and other unnamable trees and said nothing for a moment. But the whispers returned to fill the void.

"Gods," moaned Hana. "Not again."

Thilly felt much the same, and it was nearly unbearable to hear disembodied voices she could not understand, when she only wanted to hear the voice of one person just then: Beaumain. She felt tiny and hopeless and small, like a little girl again, away from her mother in a great vaulted place, and yet she had not been closer to her mother than she was just then in many years. The words *"You're not ready"* rang in her mind even as other whispers floated around her.

And then, quite suddenly, she understood some of them. She sat up, her arms around her knees, and listened. The two girls were deep enough in the woods that she could hear muffled shouts, but nothing else of whatever battle lay ahead that Evgrent had charged into. She did not see anyone else of their party, and worried for Mrs. Florence and Birkswood. But she heard a name in those whispers that she recognized.

*Antimon.*

And another.

*Meteor.*

"Do you hear that, Hana?" she asked quietly.

"All I hear's those damned whispers," said the girl, and then she clapped her hand over her mouth. "I'm so sorry, Your Highness! That was rude and crass and—"

Thilly managed a smirk and replied, "Not to me. Speak plainly around me always, if you wish, Hana, because that's how I prefer it." Hana still looked mortified, so Thilly said, "I heard two names."

"What names?" Hana asked, owl eyed.

"Antimon and Meteor."

Hana blinked. "What, like the dragon myths?"

Thilly nodded. She listened again.

*Jadesilver.*

Her eyebrow perked up.

*Sunder.*

She nodded.

*Nistraan.*

She waited…

*Antares.*

The dragon of Vickery, her home.

She listened again, and the names repeated, along with other names she did not recognize, or perhaps they were nonsense, for she did not recognize the speech. But then she heard something that sent a shock through her.

*All seven. You need all seven.*

It was as clear as if someone had spoken next to her, but then it became almost an echo of itself. *Seven-seven-seven. All seven-seven-seven.*

~ 200 ~

She stood abruptly then.

"Who are you?" she called out. "Who are you that tells a princess of Vickery what I need? Are you Absinweald itself, or are you of the Covenant? Who? Speak plainly to me!"

The whispers trailed off as if going around a curve, and only the wind answered Thilly, moaning and creaking among the treetops. She looked back at Hana, who stood now also, her face in awe of Thilly, and the princess tilted her head at her.

"What is it?" she asked Hana.

"You, Your Highness," said Hana, eyes wide. "You scared them off!"

Thilly snorted. "I did no such thing."

"I saw it!" exclaimed Hana. "Well…heard it, anyway. You are powerful."

Thilly shook her head. "I'm only a girl. We're just girls, up against something terrible."

Hana's lips twitched at the corners. "You're no girl, Your Highness. You are the Princess Githilien of Vickery, and one day you will be queen."

Thilly turned away from the girl's admiration and pressed her hands to her forehead.

"I will be no queen," she whispered into the depths of the forest. "But I want my friend to live and be king one day."

So she stood and let the darkness of the forest envelop her, and felt the ground tremble again, and she tried her best to wait patiently for what news, she did not know, and she felt she could never be ready to know, either.

# CHAPTER 23

## *HEAVY IS THE HEAD*

A sharp snort broke the strange forest sounds, and Thilly jumped and looked at Hana, who stepped quietly over to her. The two young women hid behind the great tree and peered all around them. Thilly could hear something shuffling, and then another snort. She peered from behind the tree and cried out in surprise: it was Umbra, huffing into Thilly's face, and the mare tossed her head as if to say, *Were you expecting someone else?*

"Oh, Umbra, thank the gods," breathed Thilly, throwing her arms around the mare. She checked the pommel and looked above them all. "But where is Blinky?"

Umbra nudged her mahogany face against Thilly's head, and she looked at the horse in confusion.

"What is it, Umbra?"

Umbra shook her head and then knelt to the ground.

"Oh!" said Thilly. "You're wanting us to climb on. But what then? Evgrent told us we should stay here."

# THE VALE OF SEVEN DRAGONS

Umbra let out a sly whickering sound, and Thilly gave her a pointed look.

"Are you suggesting we disobey?" she asked the mare. She glanced at Hana, whose lip curved in in a lopsided grin.

"I think she does, milady," Hana agreed.

"Well," Thilly observed, stroking the rich red-brown face of Umbra, "there's more to you than meets the eye, I suppose. Hana, let's get on." So they clambered onto the saddle, and the horse rose again and then turned to face a path opposite the one they had arrived by.

"Oh, let's not go that way," Thilly objected. "I don't want to go far, or Evgrent will be angry at all three of us."

"Your Highness," said Hana suddenly, "when has that ever stopped you before?"

Thilly gave a rueful half-laugh. "You've got me figured out, I think, Hana. So…where to, then, Umbra? I'll let you walk us a bit, but we should be back before long, all right?" Umbra tossed her mane in response.

The horse carried the two girls through a dense section of the forest, full of phosphorescent lichen and fungi, and glowworms traversing the immense old-growth trunks of huge trees. Epiphytic orchids wound their way around trunks reaching so high that it hurt Thilly's neck to try to see the treetops. And then, by and by, Umbra led them into a segment of Absinweald that grew lighter and lighter, and as it did so, Thilly felt herself start to relax a tiny bit. She had not realized how much she craved proper daylight until then…at least one without a monster descending from the sky.

A clearing appeared ahead, and Umbra walked slowly toward it. Thilly instantly found why the horse had slowed: there was a sheer drop, where the plateau Absinweald stretched across fell sharply in an escarpment.

"Look at that!" gasped Thilly, gazing out a vivid green expanse of a great valley, with a silver thread of a river twisting among both evergreen and deciduous trees, with some still bearing autumnal gold or brown leaves. Beyond the valley a strangely patterned fog stretched like fingers to a grey smudge, and Thilly squinted to try to see what lay in that smudge.

"Islands!" said Hana.

"What?" Thilly said incredulously. "I don't see any islands. Just a grey streak...the Stellar Sea, I presume?"

"Yes," agreed Hana, "but there are several islands out there. Can't you see them?"

Thilly strained her eyes, rubbed them, and looked again. *Maybe I've been reading so many books that I don't know how to focus long distance anymore,* she mused. She could see no islands.

"But Hana," Thilly remarked, "they're *Veiled* Isles. Nobody can see them, so the stories go."

Hana shrugged. "I don't know what to tell you, milady, but I can see them, all right. And the fog looks like it's moving, like it's—"

"Thilly!" a voice cried out, and she turned swiftly. Mrs. Florence came running at her, Birkswood alongside.

"Thank the gods you're all right," Birkswood said, and he and Mrs. Florence exchanged relieved glances.

"Gods!" cried Thilly, "What's happened to you both? Are you all right?"

She slid off Umbra's back and ran to the pair. They were lashed with dried blood on their clothing and with splatters of blood on their faces. Mrs. Florence's skirt was torn in parts, revealing a bit of her layers of petticoats, and not for the first time, Thilly questioned the necessity for such things that she also had to wear, but secretly rarely did, if she could get away with it.

"Where are the others?" Thilly asked them.

## THE VALE OF SEVEN DRAGONS

Mrs. Florence's shoulders lifted as she inhaled, and she made an unusually vocal sigh and said, "Well, we've seen more than we cared to, and we've lost some of our people. The rest went flying, and I urged Birkswood to as well." She pierced the tall butler with a sharp look. "I know he only did because he needed to know *you* were safe; else he'd have stayed and likely suffered the same fate as everyone around that...thing."

Thilly pressed her hands against her lips and felt her stomach churn. "Who...who was...taken?" she asked.

Mrs. Florence sighed again, and Birkswood put his hands behind his back and lifted his chin.

"Truth be told, Your Highness," he said to her, "we aren't quite sure. The thing from the sky maimed whatever it took...I regret to say, beyond recognition."

Thilly shuddered. "The prince? Evgrent?" she croaked.

"The last I saw of Evgrent," said Birkswood, "was of his running toward the fray, sword in hand, and he asked if we'd seen the prince. But apparently, none of us had."

Thilly vibrated all over from fear and nausea.

"He—he seemed like he was in a trance," she said, swallowing the taste of bile building in her mouth. "He kept going towards it, as if drawn to it." She balled her hands into fists and rubbed her eyes with them, as a young child might. "I think I doomed him."

Hana exclaimed, "You never! Your Highness, he was clearly not right in his head."

"It's not that," gasped Thilly. "It's that the thing...the thing was...I don't know how to say this. His mother, Queen Maulielle...I saw her. I saw her in darkness, and she was not herself. She had shadows in her eyes and she...oh, Birkswood," she wailed, "she's one of *them*."

Birkswood, Mrs. Florence, and Hana stared at her. A long moment passed, awful for Thilly, for she felt the extreme guilt of having kept the secret wring her dry, while at the same time she felt a wave of catharsis from admitting it at last.

"How can that be?" Birkswood asked. "She seemed quite normal to me."

"And to me," said Mrs. Florence.

"I wouldn't know," Hana remarked thoughtfully, "as I'd never seen her before your coming out ball. She seemed quite beautiful, but cold. It...didn't feel pleasant to look at her, d'you know what I mean?"

Thilly blinked at Hana, and answered, "Yes, I do. She hates me."

"Oh, for heaven's sake," scoffed Mrs. Florence. "That's nonsense. I know the queen has always thought highly of you your whole life; it's nobody's fault you and the prince didn't gel."

"No," said Thilly firmly, feeling the blood return to her face. "She more than disapproved of me. She ridiculed me, tried to shame me, tried to insult my mother for abdicating. Claiming she'd left me."

"Your mother did leave you," Birkswood said, and Thilly gasped. "Well, there's no sense softening that, is there? It is a known fact. It wasn't a wanton act; it was purposeful, and yet the fact remains, and I've seen how it's affected you your whole life. That being said, the queen had no right to bring up that old pain. Still, it does not make her a monster."

"You don't understand," Thilly pressed, "there is something monstrous in her. She was not her old self! I remember she had always been overly stiff and formal, and a little too fancy and tuned in to fashion for my own tastes. This was different. Something happened to her. Do you remember, something about her being at the coast? And she didn't have her usual maids, for they'd fallen ill? We had the rider from the coast raving about some tempest. Then we get that extraordinary man: the pirate, Aldebaran Copperbox, and the vile head he threw at our feet! Do you see, now? The queen had also been at the coast. Something monstrous *was* there, and I believe it overtook her. That may not even be the queen at all."

Mrs. Florence held her hand over her heart and had gone so pale that Thilly feared she might drop on the spot.

"Your Highness, if you are right," she whispered, "and we cannot know for certain that you are! But *if* you are, then Catellaith may be doomed."

Birkswood added, "If Catellaith is doomed, perhaps Vickery is as well. I pray that your mother's protections have held there."

Thilly jerked her head up to look at him. "Father!" she murmured helplessly. "And what protections?"

Birkswood and Mrs. Florence looked at each other and both sighed in unison.

"This is one of our most private secrets that we've kept," said Birkswood. "Hana, we are entrusting you to keep it this way." The girl nodded in open-mouthed awe. "Priestess Woadlynn has always projected a protective enchantment over Castle Taugan."

"Or so we thought," noted Mrs. Florence.

Birkswood looked miserable. "Princess, if you are right about Queen Maulielle, then the protection did not work fully."

"Maybe it did," said Mrs. Florence, brow pinched. "For this…creature could easily have overtaken the castle otherwise. Why hold back if she were the monster?"

"Maybe," Hana spoke up, blushing, "maybe she…or it…was counting on the prince marrying the princess, binding the kingdoms so she'd have more power, and that didn't happen. So she was weaker than she thought she'd be: you hadn't"—Hana turned almost magenta in embarrassment— "you hadn't unified. I don't know anythin', though, so feel free to ignore me!"

Birkswood said, "No, I think you might be circling the truth of it, good Hana." He leaned against a tree and thought, right arm folded across his chest and his chin in his left hand, deep in thought. "There is a powerful, unequivocal bond to royal marriage—to any marriage, of course, but especially to royals, in our realm at any rate. And Woadlynn's protection as a mother, a wife, and a sorceress is considerable. Not enough to prevent your knee scrapes and getting into trouble, dear Princess, as well I know. But enough to offer, even from that great distance, some aid."

"My picture of her," sighed Thilly. "Maybe she used that."

"I daresay she did," said Mrs. Florence. "As she also used a mirror to speak to your father in private."

"You knew about that too?" cried Thilly.

Mrs. Florence threw her hands in the air. "Well, all the secrets are coming out, I suppose!"

"Now, Your Highness," said Birkswood in a warning voice, "do not assume that your mother didn't care for you and that she kept herself from you for selfish reasons. I can see the thoughts spinning in your eyes. No, Woadlynn had a greater goal. It was not a joy for her to abdicate, it was for duty, for protecting the realm, and for protecting more than that. And somehow, we must get to her, for even though that hole in the sky is sealed, it's proof those vile beasts can get through. And if they've got through to Aceltia, they can get through anywhere."

"Well," muttered Mrs. Florence, "perhaps not Osthadon."

"Hmmph," grunted Birkswood, sounding disgusted. "A land whose monsters are its own citizens, or at least its ruling class. Perhaps the things will have met their match."

"We've got to find Beaumain," Thilly insisted, "no matter what. If that thing overtook his mother, then I don't know—maybe the other monster from the sky lured him somehow to it."

# THE VALE OF SEVEN DRAGONS

"Whatever the case," Birkswood said firmly, "we will not go back down there. The fae and Evgrent were part of the fray, and they are more prepared for such a thing than we—if anyone can be."

"Mother stopped me from following," Thilly said quietly. "I ran into a wall, one I couldn't see. And…I heard her voice telling me I wasn't ready."

"Certainly you weren't ready to go up against any monsters," Mrs. Florence said forcefully. "So your mother was right about that!"

"We can't leave Beaumain," pleaded Thilly.

Birkswood took her hands in his and looked down at her with great affection, as someone who had known her since birth and cherished her, and he said, "Dear child, he would want you to. He did his duty: he escorted you here so that you could go to your mother. And my and Mrs. Florence's roles are to make absolutely sure you get to her. So that is what we will do. The sooner, the better."

"We've got a bit of a hike down," noted Hana, pointing toward the clearing.

Birkswood looked up, released Thilly's hands, and walked over to see. Umbra grazed some of the softer plants at the edge environment of the precipice, but she turned to look at him and snuffled his shoulder.

"Yes," said the man thoughtfully, gazing out the expanse below, "we've got some narrow paths among cascades to get down there, but the valley is the surest sign that we are near the Veiled Isles. It's been many a year since I've been there. Hopefully I've not completely forgotten how to get to them."

"They're right there!" exclaimed Hana. "You can see 'em plain as day."

Birkswood sniffed. "Hana, dear, they're called the Veiled Isles because they are veiled to the sight of normal humans."

Hana gave a short laugh. "Well, I'm the most normal person I know m'self, and I can see islands out there in the sea. There's a strange fog headed out to them, like a comb, but I see them just fine."

Birkswood turned his eyes to Mrs. Florence, and Thilly watched their subtle facial twitches. She raised her right eyebrow at Hana, who rummaged through her pack for snacks and pulled forth some hard little oatcakes.

"Hmm," said Birkswood simply, turning away from the girl and looking back to the northwest. "At any rate, we had better take Umbra and get to the path down to the valley and hope for the best. If anyone has made it out of that attack, we'll find them sooner or later, but we must press on."

"We've lost the prince of Catellaith, and my friend," sighed Thilly, looking down at her scuffed shoes and the burrs caught in her skirts. "We've lost gods know how many of our party. We've lost all our horses, save Umbra here." The horse's ears perked up. "I hope that my mother has everything we need, and we get to her before we lose anything or anyone else."

"Heavy is the head, as the saying goes," sighed Mrs. Florence, patting Thilly's shoulder affectionately. "First, eat and drink, and then we'll go. Food is energy, and we're going to need a lot of it to make up for whatever we find along the way."

*Heavy is my head indeed,* thought Thilly. She said aloud, "Every day and every minute, I want a crown less and less."

Hana said to her, handing her an oatcake, "Your Highness, maybe you don't want the crown, but we need someone to lead us. And would you rather have it be monsters, or you?"

Thilly swallowed in anxiety. Then she said, "I'd rather kill those monsters and lead nobody."

"Well," Birkswood observed in his booming voice, "you'll not be able to do either if we don't get to your mother soon."

# THE VALE OF SEVEN DRAGONS

"You don't have to tell me twice!" Thilly said. She pressed her fingers to her lips and looked out to the soft silver-grey horizon where the sea heaved obscured. "I just pray to the stars above that we find Beaumain safe, and Evgrent," and her voice changed pitch when she said his name, "and everyone else on the way. Let's go, then. To doom, possibly, but to my mother, absolutely."

# CHAPTER 24

## *LOST*

She had hoped that Evgrent would find them as they made their way back to the great trees, but he did not. It took every ounce of stubbornness she could muster to refuse to believe that he or Beaumain could be gone, but she could feel her grip on positivity slipping away with each step. And then a great flash burst in the sky above them, brilliant enough to shine down through the tangled dark fir boughs and penetrate the floor of Absinweald. She gasped in shock, Hana shouted in fear, and Umbra jumped and whinnied. Then the light vanished. Mrs. Florence and Birkswood briefly clasped each other's hands.

"What—was—that?" she cried, but before her stunned cohort could attempt an answer, she heard a furious flapping of wings, and a wood parrot burst from the treetops and aimed right for her breast.

"Ack, Blinky, gods!" screamed Thilly, and the bird was wild-eyed and clearly frightened, but had that spark in its eye that she recognized. The bird looked ready to take flight again as it swayed back and forth on Thilly's wrist, flicking its wings. "What is it, what's happened?"

"Fae fire! Fae fire!" cried Blinky, and then the bird leapt onto Thilly's shoulder and trembled under her voluminous and feral hair.

Birkswood stared at Thilly.

"We'd better get in sight of that battle, but only just," he said cautiously, "and see what has happened. And then, Princess, we *must* get to the valley and make haste for your mother."

"Agreed," Thilly answered, and they walked quickly, with Mrs. Florence riding Umbra at Thilly and Birkswood's insistence.

And despite her initial protests, Mrs. Florence said, "I daresay we'd make better time this way after all, given my left ankle knows we're in the far north, and I definitely pressed my luck with it back in my youth."

"What, doing tricks?" Thilly said before she thought. Birkswood wheeled upon her and caught her in an eagle-eyed stare, and she went pale. "Sorry," she mouthed to him.

Mrs. Florence, keen as ever, snapped, "The only trick to speak of is getting us safely to your mother, Your Highness. And I'm afraid that other than guiding you and making sure you're fed, I've no hat to draw a solution out of to hasten the trip."

And so for that time, Thilly said nothing more about Mrs. Florence's magical history.

They edged the furrow where the great black column had descended and been cut, and Thilly could hear horrible groans, but no screams, and the scent of sulfur was strong in the air. The gully was thick with dark grey smoke, and she heard coughing among the groans. She saw a shadow and looked up, and Ki'roth hovered above her and lowered.

"Thank the gods," said the fae, whose face was streaked with ash and the passage of tears.

"What has happened, Ki'roth?" Thilly asked, meeting him when he stepped back up on the earth and clasping his hands.

"We've lost Mal'treth," said Ki'roth, lower lip trembling, "and Val'dreth is badly burned."

"What of the creatures?" asked Birkswood, his dark eyes darting to and fro for any sign.

"Mal'treth," said Ki'roth with a strained voice, "made the sacrifice. Our fire arrows took purchase, but the thing was too strong, and even though we sent all our arrows it was not enough. And so—and so—" Ki'roth covered their face, and Thilly lay her hand on their shoulder in concern. "Mal'treth brought forth a fire conjuring, which consumed them entirely, and so consumed the enemy. And both are destroyed."

"Gods," whispered Thilly. "I am so sorry. Such a brave sacrifice. Oh, but Val'dreth...how are they?"

"Ul'trok has them stable for now, but I fear without proper care, we will lose Val'dreth as well."

"Are you quite sure the thing is beaten?" pressed Birkswood. "Where is Prince Beaumain, and where are the others? Are there any other survivors?"

Ki'roth hung their head.

"The last I could see was that anyone who had not been consumed by the thing fled to the forest, as you did. I have not seen the prince at all."

Thilly's entire body began to shake. "Not at all," she repeated. "And Evgrent?"

"No sign of him either."

Thilly reeled, and Hana caught her. "What could have happened? Do you think—could the thing have—"

And she did not want to ask what she most feared, so she let her words hang unfinished in the smoky air, which stung her eyes along with her own tears.

Ki'roth shook their head, sending their ash-coated cables of hair dashing back and forth.

"If the thing took them, they perished in that fire with it."

"Do not speak so in front of the princess!" hissed Birkswood, teeth bared. "We must cling to some hope even in the darkest moment!"

"No," said Thilly, her voice flat and dull. "Ki'roth, speak plainly: I ask that everyone do this for me. Birkswood, I know you are trying to protect me, but words can only go so far right now. Let us try to find anyone left, and go to my mother, including Val'dreth. We will rig a sled or…or something, I do not know, to carry them."

She shook her head, thinking of the miles that lay ahead of them to the sea, and wondered how they would get on.

"Can the river take us?" she wondered, remembering the twisting waters she had seen from above.

"For some way, perhaps," Ki'roth replied, "but between here and there are cascades and harsh rapids. I think we will fare better along the river path than on the waters themselves."

"Gather everyone we can find," Thilly told everyone.

Hana nudged her and asked, "Is the monster defeated, then, at least?" she asked.

Thilly lifted her stricken eyes to the girl and said, "I wish I could believe that. I think we've only cut a cord away from a much larger monster."

Ki'roth said, "We agree. It has taken many forms now, but at least Aceltia is free of it for the moment. At great cost."

*How much greater a cost will there be?* Thilly wondered.

They avoided the site of the battle, for beyond the smell of sulfur, the scent of death and a horrible, unknowable scent of *other* hung in that hollow. Thilly felt a powerful urge to get as far away from it as possible. She had no need nor desire to see maimed and warped bodies. She had seen the head Captain Copperbox had thrown before her on that night that seemed a thousand years ago. She did not want to see her own people mutilated.

As if in answer to her thoughts, Ki'roth declared, "Absinweald will see to the dead in its own ways. Of that we can be sure."

So they carried on, around and up and through the opposite side of the cleft in the forest, now scarred and burned and a place of misery and death. Absinweald's whispers returned as they walked along an ancient path, marked at times by pillars of stone, and the further west they traveled, more elaborate, moss-covered stone structures emerged from the undergrowth from time to time.

"What are they marking?" Hana asked, touching one of them, which looked rather like a mix between a cat and a fox, and had been etched from centuries of tree-filtered rain.

"Journeys," answered Ki'roth, adjusting Umbra's sling for Val'dreth. The injured fae had gone quite pale, flickering between consciousness and pained sleep. The third fae, Ul'trok, kept their eyes downcast and their forest-green cloak bound tightly around them, and spoke in a quiet voice words that Thilly did not recognize, over and over. She wondered if they were prayers. "Journeys, distance; perhaps in your land, distance matters more, Your Highness. But those who venture in Absinweald experience something other than measurement, and so marking miles matters less."

They found a small tributary of the River Titeltian and were about to stop for a break and to refill their flagons when a rustling among the trees startled Umbra, and Ki'roth and Ul'trok readied their arrows.

# THE VALE OF SEVEN DRAGONS

"Oh!" a woman's voice cried.

"Keep back!" a man hissed.

*I know that voice!* thought Thilly, and her heart bounded.

"Who's there?" she called out.

The woman then erupted from the bushes and fell at her feet. It was one of her own housemaids, Kaydra, a woman in her twenties who served directly under Mrs. Florence.

"Kaydra!" cried Mrs. Florence. "Oh, thank heavens…are you alone, dear?"

She was not: another few maids and footmen stepped forth gingerly, their eyes large and uncertain, and some wept openly at the sight of Thilly, throwing themselves on the ground and bowing.

And behind them stood Evgrent, holding onto a standing man, and bodily turning the man around to face Thilly. It was Beaumain.

She cried out and ran toward both, but Evgrent stepped in front of the prince and stopped her.

"Your Highness," he said, his voice thick with emotion, "he is not the same."

She stopped then, and looked into Evgrent's eyes, and saw sadness and exhaustion there. She stepped around him to see Beaumain, and she tried her best not to react strongly.

He was intact, insofar as he was not visibly injured. But he was, as Evgrent said, not the same. He stared vacantly ahead, as if not seeing her.

"Beaumain!" she said. "It's me, Thilly!"

But he did not react. He stared unblinking into nothingness, his lips dry and partly opened, his blue-green eyes clear but nonreactive.

"Has he lost his sight, his hearing?" Thilly demanded of Evgrent.

"I do not think so," Evgrent said, and he took Thilly's hands in his. "My Princess, he has lost his mind."

# CHAPTER 25

## *BRIDGES*

Thilly stayed stalwart in front of her and Prince Beaumain's subjects. Everyone looked by turns fatigued, in shock, or some combination of both, and she felt both as well. And although she loathed duty and honor and expectations of her, at that moment she knew that she must rely upon all the training that she had received in her life to become a queen; finally, she understood that even during moments of boredom and longing, she had been educated for a specific task. Today she had to rise to it, even though she had never felt further from doing so.

She led the prince back to where Hana, Mrs. Florence, and Birkswood stood comingling with the other members of their house, and Blinky perched atop Umbra's head and groomed the horse, who tolerated the action, whether she actually liked it or not. Birkswood and Mrs. Florence held their expressions neutral, and Thilly felt tremendous relief from their doing so. She could see that they knew, like she did, that they must not react strongly to the state of the prince. Hana barely held her mouth shut, but she clenched her hands together in front of her until they turned dark red, and so Thilly knew the girl was horrified as well. Her eyes locked with Thilly's, and the princess recognized the great concern the girl had for her. Thilly closed her eyes for a split second in acknowledgment and opened them again. She lifted her chin proudly.

"Good people of Vickery and Catellaith, rejoice in the survival of Prince Beaumain, but quietly," she added, as they all murmured and exchanged looks of relief and confusion and, in some cases, alarm. "I think I speak for all of us when I say that we have each been through an extraordinary ordeal. But the fae came to our aid and saved us. We thank them," and she inclined her head to Ki'roth, who bowed, and to Ul'trok, who barely tilted their head down at all, "for their sacrifice and their protection, without which…I dare not speculate. We are tired, we are injured," and she glanced at Val'dreth, sleeping fitfully in the sling, "but we are alive. For the moment, that is all that matters. We must carry forth to the Veiled Isles to my mother, and to the healing powers of the Covenant to which she belongs. To that end, we cannot wait."

She gazed into each person's eyes, and she said, "That thing we saw was but one piece of a larger whole, or several, which has attacked our shores and now the lands of the north, and by all accounts, possibly our homes by now as well."

She heard soft sobbing. "But we are alive. And we will do all we can to keep all our people, here and at home, alive as well. Let us march forth and face together what we must and find a way to stop these monsters."

"How?" called a male's voice. She looked and found one of the footmen of Catellaith.

"Yes?" she asked. "Speak, good sir."

"Look at our prince," he said, and she could hear a mixture of bitterness and sadness in the man's voice. His eyes were red, his hooked nose running and raw, his dark sandy hair bedraggled, his clothes torn; yet she could see the livery of Catellaith on him, gleaming silver and blue in the semi-darkness of Absinweald. "What have we to go back to? Are the king and queen even still alive?"

Thilly shuddered and tried her best not to show it.

"We must assume that they are until we know otherwise," she answered. "Else we'll go mad. I, for one, am going to focus on what can be done to help them going forth."

"Your Highness, what could stop that thing?" asked another man. "There are only so many of the fae, and to ask of them another sacrifice...it wouldn't be enough, and it wouldn't be right beside."

"No, you're right," Thilly agreed. "I'm working on a plan."

Whispers rang into her ears just then, and she turned her head swiftly to Hana, who nodded. *You can hear them too.*

The party closed ranks around Thilly and the prince, looking nervous.

"Can you hear that?" she asked them all.

"I hear nothing, Your Highness," answered one of her maids, "but I feel a cold dread, I do."

"I hear them," said Hana.

"As do I," said Evgrent.

Thilly looked at Beaumain, and he stood stock still, registering nothing. She sighed.

"I heard words among the whispers, has anyone else?" she asked.

Her listeners shook their heads.

"I can't understand them," Hana said.

Thilly said, "I see. I can understand some of them, and what I can gives me courage. But we must make it to the Veiled Isles and see if this courage leads to hope. For now, rest. We will camp here tonight. Our walk is a long one, and we will need to take turns to help the wounded. Remember too, not all wounds are visible from the outside. Be good to yourselves."

They then scattered to make camp, and Thilly felt her shoulders droop and all her confidence seep out of her. She looked at Beaumain, still standing, and envisioned him as one of the forest markers, growing moss over time. She shivered.

"My friend," Thilly said to him softly, next to his ear, hoping somehow that he heard her. "I don't know what happened. I can only guess that it was her, or it, trying to lure you. But that isn't your fault. I'm just so, so glad you're alive."

She called two footmen to help ease Beaumain into a sitting position and to attempt to feed him and get him settled for bed. He was still unresponsive. His lips grew dryer.

Birkswood then leaned down to her and said, "If he cannot eat, that is one thing, but he must drink water, or he will grow dehydrated and perish. Everything else can wait."

"How do we get him to drink?" Thilly whispered to him.

Without answering, he found a cloth and soaked it with water from the stream. Then he gestured to a footman to hold the prince's body flat, with his head tilted back, and Birkswood squeezed water from the cloth into Beaumain's mouth.

"This is what you must do from time to time," he told the prince's footmen. "His survival depends upon it."

They nodded and took over.

"Can he sleep?" Thilly wondered.

"Gods know," answered Birkswood.

Mrs. Florence approached them and said, "Your Highness, one thing is for certain, and that is *you* must hydrate yourself, and *you* must sleep. We've miles yet to go and you need your strength. Let us take care of the prince. Get some rest, dear child."

Thilly almost instantly grew so sleepy that she had trouble standing. Hana came and led her to a small tent.

"I'm afraid we have to share, Your Highness," lamented Hana, "as we've lost so much of our equipment."

"That's all right, Hana, that's all right," and before Thilly could even take off her now filthy dress, she sank onto the bedroll in the tent and fell asleep.

The morning arrived in a rude fashion, as another earthquake woke anyone still sleeping. Thilly jerked awake, flung her hands out, and felt something soft and warm, and she started to yelp. She realized then it was Hana, and the girl also panicked for a second as they both remembered their circumstance.

"Another bloody earthquake!" Thilly hissed. "Fucking *why*? I'm so tired of them, I'm so sick of this. Oh, gods, Hana, I'm sorry. I shouldn't have said that. I'm just...I'm tired."

Hana sat up and said, "Now, Your Highness, how could you be anything but tired? And not just from all the walkin' and runnin' and generally tryin' to survive this mess. You're also grievin', missin' your dad the good King Gathlade, I know you are. And now to have the prince in this state, not knowing if he'll get out of it? I truly don't know how you carry on at all. And that speech you gave, milady. You'd have called up a thousand knights to your banners, had they heard it."

Thilly snorted at that, but Hana looked surprisingly stern in response.

"You're a leader and a future queen, milady," said Hana stubbornly. "Maybe you don't want to be. But that's what you are. And we'll fight for you and with you through anythin' so just know that."

Thilly softened and reached out to clasp the girl's hand.

"You're a true friend," she said to Hana, and she meant it. "Thank you."

Hana looked radiant then and ducked her head. "Thank you, Your Highness."

"I think it's safe to call me Thilly, Hana," she said in return.

"Never," said Hana.

Thilly shook her head. "You are most stubborn, but I won't fight you. It's time we ate and got going."

Thilly washed in the stream in privacy, guarded by Hana and Mrs. Florence from any prying eyes, but everyone was too tired and weary to bother doing anything but eat and drink. Thilly was relieved they could do that and worried incessantly about Beaumain. She knew that Birkswood was right, and that the longer they waited to seek aid, the closer to death they might all be, but in particular, Beaumain and Val'dreth. That fae, looked after by Ul'trok most tenderly and by Ki'roth as well, wavered back and forth in consciousness, at times raving. Their wounds were great red weals, burns from being in proximity to Mal'treth's immolation.

Thilly sought Birkswood and Mrs. Florence.

"Is there anything we have that we can give Val'dreth, among your stores?" she asked quietly, out of range of the hearing of the fae.

Mrs. Florence shook her head. "Nothing we have would be as powerful as what the fae might carry."

"Your Highness," said Birkswood, "Absinweald itself contains many hallucinogenic and analgesic substances among its herbs and fungi, and you can be sure the fae know this."

"Then why can't they help Val'dreth?" she wanted to know.

"Because Val'dreth is suffering from multiple things, and while burns can be treated and inner wounds can be aided, a fight with something like that back there, in which you lose someone dear? That is beyond what any of us can help with. We're battling with something from another world, another place, I don't know. But it is not of *this* world, and I fear that its effects are beyond anyone's, save the Covenant's."

"Let us hope and pray," murmured Mrs. Florence, following the gaze of Thilly from Val'dreth to Beaumain, who now stood fully cleaned and dressed by his people, yet remained unreactive. She thought perhaps his color looked healthier today, but she did not know if that were really true or if she merely hoped that it was.

Evgrent helped set the prince upon Umbra to ride, and adjusted the sling that Umbra pulled. He muttered something into the horse's ear and stroked her cheek and offered something for her to eat. He sighed, and Thilly heard him. He glanced at her and then turned his head away. He then walked around Umbra to retrieve something and returned with a bundle.

"Try not to drop it again, will you?" he said to her simply, handing the bundle to her.

She unwrapped the bundle to find her sword gleaming in the strange dim dawn of Absinweald. She heaved forth a shaky sigh.

"Thank you," she told him. "I don't know what good it will do now, facing monsters and all that."

"It would be good for you to practice, at least," said Evgrent, adjusting the straps of Umbra.

"When? And where?" Thilly wondered.

"Soon," answered Evgrent, "and we'll find the right place for me to train you."

"Oh," said Thilly, blushing. "Haven't you quite got your hands full?"

"I do," said Evgrent tersely, pushing his lank hair behind his ears, "but I'm going to prioritize giving you lessons in case any other fuckery piles onto my plate."

With that, he marched around to the front of Umbra and urged her to begin the trek forward, and he did not look back at Thilly.

# THE VALE OF SEVEN DRAGONS

They proceeded through narrowing paths that began to descend, and the former stream had joined the Titeltian, which ran in a great torrent by their path. Waterfalls roared alongside them as the party picked its way carefully around rocks and tree roots. Umbra managed fairly well, but by the looks of her ears, she clearly did not prefer such a place. On they all pressed, however, the crush and dash of fast water chasing their anxiety away, the mists of the river soothing them, and Absinweald providing its own sort of healing properties in that way. Thilly, despite everything, felt glad of heart to be traveling, to be using her muscles, and even when she almost turned her ankle traversing a tricky spot with slick, decaying leaves and mist-soaked moss she felt alive, and glad to be so.

They came upon more rocky outcroppings as the land descended, and at last they reached an arched, ancient stone bridge, where the Titeltian bent to the north before buckling back. Huge boulders ended their current path, so they needed to cross the bridge to continue. It was set before a huge, tall waterfall, and looking up, Thilly could see a shaft of light enter the great forest and set the billowing droplets from the waterfall's foam into a rainbow.

Next to the bridge, another old stone marker stood, this time in the shape of what closely resembled an owl, but Thilly could not be sure. Blinky hopped over to it and inspected the thing, nudging its beak around on the mossy face of the statue and revealing a stone beak of sorts. Blinky then lifted its head back and laughed raucously at the thing.

"Fake, fake, fake!" said Blinky in a singsong voice, and Thilly laughed despite herself.

She looked at Beaumain to see his reaction and remembered anew, and still with a shock, that he could not register what she might say. She sighed.

Everyone rested before crossing the bridge except for Evgrent, who groomed Umbra.

"Well?" Thilly called. "Is now a good time?"

She unsheathed her sword and waived it around.

He glanced over his shoulder at her and harrumphed. Then he brought forth his own sword.

"Yes, why not?" he said to her, walking toward her with his sword drawn. "We've no idea what's ahead and nothing's better than a fucking risky bridge in front of a waterfall to give you a proper lesson."

He charged her, and for a second, she stood still in surprise, but then she readied herself and brought her sword up. He easily dashed it out of her hands, and then pointed at it and her and said, "Pick it up!"

Then they had a crowd watching them, and they parried back and forth on the bridge, the spray and the waterfall dazzling Thilly's eyes, and she was soaked to the skin and cold, yet she felt vibrant and electric as Evgrent barked orders to her.

"Not like that, you snippet!" he cried, and she knew then that the roar of water covered their speech. She felt freed by the knowledge and laughed at him.

"Oh yeah? Fuck you, then!" and she charged him next.

The ringing of their swords was drowned by the water, and Evgrent shook off the droplets from his hair. Thilly's own hair frizzed in the humidity, and her hands were slick. At one point she lost her grip on the sword, and it skidded close to the edge of the bridge and the roiling waters below it. Evgrent came at her then, but she leaped and landed on her front. Yet in the blinding pain from that action, she still managed to seize her sword and thwack him in the backs of his knees, so that he sprawled.

"How the fuck did you do that?" he yelled. "And where did you learn it? Dirty trick, that!"

Thilly laughed and then sighed.

"I learned it by watching your brother," she told him.

Their swords met, inches from their eyes, and they stared at each other. Then Evgrent blinked and stepped back and bowed extravagantly. Thilly could faintly hear cheers from their party.

"You got me," he called to her, and he sheathed his sword and turned away from her, to return to his horse and her passengers, without looking back.

Thilly, soaked and sweating and sore, sheathed her own sword and walked back toward the camp.

"So!" cried Hana before everyone. "Not only is our princess a great leader, but she's also a fighter too! I'm thinkin' we're gonna be all right!"

Another cheer rose from the crowd and Thilly, cheeks scarlet, grinned and waved them off and headed for a disapproving Mrs. Florence, who stood ready with a set of clean, dry clothes for her, plain but serviceable. As it was a bit loose, Thilly tore a ribbon off her old gown and tied it around her waist, so that it was the lone red item on her beige outfit, signifying her home country. Thilly was only too glad to be rid of her last decent gown, which was now ripped and soiled beyond repair. Wearing the new, simple clothes, she felt invigorated and strong, like she had crossed from her old life into new territory within and without and donned something more than clothing, something immutable and true.

# CHAPTER 26

## *BRUME*

It was slow going in the descent to the valley, yet it grew warmer, and for that, at least, Thilly was glad. She did not, however, enjoy the increased humidity. The epiphytes of Absinweald clearly loved it, though, as more and more climbing vines and orchids and bromeliads began to cluster around the tree trunks. There were also more deciduous trees, including oaks, aspens, elms, and beech, with a few brilliant scarlet maples scattered among them, spiking the lower elevations with fiery color as the last hangers-on for late autumn.

At one of the maples, Ki'roth halted, placed a hand upon the trunk, and murmured something. The fae pressed an ear against the tree and nodded. Exchanging a look with Ul'trok, Ki'roth unsheathed a tool from a belt pocket and placed its sharp end along the trunk. Ul'trok picked up a fallen branch and cut a small piece off and began to whittle it.

Ki'roth said to the assemblage, who now all halted their paths to watch him, "This maple has granted me permission to drink of its sap, to aid us in our journey. The drink will refresh us and aid in healing both body and spirit, so I invite all of you to taste of it."

Then Ki'roth used the little augur to bore into the tree, and Ul'trok stepped forward with the small tap, freshly whittled, and pushed it in. The sap began to flow soon after, and Ki'roth nodded to Mrs. Florence and Birkswood. Mrs. Florence brought forth a tin cup, the finer royal wares long abandoned, and gave it to Ki'roth.

The fae filled it and walked to Thilly and bowed.

"For you, Princess Githilien, to give you the strength to lead."

Thilly took the cup and sniffed the clear contents. She tipped her tongue delicately into the liquid and tasted its light sweetness. Then she handed it back to Ki'roth.

"For Prince Beaumain and Val'dreth first, please," she urged.

Ki'roth bowed and smiled. "Thank you."

"And then you and everyone else after," Thilly said, adjusting her new red belt and hooking her sword scabbard on it. "I will take the last cup only. That includes Blinky and Umbra, please."

Birkswood managed to tip some of the sap into Beaumain's mouth, and carefully wiped his lips while Thilly held her friend's hand. The prince continued not to react, but simply stared upward at the brightening sky, to a canopy less dense than the heart of Absinweald. Thilly watched his slow pulse.

"It's almost like he's in torpor," she murmured.

Val'dreth, more awake and alert after sipping the maple sap, said hoarsely, "It is like he is trapped in amber. Yet he lives."

"I hope my mother can help him," sighed Thilly, smoothing the prince's golden-brown brow. She knelt and blushed a little and kissed him on that brow. He did not react. "Ah well," she said. "I hoped the old fairy stories might be true."

Val'dreth chuckled weakly. "Many fairy stories are not true," said the fae, "chiefly because fairies tell them."

Thilly giggled at that and reached over to squeeze Val'dreth's hand.

"I of course hope my mother can aid you as well," she said warmly. "Thank you so much for helping us all. I know you must be in such pain."

Val'dreth closed their eyes for a moment. Their vibrant hair drooped now, and their skin looked palest gold, almost translucent.

"Pain is relative," said the fae. "Yes, the burns hurt. But the loss of Mal'treth hurts far greater. And yet no life must remain forever."

"I am sorry," said Thilly. She felt out of her element with grief, even though she felt it constantly. She could hardly bear to think about it, so she pushed it aside. "If there's anything I can do, anything *any* of us can do, please ask."

Val'dreth nodded. "I am most grateful, princess." And then the fae dozed.

At the last, Blinky and Umbra were given dishes of the sap; Blinky's was a thimble that the parrot first dipped its tongue into, much like Thilly had, and then seized the edge of the thing in its beak and tipped the whole thing back like a cup. Blinky then fluffed up all its feathers and splayed its wings and bobbed its head, blinking.

"Good shit!" said the bird.

"I do think you've spent some time around pirates, Blinky," chided Thilly with a grin.

"Good shit! Good shit! Good shit!" sang Blinky.

Umbra seemed to agree, flicking her tail and prancing in place, clearly ready to go.

Thilly thanked Ki'roth and Ul'trok and then she placed her hands upon the great maple tree, mesmerized by its remaining vibrant deep red leaves, some of which fell around her as she stood there in her pale dress and red sash, with her hair once more gone wild and curling in all directions. Evgrent glanced at her, and his lips curled downward.

"Thank you," she said to the maple.

They set forth again, lighter of mood than they had been in several days. Some of their party were even singing softly, but there was no outright jubilance, more cautious relief. Still, loss hung about them all like a prickly cloak. Thilly wanted to believe that things would surely be better in her mother's stronghold, but she began to wonder about that.

"We're getting closer every moment," she noted to Hana, who had perked up enough from the maple sap that she hummed a folk tune while walking alongside Thilly. "I'm both relieved and worried at the same time."

Hana looked thoughtful and said, "I suppose that's natural. You've been through a lot."

"Not alone, thankfully," said Thilly with a half-smile.

"Never," agreed Hana. "I'll be there with you, milady, supporting you. And not just me. What you did back there was a good thing. They'll remember that."

Thilly shrugged. "I just want everyone to make it out alive and well." She looked ahead at Beaumain, stiff on Umbra's back, as Evgrent led the horse along. *I might have to redefine what "well" means.*

Just as they had all grown more accustomed to warmer weather, it abruptly ended as they began their descent to the delta of the River Titeltian. Thilly could see broad swaths of fog making a strange pattern in the river plains, and noted they curled at the ends, and therefore redistributed back into the upper reaches of Absinweald.

"How odd," she murmured, but she thought nothing more of it during their descent until later, when they had reached the lowlands and exited Absinweald's boundaries. They stopped for a break by the riverbank, where the Titeltian became a sleepy expanse as a tidal river intermixing with the sea. Several birds sheltered along its banks and plunged their sharp beaks into the coastal mud, drawing out crustaceans and worms by turn. Dotting the landscape to the west, large morros jutted out of the land, and she thought, but could not tell for certain, that they must extend into the sea. Out of one of them, there were five low caves, dripping with coastal plants and desiccated bird droppings. And the fog seemed to flow out of those caves and blend with the coastal marine fog. The cave fog seemed somehow warmer to her, and smelled off, much as the air of all Aceltia did, but even more so here at its edge. She was not sure she quite liked the mixture of that scent with the sea brine and festering kelp smells, either.

"Beautiful out there," observed Hana, looking to the west from where she sat eating dried bread upon the edge of the river, her legs dangling over the edge, her old skirt tattered at the hem.

"Quite foggy," replied Thilly, "though I suppose if you like fog, it's lovely."

"Not the fog," replied Hana. "The islands."

Thilly looked back to the west, and the horizon gleamed pale gold only on the underlying edge of one set of steel-grey low clouds, whereas the shore itself was quite obscured.

"I don't see a single island," said Thilly with a frustrated sigh.

Hana gawked at her. "Can you really not see them? They're huge, some of them! Like that big rock there," she added, pointing at the morrow with the five caves. "Several of them all in a chain going out as far as I can see."

Birkswood overheard Hana and remarked, "There is indeed a chain of islands out there, but I cannot see them, and I have visited them! Hana, how is it you're able to see them?"

Hana looked confused. "I don't understand. I just see 'em. That's all. Plain as day they are! Right there!" and she pointed.

Evgrent stepped up to them and said, "No one but you can see them, Hana, I guarantee it."

Hana looked startled. "Why would that be?"

Evgrent put his hands on his hips and tilted his head at her. "Where are you from?" he asked her.

"Why, Vickery, of course," Hana said, surprised.

"Always Vickery?" he pressed.

"Well, I—" Hana began, and she looked at Mrs. Florence and Birkswood, whose eyebrows were raised. "Well, now, I was never told otherwise, but I've never had family, you see. I was raised on a farm in the Hilltocks along with other orphans."

Thilly turned to stare at Evgrent.

"Speak, Evgrent. What are you implying?" she demanded.

Evgrent lowered his eyelids and shook his head. "Only that there are not many with such far sight, not among humans," he replied.

Hana giggled. "I'm as human as anyone!"

"Aye, perhaps," Evgrent countered, "but there are some…are you quite sure you were born in Vickery? Now I'm considering it, you look a bit like a Gamdon."

Hana gasped. "Gamdon! You mean of Osthadon!" She laughed then. "You're a good one for telling tales, sir."

"Certainly you're no Thaddon," added the man, "and for that we can all be glad."

"Cheers to that!" hollered one of the footmen. "Worst people on the face of the earth, Thaddons!"

Then the footmen fell to complaining and telling dreadful stories about the ruling class of Osthadon, a pale group of people known for xenophobia and classism regarding the Gamdons, the minority group of the country. The Thaddons looked more elfin, with narrow features and dark violet rings around nearly white irises, whereas the Gamdons tended to be more rustic and jovial farmers, rosy and fond of song and food, and were quite in tune with nature. Some indeed had highly keen eyesight. Now that Evgrent had asked, Thilly could not unsee Hana's features.

"We are not so far from Osthadon, are we, up here?" she asked the group.

"Not at all," answered Ki'roth. "There's a thin band of Valetheant separating Aceltia and Osthadon to the north; that is where the great beacon is, shining still after centuries, guiding sailors. The border to Osthadon is closed, as ever it has been in recent memory, save to licensed trade. A strange land, indeed. I wonder what fate has befallen them in all this?"

"Would Osthadon even know the difference between one of them and a monster?" a footman asked, and Birkswood's eyes blazed.

"I'll not be having that kind of talk amongst you!" he bellowed. "Consider, too, that if good Hana is of Osthadon lineage, you insult her by doing so. Enough!"

A shamed silence fell upon the footmen then.

Thilly stood, and the crumbs of her old bread scattered, to the delight of many gulls who had wheeled over their party as soon as they had descended. She watched surf scoters and gill-de-wakes skim the surface of the river as the tide poured in. It was late afternoon, she reasoned, and soon they would need to camp. She watched the fog stream in, mixing with the warmer fog from the five caves, and she then turned to look back at Absinweald. It was now engulfed in fog and out of sight.

"Well," she said to everyone, "it's getting late in the day, so if we can make it to the shore, perhaps Mother's people will be there to greet us."

Ki'roth stood stock still, and Evgrent put his hand on the hilt of his sword. Ul'trok pulled an arrow from their quiver.

"What is it?" hissed Thilly.

# THE VALE OF SEVEN DRAGONS

"Someone approaches," said Evgrent.

The fog billowed in then, and she could see nothing save her own party. She could hear the slap-slap of gentle waves of the tidal river and the slow rush of the tide of the sea spilling in. And then she beheld the slow bobbing of yellow and green objects emerging from the fog in blobs.

"Not them again!" wailed a maid.

"Gods," someone else groaned.

Thilly recognized them too as the strange mix of creatures they had seen, and whose visions had disrupted the party days before. She felt herself grow cold, despite the warmth of the five-cave fog pumping out toward them all. She also experienced a strong desire to run, but there was nowhere to do so safely, and she was in no position to give up her post as the leader of her people. Here they faced another obstacle. Thilly hoped it was a familiar one.

"Mother?" she said feebly, as one of the glowing objects neared her.

"No," said a voice, deep and resonant and layered with whispers.

"Then who are you?" she demanded. "Show yourselves."

"To do so would bring madness to you all," said the voice, which never materialized into a person that she could discern. "Come with us."

"Not until you tell me who you are!" cried Thilly through gritted teeth.

Evgrent and the two fae shouted as their weapons were loosed from their hands by an invisible force and hovered in the air.

"We are the ferry folk of the Veiled Isles," the voice said. "You will come with us as we guide you to the islands."

Thilly turned quickly to Hana. "Can you see them?" she whispered.

The girl trembled head to foot.

"You don't want to see 'em, Your Highness," she whimpered. "You don't. But we'd better follow 'em."

Thilly felt a surge of emotion and anxiety as she turned back to the glowing host and said, "Take us to my mother."

# CHAPTER 27

## *OVERSEA*

There was a sensation of moving: Thilly indeed walked, but she became so disoriented in the thick fog that she could not see in front of her or behind her. She could not see Hana, Mrs. Florence, or anyone else. She could only see the bobbing forms all around them, guiding the way. At one point she heard what she felt sure was the whinny of a horse, but it did not sound like Umbra, so she wondered at that. She heard other voices: undulating murmurs and muffled sounds, and then quite suddenly, she heard a low moan and a clanging sound, and the air smelled heavily of seaweed, to the point that she gagged.

The fog lifted then, but only a little, and she could see a shape before her: a pier, stretching as a long dark smudge ahead of her. At the end, an oblong object glowed yellow-green in places, and she gawked at it.

"Is that a ship?" she wondered aloud.

# THE VALE OF SEVEN DRAGONS

One of the glowing beings approached her, and she held her breath. She still could not see what sort of creature dwelt in its light, and it made her dizzy even to try to look at it, as if she were watching something moving very fast in all directions yet held into one place before her. She licked her lips and swallowed and tried to breathe deeply, for the effect was nauseating. The dock itself was disorienting as well. She heard the moan again and realized it was a foghorn, somewhere out in the water. And then she heard something else: singing.

High and low and fair were the voices traveling across the water to that dock, with waves unusually calm for an ocean coast. She listened intently to those voices, her ears searching for one, and then she found it: the familiar pitch, the sadness, and it was unmistakable: the voice of her mother Woadlynn, traveling across the water, amplified in some way Thilly could not understand. She closed her eyes and focused on that one voice among the many, and it calmed her to do so. She turned and found her people thronged behind her, with Umbra in front, led by Evgrent, and Beaumain sitting tall and still on the horse's back. Thilly fought tears that threatened to pool in her eyes. *Soon, dear Beaumain,* she thought.

Blinky, who had been riding on Umbra's pommel, flitted through the fog over to Thilly's shoulder, and she was glad to have the bird there. Ki'roth stepped forward alongside Birkswood and Mrs. Florence, and Hana rejoined Thilly at last. The maid looked perturbed and disoriented, and Thilly could understand that, although she could not see into the light beings the way Hana apparently could. She would have liked to have learned more about that, but one of the beings spoke to her.

"The-the-the Covenant-ant-ant awaits-aits-aits," the echoing, layered voice intoned, and Thilly shuddered, for it sounded very strange to her, operating in pitches with which she was unfamiliar, and feeling otherworldly. But not in the way of the monsters; in some other unexplained fashion: of the earth, but not of people the way she knew people.

*Githilien.*

*Githilien.*

*Githilien.*

Her mother's voice zeroed in on her ears, and Thilly pressed her own cold hands to her cheeks, and her heart hammered.

*I'm here at last, Mother,* she thought.

The speaker from before then said, "Enter-er-er the ferry-erry-erry, Princess-cess-cess Githilien-ilien-ilien."

"Princess," hissed Evgrent then.

Thilly wheeled around to find him behind her.

"Do you have your sword?" he whispered in her ear.

"Yes, why?" she whispered back, patting her side.

"Good," he answered, and then he stepped back and nodded to her.

Thilly looked back at several glowing shapes hovering in the air and glanced at Ki'roth.

"Thus, we must be guided," the fae said to her, "for no one can know where the stronghold of the Covenant lies."

Thilly slowly turned her head to look at Hana, who avoided her gaze.

*One of us knows for certain,* Thilly thought confidently. Then she took a deep breath and walked down the ancient wooden dock, her scuffed heels ringing on a wooden surface for the first time in many days. She might have found the sound comforting, elsewhere. But not here; it only unnerved her more. She walked to the boat, gleaming just as the unseen beings who shepherded her to it, but she could at least see that it was indeed a quite simple longboat of sorts. Its seats were rudimentary benches, but worn and sleek, made of a pale grey wood like the rest of the ship, despite the phosphorescent glow giving it a greenish tinge.

"I will stay," Evgrent said suddenly.

Thilly stared. "There is room for Umbra."

"Ki'roth," Evgrent called to the fae, "help me with the prince and Val'dreth."

"Wait, you have to come!" insisted Thilly. "You'll be safer."

Evgrent did not meet her eyes, and she wondered at his strange behavior.

"I do not know that I will be safer, Princess," he replied, still avoiding her gaze, "but certainly I will be unnecessary. I bid you farewell."

"No," Thilly huffed stubbornly, "you do not. You are under my command, and I order you to get on this boat with Umbra and come with us to my mother's stronghold."

At that, one of the hovering glow-beings approached Evgrent, and his eyebrows shot up. Umbra twitched and made nervous sounds. "Enter-er-er," it said to him. Swallowing, he took hold of Umbra's reins.

"Easy, girl," he murmured, and he shot Thilly an odd look with a furrowed brow.

*He looks...troubled*, she thought.

She had no more time to wonder why he was so uneasy, however, for the rest of her company began to board the ship. It scarcely bobbed at all, and she wondered at the calm sea. She sat at the head of the boat and watched as all the glowing beings aligned upon the bow on either side of the craft. Then it moved forward, with no rowing and no sails, and she suspected the beings themselves must be towing it, but she was not sure.

She looked out over the water and found the air as clogged with mist as the shore had been, and she began to sweat. No one spoke, and so the only sounds were the boat rushing through the water, and the distant murmurs and songs of the Covenant.

"Is the sea always this calm?" she finally asked Ki'roth, and the fae shook their head.

"Never," said Ki'roth.

"It is the enchantment," Ul'trok spoke up then in a cold, clinical voice. "The strongest waves are blocked by the Covenant's protective dome. I fear it inhibits wildlife, but I do not understand the workings of its power, if it serves as a filter or what."

At that, one of the glowing beings moved from the bow of the ship to hover just above Ul'trok and made a strange, whistling sort of noise that sent shivers up and down Thilly's spine. Blinky crawled all the way under her hair to the nape of her neck, the parrot's toenails tickling her skin, and she shuddered. Ul'trok looked up with large eyes and closed their mouth with a snap. The being then moved away, and Thilly decided perhaps it would be best to say nothing.

She wanted to ask Hana what the girl could see, but Hana only looked down, and her face had gone a peculiar shade. She could see *something*, and she would not say what. But for Thilly and everyone else who had stepped on that boat, the isles were veiled indeed.

# CHAPTER 28

## THE VIOLET GROTTO

Across the fog-laden sea the boat sped, its glowing pilots commanding it along and hovering at the same speed along the bow, and by and by, Thilly could hear the splashing of something in the water. She looked out to see coral-hued dolphins cavorting and chasing the shimmering boat on either side, and they looked for all the world as though they were smiling. Blinky watched them with intense interest and began to make a sort of crowing and wordless song whenever they would leap beside the boat.

This made Thilly laugh, and for that she was grateful, for her nerves were wound as tightly as harp strings. To have silly Blinky breaking the strange silence was a blessing, she thought, and when she looked over her shoulder at her subjects, she found their faces more relaxed. The spray of the sea was gentle, for it continued to be oddly calm, and she suspected Ul'trok must be right, and the Covenant's protective barrier extended over land and undersea, and perhaps underground as well.

# THE VALE OF SEVEN DRAGONS

*Is it a protective sphere?* She wondered, recalling how the invasive thing had coursed straight from the sky to burrow into the earth. She looked somberly at the three remaining fae, thinking of the sacrifice of Mal'treth and how they likely saved the entire country of Aceltia. Yet the Covenant's reach did not extend to all the Vale, and this gave Thilly pause. She wondered just how much protection her mother's people could manage, and for how much longer. If the monster broke through once, it likely could again. But her thoughts were spinning, and she was bone-tired, and she had to keep up a brave face for her own subjects and guests. She only hoped the Covenant could heal Beaumain and Val'dreth. For if they could not, she suspected no one could.

While most of the journey had been quiet save for the leaping chatter of the coral dolphins, accompanied by Blinky's zealous vocals, Thilly began to hear songs again, warped as if they passed around shapes. This was how she first knew she had finally reached the Veiled Isles before she could even see the steep morros jutting out of the sea, and the archipelago of smaller islands surrounding those, each connected by countless tiny bridges made of cemented shells and jewels that the lifting fog began to reveal. At last, the sun broke through the thick marine layer in shafts, with flints of gold light dancing upon the dark grey water of the Stellar Sea. The dolphins swept in and out of the water and then broke away, chattering in their squeaky speech, leaving the glowing boat to skim alone toward a large island with a cave mouth just large enough to enter.

As they passed into the cave, the water beneath broke into brilliant violet color, and everyone on that ship gasped…even the few who had been to the Isles long ago.

"That never gets old," Birkswood declared, the violet light flickering upon his face.

"What is this place?" Thilly asked.

Ki'roth, dark face glowing violet also, said, "This is the Violet Grotto, the entrance to Isle Corcra, the capital of the Veiled Isles, home to the Covenant keep."

The stunning violet flickering of the water below and the glowing yellow-green of the ship dazzled Thilly's eyes, but she felt a deep thrill and happiness and nervousness all at once to be so close to her mother. And the singing!

Songs echoed and undulated throughout the great Violet Grotto, mesmerizing the passengers of the boat. Blinky tried to whistle to them, and then gave up and decided to sway on Thilly's shoulder instead.

"Blinky," she said to the wood parrot, "would you be a dear and perch on Umbra again, and let me know if the prince needs anything?"

Blinky flicked its wings out and flapped over to the horse, who raised her head to glance back. They were quite accustomed to each other now, and Umbra seemed to like Blinky's grooming.

The boat drifted into a slot of stone just wide enough to hold it, and bobbed there while the glowing beings pulling it drifted up and away from it. Thilly jumped. Something had seized the boat to anchor it as if held by unseen hands, and the glowing host drifted up hewn stone stairs partially lit by them and by the violet glowing of the water in the grotto. Thilly breathed in the air, finding it pungent with sea brine, and somehow with floral sweetness, though no flowers could be seen anywhere in the cave.

"You-ou-ou must-ust-ust exit-it-it," the glowing beings all said in unison.

Realizing they were addressing her specifically and her party generally, she stepped from the still boat to the stone landing where it berthed. The second she set foot upon that stone, sconces burst into flame all up and down the stairs, off to a lit archway above. Along the stairway, she could now see a wrought iron banister leading upward, shaped in curling patterns that at first, she could not discern. As she approached them, she discovered they were of dragons and flowers and vines…as well as various strange and even hideous creatures that she did not know, and then she thought about what Hana had said, about not wanting to see the hovering beings earlier. Perhaps the beings were the same as the ones from the Gloaming Grove, but perhaps, she thought, they were something else entirely. Nothing in Aceltia seemed to resemble anything else in all the Vale; that much Thilly had learned so far.

Evgrent broke her thoughts by murmuring to Birkswood, "How do we get them up those stairs?"

Thilly turned to see the two men on the landing with Umbra, considering the stock-still Beaumain staring into the dark cave, not comprehending anything. She winced, for she would have loved for him to have seen everything there. Ul'trok and Ki'roth formed a sort of chair with their arms for Val'dreth, who did their best to try to stand, their face soaked in sweat from the effort.

"Can we take them up first?" Thilly asked Birkswood and Evgrent.

"I think you had better go first, Your Highness," Birkswood said, his deep voice bouncing off the walls of the cavern.

The glow-beings had vanished beyond the archway above, but just then a group of women arrived, their faces obscured by glittering veils of gold, silver, and copper, and they descended two by two down the stairs. Assembled before Thilly and her company, they bowed low, and without speaking, they moved toward Val'dreth and the prince, and effortlessly lifted the latter from Umbra, who sat upon the stone landing for them.

Beaumain stood and walked with two of the women, still not registering anything else, but able to move at least, and for that Thilly was relieved. Val'dreth permitted two other women to guide or offer assistance up the stairs, but the fae clearly suffered from movement.

Blinky flitted to Thilly's shoulder and nibbled on her earlobe, saying, "What's for tea?"

"Oh, Blinky," she murmured, "I don't think it's quite time for that."

One of the shrouded women then said, "We can lead all of you to refreshment first and to housing after that, if you wish, Princess Githilien. Your mother has instructed us to do as you command."

Thilly raised her eyebrows. "I appreciate the gesture, but this is not my land, and I do not want to overstep on anyone in the Covenant by being here."

"Nevertheless," said the woman, with a bit of an edge to her voice, "the Priestess Woadlynn orders it, and approval comes from on high. Please," and she gestured to the stairs.

Thilly thought that was a rather strange attitude to greet a royal with, not that she really cared; but it did intrigue her.

*Just what sort of hierarchy exists here?* she wondered.

Up Thilly strode, one foot after the other, holding her skirts up a bit, and making the unfortunate error of looking down as she climbed. The drop fell sheer to the flickering violet depths of the grotto below, and the shift from light below to darkness above disoriented Thilly. The sconces crackling at the top of the stairs provided a visual anchor for her. Two of the veiled women stood there waiting for her, and she realized these two wore not only veils, but also helmets and armor beneath them. The veils themselves, she found, were made of the finest mail she had ever seen, making them appear to be fabric from a distance, but up close, they were wrought of a delicate, silvery-gold substance in links of thousands of tiny stars. A great seven-pointed star shone on the forehead of each smooth metal helmet, through which she could see no features at all. This chilled her, despite the warm fizzing of sconces on the wall next to them, the flames dancing on their mail and their faceplates.

They said nothing to Thilly, but turned and clapped their arms to their sides, their raiment tinkling, and allowed her passage through the archway.

"Raaaawwwwk," crowed Blinky, stretching its head back and forth and blinking several times, and just then, Thilly could find no better way to describe what she beheld.

She walked into a chamber so immense that it gave her more vertigo than the stairs in the cave had. It was lined with iridescent black crystals that shifted between green and purple and back again. All throughout were stairs and bridges heading in different directions, but all curving upward to the top, where a large antechamber glowed pale green. At each stair landing, veiled women knights—for knights Thilly decided they were—stood on either side of the glowing beings from the boat. The effect of the pale metal, the yellow-green glowing, and the green-purple-black crystals both dazzled and unnerved Thilly.

But most unsettling of all was the singing.

A blended chorus of song looped repeatedly, and the acoustics of the room focused it, and when Thilly turned to see what they all faced, she could not quite grasp what she saw. It resembled a black morning glory embedded in the crystalline wall of this chamber, with a bottomless-looking mouth stretching somewhere deep in the rock wall of the place, to where, she could not guess. She realized then the songs funneled through that hole, a dark blossom channeling the haunting song to a destination unknown.

Turning back, Thilly looked up at the high antechamber and could see a person standing there, all in silver, with a crown of brilliant silver stars and silver chimes dangling off it. Her heart pounded, but she knew instinctively this was not her mother. There stood a figure behind and to the right of that woman, in shadow.

*Come forward,* she thought, *and let me see you.*

Because she knew: down to her marrow, down to her soul's terminus, she knew. That shadowed person was her mother.

Suddenly Woadlynn stood before her, as if from nowhere, and Thilly gasped. Her mother shimmered a bit, and Thilly quickly glanced back up to the balcony high above; the woman there still stood in shadow behind the star-crowned priestess.

*You are correct,* Woadlynn said to Thilly. *This is how I look. But I cannot move from where I stand.*

"What?" Thilly asked aloud, looking up again.

*I am projecting to you.*

"Why can't you move? I want to see you in the flesh!" Thilly cried, starting to shake. She wanted desperately now to run to her mother's arms, and not to a vision of her.

*I cannot move because I am singing.*

"Can you…stop? And take a break?" gasped Thilly.

*I cannot stop singing right now.*

"Why?" Thilly asked, eyes round.

Woadlynn raised her hand to point behind Thilly, and so the girl turned and looked back up at the dark flower-like chasm in the wall.

*Because it will wake the dragon.*

# CHAPTER 29

## *ASTRIDAE*

Thilly's mind tripped over the words of her mother's projected image. Nothing about Isle Corcra seemed real just then, and Thilly would not have been surprised if she had ingested something in Absinweald that set her on a hallucinogenic journey. But she knew that this place *was* real, if for no other reason than her friend Beaumain was still frozen in a catatonic state. That was nothing she ever could have conjured in a dream or in delusion. Yet before her stood several levels of singers filling the inside of a sea mountain with song aimed at…

"Did you say *the dragon*?" she asked.

A slow, wry smile crept across the face of Woadlynn, showing the little crinkles at the corners of her eyes, hazel like her daughter's, and around her mouth.

"I did," Woadlynn answered, "but that can wait. I know that you have been through an ordeal and that your friends are injured or tired or both. You will have time to rest and recover, and we will catch up."

"Can you help them, then?" Thilly beseeched her, hands clasped under her chin, feeling very like a little girl again, asking her mother for something long ago.

Woadlynn's image shifted and flickered, much like the curtain of an aurora, subtle yet obvious at the same time.

"I will do what I can," she answered, and her smile faded.

Thilly did not like that.

Even so, she swallowed her uncertainty, turned to her companions and said, "You will have rest and comfort now. You are safe."

When Thilly swiveled back to Woadlynn's image, the smile was long gone, and a haunted look passed over the woman's face. Thilly went cold, looking at it. She glanced up above at all the priestesses and knights and they sang evermore.

"When can *you* rest?" she asked her mother.

"Soon," said Woadlynn. "I have the golden hour and the beginning of dusk, and then the shift changes. We are all working harder than usual, too, because of the attacks. But let us not speak of that here, darling. My ladies will take good care of you, and we will work on a treatment for the prince and the fae."

After saying this, the vision of her mother vanished, and the singing continued.

Thilly had not realized she had been breathing in shallow puffs from anxiety, and only then did she finally exhale and feel as though she *could* rest at last. So the knights guided Thilly and her company through long hallways glittering with dark gems yet cast with soft rugs, and several doors along the walk revealed branches extending up or down the inside of the great morro, each full of strange wonders and creatures and beings of all sorts, and no shortage of puffins, Thilly discovered, at which Blinky hissed furiously.

"I would have thought you'd *like* puffins," Thilly grumbled. "What's got into you?" She tapped her finger softly on Blinky's beak, and the bird responded by bonking her nose. "They're just puffins."

"Blinky hates puffins!" squawked the wood parrot, to which several said puffins turned and glared at the bird from its perch on Thilly's shoulder.

Thilly shook her head and looked behind her at the procession of murmuring friends and staff, and she felt glad at least that they would all get a proper night's sleep compared to what they had endured for several days. She drooped a bit, weary and hungry and covered in sweat and dried sea spray and grime from her travels. She knew she reeked, and her scalp itched. Yet even though in Castle Taugan, far away and seeming long ago, she could have had a luxurious bath and never ventured beyond the confines of her own country, she marveled at how preposterous her life had been there, how removed from trouble she had really been. Here she was in the stronghold of her mother's people, the mysterious Covenant, after undergoing much strain. A bath would have been nice, yes, but she was just glad to be alive and glad that most of her party was too. She avoided that horrible pit in her thoughts where the deaths of people she and Beaumain ruled over threatened to siphon her down into darkness. She was too tired to let it, too stubborn, and in denial, all at the same time.

*My people died on my watch*, was all that she allowed herself to think, and then she shoved it away. *My goal is to let no one else.*

The Covenant knights drew her into a great hallway with many archways branching off it, and then to a chamber set with a long table. In that chamber hung stalactites of green and purple crystals, and some of the stalagmites from the floor of the place had been carved into sculptures and tables. The air smelled slightly damp but also filled with floral incense, much stronger than she had smelled in the

Violet Grotto. The walls gleamed with sconces reflecting off all the crystalline facets in the room, and the long table was laden with platters of food of all sorts, many of which Thilly did not recognize.

Set off from the dining table was a splendid silver trough, and one of the knights gestured to Evgrent to lead Umbra to it. The mare gladly stepped forward to eat, and two pages, young people who looked to be in their late teens like Thilly, came forth to brush and clean Umbra. Next to the trough, an elaborate silver perch, formed like the forked branch of a tree, stood gleaming, with a platform piled with seeds, nuts, and fruits. Blinky wasted no time in gliding over to it, and finding also a bowl of water, promptly bathed and splashed between munches.

"Blinky!" Thilly mouthed to the bird, who momentarily ceased the noise, but not for long.

Evgrent stepped back, caught Thilly's eye, and sauntered over to sit at the table. He looked troubled, but Thilly had no time to dwell on that. She watched as Beaumain and Val'dreth were given pride of place and attended to by more pages. They were even keeled, and the only expressions they bore were those of respect and perhaps admiration, but nothing fawning. They had work to do, and they did it without question.

"Thank you," she said quietly to one of the pages, and the young man simply nodded.

This was when she realized fully that she was not going to be treated like a royal here. She was a guest of Priestess Woadlynn, and the Covenant itself. Whatever societal rules they had, she decided it was not based on deference to outsiders. Also, everyone else in her party were treated as equals to her. She received no special treatment for who she was here, beyond being allowed in. It was a strange feeling, yet freeing, somehow. It reminded her of the contingent from the Republic of Montadanthe who had attended her gala. Equal footing, no royals…she could get used to it. But it was a covenant, and so she wondered what residing there entailed.

Birkswood and Mrs. Florence watched her, though she did not realize it. Hana sat to her right, and covered her mouth in between large scoops of food, for she was ravenous and tired in equal measure.

"I'm so sorry, Your Highness," she gasped when she realized she had slurped her drink.

Thilly giggled. "You can let the titles go and enjoy your food and drink. We're not royals here; we're equals."

Hana looked deeply suspicious at that remark.

"I don't know about that, milady," she whispered to Thilly. "Maybe they think us equals, but I still serve you."

Thilly cringed. "I know that," she said, "but you don't have to be that way here. They operate by a different code."

"One that makes most of them knights," observed Hana, her brow pinched together. "Why would they need so many knights? Who do they expect to invade?"

"Well, aside from monsters? Who knows."

She turned then and said, "Isn't this weird?" to Beaumain, and then she blushed and felt sad, for she just wanted to talk to her friend, and he sat still. The pages had done their best to hydrate him and keep him clean, and two hovered nearby, watchful and attentive.

"Shall we take him to his quarters?" one of them asked Thilly.

"Will he be looked after?" Thilly asked the page, this time a young woman.

"Of course," she answered. "High Priestess Astridae has ordered it so, and she plans to visit him herself to assess how to help him."

"Is the High Priestess the woman with the star crown?" Thilly asked, and then the page straightened stiff as a rod and backed away.

# THE VALE OF SEVEN DRAGONS

Thilly turned the opposite direction and beheld the very woman standing at the head of the table, her raiment stunning, with stars and sun ray designs stretching from an elaborate crown headdress, her shoulders broad and glistening with sun ray epaulets reflecting against her dark brown skin, and her eyes green and ringed with violet. Her face looked chiseled from crystal, sharp and keen and elegant, and not to be taken lightly; Thilly understood that immediately. There stood real power in all her stellar radiance: the High Priestess Astridae.

"Greetings, Princess Githilien of Vickery," said the High Priestess. "We are honored by the presence of Woadlynn's daughter, come of age."

"Thank you, High Priestess," said Thilly.

Astridae displayed no emotion whatsoever, and then said, "You are here under duress during an extraordinary time. The Covenant has placed a barrier sphere over and under the land." She gazed out at everyone sitting at the table, and her eyes lingered on Val'dreth and Beaumain. "We face an enemy the likes of which we have never seen before, and desperate actions have been taken, but they are impermanent, and we must find a solution before the barrier breaks down completely.

"To the people of Vickery and Catellaith, we offer you shelter, but we cannot guarantee your safety, given the unnatural threat," and she paused to let the unsettled murmurs dissipate. "We have held the line against many foes for many centuries, and we have kept quiet the beast that resides beneath the earth, the dragon Maelwyrm."

Gasps of surprise, awe, and disbelief undulated around the table. Even Evgrent, Thilly saw, raised his eyebrows. Birkswood and Mrs. Florence, of course, sat impassively.

"I had thought the dragons were long gone, or actual myth," Thilly remarked, and she heard mutters of assent and saw nods as well.

"Actual myth!" exclaimed Astridae, and her expressionless face finally broke into a wry smile, revealing bright white teeth. "Myth, however, always interweaves with fact. The dragon is very much real, and in repose, for the Covenant is entrusted to his safety and his rest. So we sing to him, and have for centuries, to let him sleep after his battles. Maelwyrm is an old dragon, and we owe him his deserved respite, for he kept the Realm safe and brokered peace among the other six dragons of the Vale."

"So there really are seven dragons?" Thilly asked in wonder.

"There are indeed," answered Astridae, and she tilted her head and let the candle and firelight twinkle upon her starry crown.

"Where are the other six?" Thilly wanted to know.

"They are each within their home countries," answered Astridae simply, holding her hands out. "It amuses and also concerns me that you did not know this, Princess."

Birkswood dared to speak. "High Priestess, it was the instruction of her parents."

The wry smile returned to Astridae's face.

"And greetings to you as well, Birkswood. We have seen some things," she said, and Thilly's eyes flew wide, watching the old butler's face tinge a darker hue. "It is good that you, especially, have returned at this time."

At last, Astridae sat in her high-backed silver chair, and as she drank from a violet goblet, silver and gold and emerald bangles clinked together on her arms. Thilly could then see that she bore an elaborate starburst design on breastplate armor molded to her curvy form, and a dragon wound around that star. Thilly wondered if it were Maelwyrm. Astridae turned to her.

"You surely experienced the earthquakes, though, yes?" she asked Thilly, her dark eyes seeming to burrow into her.

Thilly recognized that look as daring her to say something amiss. The High Priestess was a commander. It was evident in every movement, smooth yet in complete control at all times. She impressed Thilly, but Thilly refused to slip into outright awe. She felt as though she were under a powerful lens and being tested at the same time.

"Yes, we did endure a number of earthquakes," Thilly replied.

"What did you think caused them?" Astridae questioned.

Thilly looked at Beaumain, and she blinked for a moment. She tried to stifle a sigh, but a bit of it escaped anyway. When she turned back to look at the high priestess, she noticed a softening in the woman's face.

"He would—he would say it was seismic activity," said Thilly, "and that it was not expected in the places we felt it. Not like in the northeast, in Osthadon. Or even Valetheant."

Astridae nodded, sending shafts of sparkles all about the great dining hall.

"Prince Beaumain is correct," she agreed. "It was the dragons, Princess, causing the earthquakes."

Thilly looked at her with huge eyes.

"But that's never happened before!" she said.

"Well, not in recent memory," Astridae replied. "And never by all of them."

"The monsters?" Thilly wondered.

"It would appear so," said Astridae. "The dragons seem to have stirred in their sleep. I have sought evidence throughout the realm, and each country has experienced the quakes. The dragons are perturbed…yet hopefully not infiltrated."

Silence spread around the table, and Thilly went cold.

Astridae raised her head and said, "If indeed the dragons are infiltrated, we are all lost."

A few cries of shock rose from the crowd.

"No, there is no softening this possibly, Birkswood," said the High Priestess, seeing the butler's scandalized face. "Your people should know."

"What should we do?" Thilly asked. "If dragons are taken over by those—those things—"

"Which is why we sought to prevent it here, and also so our Covenant is not invaded," said the High Priestess. "Unfortunately, we are strained to our limits with protection spells and trying to keep Maelwyrm at peace."

"It is most appreciated," Thilly told her. "What can you do to keep up the enchantment?"

Here Astridae then sighed and lowered her head.

"We cannot," she declared. "We will begin to break down; we already have. Another attack might be the one to finish us. But we also cannot do this to our wildlife, Princess. We have disrupted the tide table, migration, and even the courses of the detritivores under the surface of the earth. We cannot trade a potential catastrophe for another."

Thilly's mouth fell open. "What will you do?"

"We will take away the protection," answered Astridae.

"And expose us all, yourselves included, to those monsters?" she nearly shouted. "How could you?"

"As I said, we are strained," said Astridae. "And it is my decision."

"They will kill you, maim you, or take you over," said Thilly vehemently, her cheeks flushed, and her fists clenched. "You would risk all of that for…for tide tables?"

"Ask yourself," Astridae's deep, resonant voice cut through the hall, "what price is worth paying, to let our environment degrade, so that we might not be attacked? Sooner or later, they will break free."

"You're abandoning the hopes of everyone here by doing this!" cried Thilly. "I urge you not to!"

"Ah, your mother's daughter indeed," said Astridae with a small laugh. "It is not hope that you need, it is strength, and we are weakening. We cannot fight this force by sacrificing our lands and our strength. Do you see that?"

Thilly shook her head.

"You might be the only stronghold left," she said, feeling defeated. "If you go, what will be left?"

Astridae spread her hands out on the table before her, her fingernails long and tipped by green crystals.

"Every nation in this realm must face this thing, must fight it," she said. "We can't hold it back, so we must meet it. You are with us now, and safe, and you will be protected by us, so long as you stay here."

"Nobody is safe anywhere," Thilly said then. "You're in denial. You don't know what those things can do. What power do you have against them? You can't sing them into submission. You can't fight them with swords."

"What do you suggest, if you are so certain?" asked the High Priestess, her eyes narrowing, and glinting deep within.

"Only one thing stopped them," said Thilly, "at the shore. Fire. But not regular fire, pitch fire. And the fae lost one of their own, Mal'treth, creating their own fire and"—she looked sorrowfully at the fae—"it worked, but it was not enough to stop them all. There are too many, and some of them are huge."

"Tell me," Astridae said, her voice like iron on stone, "what do you suggest?"

Thilly stood, and just as she did so, her mother entered the room and stared at her.

The High Priestess Astridae stood then, between Thilly with her hair wild and her red sash like a gash of heart's blood across her body, her sword on her hip, and her mother Woadlynn, pale, tall, golden, and covered in the fine stellar mail.

Looking at her mother and shaking, Thilly swallowed with a very dry mouth.

"Stop your singing. All of you," she said. "And wake the dragons."

# CHAPTER 30

## OF SONGS AND MEADOWS GONE

"And thus spake your daughter, Woadlynn of the Isles," said Astridae. "Will you silence the singing of the Covenant? You must decide soon, for we will untangle the enchantments for the barrier at dawn. I will sacrifice no more of home than I have already done."

Everyone stared at the three of them until Woadlynn motioned for Thilly and Astridae to leave the room.

In an adjacent hall, Woadlynn said, "You would sacrifice us all, then," and her voice was like a sword itself, challenging. "If we let the dragons wake, what will they feast upon? All of us? The farms of the Vale? Do they crave monsters from the void? Or will they become like them, and doom us further?"

"I do not have answers for the hypotheticals," declared Astridae. "We will abandon the protection and we *will* fight. Your daughter is correct: we need to wake the dragons, and we need to do it soon. Starting with our own.

"And now I bid you goodnight, Githilien," she continued. "I will see how we can aid Prince Beaumain, and your people will be attended to, including Hana of Osthadon; for although that land is no friend of ours, it is clear she is a bright child of them."

Thilly stared at the high priestess in shock. "How did you know?"

"I know, Githilien," answered Astridae, "an abundance of trivia, much of it useless, all of it interesting, and some of it helpful after all."

Thilly shook from head to toe, standing there. "Mother," she said, her voice quaking, "we have to do this. It is not just for Aceltia. It is for Vickery. It is for Father."

"Your father is well and safe," countered Woadlynn, "for I have made it so."

"In so doing, Woadlynn," said Astridae, "you have also sheltered him from growth, from evolving, and he has grown soft."

That stung.

"My father is not a soft man," said Thilly with a heated voice. Yet even as she said the words, she felt her stomach drop. Astridae was not entirely incorrect, and now Thilly realized in full what her mother had done.

"You...sheltered all of us until these attacks, when you had to form protections up here, didn't you?" she demanded.

Woadlynn lifted her head upon its long, slender neck.

"I protected my husband, and I protected the dragon," she countered. "I was duty bound to do both."

Thilly trembled. "I—I think you put us all at greater risk, Mother."

Woadlynn shook her head.

"Enough of this, daughter," she said in a prickly voice. "You are tired. You must bathe and rest and we will speak again in the morning. High Priestess," and she bowed.

Astridae tilted her head with its many sparkling points upon the crown and left Thilly alone with her mother.

Woadlynn wore a long cloak with a gossamer hood woven of stars and flowers, some of which reminded Thilly of her own star-flowers, and she thrust her hand in her pocket to clasp the little embedded flower from Vyrent and saved by Evgrent. Thilly found her mother ethereal and canny, familiar and overwhelming at the same time. And here they were, face to face, finally.

Everything froze: every second, every mote of dust, perhaps even every molecule there save the spaces in which Thilly and Woadlynn dwelt together, breathing the same air for the first time in over a decade, yet stitching those years together in real time and in the same place at last. Thilly shook all over, and she could see despite what must have been decades of training by the Covenant to seem restrained, that her mother trembled some too…it was barely perceptible to Thilly, but she *knew* her mother, knew every twitch of muscle in every pore of the woman's face, and had since the day she was born. How could she have forgotten this incredible woman, with whom she both disagreed and admired so much?

*It is not that you forgot,* her mother reminded her in her thoughts. *It is that you* chose *not to remember. The same as I chose not to remember the two greatest pains of my life: that of childbirth and that of leaving you behind.*

And then the tears flowed from Thilly, beginning with a slow welling as the wonder of her mother grew in such clarity and focus and returned to her memories in full color and love and heartache. That slow welling became a runnelling of tears, and finally a torrent, as Thilly bent over in half, choking, gagging on her own tears and snot and then she clenched her fists and bayed.

"How—how could you?" she shouted at Woadlynn with the force of years upon years of her own turbulent nature and her own denial over her grief. *"You left your baby behind."*

Those words she drew from her soul the way she might pull her sword from its scabbard, except she knew better how to wield words than any blade, and she knew how to strike them true. So she did, and Woadlynn's starry chainmail veil shimmered as her body responded viscerally to the anger and the hurt roaring forth from her daughter like a bonfire unabated.

Woadlynn did not look away from her daughter, and instead stood very still.

"Thilly," she said in her low voice, "I am sorry."

Thilly felt so small just then, so vulnerable, that she found it unbearable. Yet her mother had apologized at last, and Thilly did not want to spend more of her life wondering if there might be a path forward with her mother. So she stepped up to Woadlynn and threw her arms about her mother and wept into her neck, much as she had done as a very little girl from some insult or injury.

She breathed in the scent of her mother, which she had long forgotten: a mix of almost citrus, spice, and dried flowers…the flowers of Vickery meadows in summer. She saw, in her memory, that very scene, of walking with her mother among the tall grasses, the stalks of poppies and periwinkle and daisies dancing in the wind, the scent of wheat fields warmed by the sun: a moment of pure bliss and daisy chains and lying on their backs holding hands, looking up at cloud shapes in a blue bowl of sky. And then she had been too tired on her little legs for the walk home, so Woadlynn had carried her, and she had buried her face in her mother's neck.

To her father, Woadlynn strode, and he released her from her mother, and laid her on a divan, and covered her with a blanket.

Gathlade had said, "Oh, must it be tonight? What will you tell her?"

And she had said into her favorite space of his neck, up against his ear, where his then-brown beard tickled her, "I will tell her nothing. I will watch over you, and you can tell me how she is."

"How can you bear that?" he had asked.

"Duty to you and to her," she had replied, "and so you must let me do what I can to protect you both as long as I can. I am of more use to the Realm itself than I am here, to waste away and wonder if I could have done more."

Thilly had heard these words among her dozing, those many years ago, but she had never understood them until now. She had perhaps understood their tone, though, and the determination of her mother, which she had never questioned.

"You see, I meant well at the time," said Woadlynn to her ruefully, "and you grew to be so independent and strong-willed!"

"They say I am like you," said Thilly, stepping back from Woadlynn, who held the girl's hands in her own aging ones, delicate and small, unlike Thilly's strong and versatile hands, now callused and cut and scraped from her journey.

"Let me guess," said Woadlynn with a twitching smile, "stubborn, willful, likes to bend the rules."

"Yes," replied Thilly, managing to grin. "How did Father ever catch you at all?"

Woadlynn laughed a deep, velvety laugh at that.

"I sought *him* out," she answered, with a mischievous glint in her eyes. "He was a good man, and so smart, and we studied together often. And, well, I fell in love."

"Why couldn't you speak to me? Like you do him?" Thilly asked next. It had bothered her since her discovery.

Woadlynn shrugged and sighed. "It seemed like a good idea to let you grow up without my interference," and when Thilly's expression grew stern, she hastily added, "and after all, I had to sing at certain times, and did not see your father as often as you might think. It seems you did well, however. I made sure Mrs. Florence and Birkswood remained at Castle Taugan with you, and it is a good thing they did; I do not think your father could have run things nearly so well without them."

"So Birkswood is...from here?" Thilly asked, marveling.

Woadlynn smiled openly. "He is," she replied. "He has known me since *I* was a little girl, and was loyal to my family as well. He in many ways served as something of a father to me, for I was orphaned as a young girl. He made sure the Covenant took me in. And they gave me family and shelter and trained me to sing. We knew Mrs. Florence for some time as well, although I did not know about her magic skills until much later!"

Thilly laughed. "Oh, I hope you didn't say anything to her!"

"I learned not to," said Woadlynn, and for a moment she seemed lost in a memory as she looked off in the distance. "Thilly," she said then, "can we start over? I want to get to know you. I want to learn about the woman you're becoming. I'm so, so proud of you, every second, every day. I want you to know it. What do you think? Can we start again?"

Thilly sighed. "Will you stop singing?"

Woadlynn blinked, and then she laughed. "My, but you are determined. I—I admit, I am afraid to stop. It has been my life, singing to Maelwyrm."

"Have you ever seen him?" Thilly asked in wonder.

"Not in the flesh, no," her mother answered. "But I have seen his breath. I know you must have as well, flowing into Absinweald."

Thilly gasped. "I thought it was just fog!"

"No," said Woadlynn, grinning, "though it must have been a good day for him, if you don't smell his bad breath!"

"Come to think of it," said Thilly thoughtfully, "the fog *did* smell strange."

"Much of it is mixed with the coastal fog; both combined create an entire ecosystem within the forest Absinweald and beyond. I suppose that will all change, too, once he is awake…"

Woadlynn's voice trailed off, and her face fell. But noticing Thilly staring so earnestly at her, she perked up, shook her starry cloak, and squeezed her daughter's hands in her own.

"There," she said. "That's enough. I'm going to be your mother here, as I should be, and insist you bathe and sleep. We'll talk about our plans tomorrow."

"And Beaumain?" Thilly asked.

Woadlynn nodded. "We will see what we can do for him. I know you are very fond of him and hate to see him like this."

"What do you think caused it?" Thilly dared to ask.

"I can't say for sure," Woadlynn answered, "but it's a form of catatonia, which makes me think he experienced a great shock…so great that he has not recovered. And Thilly, it is possible he may not. But! Do not worry for now. We will try everything we can."

When Thilly was led by her mother to her quarters, she found a golden little shell of a room, beautiful and cozy, and a tall perch stood next to the bed. She found Blinky there, head tucked under wing, dozing. Woadlynn kissed Thilly on her cheek and left. Thilly found a small washroom and a basin of hot water full of bubbles, which she soon sank into and sighed in both discomfort and pleasure at the same time. Then she dressed in a robe and became so drowsy that she fell asleep with her wet hair sprawled on her pillow and blankets up to her nose.

She woke the next day to a knock on her door that startled Blinky, who let out a raspy sort of bark.

"Oh, Blinky," she groaned, "must you bark like a dog?"

Blinky fluffed up and scratched behind its ear and blinked at her and barked once more.

Grumbling, Thilly opened the door and found Hana there, looking red as a beet, as though she had scrubbed off layers of skin. She seemed quite proud of it, too.

"Wait until you see the tea," Hana gushed, beckoning Thilly out. Thilly found a long-sleeved white shirt and a simple tan tunic on the foot of her bed, and a clean new red sash, rather than the one she had torn for herself. There was also a pair of tan pants to go under the tunic. She tied the sash about her waist and felt quite ready to tackle anything. Then she searched the room and found her sword leaning up against a wall. She attached its scabbard to her belt and patted it. Blinky flew to her shoulder, and she walked with Hana to the dining hall.

There sat everyone except Beaumain, and Thilly wondered where he might be. Woadlynn met her and kissed her cheek, and the scent of meadow flowers rose from her hair as she hugged Thilly.

"He is being examined by the High Priestess," she whispered, sitting next to Thilly.

Thilly nodded in relief.

Val'dreth sat looking refreshed, arms bound in clean attire and face brighter, and the looks on both Ki'roth's and Ul'trok's faces shone in relief and gratitude. Everyone looked as though they had finally slept well for the first time in weeks, except for Evgrent. He sat alone, close to Umbra, and then when he saw Thilly, he rose and led Umbra out of the room, avoiding her gaze.

*Such a cranky man*, she thought, rolling her eyes.

She enjoyed her tea and scones and grain-sausages, and the wealth of Aceltia jams glittering in silver jam pots. Most of all, she enjoyed the moment of peace.

But it did not last.

The earth shook, first a small tremor, and then with greater fervor. The next shaking grew so violent that everyone dropped to the floor and held to the table legs.

"What is happening?" Thilly cried.

Woadlynn called out, "We stopped singing! Maelwyrm awakes!"

# CHAPTER 31

## LEATHERED WINGS AND DARK THINGS

Thilly felt her stomach lurch along with the earth.

"That didn't take long!" she cried, staring at her mother under the table.

The shaking stilled finally and Woadlynn stood.

"I gave the order last night," she declared.

Thilly smiled in gratitude. "Thank you. Now we have a chance."

Woadlynn pressed her lips into a line. "I hope so, Thilly. Maelwyrm is quite old. Perhaps he has a few embers left within him after his long sleep. At any rate, we should be there to greet him when he awakens, so that he may know us…and perhaps, if he's quite ornery, I can sing a few notes to him to calm him."

"What then?" Thilly asked, and Hana leaned closer to her to hear the answer.

"Then," said Woadlynn, looking back and forth between the two girls, "you fly! And go find the other six dragons. I think it best if you venture to Osthadon first; I have a feeling that you'd be faster finding Antimon than Jadesilver. I think she's to the south, not up at this end of the Vale."

Hana went pale. "Isn't—isn't Antimon the mean one? And isn't Osthadon...mean also?"

Woadlynn bit her lip. "Well, yes and yes, I'm afraid," she replied. "So you'll be essential, Hana, in brokering any peace."

Hana burst out laughing. "I don't know a thing about any o' that!" she cried, giggling so hard that she had to fan herself.

"You might surprise yourself," Woadlynn said warmly.

"Are we leaving the Isles, then?" Thilly asked.

"I think it's a good idea, Thilly," said her mother.

"What about Beaumain?"

"I can answer that," said a deep woman's voice.

Thilly turned to see High Priestess Astridae, smiling, wearing a violet and silver star crown and sparkling silver, blue, and indigo robes embroidered with glittering stars. She held her hands together in front of her and looked most regal as she took in the assemblage in the dining hall.

"Prince Beaumain is restored," she announced, "after a fashion." Shouts of joy and relief rose, and Thilly clasped her own hands under her chin in happiness. "You should know, however, that the price was steep. He has knowledge now that he did not before: some of it base and brutal and incomprehensible. Knowledge of the enemy."

Thilly felt cold spikes travel up and down her back, hearing this.

"This enemy is far worse than what we could have imagined," said Astridae gravely. "And I know that the sacrifice we must make for our lands means we are going to be at great risk. But we shall not hide. We shall fight!"

The knights of the hall clattered their staffs and shook their raiment, and although Thilly could not see their faces, she imagined they must look exuberant.

"But where is the prince?" she asked Astridae.

The woman then spread her arms wide, making her robes look like blue, purple, and silver wings, and then she stepped aside. From the shadows behind her strode Beaumain, and he was met with cheers. But not by Thilly.

He turned his gaze to her, and his look felt like a slap across her face. His eyes were as beautifully aqua as ever, ringed by red-gold lashes in his light brown face, and he was quite handsome and emotive, but not in the way she might have hoped. He looked coldly furious, and thinner in the face, and not happy to see her at all.

She stood and faced him, and he turned away from her.

"I think," Astridae declared, "that it has been long enough since the prince did without his tea, so let us share with him in that and in healing!"

More cheers erupted, and Beaumain sat down the table from Thilly, next to Ki'roth and the other two fae.

*What has happened to him?* Thilly wondered. Hana touched her elbow.

"He will be all right," she whispered encouragingly.

"I hope so, Hana," Thilly whispered back.

Unnerved, shaken body and soul, Thilly downed her breakfast and stood. Blinky hopped onto her chair and promptly siphoned up every crumb that had fallen from her outfit. Woadlynn caught Thilly's eye.

"Something has happened with the prince," she said quietly. "I can try to find out, if you like."

# THE VALE OF SEVEN DRAGONS

"No," said Thilly instantly. "He's been through enough as is. He'll come around." She said that to try to fool herself into believing it, but she knew anger when she saw it, and his gaze at her carried it.

Woadlynn joined Astridae where she stood, and the High Priestess announced, "We will send a contingent to Maelwyrm, and then we must relinquish the boundary to let our lands and sea restore back to their health. So let us be ready to fight or flee, as needed. But we have a *dragon*. Let us hope he is willing to ride under any banner and fight these foul things out in the world."

She turned to Birkswood and arched her eyebrow up at him. He stood and inclined his head and approached her and Woadlynn. He glanced down at Thilly.

She asked him, "Is there something you'd like to tell me, Birkswood?"

He stood straight and tall and lifted his chin.

"Not so much, Your Highness, no," he answered. "All in good time."

She shook her head. "Well, then I guess we'd better be off. Do we have to ride with those strange light-beings again?"

Woadlynn laughed and glanced at Astridae, who frowned slightly. "The chaorids are...interesting, are they not? They are the ferry captains of the Isles, however, and we must abide by their domain. So let us head to the grotto and set sail to our dragon."

These were all words that Thilly never imagined she would hear, let alone act upon, and she felt a thrill of purpose and excitement. Maybe they could sweep forth across the Vale and join up with the remaining six dragons and soar through the sky to meet the foul other-creatures with a torrent of flame, she thought, eyes glazing over.

A bump into her shoulder jarred her out of her daydreams.

"You should have told me," said a voice to her. She turned and looked up and found Beaumain. He avoided eye contact with her.

Thilly then knew that whatever Astridae had done, while she had certainly restored the prince, she had opened him up to something traumatic. And she had a good feeling she knew what and who it was about.

"Did you see your mother?" asked Thilly urgently. "In Absinweald, during the attack?"

Beaumain, still looking away, answered in a neutral voice, "I did. She lured me. Evgrent rescued me, but not before I felt...I could feel her...it...chewing at the edges of my thoughts, trying to get in. And then I did not know where I was. Until this morning. You should have told me, Githilien."

"And what exactly should I have told you, Your Highness?" growled Thilly, breathing more quickly.

Beaumain turned then and looked at her with such intensity that she flinched.

"That my mother is dead," he replied, his voice like hammer blows. "She is replaced by a creature not of this world. And what signature of my mother remains will seek me—and us—always. We are damned, Thilly. You should have told me."

He turned away from her and stalked off toward the grotto, not waiting for her to catch up and not wanting to speak to her at all.

She turned to Astridae. "Tell me what happened," she pleaded.

The look on the woman's face unsettled Thilly.

"Let us walk together, before you depart," she said to the princess.

She led Thilly into one of the many chambers along the great hallway that led to the grotto. In one of them, a library stretched preposterously high above them in a cylindrical room, threaded with

# THE VALE OF SEVEN DRAGONS

a little spiral elevator atop which a librarian knight gathered ancient tomes high above their head.

Thilly gave the library one glance of appreciative wonder, but quickly turned back to the High Priestess.

"Child, I do not wish to frighten you," said Astridae in a softer tone than Thilly had heard from her before.

"Risk it," said Thilly. "I beg you. I need to know. He is my dearest friend," and in saying so, Thilly fully realized that crucial truth. Not having him by her side hurt.

Astridae nodded and sighed. She looked with great feeling at Thilly.

"His mother is lost," she said.

Thilly's shoulders sank. "I feared this. I hoped it was just—a trick of the light, or her wanting someone else for him to marry, other than myself."

"Perhaps the real Queen Maulielle harbored such feelings," pondered Astridae, "but you will never know fully, because she is completely and utterly destroyed, and yet remade, scaffolded into a hideous decoy. Such is the way with these creatures, in some instances." She looked disgusted then. "It makes them far more dangerous than any beast in the world. And that is how I know they are not of our world."

"But where did they come from?" Thilly asked.

"We do not know for certain," Astridae answered, and by the tiniest twitch in the woman's cheek, Thilly suspected this frustrated the otherwise unemotional High Priestess a great deal. "If we knew that, perhaps we could do something meaningful about it. Perhaps we could learn a weakness other than extraordinary fire. I fear the destruction upon our Realm from within and without, Githilien. The dragons may well be our only hope."

"Will he be all right?" Thilly asked her.

"I do not know, dear child. He was deeply catatonic, and I bonded with him through thought to try to coax him back. It worked, but what a price... for I could see what he saw before he slid into that blank state."

"What was it?" Thilly pressed, her mouth gone dry.

"He saw his mother as she was before," answered Astridae grimly, "and he could see her transformed and murdered at the same time. He was held in thrall by this thing, for it broke his mind to consider. And he could also see some of that creature's thoughts, so that is how he knew that you had seen the faux Maulielle as well."

"Antares preserve us," gasped Thilly. "But I didn't know for sure, so how would I have told him?"

"Githilien," said the High Priestess seriously, "know this: grief takes many forms. Anger is often one of them. Prince Beaumain has undergone an incredible shock. I confess I do not know why that being did not outright kill him or make him one of its own. I suspect it needed him alive for nefarious purposes, however, and so I shall not be sad to see you both leave, I am sorry to say. But dear princess, be careful. He is easily triggered now. He might be sensitive to those foul creatures, or he might be more vulnerable. You won't know until you are up against them, and I fear that is a certainty. So go forth, wake Maelwyrm and let him bond to a rider... he will choose among you... and then seek the other dragons. I hesitate to recommend your going to Osthadon first, but it is closest to us, just with a bit of Valetheant to go through to the north. I pray we meet again one day, child, but not until the Realm is safe. Go well, Princess Githilien of Vickery, daughter of Woadlynn and Gathlade, and keep that fiery spirit of yours going, no matter what happens next."

Thilly bowed her head. "Thank you, High Priestess."

With that, she rejoined her companions in the Violet Grotto, and she felt disorientation from seeing the vivid colors of the water and the presence of the glowing Chaorids. Despite Beaumain's coldness toward her, Thilly was glad to see him animated again. If he was not his old self, he at least was alive and functioning. She hoped he would not hate her forever.

While Beaumain avoided her gaze, Blinky kept Thilly distracted, at times flying just above the boat, which was pulled by the Chaorids toward the shore but also tugged by the released waves, with the tide going in. The ride was turbulent this time, the sea choppy with whitecaps, and the breeze nearly gale strength and full of the cold, fresh air that had been held back by the Covenant's protection, now dissolved. Thilly sat beside her mother, who placed her arm around her daughter in the chilly wind and kept Thilly warm.

She felt comfortable and drowsy within her mother's arms, and that helped her move on from her thoughts about both Beaumain and Evgrent, who sat at the back of the ship with Umbra. It was time to stitch back together her relationship with her mother, and while she still felt some hurt over their missed years, part of her spirit had begun to heal by being with Woadlynn again.

Birkswood sat in front of them but turned back often, as did Mrs. Florence, and then they would look at each other with glints of satisfaction.

"It is good to see you together again, ladies," said Birkswood over the rush of water and spray.

"Indeed it is," seconded Mrs. Florence. "Here's to many more years of this going forward!"

Woadlynn smiled and hugged Thilly to her, saying, "It feels so strange. Like not a day has passed, and yet here I have a grown young woman of the world! I am so proud."

Thilly beamed. But when she glanced at Beaumain, he kept avoiding her, and his shoulders drooped. She felt heartbroken for him.

*How sad that I should regain my mother and he should lose his. Nothing about this is fair.*

Woadlynn thought back, *You cannot blame yourself for what has happened. There is only one enemy that we face, and they did this to him. No one else but them.*

Thilly heaved a great sigh, adjusted her sword, and watched the fog fly by them, tinged coral in the morning sun of late autumn. Soon it would be winter, and there would be little sun in the far north here. She was quite ready to leave Aceltia and begin whatever path necessary to get to safety and to her father and Vickery.

The fog broke up to reveal the shore, with the deep green-grey sea breaking in billowing white surf, and Hana cried, "Look!"

Thilly strained to see what the girl might be looking at, but she only found the misty coast, with the dark streak of Absinweald on the horizon. She could see the sea rocks covered with barking seals and birds wheeling in, ecstatic to have the tides back.

"What do you see, Hana?" she asked.

"Well," said the maid, "many things, but look, don't you see *that*? All that sand and dust flying up?"

Thilly leaned forward and squinted. "I see a cloud of something, I suppose," she answered doubtfully.

"I'll bet that's the dragon!" Hana exclaimed. "Waking up!"

"Oh!" cried Thilly, and Birkswood looked as well with great interest.

"Ah, good Hana!" he said, "you have eyes like a spyglass. I can't see much of anything!"

"But that's not all I see," said Hana excitedly. "Look down a bit, in the valley!"

Thilly grinned. "Hana, we really can't see what you can. Just tell us!"

## THE VALE OF SEVEN DRAGONS

Evgrent then called urgently, "There's something to the west behind us," and Thilly whipped around and locked eyes with the man. She shivered, for he looked frightened. She looked to the horizon and could see a dark streak, like a long cloud or strand of horizontal smoke. "Hana," he said, "can you tell us what *that* is?"

Hana turned and looked, and her face went nearly grey.

"Gods," she whispered. She turned to Thilly. "Can we make it to shore faster?"

"Is it them?" cried Thilly, but she did not really need to hear the answer. Hana could see.

Woadlynn rose from her seat and worked her way to the front of the speeding boat. She spoke in a resonating voice to the chaorids, and then she braced, for the craft surged ahead even faster.

"Hold on!" she called to the passengers. "Face forward, not back! We will make it to the shore. Focus on that."

But the cloud was fast…alarmingly, disturbingly fast, and it began to fill the sky to the west. The morning sun to the east beckoned, and Thilly hoped against hope they would indeed make it to the shore.

"Can we change course?" shouted Hana, shocking Thilly.

"We must make it to shore," Woadlynn answered, her face drawn and her brow furrowed. Thilly crawled with dread at her expression. "We have to make it to the dragon! Otherwise we're lost! *Hurry, hurry!*" she yelled at the chaorids.

They raced forward, the boat bouncing over the waves, its passengers by turns crying out or vomiting, or clinging to the sides and seats. Blinky rose and burst forward, and Thilly cried, "Blinky!" but the bird wasted no time and pumped its wings, headed straight for the kicked-up dust.

"But we could be a bit south and—" Hana began.

"Hana," said Mrs. Florence with a hard voice, "you heard the Priestess Woadlynn. We must make it to the dragon."

"But Mrs. Florence, there's—"

"It can wait, Hana!" cried Mrs. Florence.

Hana looked fit to be tied, but before Thilly could ask what was so important, her eyes fell on Beaumain, who had turned and stared back at the incoming tempest.

"Beaumain!" she shouted at him, and he turned to her with a stern face. This relieved her, for she had feared he would slip back into catatonia. "Don't look at it," she told him. "Please."

"It's coming for me," he called back. "Why not just let it have me?"

"Fuck off!" yelled Thilly, and Hana gasped. "I'm not letting anything have you!" She put her hand on her sword hilt, and then the boat skidded onto the shore suddenly and with a jolt, and she fell forward into Birkswood and Mrs. Florence.

"Get off!" screamed Woadlynn. "Run for the dragon!"

"Thilly, Thilly!" a nasal little voice shrieked, and as Thilly leapt from the boat onto the shore, she could see little Blinky flapping anxiously, circling over a great chuffing and huffing in the earth.

And so they all ran or were carried as fast as they could, away from the sea, and Thilly beheld a most unusual sight: the chaorids rose into the sky and surged toward that dark cloud to the west. Now it was more defined, roiling, colling, spinning with wings and teeth. The glowing chaorids met high above the water, now in full shadow, with the dark beings, and one by one, their lights winked out, and they were smeared across the sky like meteors, obliterated.

"Gods," moaned Thilly, but she sprinted toward the immense clouds of dirt as the earth shook under her. Evgrent, on Umbra, galloped up beside her.

"This is where I leave you," he called down to her, and he glanced off to the south, where Hana had looked earlier.

"What?" cried Thilly.

"My job is done, Princess," growled Evgrent. "I did not sign up for any of this."

Thilly halted in her sprint and gawked up at him.

"What the fuck!" she yelled at him. "What do you mean?"

He looked coldly down at her and patted his saddlebag. "I'm a mercenary. It's what I do. I got my payment, and now I'll be off, thank you, because my work is done."

Thilly pulled her sword forth. "You fucking coward!" she screamed. "Leaving when we need you most!"

"You never needed me," he hissed back, as Umbra began to whinny and jump. "I did a job, I got paid for it, and now I'm out. Goodbye."

Thilly's jaw dropped, and Evgrent said something in Umbra's ear, and she leapt up, and they raced away to the south at great speed. Thilly watched them go, breathless, her eyes stinging in shock.

"Thilly!" her mother cried. "Get behind the dragon. Here they come!"

And with a great, ear-shattering roar, a beast burst from the tidal flatland and heaved its great leathery wings aloft. It was brown and green, and it bore front legs with grasping claws, and thick hind legs. The wings were separate and broad and scarred, jutting out from the creature's back. Its gnarled, ancient scales were dirty, even a bit shaggy from old wear and tear, but solid, and ranged from platter-sized on its back to hand-sized on its head. The beast's head was deeply grooved by scars, with old, weathered rows of horns on its crown. It had a grizzled and aged look, with some sagging of its jowls, as if they formed a goatee. It towered above them all, easily the height of two elephants while standing on all its legs, and it looked as though it could swallow a child in one gulp.

"Oh my," wailed Hana, "he looks angry. Or hungry."

"Never mind," shouted Thilly, "get behind him! Let him take his anger out on those things out there!"

Woadlynn and Ki'roth herded everyone behind the dragon, and Woadlynn stood at his feet, and she sang up to him a high song, and he turned his immense green-brown head down to her and snorted, and puffs of sulfurous smoke billowed out. Her eyes watered and she laughed. "Hello to you too, dear Maelwyrm!"

She stood back, smiled at Thilly, and then she jerked where she stood.

Thilly stared at her.

"Mother?" she called to Woadlynn.

A black spike burst from Woadlynn's chest, spraying blood everywhere.

Thilly screamed.

Strong arms seized her and pushed her face into his shoulder: Beaumain.

"Don't look, Thilly," he said urgently, holding her tight and running backward with her beyond Maelwyrm.

Thilly heard a gurgle and a shriek as the black, twisting things ripped Woadlynn apart, spraying her blood across the sand.

Maelwyrm, in shock and rage, set forth a blistering column of fire, incinerating her remains and the foul things with them, and then lifted his head and howled at the sky, with fire and ash raining all around him.

# CHAPTER 32

## RIDERS OF SKY AND SURF

Maelwyrm whipped his head back and forth, spraying fire everywhere, and snapped at the air for any of the stalks sprouting from the cloudlike mass of creatures above. The flame seared the monsters at great temperature, and they seemed confounded by the sheer power of the dragon's fire. They recoiled and shrank into an oblong oily-black shape and then rose at incredible speed into the sky, above the cloud deck and out of sight.

Shouts of elation rose, and Maelwyrm then sank down and lay his head on the cauterized mud flats and sighed like a great dog, puffs of smoke spilling out of his great nostrils.

Thilly could not hear the cheers. She could only hear, on loop, the sound of her mother dying, and of her own screams.

Beaumain held her close, and they sat pressed up against Maelwyrm's abdomen as he rested. Beaumain stroked her frazzled auburn hair and rocked her as she sobbed. At times she would let out a sharp cry of deep anguish.

Birkswood, Mrs. Florence, and Hana hovered close by, their faces stricken and stained with tears and soot. While the two older helpers had known Woadlynn, Hana had not, but it pained her to see Thilly hurt.

"If there's anythin' we can do, milady," she said softly. "We're right here."

It was Birkswood who seemed most winded by Woadlynn's death.

"I'm sorry, Your Highness," he said, choking on tears, "I'm just so very sorry."

Mrs. Florence patted his arm and shook her head.

"Child," she said to Thilly, who still buried her head up against Beaumain's neck and refused to look up at anyone, "there's nothing to make sense of here, and nothing I can ever say will take away the pain. Just know that we *love* you, and we always have, and we always will."

With that, she gently pulled Birkswood and Hana away.

Thilly could hear her whispering something to them and felt a spike of anger shoot up inside her, and for a moment she clung to it, because it was something she understood. She *knew* anger. She did not know true grief.

And she knew just where to turn her anger with as much focus as Maelwyrm's spouting flame: Evgrent.

"Why did he leave?" she muttered, finally lifting her head from Beaumain's shoulder but not quite willing to let him go just yet.

He held onto her also and looked into her stern face and her bloodshot eyes.

"Who, Thilly?" he asked gently.

"That damned Evgrent," she said. Then she rose and stood and dusted herself off. "I'd like to give him a piece of my mind, going off like that. Saying he was paid to help see me up here. Then he goes off."

She was raving, and Beaumain knew it. He stood and watched her puffy face and noticed her balled fists, and he sighed softly.

"Well, he was always going to do that, wasn't he?" he asked. "It seemed clear to me. Why else would he have stayed with us as long as he did?"

Thilly turned her head to look down the coast, and shielded her eyes from the sun, now arcing overhead at its low, late-autumn angle even close to noon. She watched ashes curl into the coastal air. Then another wave of horror rollicked through her, thinking suddenly again of what had just happened. She fell to her knees and vomited.

Birkswood watched her closely through his grief-tired eyes but did not interfere. One of the footmen spouted off, saying, "We've got ourselves a dragon! Those things won't mess with us anymore. I'm ready to head home."

"Proper show, that," another said.

"Will you shut your mouth?" Birkswood's voice cut through like an axe.

The footmen stared at him with wide eyes.

"You will never say such disrespectful things in front of the princess and the prince," he bellowed. "The princess has lost her mother; the prince also learned he lost *his* mother. I want you to go to them both and apologize or find your own ways home." They scrambled to attention and sputtered, apologizing generally, and Birkswood said, "As for the creatures 'not messing with us,' tell me, how do you know?"

One of them, a tall gangly fellow with pale blue eyes and dull gold hair, stammered, "I just thought that with the dragon, you know, because nobody thought they were still around, and…and it's a *dragon*."

# THE VALE OF SEVEN DRAGONS

"Yes," agreed Birkswood, "you've got enough rational thought left in your hollow head to see that, at least. But unless you're holding back some bit of knowledge we don't have, we don't know where those things came from, or by how many more there *are*. And we have one dragon, an old one"—he reached out to pat Maelwyrm's brownish-green scales—"and we don't know where the others might be. We had better hope those things don't come back with a greater force. We should get going. And you lot," he added with a face full of disgust, "will pack everything up and carry as much as you can on your own backs. Dismissed."

Fuming, the older gentleman patted the flank of the dragon. Blinky fluttered over to his shoulder to get a good vantage from below, having scoped the entire dragon camp from flying in a figure-eight formation above it several times.

"Biiiiiig Blinky," said the bird, blinking up at the dragon, who seemed to be snoozing.

"Yes, indeed," agreed Birkswood.

Beaumain stood straight and tall, dusted himself off, and said, "We need to decide quickly what we will do next. The day grows short. We need shelter, we need food. Do we go back into Absinweald? We can't make it to Osthadon before dark at this rate even *with* a dragon, which brings me to my next question. How in the hells are we going to get all of us where we need to go, when we only have one dragon?"

Maelwyrm let out a long, grumbling sigh and turned his head to look at Birkswood. Blinky tugged at the man's earlobe, much to his chagrin, and said, "Big Blinky *hungry*," and Birkswood growled much as a dragon might himself.

"Quite," he said irritably, "just as we are all hungry, as the prince notes."

Birkswood sighed, feeling that all eyes were on him, when he watched Thilly out of the corner of his. Then he turned to face Maelwyrm. And his eyes went wide.

A deep, hoarse sound rumbled out of the dragon's mouth, and he said in a voice like a sea gale funneled through a huge bellows, "YOU!"

Everyone went dead silent, and Thilly, lost in her own thoughts and shock and grief still, turned to look at the dragon staring down at Birkswood. Blinky looked very pleased with this turn of events and began preening from Birkswood's shoulder. The man looked utterly bewildered.

"Yes?" he answered, as calmly and steadily as he could. Thilly knew that voice and she felt comfort in its solidity, but also knew that for Birkswood, that was his nervous voice…as much as the man had or that she knew of, at any rate.

Again the rumbling, and the windy, deep voice of Maelwyrm, deeper even than Birkswood's considerable baritone, deep as the decibels of a great, thundering waterfall, said, "You are the RIDER, descended of RIDERS."

Then Birkswood did something Thilly had never seen him do before. He blushed from the roots of his hair to the collar of his travel-worn yet tidy cravat. He glanced around at the assemblage of people watching in awe of this conversation. Mrs. Florence lifted an eyebrow at him.

"Is there something you'd like to tell us, Birkswood?" she asked, and Thilly thought she heard an impish and knowing lilt in her accent.

Birkswood put his hands behind his back, lifted his chin, and declared, "Yes. Fine. If you must know, I am indeed descended from Aceltia's dragon riders of old. Not, mind you," he said to the gasps, "that we really believed they existed during the generations since. But. Here we are. That is all."

# THE VALE OF SEVEN DRAGONS

Ki'roth beamed at their fellow fae, who all encircled Birkswood then.

"Maelwyrm has chosen you to be head rider, then," said Ki'roth.

"This is a tremendous honor and duty," said Ul'trok solemnly.

Val'dreth grinned, looking more refreshed than they had in days, and remarked, "How perfect!"

Birkswood drew himself up and said, "I thank you. But I do wonder, grand Maelwyrm, am I not too old for the job?"

Maelwyrm's grumbling turned into a rattle and then little spirals of smoke shot out of his nostrils, making Blinky take flight to avoid them. And so the dragon *laughed*.

"If YOU be too old, dragon rider, then WHAT might I be?" he boomed.

Birkswood smirked. "Fair enough. But how can we make this work? We've too many to carry."

"I must EAT," Maelwyrm said in a slow and rich voice.

"Well," one of the footmen quipped, "I hope you don't mean to eat *us*."

Nervous laughter rippled among the footmen, and wide-eyed stares were exchanged among the maids.

"I do not eat MAMMALS," huffed Maelwyrm. Upon hearing that, Blinky darted over to Hana's shoulder and looked up at the dragon with feathers all drawn in tightly. "I have fasted LONG but that remains true." The dragon turned to Hana and Blinky. "I do not eat WOOD PARROTS, little one," he added. Blinky then fluffed up and squawked appreciatively. "Long have I rested in the SONGS of the COVENANT," and he turned his great, reptilian gold eyes to Thilly. "My favorite song has ENDED, and I am SAD."

Thilly shook where she stood, and Hana stepped near to her, but she held her hand up to the maid. She did not want to speak to anyone, did not want anyone near, not just then. All she could do was stand there and watch in her pain. But with the dragon's words, the tears came again; quietly this time, over her now-stony face.

"What can we feed you?" Birkswood asked the dragon.

"Not seals, I hope," Hana said plaintively. "I can't bear that now."

Maelwyrm huffed. "Not SEALS, not WHALES, not MAMMALS of any kind," and then he turned away from them all and shuffled, kicking up dust and ash, over to the river mouth. He clambered down in, raised his great, green-brown leathery wings, and settled his bulbous old belly down into the river and rested, holding his mouth agape, letting the water flow through it.

"He's gone fishin', he has!" exclaimed Hana, with a delighted chuckle.

"Perhaps we should as well," Beaumain said with a sigh.

Ki'roth and the other two fae nodded to each other.

"We will find food," said Ki'roth. "Sit and rest and make camp. No one will go hungry on this difficult day."

Ki'roth then looked meaningfully at Beaumain while glancing at Thilly. She simply hugged herself and faced the sea.

"That solves one problem, and we thank you for it," Beaumain said gratefully. "But as for the other, our transport…how will we do it? We cannot venture forth on foot again. We are spent, and that is too slow."

Hana wheeled around and looked to the south.

"Oh!" she cried, and she covered her mouth.

Beaumain stepped over to her, alarmed, and said, "What is it? What do you see?"

Hana took her hand away from her mouth to reveal a smile. Tears shone in her eyes.

"I think you can see now," she answered, pointing.

# THE VALE OF SEVEN DRAGONS

Everyone turned except for Thilly, who could hear everything but wanted only silence.

Then she heard the whinny of a horse.

For a second she felt enraged. *Has Evgrent come to get more money from us?*

But then she heard another horse, and another, and before long the sound of many horses and their splashing through the surf line. She turned to look then, and saw Evgrent on Umbra, his hair swept back and his face as taciturn as ever, leading their lost horses back to them.

# CHAPTER 33

## *RENDERED*

*Am I standing in my mother's ashes?* she thought absently, watching Evgrent approach her, and feeling a swirl of sadness, shock, and anger, again with much of that anger directed toward him. It was easy, and she wanted to do nothing hard just then. She had just been through hard.

Now she watched him approach on sleek, ruddy-brown Umbra and felt a bitterness so pure she could have bottled it as a tincture. She hated him just then. And when he rode up to the dragon camp, she planned to make sure he could see that she did.

He avoided her gaze and swept his grey eyes around at the cauterized mud, and some of the sand turned to glass by dragon fire, and lifted his eyes to the riverbanks to see Maelwyrm tilting up his great jaws full of water, a few fish escaping out the corners of his mouth. Evgrent approached Birkswood on horseback, and the two looked at each other for a moment. A flicker of something passed over Evgrent's face as he slid off Umbra.

"It was good of you to bring the horses back to us," Birkswood told him.

"It was nothing," replied Evgrent with a small shrug. "I was passing through and saw them. I can be on my way again."

Mrs. Florence and Hana strode up to him. "Not yet, sir—Mister Evgrent," said Mrs. Florence. "You must stay and let us feed you before you're off again. Let us do that as a thanks. You've brought the horses just when we need them most."

Hana turned to look at Thilly, and Beaumain stood in between Evgrent and Thilly, close enough to watch the man's stern eyes as he turned slowly to her. She avoided turning to him, though.

*I do not need to see him just yet. I do not need to leave this spot. Not just yet.*

She looked up at the leaden sky, the sun now behind clouds as it began to sink further toward sunset.

*Some people believe Mother is in the halls of the cloud tops,* she mused. *I wonder where she is. What she believed.*

Evgrent turned back to Mrs. Florence. "I should not be here," he said quietly.

"Nonsense," answered Birkswood, loudly enough to ensure Thilly heard. "The houses of Vickery and Catellaith owe you a debt of gratitude, and we must repay you."

"Why?" Thilly said then, her voice cold. At last she turned and made eye contact with Evgrent.

He flinched, and his eyebrows flicked up.

*I hope you see,* she thought. *I hope you see and feel how much I hate you.*

But something in his eyes made her slip a moment. Something there she had not seen before, a sort of recognition. It confused her, but she recovered and tossed her wild hair. She marched up to him and lifted her face to stare into those sea-grey eyes until he blinked.

"Why should we repay him?" she asked. "When he told us—*me*—quite clearly that he was a mercenary, that he only helped us for money. It would seem there hasn't been much opportunity for him to *spend* it already. So why?"

"Your Highness—" began Birkswood.

"No," Evgrent interrupted, holding his hand up. "I will stay only to give Umbra refreshment, and take none myself, and then we will go."

Beaumain walked up to him and said, "Where will you go, then? What place is it that you call home?"

Evgrent lifted his chin and lowered his eyelids while regarding the prince.

"My home," answered the man, with one hand on Umbra's back, "is where my horse and I choose to go. We do not live in castles, or kitchens, or villages. And soon, maybe, none of you will, either. So it is for the best that we ride on."

"Perhaps," answered Beaumain, his voice even, "but we won't see you go hungry. The fae just returned with a bounty of fish. Stay one more night with us and then part if you must. We would be most grateful, though, if you could lead our people home. We know you know the way. And you've a fine horse; the other horses clearly feel safe with her. Please consider it."

*The words of a future king indeed*, thought Thilly, and for a moment the little kindling of shame flared up in her, but she beat it back.

Evgrent looked as if he would rather have been anywhere but there just then, but he gritted his teeth and replied evenly, "Thank you. I will consider it."

The footmen helped rally the horses and keep watch on them, which Birkswood liked to see; "Keep them busy and keep their tongues from wagging," he grumbled.

The shared effort in building a great bonfire was lost on Thilly. She knew she should be grateful, but she could not even quite take in what everyone was doing.

"You're in shock, milady," said Hana softly. "It's all right. But come closer to the fire, will you? It's gettin' cold with that sea breeze. And Maelwyrm's coming back. Tomorrow we'll leave this godsforsaken place behind. Tonight, let's honor your mum."

Thilly sighed. "But what about Father?" she whispered very, very quietly.

Hana squeezed her limp cold hand. "We'll go to him when we can. But your mum wanted us to find the other dragons first. We'd not be much good for your dad if we didn't do that, would we?"

"I..." Thilly began. "I don't have the heart to tell him."

"You don't have to be the one that does," Hana said. "Let's just make sure we can live long enough to do it, though, because what if Birkswood's right? What if those things come back?"

"I know they will," Thilly said in a somber voice. "What's the point, then?"

Hana then shook her head and huffed out a great sigh. "Your Highness, what's the point of anythin' then, if you're going to be like that? The point is, *we help each other*. That's the only point there is at the end of it all."

Thilly blinked at Hana, who let her hand fall to her side.

"You go on," she told the girl. "Get something to eat."

"I'll bring you food," promised Hana. "Will you eat some?"

"I don't know," she said truthfully. "I just...I want to be alone for now."

She wanted to hear the pounding of the surf and look at the darkening sea, at the deep grey-blue twilight. Her mother had been a woman of gold and light and song, and now she was gone; she was ashes. And she felt then a spark of gratitude for Maelwyrm, and she shuddered, for at least she was spared, and so were the others, having to bury Woadlynn after the way she was killed.

"Thilly," called Beaumain.

"Not now," she called over her shoulder, sinking into the sand and wrapping her arms around her legs. She stuck her sword point-down deep into the sand. She was tired. So tired; more tired than she had ever been, and she felt a flatness, a resignation. She felt aged, suddenly, as if all the charming little things she had once enjoyed had fallen away.

As she sat there, she smelled the scent of fried fish and briny seaweed, and she could see someone sit next to her in the darkness, with firelight glowing on the back of their head.

It was Evgrent.

She nearly scrambled up just then to run from him, but he simply sat there, eating, staring out at the sea. She ground her teeth.

"When I was ten years old," he said suddenly, and quietly, "I was waiting for Father to come out of a shop. I thought it was a shop, anyway. I think maybe it was a saloon. Anyway, I had my little brother with me, and he was four. We were swinging on a rail and then we dared each other to climb along its top. The things kids do at that age."

She turned away from him so that she could not see him.

"We're playing outside and making a fair bit of noise," he went on with a low voice. "And there's a commotion at this place, this shop...saloon, or whatever it was. Father comes tumbling out and doesn't see us, but we see him, and he just barrels into the street, looking confused. I am pretty sure he was very drunk. He didn't watch what he was doing, and he was struck by a coach. A coach! And he flung onto the road and another coach struck him."

Thilly sat very still.

"I saw it all. Vyrent didn't, and I stepped in front of him so he couldn't, and I pulled him around the side of the building, and I asked him to tell me his letters and numbers. I kept doing this over and over for a long time, and we made it a game, though I didn't have the heart to play. I knew Father was dead. So we waited, and Vyrent got fussy, and then our mother found us, and she lashed into us and screamed and carried on. Our lives were very different after that. They didn't have the happiest marriage, but it was solid. But once my father was dead, Mother turned to the drink herself, and we saw less and less of her. Even when she was home, she wasn't her old self again. And then she died."

Thilly felt a pang deep in her. Vyrent had never told her any of this, not that they had much time for such a revelation. She wrestled with her feelings. But she needed to know.

"Then what happened to you?" she asked.

Evgrent wiped his mouth with his sleeve and said, "We were passed from relative to relative, and we never saw our old home again. It wasn't much. Just a shack. But it was ours. That was the last true home I ever had. I didn't want Vyrent to live like that, though, so I started working and helped get him into school. And just…I just wanted him to have better than that. That's all. Eventually, he did. He was witty and pleasant, and he could charm anyone who knew him."

Thilly closed her eyes and remembered the tingling of her neck from Vyrent's kiss.

"So he had a good life," Evgrent remarked. He slowly scooted over to Thilly. She did not move. He set his food in her lap; it was cooked fish wrapped in a large, leathery leaf, with seaweed alongside. She sighed and pulled off a big flake of fish, put it in her mouth, slowly chewed it, and swallowed it with a tear-swollen throat.

"I saw it in your eyes," he said to her. "Nobody had to tell me. I knew what happened to you. Because it happened to me."

Thilly's shoulders began to shake, and her tears streamed again.

"I'm sorry," said Evgrent. "I left because I thought it was for the best. You had the prince back, I thought things would go better, and

I—I wish I had been here. I wish it had been me instead of your mum."

Thilly whipped her head around and stared at him.

"No," she said. "Don't ever wish that. No matter what happens, I wouldn't wish that on anyone."

Evgrent looked sad, and he looked out at the sea before turning back to her.

"It was your mother," he said softly.

"What?" Thilly asked, confused.

"Your mother paid me to make sure you were safe," he told her. "I could have gone to my dying day not telling you that, but given what's happened, I wanted you to know. She would have done anything to keep you safe. Even hiring an old, bitter reprobate like me."

Thilly felt her shoulders relax, and she hung her head for a moment. Then she rose, and she moved over close to Evgrent, and she stared down into his eyes. Then they both blinked.

"Don't leave again," Thilly said to him.

Evgrent shook his head. "I can't stay. I have to help your people."

"You don't have to," Thilly replied.

"Yes," Evgrent said, "I do. I will do this. This is all I can give you, Githilien."

Her heart hammered in her chest. "I think I hate you, Evgrent," she said, swallowing and blinking rapidly.

Evgrent grinned up at her. "Then I'm glad you feel something, at least."

He stood then, picked the wrapped fish where she had left it, and pushed it at her.

"Eat this," he said. "And for the sake of the gods, don't forget that fucking sword again."

Thilly let out an exasperated groan and seized her sword. She sheathed it and took the fish.

# THE VALE OF SEVEN DRAGONS

"So we'll say goodbye again in the morning," she said. "How many times will we say goodbye?"

"As many as it takes," Evgrent told her. "So long as we can say hello again. You have a friend for life, Thilly. I have never had a friend before now. Well, aside from Umbra."

Thilly seized his hand and held it, and they stood watching Maelwyrm turn around like a great dog three times to settle in near the bonfire, which had begun to wane.

"The only goodbye tonight, though," said Thilly, "is to Mother. Will you join us?"

"For you, anything," said Evgrent, and he let her go. She walked back to the fire, sure that her face burned hotter than it did, toward Beaumain and his own ginger hair glimmering in the reflection of the flames. She did not look back at Evgrent that night, and she stared into the fire, the heat on her face, her heart rendered into tears that evaporated or were caught by the ocean wind, and she could not remember what she or anyone else said about her mother before making offerings to that fire. She watched the little sparks fly orange-gold-white in upward spirals toward the indigo clouds above, and she said, "Goodbye, Mother."

# CHAPTER 34

## *WINGING IT*

She was damaged and she would never be the same again, but when Thilly rose from her sleeping pack the next day reeking of smoke and sea, she felt something new: determination.

"I will see Father again," she announced over their rudimentary breakfast as she sat on a bleached driftwood log and finished a weak bark tea in a collapsible tin cup. "If these things were on the coast before, we've got to assume they've remained, and maybe attacked the rest of Vickery and Catellaith by now."

"Your Highness," said Birkswood, "I know your father well. The king will not allow any incursion; he's creative, and he'd find a way to keep things battened down."

"Except for my mother," Beaumain pointed out. "She"—and he swallowed—"it was there, the night of the gala. Why didn't it attack anyone?"

"Nothing those things do makes any sense at all," Ki'roth declared. "I do think that they took your mother's form to manipulate you, maybe even to find weaknesses, learn about you, and about all of us, perhaps."

Thilly shivered. Blinky, cozy on her shoulder, fluffed its feathers too.

"The only thing we do know for sure," Thilly said, standing up and putting her hands on her hips, "is that they hate dragon fire; it destroys them, as does pitch fire. We don't have the means to launch pitch fire of much volume at the things. But we have Maelwyrm. And presumably, there are still six other dragons. Somewhere. It's time we found them. Birkswood, Ki'roth, and Ul'trok, have the footmen rig a dragon coach, if you will, for us to ride. Evgrent, if you'll take everyone else home," and she felt a lump in her throat, regarding him and Umbra.

They did recognize each other now: bound in tragedy forever.

"May the gods bless you on your journey," she said to him publicly.

Privately, as everyone worked to prepare for their trips, she said to him, "I know you don't believe that shit," and he chuckled at her.

"I know you don't either," he said, snapping buckles on Umbra's back.

"Take care of yourself," she said to him. "If we can meet again, then I hope it's for a good reason, and soon."

"I'll see what I can do, princess," said Evgrent. "Keep that sword with you at all times. You won't make a proper knight *or* mercenary without it."

"I can't have one without the other," Thilly blurted out, and then they turned away from each other.

She marched then with a heavy heart and an eagerness to leave this land forever, for it had taken her mother away, and a part of her as well.

Hana walked up to her, looking nervous, and said, "Mrs. Florence is rounding us all up to leave."

Thilly gazed over to see Birkswood saying goodbye to Mrs. Florence, and she wondered exactly what they were saying to each other in their stiff, respective ways. She tilted her head at Hana. "Not you, though," she noted.

"Well, she did ask," Hana said, twisting her skirts in her hands.

"I want you with me at all times," said Thilly.

Hana exhaled and threw her arms around Thilly, who yelped. "Oh, thank you, milady!"

"Ack! You're welcome!"

Thilly and Beaumain saw the contingent of horses and riders and footmen off, with Evgrent at their head and Ul'trok at their rear, to see them to the border of Aceltia.

Ki'roth turned to Thilly.

"I would go with you," said the fae, "but Val'dreth is not completely healed. We will return to the Covenant and seek more healing there."

"That's all right, Ki'roth," said Thilly. "You've done so much to help us. I hope we meet again soon."

Ki'roth and Val'dreth bowed low, and they set off up the coast.

Thilly, Beaumain, Hana, and Birkswood faced Maelwyrm, who stretched and shook his head. Blinky sang and bobbed back and forth, clearly feeling adventurous in the bright morning of mixed clouds and sun.

"How is the coach?" Birkswood asked the dragon, inspecting the ropes around Maelwyrm's belly and the makeshift set of rudimentary seats and a cover over those.

Maelwyrm leaned down and said, "It is FINE. It ITCHES, though. Climb aboard before I change my MIND."

# THE VALE OF SEVEN DRAGONS

He lowered down and lay his head flat on the ground, and the four of them climbed aboard the beast and sat in their seats. Blinky at first nestled under Thilly's hair, but quickly decided to hop down between her feet, and burrowed a bit into the ropes to secure its little body. Little ropes across those seats served as belts to keep them strapped down. Hana looked green for a moment, suddenly considering what they were about to do.

"I could call Evgrent if I screamed loudly enough," Thilly offered.

"No," Hana said, shaking her head vigorously. "I'll be all right. Or I won't. But I'm coming."

"Good," said Thilly with a tired grin.

She wanted to feel more excitement than she did, remembering her dream of riding alongside Beaumain. Only in that dream, they were on separate dragons. Alone. Pondering this, she tied herself into her seat and held on as Maelwyrm pumped his great wings, took a breath and pushed upward into the sky.

Hana howled, and Thilly joined her for a moment, and they swerved and adjusted in a nauseating fashion as the world fell away from them. Maelwyrm let forth a contented sound, not unlike a cat's purr, as he rose above the clouds and swerved away to the north.

Thilly, chattering in the chilly wind, looked down and beheld the beauty of being between land and sky, and she could see the peaks of the tall morros stretching from the dark forest of Absinweald all the way out to the Veiled Isles.

"Can you see very far, Hana?" she asked over the wind.

"Farther than I've ever seen before!" marveled the girl. "Those great big rocks go for miles and miles, to the sea of the north!"

"That's Valetheant," called Birkswood. "Its northern shore, anyway, the only little neck of land between Aceltia and Osthadon. "If you see the beacon, that'll be a sign we're nearing Osthadon. There's a lighthouse on the border of Valetheant on top of one of those morros."

"A lighthouse?" asked Beaumain loudly. "For whom? There's no great harbor on the northern border of Valetheant!"

"Aye, Your Highness, there isn't," Birkswood replied. "It's for travelers from the far north."

They all gasped as Maelwyrm suddenly banked to turn east. Thilly focused on her breathing and did not look down.

"And what sort of travelers are those?" Beaumain asked.

"Nobody I'd want anything to do with, by the sound of them," answered Birkswood, frowning. "If you thought Aceltia was strange, the north is even more so. It's their descendants in Osthadon…the Thaddons carry some of that blood. Changelings, so the legends tell. And maybe why Osthadon is infamous for its experiments. But then again, we don't really know; they rarely venture into the Vale, and only do commerce if absolutely necessary through their crops. I think they mainly focus on trade with the north. A secretive bunch."

"I can't say I like the sound of that," admitted Beaumain over the wind's whistling.

"Nor can I," agreed Thilly.

"Quite," said Birkswood, "but they've got a dragon, and we need one."

"Any ideas how we're going to *get* that dragon?" Thilly wanted to know.

"None in the slightest," answered Birkswood in a grim voice. "We'll have to rely on our own dragon and sheer luck, I'm afraid."

"I'm glad you told us this *after* we launched into the air and headed toward people who don't like us," Thilly said with a sigh.

"No good deed goes unpunished, Your Highness," said Birkswood. "But I must say, I'm enjoying it."

And despite her pain and exhaustion, Thilly laughed at that.

# CHAPTER 35

## ROOK, PARROT, DRAGON

With the bracing north wind only shielded by a rudimentary cover over their seats, they might have frozen had it not been for the warmth of the dragon himself. His body radiated heat upward into their feet where the four of them sat (and Blinky nestled close to Thilly's feat, thereby having the warmest seat of all). Maelwyrm would occasionally puff out a little bit of his fire, just enough to heat the air around him, and that hot air flowed from his snout, over his head, and then to his passengers. Thilly had been adjusting to one strange thing after another on her journey, but flying on the dragon made her feel pure wonder, awe, a few doses of terror, and most importantly, the sensation of being totally and completely present.

The moment her thoughts went dark, and she could hear her own grief with the sound of her mother's death and her own voice crying out, Maelwyrm switched his flight, or was buffeted by the wind. She was jolted back to the moment, even if nervously. Beaumain glanced

# THE VALE OF SEVEN DRAGONS

back at her occasionally, but also admired the view and clutched his coat about him.

Birkswood chatted on and off with them all when they were in smoother flight, and eventually, Hana joined in as well, after having endured a few bouts of air sickness.

"Do you think all dragons are so…bumpy, milady?" she asked as quietly as she could.

But the dragon heard her, tilted his head back a bit to look over his shoulder, and said in his bellows voice, "I am a tad SLOW and OLD and out of PRACTICE. Also, I need to EAT. So I will set down by the water and FISH."

By mid-morning, Maelwyrm wended his way down in a long, slow spiral to the northern coast of Valetheant, and came to rest upon a pebbled cove close to the great morro with the beacon. He cleared his throat and coughed, sending little balls of spark and flame out onto the beach, startling some sandpipers, whose frightened chirps unnerved Blinky. Still, the parrot was happy to have stopped, and hopped around the rocky beach looking for food, mostly among the sea oats and beach grasses gone to seed, bent and broken in pale gold stalks. The water in the cove was a brilliant cobalt blue, and out beyond its breakwater the sea frothed with whitecaps that shone like diamonds whenever the sun broke through the clouds. Thilly, Hana, Beaumain, and Birkswood clambered down from the dragon's back, and each took a moment to adjust to the solid ground, with Thilly swaying so badly that Beaumain had to catch her and hold her steady.

"You've not slept well," he noted, and she looked up at his comforting face. "It affects your balance more if you don't."

"I would have thought it had more to do with being on a fucking *dragon* who's not flown in eons," she snapped.

Beaumain's eyes twinkled.

"I'm glad you can spar with me," he told her. "It's reassuring."

"Well, don't get too cozy," she said, almost more at herself than him. Then she seized his arm.

"There's a man over there!" she whispered, pointing to the seaside front of the morro.

He had not seen them yet, as he faced north, away from them all, and in the shelter of the morro, which was considerably larger than Maelwyrm. The dragon, meanwhile, had slid on his abdomen into the sea, and he waited in the shallow water with his mouth agape, letting the water come and go, and he sat very still.

"Look at him!" Birkswood exclaimed, and Thilly grinned at the tall butler, who watched Maelwyrm with a pride like one might watch one's child succeed at school. "He's figured it all out." He caught Thilly's gaze just then, and his eyes traveled to the fisherman.

Thilly wondered if they should warn the man, but soon he turned around, and then he jumped. She stifled a laugh. The man dropped his fishing rod, took off his hat, and put it on again.

"He won't be happy about the fish situation," Birkswood said with an uncertain voice.

The man approached them, and as he drew closer, Thilly could see he wore a dark green woolen cap over his head that covered his ears. His face was deep reddish brown, and the rest of him was bundled in very warm-looking attire of green and grey and thick, waterproof black boots. He wore a bright smile and some of his black hair poked around his neck in the form of a braid. Maelwyrm ignored the man for the moment, cozy in the water, mouth agape, patiently waiting for fish to drift in and then tilting his head up and sieving out the seawater through his teeth.

"Hello!" the man called, and he laughed. "I see now why my lines aren't pulling. Oh, wow! Oh! Shit, look at that! A dragon! A real, honest-to-gods *dragon*." And he stood back, hands on his hips, and roared with laughter.

Thilly and Beaumain exchanged quizzical looks. Hana grinned. And Birkswood strode forth to the man, towering over him as he did everyone Thilly had met aside from Maelwyrm.

"Hello, good sir," Birkswood said amiably. "We apologize for the...fishing incursion."

The fisherman took his hat off again and held his free hand out, much callused and dried, to shake Birkswood's.

"My name's Rook," he said, still smiling broadly. "And it's worth it to see that dragon. Oh, wow! Maybe he'll leave you a few fish behind, too."

"Rook," replied Birkswood, "we'll be happy to share to make up for what you've lost. I'm Birkswood, head butler of Castle Taugan, and I serve the Princess Githilien of Vickery. Alongside her, Prince Beaumain of Catellaith. And this is Hana."

"Just Hana," grinned Rook, and he shook her hand first. Then he bowed respectfully to Thilly and Beaumain.

"Call me Thilly," she said quickly. "Titles don't matter outside my country, and honestly, I don't like them in it!"

Birkswood looked scandalized, but Rook laughed. "I like you!" he declared, and with a jovial shrug he leaned in to shake her hand vigorously.

Beaumain stood stiff and a little aloof, measuring up Rook, who looked up at him and said, "Catellaith! Used to go down there sometimes to meet my brother in Nistraan's Wold." He held his hand out and Beaumain took it gladly and with a smile, and they shared a good, solid handshake.

"Rook!" cried a small, nasally voice, and out from under Thilly's hair emerged the wood parrot, turning its head side to side to get a better look at the man. "Not a rook," decided Blinky.

Rook laughed long and loudly. "Only by name," he agreed. "And what is *your* name?"

"Blinky," said the bird. "Best Blinky." And the parrot fluffed its feathers and groomed its wings.

"Well, Best Blinky," Rook said with a chuckle, looking from the parrot to the dragon to his four passengers, "you're the most interesting thing I've seen up in these parts in a long while. I'd have guessed you're from Osthadon," and he glanced at Hana, "with all the things they get up to there with animals"—he shook his head and sighed—"but your animals are *happy*, so I'm glad you told me where you're from."

Thilly wondered about that remark, as Osthadon was a mysterious, secretive nation.

"We're headed to that country next," she declared. "Is there something we should know about it?"

Rook turned his hat over and over in his hands and whistled.

"If you didn't have to go," he answered, "I wouldn't recommend it. Not sure they'd let you in, anyway."

Thilly tilted her head to her side and glanced purposefully at Maelwyrm.

"I think we'll get in whether they let us in or not," she said.

Rook opened his eyes widely and he laughed. "You're a bold one, Your Highness," he added sheepishly

"Thilly," she insisted.

He nodded. "Thilly."

She could almost feel Birkswood and Hana's disapproval, and that made her feel quite satisfied. Beaumain then said, "And just call me Beaumain."

"That's a mouthful," admitted Rook. "Why not just 'Beau'?" Beaumain's forehead went squiggly. Thilly's throat tickled with the urge to laugh. "And...are you... *her* Beau?"

Beaumain shook his head politely. "Friends only," and Thilly caught his eye, and they both nodded.

# THE VALE OF SEVEN DRAGONS

*That does feel good,* thought Thilly.

"Looks like your dragon is done fishing," observed Rook.

A great, slow splashing of waves signaled that Rook was right as Maelwyrm shuffled back ashore, dripping. He puffed his breath out a bit and they could feel the warmth off him. He ambled over before them all and opened his mouth wide, and several fish came flapping out.

"Wow!" cried Rook, laughing. "That's a good haul."

"We're not going to eat 'em, are we?" Hana exclaimed. "Right out of his mouth and that?"

Rook guffawed. "I'd say they're probably half-cooked as it is, Hana," he said. "And what's not cooked yet, I can take care of."

"Who are YOU?" Maelwyrm asked the man, settling on his haunches and folding his wings about him, patting his belly with his front arms.

"Rook," said the man, setting to work filleting the fish. "And you?"

"I am MAELWYRM," said the dragon, "the eldest of the SEVEN."

Rook looked up at him, his expression thoughtful, and said, "So there really were seven."

"There ARE seven," answered the dragon. "We will find the others."

"Strange days," said Rook. "It's odd," he continued thoughtfully, "as usually, I see more ship traffic out to sea, and more birds and seals, and lately...almost nothing. The fish seem plentiful, at least. I wonder what's happening?"

Thilly and her companions exchanged looks.

"So you've had no attacks, or sightings of anything unusual?" she asked.

"Other than you five?" said Rook. "No, but that's strange enough. Usually, you can see ships from a distance, coming from the north, headed to Osthadon's ports. Not lately."

"This is a remote place," Beaumain said. "Maybe you've been spared because of that."

Rook's face twisted as if he'd tasted something unpleasant. "Well, I don't like the sound of that. Why? What's happening, why are you here, and why do you need to go to Osthadon?"

"Why don't we have our lunch first," Birkswood suggested, looking at Thilly's troubled face.

So they ate the fish, filleted and grilled and seasoned with some spices from Rook's fishing pack. It was simple yet delicious fare, and Thilly hadn't realized how badly she needed someone to look after her and give her food and comfort. Beaumain, Birkswood, and Hana let her simply be while they recounted their harrowing adventures. Rook whistled a few times and then at the end, he turned to Thilly, and he knelt before her.

"Princess Thilly," he said earnestly, his hands in a prayer pose, "I am so sorry you've lost your mother."

She still did not want to hear those words, for they sounded so final. And she had just begun to understand the half of her that belonged not to a kingdom but to a realm faraway and wild and strange. And now, it seemed, gone forever.

Still, she said, "Thank you," in her flattest voice, and she felt vacant and out-of-body.

Rook put his hat back on after everyone had finished eating and said, "You're not getting into Osthadon without a challenge. If you're looking for their dragon, I guarantee you it won't just be out on some hillside waiting for you to find it. *They'd* have found it. Like they find all animals," and he glanced sidewise at both Blinky and Maelwyrm, "and gods know what they'd do with it."

"Antimon," said Thilly suddenly, startling them all. "The dragon's name is Antimon. She's female, I think."

Maelwyrm heard the name and turned his great, scaly head with its long snout and said, wheeze-bellowing, "We must FIND Antimon, and FREE her."

"And then head south to Montadanthe and find their two dragons," Beaumain remarked.

"SUNDER and METEOR," said Maelwyrm, stretching his wings. "Sister and brother dragons. SUNDER has a TEMPER. Meteor is the YOUNGEST of the seven and FOOLISH."

"Valetheant's dragon too," said Hana. "Isn't that the big, long one in legend?"

"Jadesilver," said Birkswood.

A smile flickered over Rook's face at the sound of the name.

"Ah, famous in the south of the Vale," he said. "Lots of family legends about Jadesilver. The farmer's dragon. Long just as the Vale is long, and in legend, as fertile as the great valley itself, but no one knew what became of her eggs; there are tales that they were all lost. The most elegant dragon! Long with two sets of wings. To see that dragon…no offense, Maelwyrm!"

"HUFOOOOOM," snorted the older dragon.

"You don't know the lay of the land," Rook said doubtfully. "They'd not keep her somewhere easily seen; they keep everything under fortress lock and key. Ugly fortress too. You'd think they'd have something attractive in their capital, but no. Everything about the Thaddons makes me suspicious, especially lately. If there's something bad going on, I'll bet they're part of it."

"What do you mean?" Thilly asked him. "Are you implying they know about those monsters?"

Rook looked at each of them in turn. "I wouldn't put it past them." His eyes rested briefly on Hana. "They're not even good to half their own people. And they tinker with things nobody understands. I wouldn't go if you didn't have to."

"We have to," said Beaumain. "We need every dragon in the vale to go up against those things; only dragon fire seems to kill them effectively."

"We do not know how many there are," Birkswood reminded them all, "or where they came from."

"I don't know that it would help to know that," Beaumain said thoughtfully.

"But what if the Thaddons knew?" Thilly wondered.

"How will you know where to go?" Rook asked. "I like all of you. I don't want you to get hurt or imprisoned or…whatever it is they do behind their ugly walls."

Thilly sighed in exasperation. "We're going. But if you're quite concerned, you do seem to know a lot about the place."

Rook shrugged. "I fish close to it a lot this time of year," he answered.

"Come with us," Thilly said. "You're more familiar with the place than we are. We could use you."

Birkswood frowned. "Your Highness, we've only just met mister…Rook."

Rook laughed and raised both his hands. "Please. Just Rook." He took a deep breath, nodded, and laughed to the point he slapped his thigh. "Well, shit!" he cried, wiping tears from his eyes. "Hells, I'll come along. I've got family to visit in the south anyway. Why not?"

Thilly felt relieved and exhausted at the same time. She could not muster a smile, although in another time she might have. She was by turns too numb or too raw; there was no space in between.

"Well, friend Maelwyrm," Birkswood said to the dragon, "it would seem we have a rescue mission on our hands, perhaps."

# THE VALE OF SEVEN DRAGONS

"Huffooooom," said Maelwyrm. "I may be OLD, but my fire still burns HOT…hot enough to melt a FORTRESS."

"I suppose we'll see," muttered Thilly under her breath.

# CHAPTER 36

## *GALVANIZED*

Rook's exuberant laughter upon Maelwyrm's leap into the sky jarred Thilly out of her desolation. He was most enthusiastic and pointed at everything he saw.

*Did I used to be like that? I seem to remember being kind of like that. Before...*

And she rested her head on her hands.

"I'm ruined now," Rook shouted over the rush of wind. "I'll never want to ride a horse again!"

"Did you have a horse?" Beaumain asked him.

Rook shook his head. "Yes and no. At my family's farm in the south, we have horses. But I don't like to deal with them during fishing season, so I usually hitch rides up through the valley as the harvests wind down. Nothing beats this, though!"

Thilly began to feel different, watching Rook, fidgeting with Blinky at her feet, and wondering how far Hana could see as they flew above the edge of Valetheant's coast toward Osthadon. The air began to smell peculiar as they approached, and Thilly did not like it.

"Ugh, gods!" cried Hana. "It smells terrible."

They all coughed, and Blinky spouted off explosive obscenities.

"That's Osthadon," said Rook, shaking his head. His smile faded then. "They bastardize everything they touch," he said, his voice surprisingly hard, given his general joviality. "There is no one to stop them anymore except at their borders; and of course, Valetheant only operates with farm conglomerates, and we don't have a king and queen like you do," and then Rook sighed. "I'm sorry," he said to both Thilly and Beaumain. "What I meant to say was, there's only Montadanthe to hold them back to their south."

"And that's why Montadanthe exists as a republic. Literally joining forces to hold off the north," remarked Beaumain.

"Eastern marauders too," Thilly chimed in. "Chamberlain used to hammer that home in our lessons. Gods, that seems like a century ago."

Maelwyrm turned then, and Hana said, "Ugh! A trail of smoke as far as I can see to the east, beyond the far coast, even."

"How can you see that?" Rook asked, marveling, but Hana could not answer, for Maelwyrm swerved very quickly as he flew lower, and then again. Something had flown past him and had nearly hit him.

"What the fuck was that!" yelled Thilly.

"I am being ATTACKED!" said Maelwyrm, and he inhaled with a crackling fire sound building in his great abdomen.

"No, Maelwyrm!" cried Birkswood. "We mustn't fire upon them. We need their help."

"If I am STRUCK by one of their TINY weapons," grumbled Maelwyrm, "you'll need more than any dragon they'll have."

"Set us down outside the gates to the capital fortress," Birkswood yelled, as Maelwyrm swerved again, throwing all of them in their makeshift dragon coach sliding.

Whatever the projectiles being launched upward out of the fortress below were, Thilly could not tell for sure, but the set of structures in the great compound unnerved her. They were all stone, blocky, and without any form of life that she could see. The northern shore of Osthadon, which curved quickly to the east and south, met the sea with a great block wall, against which the ocean pounded but never penetrated. She could see no natural beach anywhere along that coast. Several tall columns chugged smoke into the sky everywhere throughout the area. It left a lingering smog over the land, and the smell was unsavory and sickening, biting, acrid, morbidly sweet, foul, and unnatural. There were no trees, but there were many bright, unusual lights throughout this fortress city, and in one open block, she saw something flashing.

"What is that?" she asked Hana, pointing.

Hana peered over the edge of the dragon as he slowly swung in his downwards spiral. "It looks like lightning," she called back, "but in a courtyard or something. Have they harnessed lightning?"

"That's not lightning," Beaumain declared. "Not exactly. But they've harnessed something all right."

Thilly felt cold all over, and not from the rushing of northern air.

"Experiments," she murmured, thinking of what Rook had said. *What were these people doing, aside from befouling their land and the air above it?* she wondered.

"Strange," said Hana, shaking her head, as they descended, waving back and forth as Maelwyrm dodged various artillery. "There's all sorts of tubing and lights shining in that courtyard."

# THE VALE OF SEVEN DRAGONS

Thilly frowned. She looked at Beaumain, whose face was pinched in a small scowl as well, his aqua eyes dulled by the increasing amounts of yellow-grey smog.

Birkswood told Maelwyrm, pointing, "There, land there, and we will quickly address any contingent we meet."

Beaumain turned to Thilly. "Do you still have your sword?" he asked, his face rigid.

"Yes," said Thilly.

"Hide it," he said urgently. "Hide it in your pants, whatever you can do."

Thilly stared back at him.

"This could go badly," she said.

"It could," Beaumain answered. "But let's try not to make it worse from the start."

Thilly stretched her right leg out and tucked her sword down into her paints leg and secured it as best she could. She felt sick at the thought of using it in this dire-looking place.

Then they all fell silent as Maelwyrm pulsed his wings to descend, and upon landing, a legion of soldiers dressed in stiff cold-grey uniforms and hats met them, carrying strange staffs that they aimed at the dragon. Thilly noticed they were all male. One of them stepped forward, the symbol of Osthadon above his heart, a slender dragon's head in iridescent pewter, surrounded by several deep maroon metallic stars, presumably to signify rank, as none of the other soldiers had so many.

"You are ordered by the Prime Sletaad to surrender," he said calmly and coldly.

The five passengers slid off Maelwyrm and stood before the dragon all in a row. Maelwyrm held his head high and his wings tucked, glaring down at the forces, smoke trailing from his nose.

Birkswood announced, "I am Birkswood of Castle Taugan. On behalf of the countries of Vickery and Catellaith, I present to you Princess Githilien and Prince Beaumain. There will be no surrender. We seek urgent aid for our counties."

No one spoke, but Thilly could hear a strange, crackling sound and occasionally saw arcs of what looked like lightning flashing from the nearby courtyard. She fought a shudder, for she did not want to shake her sword loose, much less alert the forces that she was at all nervous.

"A strange contingent," said the Osthadon captain. "We were not alerted to your arrival by bird or post."

At that, Blinky emerged from Thilly's hair and said, "Vickery and Catellaith call for aid!"

Everyone turned to stare at Thilly, and particularly at Blinky, who stood straight and proud on Thilly's shoulder. Thilly beamed at her feathered friend.

"An unconventional message," noted the captain. "Remain here. I will consult the Prime's office. You are not to move; and if you do, you will meet with our light sterzhers."

The legion brought their rods forth, slapped from one hand to the other, pointed to Thilly and her companions, and then thrust them vertically against their shoulders in one long, coordinated clatter. Not a single soldier made eye contact with them. But Thilly could see they were all quite pale, and some had deep violet-blue eyes, while others had violet-rimmed, almost white eyes. The hair on the back of her neck rose at that, and she glanced at Hana, with her rosy face and shiny brown curls. No one in sight looked remotely like her.

*The Thaddons*, she thought.

The captain had turned and marched with disturbing crispness toward a spare-looking gate, his booted heels ringing on the concrete.

# THE VALE OF SEVEN DRAGONS

The entire place looked boxy and unnatural, devoid of any art, save the lovely dragon insignia for what Thilly reasoned must be Antimon.

*And where is* she? she wondered.

The crackling sound zapped again, and Blinky looked all around the area.

"Big cage," said Blinky, and the bird suddenly flew off and up toward one of the high turrets and out of sight.

"Blinky!" hissed Thilly, but Hana gave her a little nudge to quiet her.

The soldiers watched Blinky go, and Thilly detected a ripple of uncertainty, but they remained around the dragon and his companions.

"Huffooooom," sniffed Maelwyrm. "This is taking a LONG time."

"Silence!" said a hard voice. It was the captain again, and with him, a sharply featured man strode alongside, his outfit dark steel-grey, his dragon insignia in the form of epaulets on his shoulders, his head bare and shaven. He was the coldest looking person Thilly had ever seen, with the except of Queen Maulielle…but she had only seemed that way, Thilly remembered, after she had been taken over. Thilly's heart beat rapidly. Were these people compromised like the queen had been? But no, she decided, she did not pick up on that inhuman aspect to them. Not in that regard, at least. They were very much human, and very much not the kinds of humans she liked to be around. There was a severity, a clinical harshness to these people, a brutal and surgical power. And the man exemplified this in every respect.

"The Prime Sletaad," announced the captain.

Birkswood bowed to the man, as did Rook and Hana, but Thilly and Beaumain did not. He walked up to them, stared briefly and coldly up at Maelwyrm, who watched him with his great, golden eyes, as if daring the man to try something. Thilly and Beaumain stood in their most regal poses, despite the condition and style of their outfits. The cold leader of the Thaddons took in every inch of the pair, and his eyes lingered on Thilly's outfit, and on her face. She felt a spark of rebellion at his examination.

"Prince Beaumain of Catellaith, and Princess Githilien of Vickery," Birkswood said again, for the Prime's benefit.

The Prime looked chiefly at Beaumain and said, "I am told you are in need of aid."

Beaumain glanced at Thilly. "*We* need aid. The entire Realm is at risk."

The Prime lowered his eyelids halfway, and they seemed to spark in violet light. "I am unaware of any risk," he said.

"We are alerting you of the risk now, then," Thilly countered, growing angry. "We need protection from invasion by a new foe, monstrous, taking over the coast."

The Prime did not look at her, and instead looked at Beaumain and said, "We are a coastal country, and we have seen no cause for alarm of any sort. Do you not have defenses in your own nations?"

*This fucker is not even looking at me now!* thought Thilly, enraged.

Beaumain's jawline bulged, and Thilly knew him well enough to see he was furious as well.

"Our defenses," he replied in a rigid voice, "have been compromised. We have sought the strength of Aceltia's dragon, from our visit there, and we aim to recruit a force of the other six dragons of the vale to fight it. It shows a weakness to dragon fire. We ask for your help by volunteering your own dragon in the fight."

"And what dragon might that be?" the Prime Sletaad asked in a chilling voice.

Maelwyrm began to grumble, and Birkswood leaned against him to try to prevent his saying anything.

"Antimon," said Thilly loudly. She waited to see if somewhere, somehow, there might be a response.

The Prime lowered his eyes further and said, "Take them into the legion hall, and prepare refreshments."

With mechanical movements, the soldiers parted to allow them to walk in.

"What about our dragon?" Thilly asked.

"I will stay with Maelwyrm," said Birkswood.

"Our soldiers will stay with this dragon," the captain stated.

"And I will stay with him also," Birkswood said in his deep voice, in which Thilly could hear his own brand of quiet anger.

"As it suits you," the captain replied.

He marched in step with the Prime toward a simple arching doorway, wide enough to let all the soldiers through, but many remained. Others separated the Prime from Thilly, Beaumain, Hana, and Rook. Rook, Thilly noticed, had lost his smile, but his dark eyes paid close attention to everything he saw. At the doorway, just as they were about to enter, two soldiers blocked Hana.

"What are you doing?" Thilly demanded.

"No Gamdons allowed inside the fortress," said the captain.

"It's fine, milady," Hana said, voice trembling.

"No it is not," hissed Thilly. "Hana will accompany me. She is my ladies' maid and duty-bound to the crown of Vickery."

"We do not recognize your jurisdiction here," said the captain.

The Prime Sletaad halted his steps, wheeled around, and said, "As a courtesy, the Gamdon may stay."

"It's all right," said Hana nervously, touching Thilly's shoulder. "I will stay behind. I'll keep Birkswood company. Rook can help you if you need."

She darted her eyes to Rook, and the man barely inclined his head, but met her eyes.

The Prime Sletaad held out his hands, "Then only three many enter our hall. We will refresh ourselves and discuss your situation."

Thilly's stalk of temper, somewhat diminished since her mother's death, began to flicker in her soul.

*How dare these people,* she thought.

She, Beaumain, and Rook were seated at a marble table shot through with veins of iridescent flaked minerals. The Prime Sletaad sat at the head of it. A tall pitcher of pale blue liquid was placed before him, along with four goblets. He gestured for a servant, also dressed in grey yet with no insignia at all, who poured the liquid into the goblets and set them before the Prime, Thilly, Beaumain, and Rook. The Prime took his up in his hand and took a sip.

Thilly stared at her goblet. It smelled volatile, like a high alcohol spirt, but also a bit fruity, and was the only remotely pleasant-smelling thing she had come across since they had entered the airspace of Osthadon. Beaumain, sitting across from her, tapped the stem of his goblet while staring at her. She looked at his finger: he placed it on the side of the glass.

*Only a little, then,* she interpreted. She took a sip, and the liquid seared her throat and her nose. She pushed her eyebrows together and fought the urge to cough. She set the goblet down. Even that small amount rapidly coursed through her bloodstream, and she felt a strange mixture of alertness and relaxation, making it different than other spirits she had tried.

"Your Highness," said the Prime at last, finally addressing her, "I do wish that we could help. But we have no dragon. We had thought until today that they were but stories. Clearly, we were wrong in that sentiment."

"The other dragons live yet," said Thilly as calmly as she could manage.

# THE VALE OF SEVEN DRAGONS

"We seek them also," Rook dared to say, and then he flinched at the look the Prime gave him.

"And you are…?" asked the Prime.

"Rook of Valetheant," said the man.

"Do you represent the Conglomerate?"

Rook did not hesitate. "Yes. And we shall unearth our own dragon as we—"

Beaumain shook his head subtly, and Rook shut his mouth.

"What of this…invasion you speak of?" the Prime Sletaad asked next, turning to Beaumain with a chilling look, as though he had seen the prince's gesture.

Beaumain shot Thilly a glance of alarm.

*Gods,* she thought. *We didn't agree on what we'd say.*

"The coasts of Catellaith and Vickery," Beaumain said slowly, gripping his goblet but not drinking any more from it, "were invaded by monstrous creatures that warp and manipulate their prey: namely, people. They can take the forms of the people they attack. They also kill without remorse."

Thilly began to shake, and she tried to stop her shaking. Her right hand fell upon the stiff, short sword in her pants, and she pressed her hand upon it. That gave her the strength to settle her trembling. *Thank you, Evgrent.*

The Prime Sletaad then said, turning to her, "We are deeply sorry for your loss."

Thilly and Beaumain sat bolt upright.

"What?" said Thilly, her voice gone high. "How did—" and again Beaumain shot her a warning look.

Thilly felt the blood drain from her face.

One look into the familiar aqua eyes of Beaumain reflected her thoughts also: *They know.* She tried to calm her breathing. *But how do they know? Unless…*

"We do sympathize, Your Highness, we do," said Sletaad, perfectly manicured, long slender fingers interlocked, dark indigo-violet eyes watching her, unmoving.

*You know nothing of sympathy*, she thought, and she grew furious.

"I wonder about that," she said in a cold voice, "but I do appreciate the sentiment. Know that we have not only come here asking for help, but we have also come here to warn you. And what is rightfully ours, we will take."

"You sound as if you declare aggression upon us!" hissed Sletaad. The room of pallid faces murmured and shifted, like so many pale snakes. "You have no right to anything among these walls."

"Prime Sletaad," said Thilly, standing up, shoulders back and down, and Beaumain and Rook stood as well, "you sit in a fortress made of the finest stone and the most beautiful denial. This is the ugliest attack our world has ever seen. If you think my wanting to fight back is an act of aggression, then perhaps you should go ahead and surrender now, because nothing will stop me from doing whatever it takes to save the Vale. Our dragon will find Antimon, and she will choose her rider."

The Prime Sletaad went stiff, arms behind his back, jaw twitching, but his eyes remained as cold as frozen marbles, and as calculating as a serpent's.

"You can leave now," he said to the three of them, "or we can escort you to the gulag. That is your choice. You and your Gamdon get nothing from us."

"We're not leaving without Antimon," she declared. Rook exchanged a look of surprise, and Thilly winked at him.

"Heretic!" cried Sletaad. "That is our dragon."

"Do you admit you have her, then?" asked Thilly archly.

"I think we should make our exit," Beaumain urged.

They all heard a ferocious claxon, and the guards of the room sprang into action and bounded out.

Thilly covered her ears. "What is that?" she cried.

The Prime Sletaad rose, and the captain of his forces whispered something in his ear. The Prime abruptly turned and left the room through a back door. Thilly ran to the window and could see that Maelwyrm flapped his great wings, and at the sight of her, he yelled, "HANA!"

Thilly gasped. "What is it? Where is Hana?"

"Thilly!" Beaumain cried.

She wheeled around to see the guards seize him and Rook.

Without thinking, Thilly reached down the leg of her pants, pulled forth her scabbard, unsheathed it, and rushed at the guards, hacking at their hands, spraying blood everywhere. Freed, Beaumain, and Rook ran toward the door, but another guard surged forward with one of the light sterzhers. Thilly leapt alongside and swung with her sword, and the blade sliced the rod in half, sending sparks flying everywhere. Rook reached in his pocket, yanked forth fishing line, and swung a piece of it around the guard's neck and pulled hard and held it fast, strangling him.

"Go!" yelled Beaumain to them as he pummeled and kicked the remaining guards.

They ran out to see pure chaos.

The sky had gone blue-purple from giant arcs of electricity beyond the wall, in the courtyard they had seen from above. Maelwyrm swung his head left and right, throwing off guards and snapping their light sterzhers. Birkswood rode upon the dragon's neck and barked orders.

"Where is Hana?" screamed Thilly. No one answered her at first. But a small, brown-green ball of feathers burst from a high turret and barreled toward her, flapping desperately, and in great excitement, Blinky landed in Thilly's hair and hung there, panting.

"Big Blinky!" wheezed the bird. "Another big Blinky!"

"Show me!" cried Thilly, and the parrot flew off toward an open gate.

Thilly chased after him and around on the hard, cold concrete through a short tunnel, and out the other side she jerked to a halt, for there stood Hana in the courtyard, cowering. And burst from the earth, towering, blue-white, lightning-bolt arcs from tubes flung everywhere, she beheld a most beautiful dragon, with eyes the color of mercury, and iridescent scales and wings, haunting, and sleek: Antimon. And Antimon bowed before Hana and said: "I have waited for you!"

# CHAPTER 37

## SKY OF SHADOWS

Thilly's eyes bulged at the sight. Blinky leapt to her shoulder and crowed.

"Big, PRETTY Blinky!" sang the bird, and it gave a wolf-whistle. Thilly laughed out loud.

"Gods almighty!" she cried, watching the gorgeous dragon through all electricity around and above it, as it rested its head before the shaken Hana. She started to walk toward the girl, but Antimon let out a long, chilling hiss, so Thilly froze on the spot.

"Arise, rider!" said the dragon.

"I—you're mistaken," cried Hana, hands over her face. "It's not me ye want! I'm a nobody!"

"You are my *rider*," said the dragon, in a velvety harmonic voice that echoed throughout that courtyard.

"I—I can't be!" Hana protested. "I'm just a maid!"

"You are a true daughter of Osthadon," said Antimon, "and I will have no other pilot!"

Thilly felt a burst of pure delight.

"Hana!" she cried. "Antimon has chosen *you*!"

"I—I only serve *you*, milady!" Hana cried, but she took her hands away from her face and stared up at the lovely beast, who blinked slowly at her.

"Thilly!" a voice yelled, and then Beaumain burst around the corner with Rook. They both skidded to a halt and looked up.

"Holy shit!" shouted Rook. He laughed joyfully. "Ah, she's a lovely one!"

Thilly turned to them. Beaumain said, "Thilly, we need to go. They're powering up some kind of weapon, and I think they'll attack Maelwyrm…in which case we're fucked."

Thilly whipped around to Rook. "Ride with Hana," she said to him.

Everyone there heard it as a command, not a question, and in that second everyone knew what Thilly had denied herself: she was their leader now.

"Hana," she said to the girl, "get on the dragon's back. Hold on to whatever you can. Rook, rig something to hold you both in."

"This one's scales are different," Rook noted. "We could sit partly inside them and hold on, I think, almost like they're seats."

"Then do it!" said Thilly.

Antimon waited expectantly, and with hesitation and help from Rook, Hana climbed on to the dragon's back.

They heard a roar then and saw the burst of a jet of flame into the sky.

"Gods! Maelwyrm!" screamed Thilly. "Hana, fly Antimon south to Montadanthe. If we get separated, rendezvous there!"

"Yes, Your Highness!" said the girl.

"Call me Thilly!" yelled the princess, and she and Beaumain sprinted back around to Maelwyrm.

"Took you long enough!" bellowed Birkswood, urging Maelwyrm to spray volleys of fire at the towers around them, from which all manner of projectiles were hurled at the dragon, and an immense cannon-looking object was wheeled out along the upper balcony of the fortress. As soon as it turned toward Maelwyrm, a great burst of wind gushed from above.

Yells and screams rang through the windows, and everyone jumped and turned to look. Sletaad stepped forward to look outside, and then immediately stumbled back and fell.

Antimon lowered into the yard next to Maelwyrm, her manner mercurial and chilling, peered into the window where the Prime Sletaad hid, and stretched her neck forward, so that she grinned horribly before them all to see.

"Put that weapon away, Thaddon," Antimon's voice reverberated through the window, "or I will reduce your tower to ash."

Everything went deathly silent for a moment, and they could see the cannon begin to glow at its end, and a metallic whine wound up. Antimon shook her head from side to side and then took a deep breath and bellowed forth white-hot flame that struck the cannon and melted it, ruptured the balcony, and sent burning soldiers flying from the roof.

"I think we had better leave," Thilly said, fastening her belt on the back of Maelwyrm.

"Agreed," said Birkswood, and he nodded to Hana and grinned. The girl blushed and grinned back.

Her face shone in awe. She mouthed to Thilly, "I've got a dragon!"

Thilly smiled back and cheered her. "Let's go, Birkswood, Maelwyrm!"

"GLADLY," boomed Maelwyrm, with a few petty bursts of fire toward any remaining visible soldiers, and the two dragons pushed upward into the sky.

Thilly heard some sort of claxons continuing to ring, but their sound grew fainter as Maelwyrm flew higher. His flight did not match the speed and smoothness of Antimon's, but she slowed for him, gliding in circles around him.

"SHOW OFF," he called her to her. "Youth," he said more quietly, so that only his passengers could hear. "She has energy now, pure adrenaline, but she will need to feed soon."

"Not on the shores of Osthadon, she won't," Birkswood declared. "We don't dare set down until we're beyond the border."

"Agreed," said Thilly.

She finally relaxed and looked down at her sword scabbard.

"I forgot to clean the blade," she declared.

Beaumain grinned at her. "Something tells me you'll need it again."

She smiled back and said, "Probably, but I hope not just yet!"

"You were amazing back there," he said to her, and she looked at him, dirty yet strong, his outfit torn, his eyes glowing in his kind and handsome face, and her gaze faltered.

She still felt a surge of her own adrenaline, but she also felt more alive than she had in some time. She felt strong and vital.

"So were you," she said to Beaumain.

He reached out his hand, and she took it. His hand was rougher now, callused and covered in cuts, strong but gentle. Holding it, she felt a measure of peace and calm she had not of late, and she felt solace, even if it was brief. Then she pulled her hand away and looked off to the horizon.

"We'll have to camp overnight," she said, loud enough so Birkswood could hear.

Birkswood turned to them with a set jaw, but a twinkle in his eye.

"I'll let the dragons figure out the right spot, somewhere on the coast," he said to the teens. "Looks a tad foggy on the eastern shores, which is probably a good thing. I'm not sure anyone needs to see two huge dragons flying over their houses in time for tea."

"Well, I could certainly go for tea," Beaumain remarked. Thilly laughed. And, she realized, it felt good to laugh.

Maelwyrm then curved his flight and flew southeast, and by and by, he began to descend. Thilly watched as they approached the cloud-tops, and she closed her eyes. She did not like descending into fog, particularly as it was growing dark, for she could see nothing; but at times Maelwyrm sent forth his little spurts of flame, and the warmth that radiated back to her made her sleepy. Blinky had fallen asleep under her hair, and the bird's warmth made her drowsy also. She fell into a doze and then woke with a start. They had made it to Montadanthe, and Maelwyrm began his landing.

Antimon was of similar height to Maelwyrm, yet slimmer, and she possessed a unique quality that he did not. She glowed subtly, having phosphorescent scales, and Thilly gawked at the lovely creature openly.

"Have you ever seen anything more beautiful!" she cried, stepping off Maelwyrm. The older dragon snorted. "Sorry, dear Maelwyrm," she added.

"I am OLD and SLOW," he admitted, "and Antimon is one of the LOVELIEST of us, but not the YOUNGEST."

Hana climbed down from Antimon looking radiant and practically bouncing. Rook looked delighted as well.

"She's a fine dragon, milady!" exclaimed Hana to Thilly. "I didn't have to do anything, really!"

# THE VALE OF SEVEN DRAGONS

Rook laughed. "Well, there was a bit of shrieking at first," he said to Thilly with a broad smile, "but Antimon is a great flyer, and it was pretty smooth! Smoother than Maelwyrm."

Antimon fluttered her wings and arched her neck in appreciation while Maelwyrm huffed. The older dragon waddled off and over a beach dune along the sandy shores of Montadanthe and set to work with his passive fishing scheme. Antimon, however, bounded off into the sea and out of sight as the light faded into twilight. Thilly gazed out to sea and beheld her plunging in and out of the ocean.

"I probably don't want to know what *she* eats," she said quietly to Hana.

Hana shook her head. "Neither do I. Best not to ask."

Birkswood and Rook set up a beach fire in a circle, and then went clamming along the shore. After the sun had completely vanished and fog began to grow cozier along the beach, they came back with packs full of clams and set to steaming them on the fire. It was another simple meal made delicious by need and place, and Thilly was grateful.

She was also bone-tired and sore, and ready to sleep. The two dragons returned and encircled the little party and their rudimentary fire, with Antimon glowing and full after her long hibernation. Thilly soon learned it had not been a peaceful sleep.

Rook asked, "What were those tubes and things where you were, Antimon?"

She let out a long, warm sigh that smelled of woodsmoke and the sea.

"I do not know," she said in her rich and resonant voice. "Some of them were attached to me," and she rubbed her long, slender snout on her elbows, where scabs shone among her glowing scales. There were several such scabs, Thilly noticed, all over her body, and older scars among her lovely rainbowy scales. "The Thaddons, I think, kept me asleep."

"They poisoned you!" cried Thilly. "Why?"

Antimon let out a whistling sort of yawn. "They wanted something from me. I am not sure what."

"Osthadon," spat Rook angrily. "Experimenting on innocent lives. But what where they doing?"

"Whatever it was, I suppose they needed me to do it," Antimon said drowsily. "I have chimeric properties like all my line; we can fuse to each other. Maybe that is why."

"Or maybe they're just terrible, cruel people," said Rook angrily. "I'm sorry they hurt you."

Antimon yawned again. "You are kind to dragons, Rook of the Vale. I must sleep now. A true sleep. Not a drugged one."

At this, she curled her head around them, her slim body forming a U-shape, her wings curled over her forearms and her scalloped tail draped over her thighs. Hana curled up against her and fell asleep instantly.

Thilly fell into a restless dream, and she heard her mother's singing, which made her sad even in the dream. Exhausted, Thilly woke to hear a great scratching sound, and opening her eyes, she found Antimon grooming the back of Maelwyrm's neck.

The older dragon let out a purring sort of growl.

"I have not been ABLE to reach THAT part in EONS!" he said. "Thank YOU."

Antimon shimmied a bit and Thilly thought that must be her form of a laugh.

They all dusted off, scrounged for food and fresh water, and worked in the broken clouds of sunrise to prepare for the day ahead.

# THE VALE OF SEVEN DRAGONS

"Now that the dragons have fed," said Birkswood authoritatively, "I think we had better head to the capital of Montadanthe and plead our case there."

"Do we know where the dragons might be?" Thilly asked.

"I'll bet they're close to the Vale," Rook remarked. "They'd not be buried in the hard limestone on the eastern side of the ridges. Besides, the Vale is the cornucopia of the Realm; the soil is softer, richer, and better. If I were a dragon? I'd want to sleep closer to that."

Beaumain waxed on to anyone who would listen about the origins of the Vale again, and how it must have been a meteor crater, filled once with a shallow sea, and then ultimately the site of the great battle between Antares and Nistraan over what was now Valetheant. When they climbed aboard the dragons and began pushing their way skyward, skimming east to the Vale side of Montadanthe, Thilly shook her head in awe of the great valley. Before her travels, she never conceived of how enormous the Vale actually was. The legends all told that it was formed by a falling star, and Beaumain spoke of having taken soil samples to study for his education. It was one thing to hear of such things or read about them in a crinkled old text from her instructor Chamberlain's musty shelves at Castle Taugan. But to *see* the scale from above of this immense valley stretching from the northern coast to the southern, ringed by mountains and ridges, was another thing altogether.

"It must have been quite the meteor," she said over the rush of the wind. "To have left such a crater."

Beaumain, who had been leaning over the edge of Maelwyrm's coach to absorb everything he saw, answered, "Quite. And notice, too, along the edges in some areas: I imagine that is from the blast, creating those walls of debris that we think of as ridges."

Thilly closed her eyes and felt the rise and fall of the dragon.

*I should like to build mountains around my own cratered soul*, she thought.

She opened her eyes and gazed to the right at Maelwyrm, who was keeping up with Antimon, but whose flight undulated more; he was indeed older, slower, and less streamlined than Antimon, whose sleek and highly aerodynamic form made for a relatively smooth flight.

Hana, in her scale-seat upon Antimon, settled into a groove, and occasionally glanced back joyfully to look at Thilly. Hana's and Rook's shared joy buoyed Thilly.

"I heard Mother's voice in my dreams last night," she said suddenly. Beaumain reached over and squeezed her hand.

"This is the last thing I ever wanted us to have in common," he said to her, and she felt resolve slip and let her teras flow. He held his arms out, and she sank into them and wept into his shoulder while he stroked her hair.

"What will have happened to Father?" she asked in a muffled, broken voice.

"We will face whatever happened together," Beaumain assured her, "and with my father as well."

They sat embraced for a long while, united in pain and loss and on the small coach atop a gleaming dragon, not knowing what might happen next, and clinging to the last vestiges of normality they could find.

But when Thilly lifted her head to look up, she could see a dark smudge on the western horizon, extending many miles north and south. She broke into a cold sweat.

"Gods," she whispered, "is that—"

Beaumain shifted and looked, and is mouth dropped.

"Hana," he called in an urgent tone. "What do you see?"

Hana looked and gulped.

Where there had been soft, morning-coral clouds, the far western edge of the great Vale crawled with a sky of shadows.

# THE VALE OF SEVEN DRAGONS

"Blimey," Hana called back. "I see something I wish I couldn't. Wings and clouds…a storm coming. Coming for us!"

# CHAPTER 38

## ADJOINED AND ASUNDER

Birkswood turned in his seat quickly to look at Thilly. She did not like his expression, which looked graver than it had since the night of her mother's death.

"Suggestions?" he asked.

"Find the two dragons of the republic?" Thilly replied. She looked at Beaumain, and his face was taut with dread.

"And how do we do that?" Beaumain asked.

Thilly shook her head.

Blinky nibbled at her earlobe, and she said, "Ow! What, Blinky?"

"Fly low! Find Big Blinkies!" rasped the wood parrot.

Antimon swung over close to Maelwyrm, and Thilly called out to Rook, "You've had quite an adventure already! Are you sure you want to keep going? It's about to get a lot harder fast!"

Rook shook his head. "I'm in it now!" he shouted back. "And it sounds like I'd have no choice but be in it anyway. So I'd rather be on a dragon for it!"

# THE VALE OF SEVEN DRAGONS

"Good point!" Thilly cried. She agreed, but she did worry for Maelwyrm. Antimon, younger and stronger, might be able to do more, she reasoned, but the iridescent dragon was perhaps stranger and still recovering from trauma.

Thilly watched Antimon curve in a descent, and Maelwyrm followed suit after her, and they swept low over the ridges on the eastern edge of the Vale. Thilly scanned the area as they raced over it and could see mostly clusters of hardwood forest with mixed evergreens, some autumn leaves remaining, the stone walls of a few hillside farms, and the telltale white spots of sheep below.

"How will we know where to find the two dragons?" she called out.

Maelwyrm's deep bellows voice rang out, "We will FEEL them!"

Thilly looked at Beaumain. "I hope it works," she mouthed to him. He nodded and mouthed back, "Me too."

"Oop," said Birkswood suddenly. "We've been sighted. Well, that's not ideal, but not unexpected!"

Thilly and Beaumain looked over the sides of Maelwyrm and could see sheep running and a farmer running after them, shouting something, but they were high enough that she couldn't make out what the farmer said.

*Something profane, I'd imagine. It's what I would do.*

"Bet he shat himself," Beaumain said, and Thilly laughed loudly. "Oh gods, it's good to see your smile."

Thilly blushed. She bit her lip.

"We're about to go through a lot more hard things."

"We can handle that," Beaumain said, looking at her.

She loosed her belt.

"What are you doing?" Beaumain asked, alarmed. "You'll fall off!"

"So don't let me." And she jumped into his arms and kissed him.

He held her back for a moment, pushing her flying hair out of her face, and stared into her eyes.

"What was that for?"

"If we're going to die, Prince Beaumain of Catellaith," she answered, holding his face in her hands, "then I'm not missing the chance to kiss you as much as I can before that happens."

"Fair enough, Princess Githilien of Vickery," he said, grinning. He drew her to him, and they kissed deeply and passionately.

Birkswood turned at that moment to look back at them and nearly lost his own seat.

"What!" he cried. "There's no time for that, we're turning! Your Highness! Get back in your seat! And that does not mean the prince!"

Shaking from their moment of passion, Thilly gave Beaumain one more kiss before making her way back to her seat next to him, and they both sighed at the same time. She tied her belt back around her just as Maelwyrm tilted to bank, and she gasped as the dragon nearly grazed his claws upon a ridge just below them.

"There, maybe!" cried Birkswood, pointing.

Antimon circled a mound on the side of a hill sloping down to the great Vale. Upon that mound, an old stone circle lay crumbling, coated with moss and lichen. Thilly looked to the west and watched the sky darken like a storm coming. It was coming faster.

"We're running out of time!" she cried.

Antimon perched on one side of the mound, and Maelwyrm landed on the other.

"You're sure?" Thilly called to Antimon.

Both dragons raised their heads and looked at each other.

"It's Sunder," Antimon declared, flicking her wings, which cast rainbow sparkles through the air. "I can smell her."

"We must WAKE her," grumbled Maelwyrm.

# THE VALE OF SEVEN DRAGONS

"Hurry!" cried Hana. "That's a larger group than we faced in Aceltia."

"Gods," whispered Thilly.

"I am sorry for your pretty decorations," said Antimon, placing her front right claws on one of the standing stones, "but we've run out of time."

The earth began to shake, at first in a small tremor, and then larger. Thilly wondered if the already fallen stones had occurred because of a sleeping dragon's movements. She did not have to wait long.

"Aloft!" cried Antimon, leaping up from the ground. Maelwyrm didn't hesitate, and Thilly gasped as he pushed upward suddenly.

The ground then exploded, sending dirt and stones flying in all directions.

"She is ANGRY!" roared Maelwyrm.

Out of the dirt and debris surged a red and black dragon with a high deafening cry, snapping and spewing flames. With sleek scales close to its muscular body more like a snake's, this dragon looked much younger than Maelwyrm by far. Its wings extended like a bat's, from shoulders to handlike claws, and it had agile, muscular hind legs. This dragon was also shorter in body length than Antimon, but its tail was whippy and sharp, and jagged with sharp points. Its red and black face was elegant and triangular, with black around its eyes almost like eyeliner, pointed red ears, prominent nostrils, and a whippy red tongue.

"Good morning, Sunder!" cried Antimon.

Thilly gaped at the dragon, who indeed looked enraged, if ever a dragon could in the way humans could understand. She was another species as well, different both from Maelwyrm and Antimon with forelimbs on her wings.

"Big angry bat!" shrieked Blinky.

Sunder snapped her teeth and whipped around, flying up and out of her former nest, and perching on top of a rocky outcropping overlooking the Vale. She spouted off an impressive yellow bolt of flame and then coughed, with little flames flicking out with each hack.

"You dared wake me!" she roared, casting her red eyes in her exquisite red and black face toward the other two dragons. "And who are these humans? I see no rider for me!"

Thilly and Beaumain looked at each other.

"They're choosy, aren't they?" murmured Beaumain.

"Quite," she whispered back.

Then she said loudly, "Sunder of Montadanthe!"

"You mean Dantheant," growled the dragon.

"Oh," said Thilly. "How long were you asleep?"

"Not nearly long enough!" cried Sunder, tail whipping back and forth like an irritated cat's.

"SUNDER!" roared Maelwyrm. "Look to the WEST. We NEED you! And your BROTHER!"

Sunder snorted dismissively and whipped her head around while saying, "What do we ever need Meteor for? If he's sleeping, let him, I say—" and then she caught sight of the dark, rolling clouds now over the great Vale, and she reared her head back.

"What is that?" she asked.

"Not something we've ever seen before," Antimon replied.

"They're monsters," Thilly told Sunder. "Maelwyrm fought them. They killed my mother. And countless others. I think they want to kill us all."

"Oh good!" shouted Sunder. "I'm awakened just in time to die!"

"She's a bit sassy, isn't she?" Beaumain whispered to Thilly.

Thilly grinned. "I rather like her already."

"You would," said Beaumain back to her. "Birds of a feather. Maybe you're meant to be her rider!"

# THE VALE OF SEVEN DRAGONS

"You heard what she said," Thilly answered, shaking her head. "Her rider isn't here."

"Gods help whoever it is, then; I hope they're still alive," muttered Beaumain.

"Right!" cried Sunder. "I'm not waiting here to die. Let's face these things."

"Sunder, wait!" cried Antimon. "You should eat something first!"

But the red and black dragon shot into the sky and by turns pulsed and glided her way toward the cloud.

"She's worse than I remembered!" cried Antimon, leaping into the air, causing Hana and Rook to yell in surprise.

"Because you are YOUNG," roared Maelwyrm, and Thilly braced while he leapt up also.

"We could've let the royals off!" cried Birkswood.

"No!" shouted Thilly and Beaumain in unison.

"I don't like it!" Birkswood yelled back, holding on to his seat.

"Noted!" Thilly called back.

But she was sick to her stomach, and not only from the lurching flight of the dragon. She was flying fast toward the forces that had torn her mother to shreds and taken over Beaumain's mother. She looked sidewise at him, and he looked back at her.

"Look, whatever happens," she began.

"I love you too, Thilly."

# CHAPTER 39

## THE PRIDE OF THE VALE

In terrifying speed, the dark cloud of horrors was upon them.

"Don't wait!" screamed Thilly. "Burn them!"

Sunder wasted no time barreling up to the clouds and spewing bright yellow flame into their twisting masses. By and by shapes broke off, roughly the size of her, and charged her. She screamed horribly, and Thilly covered her ears. The ferocious red and black dragon then sent out a cry that chilled Thilly to her marrow and seemed to reverberate up and down the entire Vale.

"MEEE-TEEE-ORRR!" Sunder screamed, spinning and skittering and tumbling among the dark masses, flames galore, until she looked from a distance very like a ball of flame herself.

Then Thilly saw her. Woadlynn's face among many faces, spinning in the blackness above, grinning terribly, eyes bottomless.

Thilly heard voices.

*"Pain. There is only pain. There is endless suffering and endless hunger and pain. You will feel it. Why do you fight it? Your life is tiny. You mean nothing. Pain is all that matters. We will feed upon you. Better to let us than to fight."*

It was cold and brutal and spoken in her mother's voice, yet comingled with the lilt of Queen Maulielle's accent.

"Ah!" cried Thilly, covering her ears, but the voices still entered her mind. She saw flashes: blood and sinew and teeth gnawing on both, long, endlessly long teeth, taller than the sky, and dark, glistening round eyes, countless eyes. Teeth and eyes and blood, feasting upon all, feasting upon itself, and the only light was the reflection of her own pain.

She was falling. She felt the sensation, she felt the wind. She had untied herself and slid off the side of Maelwyrm, who sent jets of his sulfurous fire into the dark cloud, where it singed red at the edges and retreated, but he did not notice her fall.

Beaumain did, and he screamed, but it was too late for him also: for he saw his own mother, in the twisting mass of rot and hatred, and he froze, his scream frozen as well. He could not tell Birkswood, but the butler knew the moment he glanced back.

He yelled at Maelwyrm: "Githilien!" just as the black clouds formed a great mouth full of endless teeth and sucked the dragons toward it.

Maelwyrm turned briefly and shouted, "I can't stop!"

"Milady!" screamed Hana from her mount on Antimon, but Rook yelled back, "Focus! Guide Antimon straight in. If we're going, let's make it count."

"I don't know what I'm doing!" howled Hana.

"None of us does!" Rook cried back. "So let's fight like hells!"

"Sunder! Catch the princess!" screamed Antimon, but Sunder was lashing and burning everything in sight, fully focused on maximum violence.

Thilly kept falling, and soon would hit the ground, but her mother's cries were in her ears, the horrible sounds of her mother's death, over and over and over.

Then she felt a jolt, and the breath in her lungs forced out, and then she was rising again. She felt pinpricks in her side, and she flailed, but then she came out of her stupor to stare up at a strange pattern of orange and violet, and she heard wind.

"I've got you!" said a loud, musical voice.

*Have I died?* she wondered, seeing the world upside down.

"You'll be all right!" said the voice again. "I'll set you down."

She felt herself fall again, but it was a controlled fall, and confused, tired, and sad, she went limp, because fighting felt too hard. Then she felt the touch of grass and then the hardness of earth beneath her. The pinpricks left her sides. She looked up, and the sunlight caught the shimmering flame-orange and brilliant violet scales of a very excited looking dragon, with something resembling a look of purest joy on its face.

"See!" said the dragon in a bouncy voice. "You're fine. I'm going to help the others now! Yell if you need me back!"

Thilly had caught her breath back and she wheezed, "Who-who are you?"

"Meteor!" cried the dragon, and he shot into the sky, the opposite of a falling star, doing air-cartwheels, whooping and hollering as though he had not a care in the world.

Thilly lay on the soft ground for a moment, and then she wept. She wept openly and loudly, and she thrashed. She was away from the fight when she was the commander. Supposedly.

"I'm fit to lead nothing!" she cried aloud, and she heard some soft footfalls and looked up to see an exquisite golden stag with enormous, luminous copper antlers, munching leaves. He blinked at her, she blinked at him, and she sat up on her elbow. She rubbed her eyes.

# THE VALE OF SEVEN DRAGONS

There was definitely a stag there, and he seemed to have satisfied his curiosity by sniffing her and moving on.

"Well," she said feebly, "good thing you weren't here a few minutes ago. There was a dragon! Really! A very silly, colorful dragon. I think."

She felt dizzy and put her hand on her forehead. Then she turned to look up at the sky, and one uncannily round cloud, dark and tumbling but stationary, grew edged with flames. She squinted and could see the bright dragon Meteor join the fray, swooping in and around the mass—if mass it could be called—with spinning jets and bursts of flame.

"How can I get back up there?" she cried.

By and by she saw a small, dark shape dropping out and away from that cloud, tumbling at first and then righting itself, and then making an undulating flight toward her, but it was a strange shape: small and round at the top, large and straight at the bottom.

"Do you see that?" she asked, and then she felt silly for asking a stag. She looked for him, but he had gone, and his footsteps left shimmering gold marks on the grass of the hill she sat on. The hill sloped down into the vale, to rich, combed fields of grey-green winter wheat and kale. A farmhouse stood off in the distance, but she felt uncertain on her feet. She was not sure what to do, so she watched the shape, feeling more helpless and useless than she ever had before.

As it looped and spun and tumbled, the object drew closer to her, and then she heard sharp staccato words:

"Fuck! Fuck! Fuck!"

She gasped and then laughed.

"Blinky!" she yelled, and then the bird flew up to her and released the object and let off a loop of spectacular profanity as it marched back and forth on the ground. But Blinky looked extremely proud.

Thilly knelt to find the object among the grass.

"My sword!" she shouted. "Oh, Blinky!"

She picked up the ornery ball of green and brown feathers and kissed the parrot's head, scratching the neck and grooming off a pesky pin feather. Blinky blinked several times and crawled to the favorite spot on Thilly's shoulder, pulling at her earlobe while doing so.

"How'd you do that, are you part dragon yourself?" she asked. She drew forth the blade, caked at its tip with old blood, and she swung it around in the air.

"Well, I'm glad you found it," she said to Blinky. "Though I don't know how much use it'll be down here."

She plunged the sword into the earth to clean it, drew it out, and then the entire hillside began to shake. She shouted as the ground beneath her gave way and she went flying on her bottom down the hill into the Vale. Blinky shot up from her and squawked in shock.

"I know I didn't just cause that earthquake!" cried Thilly.

But the ground shook again, and this time it was so jarring that long cracks formed in all directions of the earth.

"Hell above and trouble below!" she said grimly, not knowing which way to run. It was the largest earthquake she had ever felt, and she had nothing to hold onto. She began to worry a great crevice might open and swallow her whole. She held onto her sword and tried using it as a staff to stand, but the earth shook again, and then a series of sprays of water rose like geysers in a long swatch in the vale, and Thilly watched an incredible sight.

A long, slithering, silvery mass shivered through the earth, tumbling like a great worm, sending dirt and water everywhere, and then out of one of the quake fissures rose a tall, silver-green spike. And then the rest of the huge shape rolled over and up and catapulted into the air, spinning and curling: a huge dragon, with elaborate scales of silver, pewter, and all shades of green and green-blue, dazzling in the sun, and its great mouth roared in a deafening blast of hot wind that set the wheat fields ablaze, until the mud formed by all the water fell back to the earth to extinguish it.

"Who. Brings. Forth. Jadesilver!" thundered the dragon.

"Oh my fucking gods!" shouted Thilly, scrambling to stand straight.

"Big snaky Blinky!" croaked the wood parrot, in awe.

Jadesilver bore two sets of wings on its long, twisting body, and its tremendous tail whipped back and forth, scooping piles of earth into the sky as it did so. Thilly found the tail quite terrifying and huge. Jadesilver was far and away the largest of the dragons she had met, and the most majestic. The dragon saw her standing with her sword flashing in the wind, her wild, frizzing hair billowing, and it dove and slid on its belly toward her.

"Oh!" she cried. "Oh shit!" and she turned to run.

The immense snout of Jadesilver, with its giant nostrils flaring and smoldering, surged through the mud toward her and then it opened its mouth and boomed, "You. Are. Not. My. Rider!"

Thilly, quaking, and noting the flames and darkness above, said, "H-hi, Jadesilver! You reputation precedes you. We...um, well, we're being attacked, and I...think I may have summoned you with...this?"

She brought forth her sword and the dragon eyed it with its brilliant, emerald-green eyes, with long catlike pupils.

"That. Is. Dragon's. Steel!" said the immense creature. "From. Roanmont!"

"I—don't know?" said Thilly doubtfully. "It was given to me by someone from Vickery."

"From. Vickery!" cried Jadesilver, sniffing the girl. "No. From. Roanmont!"

"What?" cried Thilly. "He's from Vickery, his name's Ev—oh for fuck's sake, can we just get up there and help them! Look!"

Jadesilver did look, and then rose from its muddy wallowing on its great front legs, stretching its head skyward and flicking out its tongue to test the air.

"My. Friends!" the dragon growled. It brought forth its rear legs and looked ready to spring into the sky.

"Wait!" screamed Thilly, shoving her sword scabbard into her belt. "Take me! I'm the commander!"

Jadesilver, expressionless, said, "You. Are. Not. My. Rider! But! I. Will. Fly. You. There."

Thilly climbed the beast's belly and found purchase between the folds of its neck.

"Blinky," she called to her bird, "I think you'd better stay here this time. I don't want you getting hurt."

Blinky flew up to Thilly and nibbled on her lower lip. Thilly kissed Blinky's beak, and the bird flew off, she hoped to safety.

She braced herself for the ride upward, and found Jadesilver's flight the most disorienting yet, as the creature flew with its front and rear wings, snaking through the fluid of air much as it had on the earth below. Fighting nausea, she held on, and they met the dark cloud with the other dragons, who looked exhausted, chased by parts of the cloud shaped like great, winged beasts themselves, and each dragon defending the others being chased, while Meteor flicked in and out, his wings batlike like his sister's, as if he were swimming through the mass. So much smoke and fire and blackness nearly choked Thilly, and she worried for her friends. And then she could see she had reason to worry; they had all fallen into trances.

"No!" she screamed. "Jadesilver, help them."

The dragon twisted, inhaled sharply, and funneled an enormous pulse of multiple fireballs into the mass of hate with a series of thunderous booms that echoed all up and down the great valley below. The voices started again, but Thilly focused only on the great dragon beneath her as it blasted its way through the clouds. Jadesilver twisted, rolled—which set Thilly shrieking and holding on for dear life—and bombed the force in bursts.

Then a layered, warped voice, lower of decibel than the lowest sound on earth, piercing enough to break through the roars of the dragons, said from the cloud: *"We have your fathers."*

A long, tapping laugh echoed into Thilly's mind. She could see the limitless teeth glinting deep in the well of her thoughts. And then the dark mass vanished completely, without a trace, leaving only smoke and pain in its wake.

# CHAPTER 40

## *GUNKHOLING*

The air cleared with a great crack like a sonic boom. The dragons swirled around, with Jadesilver centered among them, and then Beaumain came out of his trance first.

"Thilly!" he yelled. "Did you hear them?"

"I heard them!" she yelled back, as swooping Jadesilver snaked by him, all silver glitter and emerald glints in a sweeping blur making a figure-eight flight around its companions.

Hana snapped out of her trance and jolted. Rook shook himself out of it too and gaped, astonished, at the new dragon.

She said, "Antimon, fly me closer to the princess!" and obliging, shimmering Antimon slipped around huge Jadesilver.

"Milady!" she called to Thilly. "They said…"

Thilly swung back around on Jadesilver, feeling sick to her stomach at the motion, and said, "I know. They have our fathers," and her voice sounded leaden in her ears.

"Your Highness," Birkswood said gravely, "what do we do?"

# THE VALE OF SEVEN DRAGONS

*I bloody well don't know what the fuck to do!* she thought, wanting to scream it.

"We've lost our mothers," said Thilly loudly. "I won't lose our fathers too. We go to Vickery and Catellaith, and we fight." And then she vomited neatly over the side of Jadesilver, Sunder just missing the spew and hissing at her. "But first, let's fly to the border of Vickery and stop. Jadesilver is wonderous, but I cannot bear the twists!"

The five dragons and their passengers sailed to the west, with Meteor hooting and crowing and making loop-de-loops in the air while Sunder chased him and argued with him, at times sparring with him with her forelimb wings. Maelwyrm grumbled and huffed, Antimon glided, and Jadesilver snaked through a sky of clouds and chilly, late autumn sun.

"There's Loch Tauganon," called Hana, pointing, and as usual, Thilly could not see as clearly as she could.

It was a full thirty minutes before she caught the shaft of weak sunlight upon a long, silver cleft of water on the far southwestern side of Valetheant, where the Vale met the western ridge above it. The dragons all descended toward the lake in their various fashions, and they did not go unnoticed in the far more populous southwest of the Realm. Startled farmers and villagers ran forth to watch the line of dragons heading toward the lake, and park-goers fled its southernmost beach as the dragons slowed and aimed toward landing.

Jadesilver came in low, setting the lake dancing with silver-gold ripples from the breeze of its flight, and then made a water landing, to Thilly's horror. But the dragon kept her aloft and skimmed along the surface, slowing its glide and pulling the water with its four wings. Then it settled its snout upon the beach and Thilly leapt off quickly and fell onto the gravel to vomit again. Meteor and Sunder landed next, teasing and chasing each other. From above, Antimon shone silver as she descended, and she arced neatly to land with great precision and calm on the beach. Maelwyrm landed last and yawned.

Beaumain ran to Thilly and pulled her gently to his arms, and then swung her into the air.

"Awk!" she cried, and she turned her head. "I just threw up!"

"Oh, sorry!" he cried, and he set her down carefully and held her a long time, burying his face in her ample hair. She felt more relaxed then than she had in some time. But she was on edge.

"We'll find them," he said to her.

"I know," she said, chewing her lip.

"I promise."

"I know."

Jadesilver began slowly sliding backward into the lake to fish when it caught sight of Rook. Then it lifted on its front legs and bowed its great head, dripping like rainfall upon the man's head. He held his cap in his hands, looked up, and laughed.

"You're amazing!" he cried.

"You. Are. My. Rider!" boomed Jadesilver.

Rook's full body reaction amused Thilly, and he looked back at her with his mouth agape.

"What!" he cried.

But Jadesilver didn't wait for any sentimental gestures, and sank into the lake and swished off, its body moving back and forth in the water as it scooped up fish.

"Save some for us, will you, Big Green!" yelled Sunder.

"Not if I get some first!" shouted Meteor, and the two sibling dragons rose into the air, siphoning off insects and dipping down to scoop up fish from the lake. Antimon then slid in next and swam along elegantly. Maelwyrm shuffled over and walked in the water over to a tree-lined cove, sank until mostly submerged, and opened his mouth wide like a trap again.

# THE VALE OF SEVEN DRAGONS

They had set down near a weir from the River Unakery that spread from the southern coast and provided a partial border for Vickery and Valetheant. The river flowed into the lake and on north up the Vale, where it was used for irrigation for the many farms of the vast valley. Here it flowed sleekly through the weir, and a lock system lowered canal boats into the lake. A jam of those boats had built up as every captain had stopped to watch the dragons cavort and fish. Finally, one of the captains called a quick meeting among the boats and shouted they would drop anchor for the night rather than risk the boats while the dragons fished. That captain strode over to the camp and, seeing Thilly, he at first squinted and tilted his head, and then he cried, "Oh!" and he bowed low.

"Princess Githilien returns!" he shouted, and a cheer rose from the boats.

The canal folk spilled forth in jubilance and wonder.

"Your Highness!" cried some of them, and Thilly was touched to see tears on their faces.

"We thought you had perished," said another, a middle-aged woman with long golden braids woven with many colorful threads, and a patchwork dress of beautiful jewel tones. "I am Merrilynn, and this is Cap'n Canopus." The captain bore a trimmed deep ginger beard and ruddy face and wild eyebrows, and friendly, copper-colored eyes. Thilly did a double-take, looking at him.

"Do I know you?" she asked the man.

"Can't say we've ever met, Your Highness," said Captain Canopus. "I'd have remembered that, for sure!"

Words spread quickly among the canal boats, now all lined up to camp for the night, and the mood turned quickly to reverence and revelry. Every dragon rider was met with a deep bow and offered plates and mugs of food and drink. Bonfires were lit along the shore and lights strung up among the boats. Drums and guitars and flutes rang up and down, and villagers spilled forth from nearby. The dragons cavorted in the lake, refreshed and well-fed from their fishing, and they slowly made their way back to their riders, to the immense awe of the villagers and canal folks.

Some of the villagers even set out heaps of food for the dragons, who snorted and snuffed and ate whatever was put before them, except for Maelwyrm, who staunchly preferred fish to all other foods. He did rather enjoy a sponge cake, which would not even have filled one of his teeth, but his eyes gleamed and he licked and ultimately crunched on the plate it stood on.

For the first time in ages, Thilly enjoyed a hot tub bath, thanks to some of the villagers, and a change of clean clothes; but she kept her scarlet belt and never let her scabbard out of her sight. The dragons curled up at the beach, radiating heat in the chilly evening, and more or less tolerating the crowds of onlookers. Sunder, however, snapped when anyone got too close to her, and it became a game for some of the older children to see how close they could get to her before she did. Thilly hoped she did not have to deal with any apologies for dragon burns anytime soon.

Sitting by the fire, gratefully eating stew, she asked Merrilynn, "Tell me, what has happened? Are there normally these many boats here?"

"No," the woman answered, her gold braids shining in in the firelight. "We've been joined by many newcomers from the coast. And not just the south...but from the west as well." The lady looked uneasily at Captain Canopus.

"Your Highness," he said slowly, pulling on his fiery beard. "How much do you...know of what's happened?"

Thilly swallowed. "Tell me everything, Captain."

The man took a deep breath, glanced at Merrilynn, and said, "Castle Taugan is...it's..."

# THE VALE OF SEVEN DRAGONS

Merrilynn said bluntly, "It's been taken over."

"What!" cried Thilly.

"There is something draped over all the land, like black slime mold and rot, and it's covered the castle. We—we don't know if the king…"

"He's alive," said Thilly simply. "I know this."

Merrilynn and the captain exchanged doubtful looks. Then they glanced at Beaumain.

"Ought we to—"

The prince walked over and sat beside Thilly. "Please, tell me what you know. I need to know about my family."

"Your Highness," said Merrilynn hesitantly, "your father traveled to King Gathlade for aid. We are not sure if he made it, or what happened to either of them after that."

"And Tantienne?" asked Beaumain urgently. "Was she…was she with my father, or"—his eyes darted to Thilly, who stared back in alarm—"my mother?"

Merrilynn shook her head. "We don't know."

Birkswood, taking in all this, said, "We must know what happened to Mrs. Florence and the others. Did they walk into a trap?"

"Oh gods," whispered Thilly, thinking of Evgrent.

"We won't find out anything tonight," said Birkswood wearily. "I suggest we all get some rest and see what tomorrow brings."

Thilly sighed. "I don't know where Blinky is," she said unhappily.

"It's all right, Your Highness," Hana soothed. "Blinky is a plucky bird."

"Sure is," Thilly said. "Maybe an inspiration for us all."

Beaumain held out his mug of mulled Vale's Crest wine and tapped it against Thilly's mug of warm cider. "What do you have in store for us, o great leader?" he asked her, half teasing, she knew, but also to nudge her.

She looked down at the spicy contents of her mug, downed it, and stood, patting the sword by her side. Beaumain clinked a spoon against the side of his mug, and seeing Thilly stand, Hana and Rook did also. The clinking spread and a few thrums on guitars and mandolins chimed in. In the firelight, Princess Githilien of Vickery stood glowing, surrounded by villagers, canal folk, her people, and five dragons of the Vale.

"Good people of the Vale and of Vickery, and good dragons," she announced, and everyone cheered lustily for the dragons, who whipped their tails around or grumbled or purred, by turns, "tomorrow I return to the land of my father the King Gathlade." A few moans and a good deal of hissing spread around the camp. Thilly looked through the largest bonfire, which set the air wavering, and then at the faces surrounding it: young, old, people of land and water, dogs, horses, and even a few goats. "I ask nothing of you but your safety, and the assurance that I fight for every one of you. I do not know what I will find, and could be, it's my own death. But those things took my mother. *Our* mothers," she added, gazing at Beaumain, who watched her with loving eyes and sympathy. "I won't let them take yours. Not your mothers, your fathers, your children, your land, or your boats." The canal folk howled in delight at that. "I will take the love of the Vale, the honor of my office as princess, and I will take the dragons, if they will join me in this fight. We've two more asleep, and it's time they awoke. It's time we flew for the Vale and fought for what's ours."

"Ye won't fight alone!" bellowed a great, booming voice.

Captain Canopus jumped to his feet. "Brother!" he shouted.

Up from a canal boat, a giant man with a wild copper beard strode forth, glowing as if lit by his own fire: Captain Aldebaran Copperbox.

"Oh!" gasped Thilly happily.

And then the crowd gasped as well. Sunder marched forth and bowed with her tail in the air, like a dog.

"You are *my* rider!" she cried.

"I've a dragon!" roared Copperbox.

"Now we have a proper fight!" yelled Thilly, and the shrieks rang forth into the night and to the stars…which blotted out into a black void over the skies of the Stellar Seas far to the west. But for that night, Thilly felt ready for anything.

# CHAPTER 41

## *FLIGHT RISK*

The next morning, the canal and village folk descended upon Thilly and her dragon team, and repaired or added seats for the passengers to ride in. Thilly had forgotten what it was like to be among the people of the southlands, and she felt at home for the first time in ages. As she surveyed the activity and drank some greatly appreciated hot tea, she felt restless and agitated, and chewed on her lower lip.

"Your Highness," Hana said, approaching her. "They've been treatin' *me* like royalty! It ain't right."

"Yes, it is, Hana," said Thilly with a smile. "Enjoy it."

Hana shook her curls. "I'll not ever get used to it," she muttered, walking off toward Antimon, who lifted her wings in greeting to her rider. Hana put her hands on her hips and looked up at the dragon's lovely eyes; Antimon dipped her graceful head down and fluffed Hana's hair, and Hana laughed. Thilly felt a surge of love for the girl.

*Protect her, Universe.*

# THE VALE OF SEVEN DRAGONS

"We look rather complete, don't we?" Beaumain remarked, surveying the activity.

"We're missing a few things," Thilly said nervously.

"Oh?" said Beaumain.

"Our dragons, obviously," she said, a little acerbically. "And a rider for Meteor. Look at him! Who could handle that dragon? He's like a great big puppy."

Meteor was, at that moment, swishing around on his back, very like a dog, and juggling a large ball with his hind legs, and two smaller balls with his forelimbs. He snorted and cavorted and all the camp's children shrieked in delight. They wanted to climb all over him, but Merrilynn forbade it.

"He seems to think everything is an adventure, and simple fun," said Thilly uneasily. "He needs someone with common sense to ride him and manage him."

A horn blew, and Thilly lifted her eyes to the trail from the western down to the lake. A line of horses descended at a brisk pace. The one at the front shone mahogany in the morning sun. She dropped her mug and sprinted away from Beaumain.

She met the riders and their leader, and he swept off his horse and walked up to Thilly, looking down at her with grey eyes full of unspoken words. His hair swung into his eyes, and he swept it back over his ears. He took her hands into his and held them briefly to his chest before letting them go.

"Evgrent," she said, her voice cracking.

"You're safe," he murmured. Then he turned and shouted to the contingent, "Your princess lives!" Cries of joy and relief rippled among the riders, and they descended. Evgrent bowed to Thilly and let them come and greet her, one by one. She looked at him, frustrated, for she would have liked a moment alone with him.

But one of the riders was Mrs. Florence, and Thilly cried out in joy at the sight of her riding sidesaddle on a white mare. Next to her, a familiar person rode a pinto horse: Jackdaw Quelle, mayor of Nistraan's Wold. His face wore an odd expression, one of mixed relief, worry, and perplexity all at once.

"Mayor Quelle!" she exclaimed. "It's good to see you. Unexpected."

"Your Highness, what a grand thing to see you well," said the mayor. "I had news from the Covenant. I am shocked and saddened by the loss of Lady Woadlynn."

Thilly shook her head. "I'm fine," she said stubbornly. Evgrent looked at her sidewise.

Mayor Quelle looked uncomfortable. "I'm afraid I bear other news," he said.

"Oh?" Thilly asked.

"Well, I suppose I'm not really mayor anymore," he told her, pulling his peacock-hued cloak about him.

"Why not?" asked Thilly.

"Nistraan's Wold is no more," he answered.

"Oh my! What happened?"

"Earthquakes leveled the town," said the mayor, fidgeting. "I should let Prince Beaumain know."

"Let me know what, good mayor?" called Beaumain. He walked up to Evgrent, nodded at the man, and otherwise ignored him. After another series of bows by the company, the prince asked, "What news of Catellaith, and my father?"

"Well, that's just it," said Quelle nervously. "Nistraan's Wold collapsed in an earthquake, and the palace...well, word is...but I have not seen, mind you..."

"Mayor," said Beaumain, his voice hardening. "Out with it, man."

# THE VALE OF SEVEN DRAGONS

"Your father and sister are missing," said the mayor. "Their last sighting was fleeing the castle for Vickery, apparently to seek refuge at Castle Taugan with King Gathlade."

"We had heard stories of this," said Thilly. "But no one has seen them at all since?"

"None," fretted the mayor.

"Could they still be on the road?" Thilly wondered anxiously. Beaumain's normally reserved face nearly betrayed his intense emotion just then. She had learned to recognize it, and knew he must be distraught.

"We've no way to know where they might be," said the mayor miserably.

At that moment an extraordinary thing happened. A raucous howl rang out and a blur of violet and orange spun over their heads. Meteor spun down and landed among the horses, sending them running, except for Umbra, who backed up but did not run. The rambunctious dragon snuffled Evgrent like a dog and then seized him with his forelimbs into his batlike wings.

"My rider!" shouted Meteor.

"What the fuck!" cried Evgrent. "Put me down, you brute! I'm not your rider!"

Meteor obliged but wriggled and spun around on his legs. "I've been waiting for you! A true son of Roanmont!"

Evgrent held up his hands while Thilly covered her mouth to keep from guffawing.

"You've got the wrong guy," Evgrent said harshly. "I've got a horse, not a dragon."

"Well, now you've got both!" Meteor said, his eyes wild, his tail wagging and whipping.

Evgrent gave Thilly a pained look, and she smirked.

"Can't you…tell him something?" he begged her. She laughed loudly.

"They choose their riders, Evgrent," she said to him, grinning broadly.

"It ought to be *anyone* but me," Evgrent complained. "What about you two?" he asked, looking from Beaumain to Thilly. "Can't…one of you take him?"

"I've tried out some of the other dragons," said Thilly, "and I'm only too glad to say no. But Meteor is the youngest and most energetic of the seven, apparently."

"Maybe too much so," grumbled Evgrent.

"We could use him to go looking for the king and princess," Thilly suggested.

Beaumain's eyes lit up, and he turned to Evgrent. "Could we?"

"Be my guest, take him," said Evgrent.

"No! That's not how it works!" exclaimed Meteor. "You're my *rider*. That means I obey your commands first. No—I know you're trying to be nice, but really, you have to ride me to command me. That's the rule."

"Oh gods," moaned Evgrent. "Must I? Princess? Prince?"

Beaumain smirked at Thilly, who shrugged. "If a dragon says something's a rule," she said, looking Evgrent clearly in the eyes, "that's the rule."

"Thank you for this," Beaumain said to Evgrent, shaking his hand. "I owe you a fine whisky."

"You're godsdamned right you do," hissed Evgrent.

Meteor nearly incandesced with excitement. "A quest!" he shouted, eyes wild with delight.

"Settle down!" said Evgrent bitterly.

Meteor knelt then to allow them all to climb aboard. "Yes. Settling down, Captain Evgrent!"

"For fuck's sake," growled Evgrent, "don't call me that."

Mayor Quelle twisted his hands together, watching them atop Meteor's back. "Be careful. At any point those things could come back."

"We know," said Thilly. "Stay here and we'll meet up again soon, I hope, and face the threat together. You've got a nest of dragons looking after you, and therefore, you're probably in the safest spot of the entire realm."

Sunder swept overheard, hauling a whooping Copperbox, and skidded to a halt next to her brother. "I've got the better rider," she hissed at Meteor, and Copperbox roared with laughter.

"I've got the better dragon!" he hollered.

"I'm in hell," said Evgrent miserably.

Thilly laughed as she sat behind him, and Beaumain sat behind her. Meteor then surged to the sky and zigzagged his way up the coast of the lake, over the ridge, and edged along Valetheant and Vickery until they approached the border of Catellaith. Thilly looked off to the west, and what looked like an endless line of black smoke stretched out over the ocean along the horizon.

"Gods," she said, "I hope that isn't what I think it is."

"What else could it be?" Beaumain said.

Evgrent cleared his throat and said, "Meteor, bring us lower. I don't want to attract attention at this altitude, any more than we already are, as you practically glow in the dark."

"No, that's Antimon you're thinking of," Meteor shouted.

"I don't give a shit. Just do it," snapped Evgrent.

"Whatever you say, Cap—er, Evgrent!"

Thilly shook with laugher and Beaumain snickered in her ear.

"I'll say one thing for this ridiculous animal," Evgrent said to her. "He's made you laugh, and that's a sound I've wanted to hear for a while."

Thilly's face went red then, and she felt a little too excited to be sitting between the two men, but she kept her eyes scanning the ground to the west while Beaumain took the east, and Evgrent scanned the north.

"Abandoned coaches," noted Evgrent. "They'll be to the west, take a look. We're inside Catellaith now, by the look of it. Gods almighty, you can see Nistraan's Wold ahead. The mayor was right. What the hell happened there?"

The pubs and outbuildings and several houses lay flattened. Thilly hoped that no one had been inside them at the time of the earthquakes. There were no signs of life anywhere, no livestock, no people, noting. That felt ominous to Thilly. She glanced back at Beaumain, and his face looked grim.

He said to Evgrent, "Can you bring us in over the Wold? I see something down there I'd like to look at."

"What is it?" Thilly asked.

"I'm not sure," said the prince. "It's...maybe metallic."

Meteor sailed into the yard outside the Dragon's Head, where even the garden looked disheveled and dried out, among all the broken stones and damage. In that yard, something silver shimmered, as large as a coach. But it was no coach. Beaumain stepped on the ground, and the second he did, a massive tremor surged underfoot, and he fell onto his back.

"Get up!" he yelled to Evgrent. "Get off the ground!"

"Up, Meteor!" cried Evgrent. The dragon jumped into the air and flapped his forearm wings furiously, hovering for a moment.

"Beaumain!" cried Thilly, reaching her hand down to grab him.

And then, suddenly, Beaumain rose of this own accord, and was bucked by the earth to a standing position. Then all from under him a great heaving shape rose, silver and blue. He fell as it rose, but he caught it.

# THE VALE OF SEVEN DRAGONS

"Nistraan!" he shouted.

For it was the silver and blue dragon of Catellaith, awake at last…her head having rested for centuries under the very pub from which it got its name.

# CHAPTER 42

## THE ULTIMATE QUESTION

Nistraan broke free of the earth and the remains of the pub and twisted her fabulous silver-blue head to peer at Beaumain. She blinked at him with cobalt eyes and long silver eyelashes, and her long and slender snout let forth pale blue smoke that smelled of pines and snow.

"Son of Catellaith!" she exclaimed. "Who might you be?"

"Beaumain, prince and heir to the throne," he answered in awe.

Thilly shouted, "She's *gorgeous!*"

And at that, Nistraan snapped her head around and let out a long, menacing hiss.

"Daughter of Vickery," she said in a low, ominous voice. "I do not supplicate to you!"

Thilly looked at Nistraan in surprise. "I'm not asking you to!" she said.

"Oh boy, oh boy," said Meteor nervously, "we don't want to fight, Nistraan!"

"If I fight this time," said the silver and blue dragon, "I will win. Not Antares."

"Antares isn't here," Thilly called. "There's no need to worry."

"Not yet," hissed Nistraan.

"Oh my," murmured Thilly to Evgrent.

"Thilly," Beaumain called from the back of Nistraan, as he tried to find a good place to secure himself, "would you like to ride with me, instead of Evgrent?"

There was a hint of more than generosity in his voice, and Thilly could feel Evgrent stiffen in his seat.

*What are they doing?* Thilly wondered.

Nistraan growled and said, "I will carry the son of Catellaith and no one else, and no daughter of my enemy shall ride upon me."

"Damn," said Thilly, raising her eyebrows. "I guess there's your answer, Beaumain."

"I guess so," said the prince uncertainly.

"Let's keep looking, then," Evgrent said impatiently. "We've covered the east, now let's cover the west, at least..." and he gazed to the smudge on the horizon, "at least at lower altitude. And work our way down to Vickery."

Nistraan said, "Must we cross the border?"

"Yes," said Beaumain, "We must."

She let out a resigned sigh and took off at a run, her arms tucked under, her blue wings wide, her silver scales glinting in the morning sun, so that they could find any sign of the Royals Catellaith. In fact, the countryside was devoid of any visible life other than plants, and even those looked dull, flat, and dormant.

"Where is everyone?" Thilly wondered aloud.

"There is a blight upon the land," Nistraan called out. "I could feel it seeping into the ground. I dreamed, and shifted in my dream."

"That explains the earthquakes," Beaumain said.

"I felt something reaching for me," Nistraan said, and that sent a chill through them all.

"Thank the gods it didn't make it," Beaumain remarked.

"Yet," said Nistraan ominously.

"It won't take you!" shouted Thilly. "Fight it. It hates dragon fire."

"We need all of that we can get!" cried Evgrent.

"And we need one more dragon," said Thilly.

Nistraan let out a growling sort of sigh.

"Are we that desperate?" she asked, tilting her wings a bit to curve around a mountaintop.

"Yes!" said Thilly.

"Then I'll take you," she said, sounding wretched. "But I'm not staying, mind. I know where he is."

"Who?" asked Evgrent.

"Antares," said Nistraan, and she pumped her wings with great vigor, and shot across rivers and lakes and found her way to a great mound north of Castle Taugan, known as Stellar Tor. Upon its top, a decrepit, crumbled old watchtower stood, atop a winding footpath that travelers only used for hiking these days. It had long been part of a beacon network centuries prior, but as it was removed from more modern towns, it had been deemed less useful and abandoned.

Nistraan sailed around this tor, covered in russet-hued bracken on its northeastern side and greener on its western side from prevailing rains. Meteor found this quite fun and chose to fly just above her as fast as he could, until Evgrent yelled "Enough! Give her space!"

She then sent a spray of white-blue fire from her mouth to the old tower, and it set the dried grasses of the land alight until the tor seemed to return to its former glory as a beacon flaming across the countryside. Thilly looked to the west and saw the line of shadows growing darker and closer. She shivered in her seat.

"You see it?" she asked Evgrent.

"I do," he answered tersely.

"We need to hurry back."

"I know. I hope whatever she's doing, it works, and soon."

They waited, and with nothing happening, Nistraan fired another burst at the tor's top. Nothing. So she let out an ear-splitting shriek and alighted on the steep sides of the tour and clawed at the earth with her great talons.

"Wake up!" she screamed. "I know you can hear me. I don't want to fight you! We have a bigger battle. The daughter of Vickery is here!"

Nothing.

"Set me down," said Thilly urgently. She pointed to flat part of the trail up the tor. "There."

"Are you sure?" Evgrent asked.

"Do it," she commanded, and Evgrent nudged Meteor, who flapped his batlike wings and settled on the trail. Thilly jumped off.

The second her feet hit the earth, the tor rumbled and shook. She lost her footing and fell on her behind, much as Beaumain had, and then she watched as the entire top of the tor ruptured, and a spout of brilliant orange flame shot straight up through it, as though the tor were a mini volcano. A great earthquake then rocked Thilly, and she tumbled end over end halfway down the tor, but stopped herself, and an explosion of rock and dirt and grass and bracken flew in all directions. Nistraan and Meteor flew up and away from the projectiles, and Thilly covered her head.

Thilly then heard a deep breathing, inhale, exhale, and steam and smoke from the hole in the top of the tor. Then the entire remaining hillside cracked and fell away, and Thilly shrieked as she rode the current of debris. Meteor dashed in to seize her, but she held up her hands. She looked up, and found an immense beast curled in place of the hilltop, scarlet and orange and gold, and he unfurled his wings and his tail and stretched them wide and long and roared into the sky, a long arc of super-hot crimson and orange flames roaring froth.

"Oh shit," Thilly whispered.

The dragon, with its terrifying, thundering breath, turned slowly and bent his head. He looked straight at Thilly then, with a piercing gaze that melted all her resolve. Still, she used her sword to help herself stand, and she faced him directly. He crawled down the crumbled hillside, one foot in front of the other, his teeth long and jagged and menacing, his eyes like rubies, and he said in a powerful voice, "Daughter of Vickery!"

"Ye-yes?" said Thilly.

"Why do you *summon* Antares?"

Thilly's heart hammered in her chest as she looked up at the dragon. The other dragons were impressive, huge, or interesting. But Antares? He was terrifying.

"Vickery is under attack," answered Thilly, voice shaking. "We have all the other dragons, but we need you."

Antares lifted on his hind legs then and jerked his huge head to stare to the western horizon.

"Those are the *poisoners* of my land," his majestic voice thundered over the countryside. "They do not belong *here*."

"No, no they do not," Thilly agreed, sweating from fear of this great beast. *Nobody warned me that he's fucking huge and scary! How was it a fair fight for Nistraan?*

Almost as if reading her thoughts, Antares dropped back down and leaned, grinning, toward Thilly. His breath made the air shimmer, and she felt like her eyelashes might melt off if he came closer to her face.

"I will fight it *myself*," he said.

# THE VALE OF SEVEN DRAGONS

*I mean, fair!* she thought. But she drew in a deep breath, slowly exhaled, and said, "We need you to fight as a team. All of you," and she looked up to see Meteor and Nistraan gliding above in opposing circles.

Antares looked up, and if ever a dragon could look contemptible, he did at the sight of Nistraan.

"I work better *alone*," he declared, and he looked as though he were about to spring into the air and head west.

"ANTARES!" yelled Thilly. "Stop! I command you!"

The dragon let out a wicked laugh.

"Do you think you could command *me*?" hissed the beast. "I have had no rider for thousands of years. What should my rider be *you*?"

"Because I may be the only royal left," Thilly said helplessly. "Because we need you, and I'm the leader."

Antares sniffed.

Thilly then felt her rage build, the fiery spark within her growing greater, and she let it taker over her.

"They killed my mother!" she screamed at the dragon. "They manipulate, they destroy, and they do not belong. You will help me end them! I am Githilien, the lone princess of Vickery! Will you, Antares, take me into battle?"

Antares, at first staring balefully up at lovely Nistraan, nearly cloud-hued above, turned his head back to Thilly, and said, "Only for the *true heir* of Vickery."

"I am the true heir of Vickery," said Thilly, certain of it finally, sure in a way she had never wanted to be before that moment.

"Then we *ride*, Princess Githilien of Vickery!" roared Antares, and he let her climb on, and he burst into the sky.

# CHAPTER 43

## *INTO THE DARKNESS NECESSARY*

Antares joined the two dragons above them, with vastly different reactions. Meteor let out a delighted, cloud-shattering, laughing shriek and swerved in and around Antares, much to Evgrent's horror and displeasure.

"Would you stop!" he shouted, and by his expression, Thilly knew he was at his wit's end with the young, vivid dragon, twirling and bouncing over hill and dale.

"It's Antares!" yelled Meteor. "Hey, big guy! Long time, no see!"

Antares grunted.

But Nistraan ignored him entirely, and Beaumain looked uncertainly at Thilly.

"I guess our bickering continues in the form of dragons!" he called to her, and she smiled ruefully.

"I hope not. We've got a battle ahead!" cried Thilly, hanging onto the bases of the quill-scales of the great dragon, who let out a guttural, deep grumble every time Nistraan flew near.

Thilly and Beaumain exchanged troubled glances. *Oh dear.*

"Antares," she said in as loud and commanding voice as she could upon the great creature, who while not as long as Jadesilver, seemed somehow the most imposing dragon of the seven, and looked the most menacing.

Antares grumbled.

She swallowed and said, "Take us over Castle Taugan, please. I want…I want to see for myself." Her mouth went dry, and her eyes began to sting, and not just from the smell of gunpowder emanating from Antares, but from fear for her father and their kingdom. "After that, we rendezvous at Loch Tauganon."

Antares said nothing but began to tilt his vast scaled and feathered wings and angled to the southwest. Thilly caught sight of both Beaumain and Evgrent watching her, and she felt the wildest she ever had: hair flying, red belt streaming, leaned into the scarlet and orange dragon, the pair of them untamed and yet determined. Thilly felt powerful, and while she did not realize it, she looked it, streaking through the sky, heart and mind upon her father, grieving for her mother, and ready for vengeance.

She noticed first the dead spots, the veins of black stretching across the land below her, and then the fetid smell, of volatile oil and staleness mixed with rot, and something burned, but not the way anything natural burned. It reminded her, briefly, of Osthadon, and the contamination, and everything unnatural in that strange land. It smelled like something that did not belong on earth. It smelled not only incorrect, but deeply obscene. It was worse than death. It was base and cruel and unfeeling, and cared not that it contaminated her beautiful country and destroyed everything it touched.

The veins spread, and she grew more disquieted, for they all branched out from one central core here, and she knew before she saw the turrets that they all led home. And yet somehow it hit her like a blunt force to see her castle coated in black ooze, dripping and growing like a vine of pure hatred, entangled in all its turrets, choking out its windows and doors. No living thing stirred outside the castle. No birds, not even carrion eaters, plied the skies above it. It was a place of throbbing evil.

Suddenly what appeared to be a black vine upon the castle walls quivered and shot with stunning speed toward Antares, who dodged it, and it whipped through he sky to try to reach the dragons. Meteor curved under and over it in a corkscrew, Evgrent hanging on for dear life, and sprayed the thing with fire. It fell away, but the rest of them trembled and began to loose themselves from the castle.

"Thilly!" shouted Beaumain, and she looked to see where his eyes had turned. To the west, the black line had risen and reshaped high into the sky above the sea, towering like a black altocumulus cloud. It moved at great speed and settled at the coastline.

She would have to search for her father another time. *If I can.*

"Let's get out of here!" screamed Thilly. "Back to the loch! We need to get the others."

Antares did not hesitate, and Nistraan snorted at him, so they gave chase, and Meteor darted above and beneath the competing pair, hurtling through the sky. Thilly soon spied the silver-hued lake, gone dull pewter in the darkening of the enemy's approach. The other dragons one by one began their takeoff, and soon they formed a great circle above the lake. The villagers and canal folk swarmed outside their homes and boats to see the spectacle of all seven dragons of the vale.

"Go in low, Antares," said Thilly, "so that I can warn our people."

Antares grunted, dove toward the water, and pulled out of the dive just above the lake, the wind from his wake sending the resultant waves crashing on the shore as if it were the seacoast. As he arced back around, Thilly called out to the onlookers, "Get indoors! Get to safety! For the Vale!"

"For the Vale!" they roared back, and she watched as they by turns turned and fled, some needing more coaxing than others, for everyone wanted to see the dragons and their riders before they faced the greatest threat the Vale had ever seen.

"Milady!" Hana called from lovely, sparkling Antimon, "So glad to see you're all right!"

"Your Highness!" called Birkswood "What is our plan?"

And Rook called from snaking, undulating Jadesilver, "Time we got ourselves a big catch, is it?"

"Let's get to fightin' those bastards!" yelled Captain Copperbox on Sunder, who let out a wicked, laughing hiss, and the pair of them looked absolutely unhinged.

Thilly nodded, her forehead pinched; she squeezed the quills of Antares and shouted to him and to her friends on their dragons, "Full speed, straight to that cloud. Turn it to ash!"

One by one they surged forward, Thilly on Antares, Beaumain and Nistraan alongside, despite her friction with Antares; Evgrent urging Meteor to fly straight and true, Rook upon Jadesilver with a wide grin, Copperbox whooping and shrieking, his fiery beard flying, upon the red and black Sunder, Hana on Antimon, and Birkswood upon Maelwyrm, the eldest person and the eldest dragon, both seasoned, but both ready for war.

As they approached the cloud, Thilly went cold, for it was huge, enormous beyond comprehension, stretching high into the sky as the day darkened, up into the stratosphere and into space. She had never beheld something so immense. And it looked both rolling and flat at the same time, for her eyes could not focus on it. It was simply there, occupying nothing and everything simultaneously.

*Where did it come from?* she wondered again.

But this time, she had an answer. She looked down, as they flew toward the massive thing, at the sea below, and several miles offshore, between the borers of Vickery and Catellaith, an object sat upon the shadowed sea.

"What is that?" she asked.

Antares grumbled. "It looks like a ship, *perhaps*."

"Not like any ship I've ever seen," she breathed. "Can you take us closer."

"Do you want us to *fight*, princess, or *sightsee*?" boomed Antares.

"We'll regroup," Thilly replied. "Just do it!"

She shouted to Beaumain, "We'll be right back!" just before Antares plummeted, and she shrieked and held tightly to him.

The dragon swooped in low on the shore side, east of the vessel, and Thilly could see that it was some sort of ship. It was cold grey, boxy, and it had an emblem on its side. She squinted, and then she recoiled. It was a livery of Antimon's head.

"Osthadon!" she cried.

And from that ship rose a strange thing: what looked like a string, a black string, incredibly straight, infinitesimally thin. If she looked straight at it, she could not see it. But from the corner of her eyes, it was there, occupying her sight or her thoughts, and it rose in a tiny line to the immense clouds above like the string of a great balloon.

"What the *fuck!*" she gasped.

She looked down at the ship again, to see where the string emerged from, and she saw something she did not understand. The top of the metal ship looked like broken glass, and within the shards rested something heinously dark, beyond all color, beyond all light.

"What is that?" she wondered aloud.

She did not have time to find out just then, for she heard screams from above.

# THE VALE OF SEVEN DRAGONS

"Go!" she yelled at Antares, and the dragon surged skyward, into the black heart of the cloud, and immediately blasted it with a flame so powerful that Thilly crept into his scales to escape the heat from it. She rose when he halted for breath and looked around them. They were in the thick of this cloud, and it was unlike any other cloud she had ever been in. It crawled with winged creatures with no eyes, with mouths snapping, with teeth hundreds of feet long, and Antares despite his size and might seemed like a firefly among such darkness.

"Gods," moaned Thilly. "Where are the others?"

Antares did not answer; he merely fired everything he had around him, and the cloud smelled horrific and toxic. She coughed and squinted through tears, and could see that around them, the force retreated from the flames. But they kept pushing back in.

She heard a yell then, and she looked, and beheld blue-white flame, and she gasped in relief.

"Nistraan!" she shouted. And to her right, a thundering volley of flame emerged from Maelwyrm.

"Thilly!" someone yelled, and she witnessed Meteor spinning and twirling, firing flame in all directions like a dog chasing its own tail. Evgrent spied her through the darkness and smirked.

She saw a silvery, shifting form and huge Jadesilver emerged among the coils of darkness, tongue flickering, and Rook cried, "We've got a bit of weather on our hands!"

Hana and Antimon appeared then, and Thilly wondered about the emblem of Osthadon she had seen, but bit her lip.

*Is Antimon to be trusted?* she wondered, and she felt scared for Hana, who looked by turns determined and terrified. Still, even in the dim light, brightened by dragon flame, Hana looked glad to see Thilly.

"It's as wild as the kitchens at teatime, milady!" she called with a nervous laugh, and then something seized Antimon's tail so that the dragon screamed in pain, and the pair of them were flung down into the depths of the cloud, shrieking.

"Hana!" screamed Thilly. "No. No! NO!"

# CHAPTER 44

## *VOICES*

With terrible purpose, Antimon and Hana hurtled from the sky, directly toward the Osthadon ship.

"Get under them!" Thilly screamed.

Thilly and Antares gave chase, to try break their fall. But the black cloud did not relent, sending whipping stalks to try to pull Antares back. He fought them by burning them as fast as they latched on, and Thilly again had to retreat to keep herself from being burned as well.

Antimon had fallen unconscious, and Hana shrieked horribly as they fell.

"Please no!" cried Thilly.

A bright, blue-white, starlike light sped forth in the water and spun alongside the Osthadon ship, and Thilly watched as a boat emerged from that light, a glowing yellow-green boat, surrounded by glowing beings, and upon its bow stood a woman holding her arms aloft. The beings shot into the sky under the falling dragon and

# THE VALE OF SEVEN DRAGONS

caught her in their glowing grip, and she and Hana fell more gently into the water alongside.

Thilly and Antares hurtled toward them and pulled up just before striking the water.

The woman still held her hands skyward, and she was a force of midnight and starlight: it was Astridae, High Priestess of the Covenant of the Veiled Isles, with the glowing Chaorids.

"Astridae!" cried Thilly from atop Antares, and the woman lowered her arms.

"Quickly!" the priestess shouted. "We must get them out of the water and to the shore. This dragon is injured, and I must treat her."

The glowing beings pulled the dragon and Hana, choking, from the water.

A volley of exploding sounds then ricocheted across the bow of the Osthadon ship.

Thilly looked to see a row of soldiers firing weapons at the Aceltian boat and its glowing beings. Then proceeded a battle between the two, and from the boat, three figures emerged: the fae, Ki'roth, Val'dreth, and Ul'trok, and each notched a flaming arrow, and shot back at the men on the boat. It caught fire, but still more bullets flew.

"To the shore!" screamed Astridae. And the boat sped toward the coast as the fae continued to launch their arrows.

Antares hovered above the ship. "I will destroy it," he said confidently, but Thilly eyed the crack above the ship, and the black line stretching from it, and it chilled her.

"Antares, I don't think you ca—" and no sooner had she uttered those words than the cloud above them suddenly descended upon them and siphoned back into that infinitesimal line and vanished.

"What!" cried Thilly.

And then it exploded. It gurgled and hissed and laughed and chattered and it burst up and out into an immense, horrible thing, a creature dripping with claws and teeth and eyes beyond count, and it stepped over the boat and reached with its great claws toward Antares as if to squash an ant.

"Fly!" screamed Thilly, and Antares did, first sending a spray of fire upward, just as the other dragons hurtled down and spewed fire on the head of the great monster as it sloshed through the sea, the Osthadon boat bobbing like a toy beneath its legs.

Beaumain caught sight of Antares and urged Nistraan to follow them, as did Evgrent and the others. They reached the shore, where the glowing boat with Antimon rested upon the beach, and they hovered above the sand, watching the monster step forward, reaching its awful clawlike hands down into the water and into the seabed, and then it lifted the sea and earth and hurled it toward the shore.

Astridae stood ready, one hand aloft, and she formed a partial barrier, upon which the tsunami struck and bounded off. With her other hand, she knelt beside Antimon and placed her fingers upon the dragon's shimmering throat. Birkswood attended to Hana, who while coughing was well enough to stand. She wept at the sight of Antimon, limp and dull.

The other dragons landed, Antares first, and Thilly slid off him and ran to Hana. They embraced, with poor Hana cold and bedraggled and soaking wet. One of the fae threw a blanket around her.

"What can we do against that?" Evgrent asked as Meteor twitched underneath him, looking up at the monster marching forward, seizing houses and towers and boats and shoving them down its infinite maw, slobbering black ooze.

Astridae said, "This dragon is too weak to fly alone, and you need every dragon to fight this."

"Oh gods," whispered Thilly. "Are we doomed, then?"

# THE VALE OF SEVEN DRAGONS

Astridae looked at Thilly with her dark, beautiful eyes, her silver and blue and purple raiment glowing even with the monster blotting out the sun, and she said, "Would that you had learned the songs of your mother, Githilien. Would that your mother were here with us now to sing them. But failing that, I will sing a song. Not a song for sleeping, but a song for joining."

Antimon jerked, and her eyes opened, and she twisted up and looked down at Astridae, and gave her a nudge of her nose.

"I am sorry to ask this of you, Antimon," said Astridae, looking up at the dragon, "for you have been attacked. You were mistreated in Osthadon and used to form chimaeras. And here I must ask you to do the very vile thing they tried to do to you."

Antimon bowed and said, "So long as good Hana is with me, I know that I will be looked after. I am willing, just this once."

Hana strode up and wrapped her arms around Antimon's neck.

"I'll be with you," the girl said.

Antimon nuzzled Hana's curly hair and said, "Then sing the song, priestess."

So Astridae began to sing, and Thilly gasped, hearing the reverberating, beautiful, resonant music, high and low and unlike her mother's, and yet like at the same time.

In her mind, Thilly heard the words: *This is the song of joining. You will all join each other or die trying; there is no other way to face this monster. You will join in mind, and they will join in body. Stay upon your mounts and do not move, no matter what you see, or hear, or think.*

Thilly felt an unpleasant tingling and then a jerk. She could see a gray space, a nothingness, neither sinister nor welcoming. Then suddenly she heard whispers. Layer upon layer, just as she had in Absinweald. Only this time she could also see, in greyspace of thoughts, every one of her companions, lying next to her, staring upward.

She looked at Beaumain, lying to her left, and Evgrent, lying to her right. On the other side of Evgrent lay Hana and Rook. On the other side of Beaumain lay Birkswood and Copperbox.

The voice of Birkswood said, "Well, this is most unusual. If we make it through this, I'm taking an entire day to drink tea and nothing else. I wonder if Gale might join me."

*Gale?* thought Thilly. *Does he mean Mrs. Florence?*

"Good gracious, Your Highness!" came Birkswood's voice. "My apologies!"

And that was when she realized the whispers were their thoughts.

As soon as she did, they did too, and then there was a great deal of noise and banter and chaos, images of the pirate Thilly wished she could unsee, Rook longing for a quiet day of fishing, Hana bent over crying saying she couldn't do this, but most revealing, Beaumain thinking desperately of his sister and father, trying to avoid his mother, and imagining Thilly in a white and gold gown with the crown of Catellaith on her head…while Evgrent saw her just as she was now, smiling at him, holding a piece of wrapped fish like the one he had given her on the beach. Their first moment of true understanding. As she turned and looked at him, he looked at her, and then she heard him whisper, "Not here, and not now."

They all realized they could hear each other's thoughts then, and their thoughts grew quieter, except for Copperbox, whose thoughts were like trumpets and tubas and raging. "What is this place?" he roared. "Give me an open fight!"

The rich voice of Astridae broke through and Thilly heard her say in her mind, *Join of mind and they will join of body. Put aside your differences, your ambitions, and your passions.*

"I'm not sure what to do," Thilly said. "I don't know how we all join in our minds, other than this!"

Rook said, "Let's link together, arm in arm."

"That's a might sentimental, innit?" roared Copperbox.

"You can drown your embarrassment in rum later," snapped Evgrent.

"Fine. Do it," commanded Thilly, and they linked together, and squeezed closer and closer together as well.

And then she could see it. She could see Antares, though his own eyes, and she felt the tingling again, and either she cried out or the dragon screamed, for there was searing and unpleasant pain. She realized she was then looking ahead, looking at the monster, and she looked down to see that Antares now formed the head of a monster himself, made of all seven dragons fused together. Jadesilver formed the spine, Maelwyrm the abdomen, Meteor and Sunder the arms, and Nistraan and Antimon the legs. In their dragon-melded form they faced the monster of the void, and the mouths of the dragons all opened at once, Antares chief among them, and they rushed at the thing, flaming and seizing and tearing and punching.

The sky billowed with poisonous ash as the two great monsters fought, the evil void creatures expanding and contracting, trying to evade and yet desiring to attack. The ocean roiled beneath their feet, and they then both rose above the sea and battled in the air, the dragon chimera flying, and the monster twisting.

Astridae sang all the while, unceasing, her song beautiful and piercing.

"What do we do?" cried Hana in their mind link. "How d'we stop somethin' so huge?"

For a moment, her doubt sent an electrical pulse among them, and the chimera dragons almost fell apart.

"We stay together," said Thilly firmly. "Focus only on that."

Beaumain said, "I see my mother," and then Thilly jolted.

"Don't think of her!" cried Thilly. "Think of the song!"

And then Birkswood cried out, "Your Highness, I am sorry!"

And she could see through his eyes. On the day of her mother's death. She could see what Birkswood had seen on that beach: not just the spike of the monster piercing her body, from which Beaumain had taken Thilly and run, but the loyal butler had seen the rest: her mother torn apart.

Thilly screamed and broke the link to cover her eyes instinctively, crying, "She left me! She left me!"

And for a moment, they all felt like they were falling. But Evgrent and Beaumain seized her arms in the mind link, and Copperbox and Rook grabbed hold as well and held fast, while Hana and Birkswood, both weeping, entwined themselves.

"We will never leave you," Birkswood swore to Thilly.

"Never," said Hana.

"We're here, Thilly," said Beaumain.

"I wouldn't miss this," said Rook.

"You're a fightin' lass! I seen it with me own eyes the night of your ball!" cried Copperbox.

"We love you," said Evgrent.

And Thilly felt a surge of warmth and hope, and she remembered then what that felt like, as a little girl, when her mother held her close and sang to her.

"They took her from me," she said then, her voice hard. "They took your mother from you also," and she pulled Beaumain closer in her thoughts. "They took your brother," she said to Evgrent. "We will never let them take anyone from us again. Push this devil back down into its hole!"

And with that, the dragon-chimaera flamed the creature from every angle, and seized it and, spouting flame the entire time, shoved it down toward the ship, down to the crack in the world, and burned and pushed and burned some more, and then it bayed the most unholy and horrific sound, and collapsed into the crack. The fissure shrank down to a tiny kernel and the force of the act sent an immense shockwave, blasting everyone on the ship, crushing their bodies and their brains to pulp, and sending another tsunami to the shore. The kernel vanished.

Astridae was ready, and now with both her arms she sang and she shielded at once, and then she caught her breath. The dragons flew apart in all directions, spinning down to the water.

"Let go!" cried Thilly in her thoughts, and they all released just in time to help pilot their dragons before they struck the surface.

Thilly and Antares skidded along the waterfront to a stop before the High Priestess, where she bowed down into the sand, draping her arms over her head, silent. Thilly ran to her and held her, and Astridae looked up weakly and smiled.

"You did your mother proud," she said, exhausted.

"Did we do it, then?" cried Beaumain, leaping off Nistraan. "Did we beat it?"

Astridae sighed and said, "Your fathers," and Thilly and Beaumain looked at each other in alarm. "Go," she gasped in great fatigue. "Go to the castle. And beware. I do not know if every part of the thing is gone."

Thilly and Beaumain exchanged glances. She sighed.

As the dragons landed one by one, Thilly turned to them all and said, "Well done! But we've got another thing to do. And I know you're tired. Are you in, or out?"

Evgrent said, "We've been in the whole time."

"The rum can wait a mite longer," said Copperbox with a grin.

Rook shrugged. "Who needs sleep, anyway?"

And Hana and Birkswood looked at each other and nodded. "All in a day's work, Your Highness," said the butler.

The fae then approached Antares, their quivers in hand, and Ki'roth said, "You might need a clean-up crew. The last I heard, dragons don't fit in castles."

"Climb aboard, then," said Thilly, and Ki'roth joined her, Val'dreth joined Evgrent, and Ul'trok joined Beaumain.

"To Castle Taguan!" shouted Thilly.

# CHAPTER 45

## *THE CASTLE DARK*

The dwindling smear of twilight sky to the west faded to a deep ember hue along the horizon of the ocean, and riding on Antares, Thilly glanced over her shoulder to watch the last light fade and the stars burst forth. To the north, clouds gathered, pale pewter in the night sky. Soon there would be rain, which was one thing she could always count on in the Realm as winter approached. It would spread from the land of her mother, from Aceltia, down through the Vale and Catellaith to Vickery. She knew from her studies with Chamberlain that any weather would meet some resistance in Roanmont, casting rain shadow effect east of those mountains, and therefore a microclimate of warmth and drier weather, where wine grapes and orchards flourished before the lands changed to piedmont and coastal tidelands of the southeast coast of the Realm.

Thilly wondered how much of her Realm knew of what had just happened, and she worried about Osthadon to the far north. What had their involvement been with these monsters? And what would her home be like? Would Chamberlain, a bit of a crank but a stickler for work, still be around? She admitted to herself that she missed her teacher. She was not sure how much of her former life she missed, however.

Antares had keen eyesight, even in darkness, and knew the Realm, as he was a great age. So by and by, he looped back around to the castle grounds. He growled. "Something is not *right*," he said as they touched down. Thilly's heart sank.

*Oh, Father...*

The castle stood dark. That was the first bad sign. For always there were torches, lanterns, and lamps of all sorts, candles in windows, and song and laughter among the training fields. She thought wistfully of Sir Vyrent, and how vibrant he had been. If he was dead, she wondered where his body might be, and if they would ever find it. She had been in such denial about it before, but looking about her, and after seeing what she had, she knew that Evgrent must be right. She sighed long and low. Now there was darkness and silence, except for one thing: a slow, slithering sound.

"What is that?" she murmured.

"Movement," answered Ki'roth, sliding down from Antares, readying an arrow.

"We need light," Thilly remarked.

Antares reared up his head and blasted a nearby pine tree, and it burst into flame.

"For fuck's sake!" cried Thilly.

"It *worked*, did it not?" grumbled Antares. She shot him a look of irritation, and the dragon rumbled and chortled. He then shambled off to look for food. "Scream if you need me," he told her as he stalked away. She did not want to know what he might want to eat, if there was anything *left* to eat.

The other dragons descended, and soon she had her companions about her. Evgrent held Meteor around the snout and said, "Quiet. I know you want to say something, but we need to be quiet. Go off and eat or something."

Meteor squirmed and his eyes glowed, and he full-body wriggled, but his sister Sunder snapped at his tail, and then they fled, swooping into the sky like great bats, siphoning any insects they could.

Thilly marched forward, her friends fanned out behind her, and she stopped and held up her hand.

"Listen," she said in a low voice.

The slithering sound began again, and only then she could realize what it was: the black veins she had witnessed from the air were drawing inward toward the castle, shrinking, and leaving scars and dead vegetation in their wake. She watched and shuddered as some of them made slurping and scraping noises, retreating up the castle's front stairs and up the windows, crawling out of sight into the darkness.

"Oh gods," hissed Hana, "they've gone down to the maid's quarters, I'll bet!"

"LET ME," boomed Copperbox, and Thilly wheeled on him and shushed him with wild eyes. "Let me," he tried to say quietly, and absolutely failed, "take a torch and poke at the bleedin' things! See what happens."

"Be my guest," hissed Thilly, feeling irritable and stressed.

Copperbox and Rook found torches and, lighting them, handed some of them to the fae as well. Now they all had them, and Thilly began her ascent up the stairs. She felt like a stranger in her own home, and she was filled with dread for what might be within that castle.

The firelight of the torches helped, and the door swung open easily, which alarmed her. There were no guards to be seen...not alive, at any rate, and the air reeked of death. She soon found guards and maids face down, and she covered her mouth to keep from screaming.

They were all warped and broken and sapped of blood, for whatever foul methods the monster had used on Castle Taugan, it showed no mercy in its wake. Thilly stood in the ballroom, the place that once held merriment and colorful skirts and intrigue, and it stood dark, its banners fluttering feebly. She held her torch aloft, and her friends began lighting candles. It flickered back to life, and she could see the black, oozing, serpentine material retreating up the stairs toward her quarters. Whenever any of them pushed a torch near the black material, it shrank away quickly.

She walked slowly up the stairs and stopped and listened. There was no sound at all inside now, save for the slithering. Until she reached the top of the stairs.

"Please, please Mother, no more," a girl's voice wailed.

Beaumain went rigid, and then began to spring up the stairs. Thilly flung her arm across his chest.

"Wait," she hissed, her hand on the hilt of her sword. She motioned for Ki'roth and the other fae to come up. Evgrent stepped quietly alongside Thilly, and locked eyes with Beaumain. The prince strained.

"I have to go in there. She's my sister!"

"We don't know that for sure," Thilly whispered urgently. "If it's one of those things, it could be a trap."

"Look," hissed Evgrent, pointing. The last of the black veins bubbled and slithered under the door of the office of King Gathlade.

Thilly drew her blade.

"Ki'roth," she whispered, "be ready to torch whatever's inside."

"I'll kick open the door," said Evgrent.

Thilly glanced down at the hall below and saw Birkswood, Hana, Rook, and Copperbox waiting expectantly, and keeping guard. She put her finger to her lips and mouthed "Be ready."

Their nods gave her confidence.

"Now!" she said to Evgrent.

He kicked the door open, Ki'roth raised his bow with a flaming arrow, and Thilly and Beaumain charged in. Evgrent and Thilly brandished their swords, flashing in the light of the torches. The room inside was dim except for one guttering oil lamp. Everything was in disarray, furniture thrown in all directions, her father's guitar face down in the middle of the floor and smashed, his little miniature figures scattered, and the black ooze had absorbed into one thing: the image of Queen Maulielle, made all of shadow, looming over three cowering figures in a corner: Princess Tantienne, King Ardenour, and King Gathlade.

"Mother!" cried Beaumain, and the thing wheeled around and opened its maw from the beautiful Queen's face, its jaw spilling down to the floor, the black, whipping ooze flipping to and fro.

Beaumain looked down, startled, as it snaked to him.

But something wasn't right. Thilly could see through the figure. Except for one spot, around what would have been the neckline of the queen, a dark place rested, tiny, the size of a small nut.

"It's not your mother," said Thilly loudly and angrily, "and it's barely a monster at all. You can see through it. It's that kernel we saw after we shut the monster away."

In response, the thing screamed at them and sent a volley of snaking tendrils in every direction. Those were real enough, but Thilly chopped at them, and while they fell away, they came back. One snatched Evgrent's ankle and flung him backward, pulling him toward that black focus.

# THE VALE OF SEVEN DRAGONS

Then Thilly heard the flapping of wings, and through the door behind her burst Blinky, and the bird barreled through her image to the tiny black sphere and snatched it up in its beak.

"Blinky!" cried Thilly, but the image of the queen vanished, and the kernel remained.

Blinky flew out into the hall, dropped it before Ki'roth, and the fae slammed down their torch upon it.

The sphere imploded with a great blast of white light, collapsed into a blue spark, and vanished.

# CHAPTER 46

## *LAMENTATION*

Beaumain ran forward to snatch his little sister in his arms, and he held her tightly as she sobbed.

"It's all right, it's all right," he said through his own tears.

"My...son," wheezed King Ardenour, who looked emaciated and careworn. Beaumain knelt with Tantienne in one arm and put his other arm around his father.

Birkswood and Hana ran into the room then and raced to aid the royals.

Thilly ran to her father, and his eyes were closed, and his mouth caked with dried spit. He looked as though he had been drained of blood and life, and he did not say anything.

"Gods," cried Thilly, "what's happened to him?"

There was a scramble then, as all her companions ran into the room. Copperbox brought a bottle of sprits he'd snatched from the great hall cupboards, and Rook cleared the bed of debris. Setting the bottle down, Copperbox helped Rook lift the two kings onto

Gathlade's bed. Birkswood fetched water, and Hana pelted down to the kitchens, torch in hand, to find any sort of food remaining. The fae prepared bowls of herb broth, sparkling in their own unique mixtures, and slowly, they all worked together to make the room a small hospital.

Tantienne clung to Beaumain, and the look in her eyes haunted Thilly. Whatever she had seen would not be unseen, and Thilly worried for her long-term health.

Birkswood noticed her look and said, "I will search for Astridae; hopefully she is still close enough by to help."

Thilly swabbed her unresponsive father's brow with a cloth brought by Hana, and let her tears fall as she held her father's hand.

"Will he be all right?" Evgrent asked Birkswood quietly.

The man gave Evgrent a worried look. So Evgrent approached Thilly.

"What can I do to help?" he asked her.

Thilly stared at him with large eyes and did not know what to say.

Evgrent gave a short nod. "I will ask the others. But know that I am here, should you need anything."

She closed her eyes and said, "Thank you," and then she laid her head against her father's shoulder as he breathed with a rattling wheeze in his lungs.

It was a long night, and full of anguish for Thilly and Beaumain, for their fathers were wounded in unseen ways and had nearly starved and become dehydrated. That part was easily fixed, but Thilly wondered about the trauma they must have endured, and what horrors had happened in that castle.

Blinky hopped into the room very late and snatched a biscuit from a tray on the king's desk. The bird then flew to Thilly's shoulder and dropped the biscuit in her lap.

"Good girl, Blinky," said the bird.

Thilly managed a grin. "So you're a girl?" she asked the bird, touching her nose to the parrot's beak.

"Blinky is a good girl," agreed the bird.

"You're right about that," said Thilly. "You deserve the whole biscuit."

Throughout the next day, she waited for her father to acknowledge her, but the best that she could celebrate was less rattling in his chest as the fae brought bowls of camphor to steam in his lungs. Astridae came later and knelt to listen to Gathlade's chest.

"He's got pneumonia," she announced. She inspected the broths the fae had made and she looked gratefully at the three of them. "You likely saved his life. Another day and he would have perished."

"Thank you," Thilly breathed, and they each bowed in turn.

Ki'roth said, "Since he has improved, we will leave our tinctures here and go forth to see what others may need in the kingdom."

Thilly nodded. Birkswood brought her tea, and she held it in her hands reverently and delicately. "Where is Blinky?" she asked then, for she had not seen the bird since its heroic act.

"Feasting on a perch in your room," said Birkswood pleasantly.

Hana came in then, dressed in maid's clothes and bearing a tray, and Thilly stared at her.

"Hana, what are you doing? You're a dragon rider now!" cried Thilly.

Hana shrugged. "I'm Hana Buellton of Osthadon, is who I am," she said. "And I'm goin' to help my friend. As for what's next, I dunno. Today's not the day to think about that, milady. So let me help you now."

Thilly leaned back against the chair she had slept in and held onto her teacup, then took a sip and set it down, ready for a proper meal, and grateful.

"Did you find any other staff?" she asked carefully.

"This an' that," said Hana stiffly. "I'll be ready for Mrs. Florence to come back; I'll tell you that. I think they all scattered."

"I can't say I blame them," Thilly remarked. "Oh, I am grateful for you, Hana. But know you don't have to stay here. We'll give you whatever you need, for whatever life you want."

Hana nodded and smiled through her rosy cheeks. "We'll see, milady."

She left then, and Thilly watched Beaumain and Tantienne. They looked sad and tired but were ever at each other's side. King Ardenour had begun to sit up, but he was emotional and confused about what had happened.

*It will be a long healing process,* thought Thilly.

She called for Evgrent, who she knew stayed outside the door at all times now.

"Hi," she said, looking up at him from her chair. She glanced at the little princess. "I was thinking…the dragons must be getting restless, yes?"

Evgrent's jaw twitched, and Thilly knew he was showing restraint.

"That's an understatement."

"So…would anyone, I don't know, like to see them? Or like a ride?" Thilly asked him, and she darted her eyes to the princess.

Evgrent pressed his lips into a line. Thilly grinned at him. She knew he hated this, but since he had asked what she wanted, she told him. So it was that he offered to escort Princess Tantienne to see the dragons, and Meteor proved to be a most willing participant in the path to the girl's recovery. She also instantly loved Nistraan, and the feeling was mutual, as the dragon of Catellaith was delighted to have a girl in the family.

Over the following days, Astridae visited the castle many times, and eventually, Mrs. Florence and Mayor Quelle made their way to

Castle Taguan, to Thilly and Birkswood's relief and joy. The castle became something of a hospital, as injured and sickened villagers and farmers were brought in. Astridae trained Rook quickly, and Copperbox provided boisterous entertainment, especially when his own brother Canopus arrived with a wagon of fresh fish for both dragons and people from Loch Tauganon.

The dragons flew each day to and from the coast, and sometimes down into the vale, sometimes to Loch Tauganon, and they indeed grew restless. Maelwyrm began to pine for the River Titeltian. Meteor and Sunder bickered and fought in between rides for the villagers. Jadesilver spent more and more time along the sea, and Antimon liked to nestle in the winter gardens of the castle, occasionally snipping off any remaining rosehips, much to the gardener's horror. Nistraan grew impatient to return to Catellaith and was elated when King Ardenour finally walked down the castle steps and outside for the first time. Nistraan then flew in elaborate patterns in the air above the castle, for her king to see, and for the first time he smiled, if briefly.

Antares bristled at becoming a showpiece. He often grumbled and grew twitchy. But one day, Thilly jumped up from her nap next to her father, still bedridden.

"What?" she cried.

She looked at her father, and his cheeks had good color for the first time. "I said that dragon needs to get some exercise. Maybe we could fly him sometime," and Thilly threw her arms around Gathlade and sobbed for joy.

They sat a long time together, weeping by turns.

"Mother," Thilly began.

He held his hands up. "I know. I knew instantly."

"I'm sorry, Father," Thilly said, sobbing.

"I am too," said Gathlade sadly.

Gathlade gained his strength back quickly from then on, and enjoyed walking with Thilly around the castle grounds, and watching the occasional dragon wheel overhead. On one morning it snowed, and Meteor went quite berserk, snapping at the snowflakes and then skidding down hillsides on his bottom. The king laughed at him. Thilly was glad to see her father laugh again at last.

"It's time we honored everyone," he said to her. "I have some new knighthoods to grant. And we must lament those we lost."

Before that happened, though, Copperbox and Rook returned one day after a trip to the coast. The pirate looked as chaotic as ever, but he held a strange box in his hands as he entered the castle.

Rook said to Thilly in the court, "We thought you might like this."

Thilly looked at Copperbox archly and said, "It's not another mutated head, is it?"

Copperbox roared with laughter and slapped his thigh.

"No, but maybe just as disturbin,'" he then said, his wild coppery eyebrows dancing. "We've got ourselves a problem in the North."

"Speak plainly, good man," urged King Gathlade. Thilly grinned at that. Her father was still a bit wasted away and had more grey hairs, but he remained the calm and welcoming dad she knew.

Rook exchanged an uneasy glance with Copperbox, and Thilly then frowned, for Rook was always smiling.

"Well," said Rook, "we found some debris washed up on the shore."

"Yer been' too diplomatic, Rook," laughed Copperbox. "I *am* a pirate."

Rook laughed. "Well, fair enough. The wreckage from that Osthadon ship has washed in, and we found this box. What's in it…might interest you. And I agree with the captain here. It's time to think about what they're doing up there, what they've been doing, and what we need to do next."

"That sounds deeply unpleasant," remarked Gathlade, his eyebrows knitting together like warring caterpillars. "But thank you, just the same. We'll take it under consideration."

The two men bowed and went on with their day. But while the gradually refilling castle returned to some semblance of normality and prepared for a celebration, Thilly wasted no time and snatched the box up. Beaumain joined her, and the three of them opened it together.

Inside there were oilcloth maps and diagrams, with unusual symbols and strange pictures. "What do you think these are?" Beaumain asked her and Gathlade.

"I think that's a seafloor map," said Gathlade, pointing at a series of ridges. "This, however, is a map of something else. And I don't know these words. It's a language I've not seen before."

"Look at that," murmured Thilly, for she found an illustration of what looked like a cracked, dark space on a map.

"A hole in the world," she said to herself.

Shuffling through the papers, Beaumain said, "I think they were working on something foul. To what purpose, I don't know. But I think…Thilly, I think Osthadon opened some sort of gateway. And the monsters came through."

"Why would they do that?" Thilly gasped. "It could have killed them all too. And where"—she shuddered before continuing—"where did the gateway *go*?"

"I don't know," Gathlade replied, rubbing the coarse black and grey goatee on his chin, "but I'm reluctant to share this with Ardenour. Given your mother's ancestry, Beaumain."

Thilly went cold. "But she's of Catellaith."

Beaumain stared into her eyes. "She's descended from Thaddons, Thilly."

Thilly clapped her hands over her mouth.

*Of course.* Her pale skin, her deep violet-blue eyes, and her general disdain for the ways of the southlands.

"But she was killed," said Thilly.

"It could be," Gathlade muttered slowly and carefully, "that she was used as a vehicle for those creatures. We may never know. But I am on alert now. Whatever Osthadon has been doing has taken them time. And you said their dragon Antimon had been experimented on as well. Foul tidings indeed."

Beaumain did keep the information to himself, for his father's grief was acute.

That evening, Thilly and King Gathlade honored the dead with the songs of Astridae, who sent their laments skyward, reading off names and casting them into the air on little sailing papers. One of the names was Vyrent, and Thilly asked Evgrent to write it with her. They had never found his body, but both knew they had to let him go. When the papers rose high into the air, the dragons all aimed their snouts in unison to burn the little papers into embers that flew high into the sky of a moonlit night.

# CHAPTER 47

## *OF THE VALE*

Evgrent refused to be knighted, on principle. Copperbox refused with a booming laugh because "I'm a pirate, and nobody'll take me seriously as a knight!"

Rook accepted the rank, but wanted to return to Valetheant before he served.

"I need to see my family," he added.

"You're always welcome here," Thilly told him. He bowed to her.

Rook and Copperbox set forth on their dragons, going separate ways. Thilly felt sad to see them go.

Then came the day when Astridae and the fae left for Aceltia.

"We will remain watchful," Ki'roth told Thilly quietly. "Osthadon is too close for comfort in many ways. But the Covenant stands, and Osthadon would not want to cross them again, I assure you."

Astridae held Thilly's face in her hands before saying farewell. "You are your mother's daughter, through and through," she told

# THE VALE OF SEVEN DRAGONS

Thilly. "And should you ever wish to act as she did and leave this place, know that the Covenant welcomes you at any time."

"Thank you," said Thilly, deeply moved by the offer. "Maybe one day."

And then it was time for the Royals Catellaith to return home, rebuild, and heal in their own country. Beaumain had remained close to Thilly throughout, walking with her in the mornings.

One day Beaumain paused in their walk in the gardens on a sparkling winter morning, with the low sun sending flickers of iridescence across mounds of fresh snow. The king had joined them, but stood off to one end of the gardens, where he laid fresh flowers at a grave marker for Woadlynn. Thilly wore a long red coat and a circlet upon her dark auburn head with the starflower emblem Evgrent had saved for her. Beaumain held her gloved hands as their breath rose in the brittle air, and his eyes were soft and kind, their aqua depths lined with red-gold lashes, and the collar of his navy blue and silver coat high. He looked most handsome, and Thilly felt the heat of his gaze and looked unflinchingly back into his eyes.

"I know what you want to ask me, Beaumain," said Thilly, and she gently pressed her gloved forefinger onto his lips. He took her hand and kissed it. And she touched her forehead to his, in many ways wanting very much to kiss him again, as they had while riding Maelwyrm. "But I am not ready. I do not know if I ever will be."

"I am prepared to wait," he said, and she felt her cheeks tingle, looking at him, as he then put his arm around her waist.

"You might have to wait a very long time, then," she answered. "I have a duty and care for my father."

"As I do for mine," Beaumain reminded her, stroking her face.

"We have different paths now, you and I," Thilly told him. "We have our countries to repair; we have a Vale looking for a leader. We have an enemy in Osthadon. I don't know that we'll see true peace again in our lives, you know?"

"I can't think of anyone I'd rather fight alongside, if it comes to that," Beaumain said to her.

"Likewise," Thilly agreed, "but for now, we help. One day, we lead. And maybe, we fight. That's enough for one lifetime, at least, don't you think?"

Beaumain nodded gently and gave a little sigh. "I suppose you're right. Very well, Githilien of Vickery, I will bid you farewell, and return to my people with my dragon at last."

Thilly stepped back from him and curtsied, and Beaumain bowed. He saluted the king and turned on his heel. The guards saluted him as he walked stiffly away from the castle, and for the time being, out of Thilly's life.

"That was brave of you," said Gathlade, watching his daughter closely as she held her chin high. "I do not want you to feel you owe me a lifetime of care, though, Githilien."

"I know you would never want that," Thilly said. "But I'm still a girl, really. And for the moment, that's all I really want to be."

"You're my dear, brave girl," said her father. "Woadlynn would be so proud; I know that she was, and she would be forever. Should we all meet again beyond the starlight, she will tell you, and we will sing together again."

Thilly felt her eyes welling with tears, and she kissed her father and walked back into the castle into the great hall.

She had one more place to go. That night, she stole out the servant's door and down the stairs outside the castle. The night sky was clear, cold, and thick with stars. She looked up at them, and then over to the patch of woods where she had kissed Sir Vyrent. It seemed so long ago to her, and somehow quaint, but that memory was happy.

# THE VALE OF SEVEN DRAGONS

She walked there, gazed from the trees down into the training grounds, and then stepped onto the open road.

She heard the hooves of a horse ringing on the frozen earth and looked behind her to see a man whose hair shone in the starlight. The steam of the horse's breath mingled with his in the frigid night air, the snow frozen solid and glimmering under the full moon. The man wore a cloak fastened with a clasp of Roanmont, shaped in the blue ridges of that land.

"Evgrent," she said. He slipped off Umbra and approached her.

He looked at the circlet upon her brow, with the embedded star-flower.

"It suits you," he said.

"Are you sure I can't change your mind?" Thilly asked him. He looked more like a knight than he ever had before.

"That is not the way for me, Thilly," he answered, but warmly. "I'm heading to my homeland. I want to see if I have any family still there. Given what we've been through, I thought it wouldn't hurt."

"That's a happy surprise," said Thilly.

They stared at each other, and she rested one hand on the hilt of her sword.

"I could use more sword-fighting lessons, though," she said with a smile.

"Aye, you could," Evgrent answered, grinning. "And what else? Do you feel that you ought to run off and be a knight now? Sir Githilien of Vickery?"

Thilly laughed, and steam rose from their chatter toward the stars.

"I am to remain a princess for now, it would seem," she said to him. "But I do not know how long I will be. This place seems small to me now, and our cares seem too large. I don't think I can be a princess of Vickery anymore, though I will try for the moment. I am

Githilien of the Vale. My heart carries me elsewhere. Maybe over mountains, maybe over sea, and certainly through the Vale. Maybe we'll meet again."

"Maybe we will. And now I'll say goodbye," he said. He knelt before her and took her hand and kissed it. Looking up at her with his starlight grey eyes, Evgrent looked calm and happy. "I would do it all again," he told her, "for free, and forever. All you need do is say the word."

Evgrent rose, bowed, and climbed aboard Umbra, and before Thilly could say anything more, he set his horse at a canter and left her standing there alone.

Thilly walked slowly back to her quarters. Everything did look smaller now, and gaudy. She missed the wilds of Aceltia and the green of the Vale. She wondered what Roanmont might be like in the Spring. She set her sword against her bed, kissed sleeping Blinky perched next to her bed, and picked up the picture of her mother from her bedside table. She turned down her lamp, held the picture against her heart, and felt only love.

# THE END

# ACKNOWLEDGMENTS

Like all epic adventures, *The Vale of Seven Dragons* became its own journey. I had always wanted to write a full-length fantasy novel, and it seemed inevitable that there must be dragons involved. Dragons should always be involved in big decisions, ultimately, because you wouldn't want to get on their bad side. Fire and paper don't get along, after all. I suspect they would look askance at phones and tablets as well. So, the consultation with the dragons was and is the best course of action in these matters. I'm pleased to say that I did, in fact, win their approval for the telling of this tale…

When I was a girl, I had the great fortune of receiving *The Hero and the Crown* as a gift from my second eldest brother, Greg. He knew I loved fantasy, science fiction, and horror. He also knew I was a very stubborn girl, fiercely independent, and highly aspirational. I must thank the bookseller who convinced him that Robin McKinley would be a good influence on me, for she was and still is.

Princess Githilien, or Thilly, owes her literary DNA to the plucky, obstinate heroines of my youth: Dorothy, Ozma, Aerin, Princess Leia, Wonder Woman, She-Ra, Jem, and so on. But Thilly is in many ways more flawed than they are, as she's closer to me. But we do share the inner fire. I have always admired those of us who looked around and asked the question, "Why can't I do that?" and then answered with a firm footstep on a new surface, declaring that we can.

I want to thank Jeremy Billingsley of Sley House Publishing for giving this traveler a home, along with two forthcoming sequels, and Scarlett R. Algee for her keen edits and feedback. Thank you to Chris Panatier for the magnificent cover, featuring in perfect detail Thilly, Prince Beaumain, and Evgrent.

There are many friends and family members I would like to thank, and although I cannot list them all here, I will mention some.

First, thank you to the Universe that I am the daughter of Fred and Janice, and the baby sister of Todd, Greg, and Brenda. Mom, Dad, and Todd are no longer with us, but their encouragement and stubbornness live on through me and my words. Thank you as ever to Pam Magnus, always my first reader and dear friend. Many thanks to James Dotson and our children together, for bearing with me and my strange writing life. Thank you to Gareth L. Powell, Helen Glynn Jones, Mya Duong, Richard Czernik, Vincent V. Cava, Pedro Iniguez, Kelly Varner, Robert Young, KC Grifant, Jonathan Maberry, Dennis K. Crosby, Michael Mulhern, Gloria Thomas (dragons at last!!), Adrian Tchaikovsky, Danika Stone, Paul Cornell, Jesse Reid, Sarah L. Miles, Ryka Aoki, Andrew K. Clark, Paulette Kennedy, Lauren Warren, Dean Powell, and so many others it would fill another book to add. You make putting down the words worth it, and the dragons give their nods of approval.

# ABOUT THE AUTHOR

JENDIA GAMMON, who also writes as J. Dianne Dotson, is a Nebula and BSFA Awards finalist author of fantasy, science fiction, horror, and thriller novels and short stories. She is also CEO of Roaring Spring Productions, LLC and Editor-in-Chief of its publishing imprint, Stars and Sabers Publishing.

Jendia conducts workshops and participates in panels on creative writing for conventions such as San Diego Comic-Con and Star Wars Celebration. She holds a degree in Ecology and Evolutionary Biology. Jendia is also a science writer and an award-winning artist. Born in Southern Appalachia, Jendia now lives in Los Angeles with her family.

Learn more about Jendia Gammon at jendiagammon.com.

# ALSO FROM SLEY HOUSE

## NOVELS

*A Mind Full of Scorpions*
*(Eyes Only, Book One)*
J.R. Billingsley

*Ground Control*
K.A. Hough

*Bad Form*
Joe Taylor

*Persephone's Escalator*
Joe Taylor

*The Cartography Door*
Sean Edward

*Black Echoes*
J.B. McLaurin

*Under the Churchyard in the Chamber of Bone*
J.R. Billingsley

*Ristenoff*
J.R. Billingsley

*Atacama*
Jendia Gammon

# ANTHOLOGIES

 *Tales of Sley House 2021*

 *Tales of Sley House 2022*

 *Tales of Sley House 2023*

 *Tales of the Sley Siblings*

 *Tales of Sley House 2024*

 *Tales of Sley House 2025*

# STORY COLLECTIONS

 *Melpomene's Garden*
Curtis Harrell

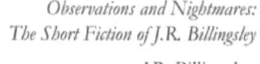  *Observations and Nightmares: The Short Fiction of J.R. Billingsley*
J.R. Billingsley

 *Your Final Sunset*
SJ Townend

See more at https://www.sleyhouse.com

www.ingramcontent.com/pod-product-compliance
Lightning Source LLC
LaVergne TN
LVHW040035080526
838202LV00045B/3351